She must not think now. Perhaps if she swam... mercy... Her mind caught the thought, *beg for Mercy*. Only yesterday she would have smiled at it. Today it was a meaningless play on words. Today she knew that to beg would accomplish nothing, except perhaps amuse the grim captain.

And how could she beg? Only by falling on her knees before him and holding up her hands in supplication. She could not speak, nor could she write down any plea. The slate that had hung at her waist since her eleventh year was gone. She had hit a pirate with it, broken it on his head. He had merely guffawed, pushed her aside and continued his slaughter.

In the past she had hit, not as hard, more men than one with it, men who thought that because she was dumb she could not carry tales of stolen kisses. This pestering had not lasted long, once they learned she could write. And now her slate was gone, though the small cloth bag of chalk and rag still hung from her belt of plaited worsted cloth. She could write on the bulkhead...

She heard heavy footsteps in the passage beyond the door and Jedediah came in with a wooden bucket of seawater, which he dumped on the table. He left without looking at her or speaking to her. However she heard through the door as he mumbled, of all things, "You needs a clean shirt."

He was answered by a cold sharp voice, which Mercy recognised. "More than a shirt."

She stood quickly and wiped the tears from her face with her bound hands. The captain would not have the satisfaction of seeing her cry. *Not yet.* Her fingers trembled on her cheeks. She bunched them together in her skirt, straightened her shoulders and stared ahead. She saw, surprised, that the light through the horn windows was dim. The long terrible day approached its end, though that was no solace. Under the cover of darkness men did things they would not dare, in daylight.

But she decided, *I will live through this.* I will not fight. I will not give him the added pleasure of subduing me. I will give him the least pleasure possible, by submitting. *I will survive.*

The Pirate And The Puritan

by

Mary Clayton

The Pirate And The Puritan

Cover Art by *Kim Mendoza*

The Wild Rose Press
PO Box 708
Adams Basin, NY 14410-0706
Visit us at www.thewildrosepress.com

Publishing History
First American Rose Edition, 2007
Print ISBN 1-60154-119-8

Published in the United States of America

DEDICATION

To my husband Arthur–
a man whom dogs and children love.

Chapter One

At first glance the pirate captain looked as staid a man as any Puritan Mercy Penhall knew. He wore neither coat nor waistcoat but his black breeches were of plain cut and his indigo-dyed shirt bore no lace. No muslin *cravate* wrapped his throat, only a plain dark stock. He was clean-shaven and instead of a periwig his own dark brown hair fell straight to his shoulders.

But he also wore cuffed boots like a soldier's and a leather belt and scabbard about his waist instead of a cloth baldric across the chest. His tanned hand held a sword with a bloodied point and he had thrust a spent brass-handled pistol into the belt.

He did not bluster or brag. He walked the line of prisoners on his midships deck and examined them swiftly and silently. His face was closed, as if he were a judge who had already passed verdict... Mercy shivered at the thought.

It was not the captain but his bearded lieutenant who lay before the sailors the choices of the captive - join the pirate crew, be cast adrift in their own longboat or resist and be slain.

"I'd as lief cut all your throats, or better'n that sell you in the Indies. But we got a gen'rous captain." His whiskered lip curled. "He says we need but t'ree, t' take the places of them we lost in th' fight. Your own cap'n shoulda surrendered when he got gived the chance. Now half o' you is dead an' your ship done for." He kicked the nearest cannon carriage for emphasis. "But the *Thalia* here, she's a lucky craft. I tell ye, a share of our booty for one season is more'n you'll see in six as honest men."

Behind his red-kerchiefed head Mercy saw the small two-masted *Jesselin*, her upper decks in flames, sinking slowly into the green summer sea. With six guns she had seemed well protected against possible French privateers for a voyage from Virginia Colony to Boston. From there her master had planned to sail in convoy with other ships bound for England. He had not believed himself at risk from sea-thieves. The war between England and France meant a presence of ships from the two navies in both the Atlantic and the Caribbean that discouraged pirates.

But a squall had blown *Jesselin* south to the Outer Banks of Carolina, and this one outlaw company, not a privateer, had found her.

Mercy felt her life was in the same state as the wrecked ship. The brave heart and sound common sense her uncle had held to her credit were of no help here. Better to have died on the *Jesselin*, by a seizure of fright like poor old Mistress Atwell, than to be the only female among the rabble of prisoners.

At least she could not scream. With the last shred of her stubborn pride she did not want these creatures to know she was afraid.

Pride was a sin. She had heard the stern ministers thunder it from Puritan pulpits when she was a child in Massachusetts Bay Province. Even the milder Separatists of kindly Virginia had said so during Sabbath day sermons. Even Uncle Jonathan had said so, though folk had said he was too easy a man in most things. But Jonathan Penhall had died the year before and it was her pride that had committed her to the voyage.

Pride had not saved her from pirates, though now it squared her small shoulders and would not allow her to tremble or weep. She had not wept her silent tears since Uncle Jonathan died, and before that not since she was eleven years old. *Face the world, Mercy,* her uncle had told her once, *always face it, never run away.*

She had run away from Virginia, her pride unable to bear being treated as a servant by her step-aunt Anne, no older than herself, and Anne's new husband. It seemed now that her pride had been punished. She was a captive, and from this place there was nowhere to run...

The captain sheathed his sword. He remained silent, grim as death, while the seamen were shoved into two groups. In the smaller were three sailors from the *Jesselin*, two of them ruffians not much different from their captors, the third a young gunner's mate hauled forcibly to join them.

But then another sailor screamed curses at his captors. The captain spun quick as a cat toward the voice, though he did not draw his blade... Another pirate's cutlass flashed downward and the scream was suddenly cut short. The captain's back stiffened.

Mercy swallowed an acid taste of fear, turned her head away to stare at the pile of captured prizes. The *Jesselin's* cargo had been tobacco, deer hides and beaver pelts, and she saw among the bales her own plain trunk. Everything she owned on earth was in there - bedding, inheritance, and her clothing layered among calico and lavender. Would her plain gowns be worn by a pirate's doxy? Would she be left with nothing but the grey wool dress she now wore and the plain white cap that hid her hair?

The pirate lieutenant had watched the killing with interest. The show over, he swaggered up to Mercy and pushed his sunburned whisker-stubbled face close to hers. He lacked a front tooth and his breath stank. Mercy longed to step backward and away from him. Pride had its uses though, for instead of retreating she pressed her hands together in the folds of her skirt and stood stiffly, unmoving.

"Ah, brothers, lookit this! A wench, an' young!" he exclaimed, as if surprised to discover a woman on board. "There's nay much of it an' it's packaged plain, but it's purty. Fine fair skin an' dolly-blue eyes, for all it's tryin' t' hide them," he leered. "I wunner now, what's the colour of its hair?

Rough fingers reached for her cap and she flung up her hands. Her hair was not for the sight of these brutes! But the lieutenant laughed gratingly, jerked her hands aside, snatched off her cap and threw it across the deck. Thick fair curls fell to her shoulders - there had been no time, that morning, to braid them.

The creature - she hardly thought of him as human - was gratified. "Ha! Yeller! It'll be worth somethin' in the slave marts, this one."

Sold for a slave... A groan bubbled in Mercy's throat that could not reach her lips. She gripped her hands together until they hurt. She refused to shudder even when the pirate fingered her locks as if they were cloth-of-gold that could be sold for gold guineas. She wanted to strike him, to bite and scratch, knew it would be foolish. After her first moments of fight on the *Jesselin,* sense had prevailed and she had played meek. But she could not bear this for long!

Out of nowhere, it seemed, a different hand, one that was long and sun-browned, pushed the lieutenant's aside. This hand took Mercy's chin and lifted it before she could think to resist. The face behind it was the captain's, lean, tanned, unsmiling and without expression. Though at least he did not leer, nor was his breath bad.

His eyes were golden-brown, a colour that should be warm, yet their gaze was sharp and cold. The eyes looked deeply into hers, as if they searched for something. So deeply and with such penetration that Mercy felt a new fear, that the pirate might see to the bottom of her soul - a worse thing.

"How old are you?" His voice was a clear and pleasant tenor that should be warm like his eyes, but like his gaze, was also cold.

Mercy shook her head, a short movement because he held her chin. She touched her mouth with a trembling finger.

"Can't speak. Frightened?"

She shook her head again, as emphatically as she could within his grip. She pointed to her lips once more.

"Mute, then. Not such a prize, Gorman," he told the lieutenant. His voice was calm, reasonable and without inflection.

"Cap'n, that would make nay diff'rence, to some buyers. Make it worth more, even. No screamin', no tale bearin'. Sell 'er in the Indies, or ship 'er to Barbary. Them Moors is mad for yeller hair an' blue eyes. An' no voice they might be pleased of, in one of them harems."

A Moorish harem! Mercy wanted to cringe, to close her eyes. But she stood straight and stared back at the captain.

The dark eyes looked her up and down, examined her costume. "You're far afield, little one, for a Puritan." He dropped his hand then uttered, indifferently, shocking words. "I'll keep this one for myself, Gorman. She can go down to my cabin." He called over his shoulder, "Jedediah!"

The mate's face twisted with anger. "Nay fair, Cap'n! She's part o' the booty!"

"I'll account her worth and take it from my share." The captain moved on, giving orders for the larger group of prisoners, the captured longboat, bread and water. The mate growled at his heels like a dog.

Mercy stared at their backs in horror. She should run after them and somehow persuade the captain by signs to send her in the longboat as well... A large hand descended to her shoulder and propelled her forward. A large voice said, "This way, liddle girl."

She was pushed out of the crowd of prisoners and prizes, toward the stern. She tried to break away but the man then seized her by both shoulders and shoved her ahead of him. Under her skirt her legs trembled. However they bore her through the doorway under the high poop deck, along a narrow passage with narrow doors either side to a larger door at its end. The man gripped her shoulder tightly while he opened it with a large key.

By the high horn windows at its far end, she judged it was the ship's great cabin. Diffused light revealed a long locker built into the hull, an oak table and two chairs bolted to the deck, a brass-bound sea chest against one bulkhead and a neatly made-up bunk fixed to the other. A straw-filled pallet lay just inside the door. The great cabin had been converted to the captain's quarters. He did not sup with his officers, then, Mercy thought in confusion.

Her guard jerked his big head at the pallet. "That's mine, most of the time. But I'll be sleepin' outside the door ag'in for a bit. Here, lassie."

He pulled her hands together, tied her wrists with cord, passed another rope through them and fastened it to an iron ring set high in the bulkhead above the pallet. Mercy's instinct was to lash out and to struggle, not to be trussed as tamely as a hen for market. But it was useless to fight, the man was too big. She must save her strength to resist the captain.

"You'm a pretty liddle thing." But Jedediah said it off-handedly, as if to a kitten. Mercy glared at him and was surprised to see the broad face, if not gentle, not savage either. "There ain't no need to be so feared, y' know. Him, he..." He scratched his head where straw-like hair stuck out under a spotted kerchief and informed her instead that there was a chamber pot in the locker beside the pallet. Then he shambled out and shut the door heavily behind him.

Mercy was alone. She allowed her knees to give way, sank down onto the pallet and let herself cry at last. Her tears were silent and no one would hear them. Yet her despair had changed in form only. She knew her fate now - attacked by one man instead of many. What could she do, when he came for her? She could fight, but men were stronger than women and to resist would only delay the ravishment. And possibly make him angry, if such a cold man could be angry, in which case he might hurt her more.

She was not ignorant of the act. Puritans were not prudish, and in this year of 1704 even an unmarried woman knew the functions of male and female. However it had never been done on Mercy Penhall's body and she had intended it never would be.

Now she must face the truth. She would be ravished and likely more than once, until the man tired of her. And what then? He would kill her, perhaps, or more likely sell her when he finished with her. A lump rose stinging into her throat and in her mind she tried to pray.

Yet God seemed very far away. Perhaps her pride had angered Him. She had left pleasant Virginia, even though she was not wanted there, to return to cold New England with its terrible memories. Her step brother Nathaniel, twelve years her senior, had offered her a home with his family years before, by way of a letter which had survived the parlous route from Massachusetts Bay Province.

But it had been a mere declaration of duty. They did not really want her. Who in the whole world wanted her? Only dear, plump, Mam Felice, Uncle Jonathan's slave from Jamaica, who had taken the place of mother in Mercy's life. Felice now belonged to Anne. And Mercy must be grateful that Mam did not share her own fate.

Mam had feared for her and Anne told her she was a

fool, to go to even a coastal town in New England. In Europe the War of The Spanish Succession was fought between France and the nations of the Grand Alliance, and the colonies of the Americas called it Queen Anne's War and also suffered. In New England pressure from the French-held lands to its north and west had already provoked a massacre, by their Indian allies, at the inland town of Deerfield only this last February.

Mercy would not see even the stony shores of Nathaniel's home at New Exmouth, now.

Beyond the *Jesselin*, before the smoke and stench of the sea battle had engulfed the day, a balmy breeze had played chase with little white clouds in a fine blue sky. At home—no, at Anne's house—roses and honeysuckle would be scenting the warm June air, and under the oaks and beeches there would be cool, dappled shade. Even in barren Massachusetts Bay Province the fields of corn and barley and the vegetable rows would be green and growing.

She must not think of them. Nothing could help her now. Perhaps if she swallowed her pride she could beg for mercy... Her mind caught the thought, *beg for Mercy*. Only yesterday she would have smiled at it. Today it was a meaningless play on words. Today she knew that to beg would accomplish nothing, except perhaps amuse the grim captain.

And how could she beg? Only by falling on her knees before him and holding up her hands in supplication. She could not speak, nor could she write down any plea. The slate that had hung at her waist since her eleventh year was gone. She had hit a pirate with it, broken it on his head. He had merely guffawed, pushed her aside and continued his slaughter.

In the past she had hit, not as hard, more men than one with it, men who thought that because she was dumb she could not carry tales of stolen kisses. This pestering had not lasted long, once they learned she could write. And now her slate was gone, though the small cloth bag of chalk and rag still hung from her belt of plaited worsted cloth. She could write on the bulkhead...

She heard heavy footsteps in the passage beyond the door and Jedediah came in with a wooden bucket of seawater, which he dumped on the table. He left without looking at her or speaking to her. However she heard through the door as he mumbled, of all things, "You needs a clean shirt."

He was answered by a cold sharp voice, which Mercy recognised. "More than a shirt."

She stood quickly and wiped the tears from her face with her bound hands. The captain would not have the satisfaction of seeing her cry. *Not yet.* Her fingers trembled on her cheeks. She bunched them together in her skirt, straightened her shoulders and stared ahead. She saw, surprised, that the light through the horn windows was dim. The long terrible day approached its end, though that was no solace. Under the cover of darkness men did things they would not dare, in daylight.

But she decided, *I will live through this.* I will not fight. I will not give him the added pleasure of subduing me. I will give him the least pleasure possible, by submitting. *I will survive.*

****

The door was pushed open, banged shut. The captain, a solid shadow in the fading light, moved quickly.

The movement was not toward Mercy. He strode past as if he did not see her, plucked the pistol from his belt and dropped it on the table. It struck a brass inkwell fixed there and the metals rang. He unstrapped the sword belt and flung it to the deck. The scabbard and buckle clattered on the boards.

He paced, then, between the table and the stern locker. His breath came harshly. To Mercy he seemed like a captive bear she had once seen in a cage. And like the bear, when he wearied of restless walking he stood and stared outward through the horn windows as if they were bars. He crossed his arms over his chest and his chin lowered until his shoulders were hunched and his head was bent to his breast.

She could see nothing but his back and a line of brow and cheek beside the dark hair. The eyelashes, oddly, were outlined against a pane of horn. They were dark and curling and as long as a woman's. They blinked up and down once or twice and that was his only movement.

Mercy had prepared herself for violence and was

bewildered. His stance was like that of a man grieving, or in despair. Yet how could he be either, when he was a bloody-handed pirate? She could do nothing except turn her face away so that he did not feel her gaze. Her breath rasped in her own ears, though he did not seem to hear it.

After many minutes the dark figure moved suddenly. Mercy's head jerked and she stepped back one involuntary pace, yet once again the movement was not toward her. He went to the stern locker, heaved up the heavy hinged seat-lid, brought out a long-necked bottle packed in cloth and a pewter mug. He dropped into one of the chairs at the table and poured liquid from bottle to tankard. The evening light fired it richly, red as blood. Wine.

He drained the mug, then sprawled in the chair and poured himself another measure. This he sipped more slowly. The light caught his gold-brown eyes. They were unreadable, though no longer cold.

If he drank heavily, she hoped he might sleep. If he did not sleep he might turn on her... Mercy bit her lower lip. Then her legs began to cramp from standing stiffly and she feared they would give way again. Carefully, within the curtain of her skirt and petticoat, she flexed her limbs to ease the taut muscles.

The captain seemed to sense the movement. He rose from the chair and swung around in the same motion, again like a big cat. His hand reached swiftly for the pistol, but the next moment halted in mid-air.

"You! I had forgotten about you." This time his voice held emotion. He was angry. Yet the anger was merely that of a man intruded upon in privacy.

Mercy's only concern was that he might see she was afraid. She clenched her tied fists in her skirt and schooled her face to be calm.

He strode toward her and she discerned his shape properly for the first time. He was slim and not tall, though easily eight or nine inches taller than her small self. But not being large did not mean he was not strong. There had been power in the hand that had held her chin. A steel rapier, a narrow rope, were also slender, but strong enough to kill... She fought to keep her mind from what he would do to her.

"No need to look like a bird in a trap." The dark lean

9

face was like a mask, as on the deck, yet he spoke testily. "I'll not harm you. You must stay in here for a few days, that is all. When we reach port again I'll turn you over to some decent folk who'll send you home. Where were you bound?" He frowned at her in the shadows of the cabin. "Ah, yes, you can't talk." Her muteness seemed to interest him as her body did not.

Mercy did not dare believe the words she had heard. It was more likely he played a cruel game and would force himself on her when she no longer feared him. Her knees trembled again. She shook her head as if to clear her ears.

"Little one, you hardly need a voice. Those blue eyes speak for you. Well, you've no reason to think I'm telling truth, but I'll not touch you." The captain's tone was dry. "I've sunk low, but not so low as that, to ravish virgins. When I find a maid among the captives, I send her home."

Mercy felt blood rush to her cheeks. How could he know such a thing?

"It's in the eyes, child." He reached out and lifted her chin, not so hard as he had on deck. "There's a different look in the eyes of a maiden than of a woman who's wed or bedded. And I see I've made no mistake." The hard hand dropped and he turned away, voice indifferent again. "You can rest easy. And eat, soon. Jedediah will bring some food. But I expect you're thirsty."

He went to the table and fetched the tankard. "Sip this, it'll restore you." When she backed away a step he snapped, "It's good burgundy from France and a mouthful, girl, is not a sin."

He knew little of Puritans, then. To drink liquor was not wicked, though drunkenness was. Mercy had thought he meant to make her drunk for easy conquest. Yet if he truly meant to spare her, it was impolitic to refuse. And she had already decided to play meek. She lifted her bound hands for the mug.

However he held it to her lips as if she was a child. She took a deep mouthful, swallowed carefully and pushed the tankard away. The wine was much heavier than she had drunk before. At home she had taken it with water. And the warm strong taste was indeed soothing, though she would not let him see that.

He drank the remainder himself, put the mug down.

10

He gazed at her, frowning. Again, as on the deck, she felt uneasy that those dark eyes saw more than she wanted revealed.

He said only, "At least I'll not need to talk with you. How do you let people know your wants?"

Pride wanted to ignore him, however sense told her to be civil. She opened the little bag at her waist, fumbled in it with her tied hands and pulled out a piece of chalk. She pointed to the loop of broken twine where her slate had hung.

"You can write, then. I recall that Puritans educate their young, even girls." With his question answered he lost interest. He returned to the table and untied the stock from round his neck, then unlaced his shirt, pulled the garment over his head and dropped it beside the water bucket.

Mercy had not expected this. Her eyes saw that his chest was leanly muscled and smoothly haired, then her cheeks burned and she averted her face. Would he strip entirely? Had he indeed been playing cat and mouse with her?

From the corner of her eye she saw him wash his upper body, then dry himself with a linen cloth. He fetched from the sea chest a white cambric shirt, a muslin neck-cloth and a long black waistcoat, drew them on and straightened them to neatness, then pulled a horn comb through his dark hair. He lifted the sword belt from the deck, buckled it on once more and locked the pistol into a flat case under his bunk. A moment later he was beside her and had gripped her grey-clad arm. She willed herself not to shrink back, but he merely inspected the bonds on her wrists.

"I'll tell Jedediah to loosen them a trice." He saw her wide eyes and laughed shortly. "Aye, you're a maiden, if you've never seen a man's chest before. Well, you'll see more than that of me, sharing quarters." He was gone, thankfully, before the blush flared to her face.

Mercy sank down onto the pallet. Her mind spun. The cabin was empty. She was alone again and as yet unmolested.

In the silence she noticed that the noise from the deck was now no more than normal ship sounds. The murdering was done then, and the longboat gone. Those of the *Jesselin's* crew that remained were now pirates themselves. She had no hope of help and was dependent for life and virtue on the word of a man she did not know.

The large Jedediah came and placed a wooden platter and two bone tumblers on the deck beside her. Muttering to himself, he dropped the captain's shirt into the water bucket, packed the wine bottle away in the stern locker, then looked about him, for all the world like a housemaid making sure her chores were done.

On the way out he inspected her bonds, though he loosened the cord only a fraction. "No more'n that, Missy. I ain't taking a chance of you doing him a mischief while he sleeps."

A faithful servant, she thought wryly. She turned her attention to the food. The plate held cold salt beef, a cooked yam also cold, rye bread not yet stale and one luxury, half a lime. There was no knife or spoon and she ate awkwardly with her tied hands. She was not hungry, yet forced herself to eat. Whatever happened, she must preserve her strength.

One mug was of water, almost fresh, which she drank immediately. The other contained a dark hot liquid with a pleasant aroma. She tasted it cautiously and recognised another luxury, coffee. Uncle Jonathan had brought some home once from Williamsburg, a gift from his merchant friend Lewis Phipps, and told her the tale of it. The beans were picked from bushes in the Dutch East Indies then roasted and imported through London. But too much of the brew, he had said, addled the senses and loosened tongues. *Ninny-broth,* he had called it.

Her uncle had talked to her more than most men did to females of their family. He had had no wife, no chick or child of his own, and Mercy could not repeat his conversations by voice and never gave them away on her slate. So he had told her how Charles the Second had tried to close down the coffee houses of London thirty-odd years before, because men had talked sedition around the tables.

King Charles was long gone, as was his brother James the Second and James's daughter Mary and her husband William of Orange. James's younger daughter

Anne had now reigned for two years. Ships from England brought news that the country was peaceful within, though at war without to prevent the grandson of Louis the Fourteenth of France from inheriting the throne of Spain.

And Massachusetts Bay Colony had become Massachusetts Bay Province, part of the colony of New England, and was now under the rule of New England's royal governors. The powerful old Puritan clergy had lost much of their authority and a woman in extremity could drink coffee without strictures even from her own conscience.

When mugs and platter were empty Mercy studied them and felt their weight. She was not certain she could trust the captain. Perhaps she could use them as weapons if need arose. She left them half-hidden in the rough woollen blanket, as if they'd simply been dropped there.

From the deck she heard orders called. She heard feet run, timbers creak, and lastly the flap of sails as they filled with air. The ship began slowly to move.

Where would it go? She tried to recall the chart of the Colonies of the Americas that had hung on Lewis Phipps' parlour wall. She remembered but two towns behind the line of islands and swampy rivers that stretched down to Spanish Florida. One was Bath on the Pimlico River and the other Charles Town, settled for little more than thirty years, in the southern part of Carolina Colony.

The Carolinians had destroyed St. Augustine in Florida two years before at the outbreak of the war and she knew ships of the Queen's Navy must be stationed in Charles Town's harbour. This ship certainly could not go there. Would it sail to the pirate havens in the Caribbean?

But surely there were few refuges for pirates in these days of war? Where could the captain release her? Had he lied after all? He could have locked her alone in another cabin, not in here with him. No, she remembered. He wanted the mate, the men, to believe he was bedding her. Yet why deceive his crew?

Her mind was tired and she could not think clearly. Her body craved rest but she dared not sleep. She was still awake, out of will power, hours later when the ship's motion ceased. It had become gentler, so they must be in calm water. She heard the splash of anchors. After that all was quiet, even the ship's timbers creaked softly. Still the captain did not come.

Then new sounds came to her ears, clunks, clinkles, thuds, and raised voices. Another voice cut across these, reducing them to mumbles. The captain's? It soon became apparent they divided the spoils.

What would become of her trunk? Most important among her belongings was the thirty Pounds that Uncle Jonathan had bequeathed to her and the fifteen Pounds Anne had sent, reluctantly, to Nathaniel for her keep. This money that had seemed a treasure was now nothing, compared to life and freedom.

Perhaps, she thought for the first time, she could ransom herself with it. After all, that was the main use pirates found for captives. But no, the mate had made it plain she was booty and the captain had not disagreed. If she offered them money, they would take it and keep her prisoner as well.

After perhaps an hour the voices swelled louder. She heard bursts of unbridled shouting, hoarse laughter, bad singing. Were they drinking? There had been Jamaica rum in the *Jesselin's* supplies. And the pirate captain liked wine. Drunken men were beasts, she had heard. It was dark and easy to imagine the worst.

Footsteps sounded suddenly outside the door and the captain came in with Jedediah, who carried a lantern. He hung it from a hook above the table and helped the captain pull off his knee-high boots with their wide cuffs of leather. The big man said something, though Mercy, her mind clouded by weariness and fear, heard only one word—*booty*.

The captain answered him and his voice, though low, carried clearly. "I told them it wasn't worth our trouble, a trader setting in to each port before heading to England. They've only themselves to blame if their shares are small. A cargo of skins does not go far among so many. Well, I have my own share." He did not look Mercy's way. "Must I always remind you, Jedediah, that this ship is not the *Teign Swan* and on it my word is not law? They're a free company and I'm their elected chief only for so long as I'm useful."

"An' find them prizes. These be lean times for piratin' but you been lucky. The prizes ever stops, they'll turn on ye like the pack of rats they is."

"Not while they need my skills." The voice sharpened. "We've talked of this before. It serves no purpose. Goodnight, Jedediah."

Jedediah muttered under his breath, but stood the captain's boots by the bunk and folded both neckcloths, the dark one and the white. He looked up at the captain. "You keep wearin' these, someday someone'll likely strangle ye with 'em."

The captain reached around for his pillow and threw it at his servant. Jedediah brushed it off, chuckled and left the cabin. He barely glanced at Mercy. She heard his heavy body settle outside the door, like a watchdog's.

She sat on the pallet with her back pressed to the bulkhead, saw the captain pull off his knitted stockings and roll them into a tidy ball. Then he stripped off his waistcoat and breeches and remained clad only in his knee-length white shirt. Hastily she turned her gaze away. Her chest tightened.

He strode over to retrieve his pillow from the deck and must have seen the movement of her head. He turned his gaze quickly in her direction. Defiantly she faced him. His eyes reflected both the shadows and the lantern light, but there was no reading them.

He said irritably, "Go to sleep." Then he dropped onto his bunk and lay on his back, hands linked under his dark head.

Mercy lay on her side along the pallet, back against the oaken wall. She pulled the rope taut with her tied hands and held the wooden platter.

Jedediah's bed smelled of stale sweat and tobacco. She did not close her eyes. She saw that the captain had not snuffed the candle in the lantern.

He breathed deeply but quickly, as if his mind laboured in thought. Slowly the sound grew more regular. She saw the white shirt move as he turned onto his side.

The voices from the deck sank into murmurs. Water lapped quietly on the ship's planking. There was a wet place on the pallet where seawater had splashed over the edge of Jedediah's bucket. It dampened her skirt but she was too weary to care. She was too weary even to pray.

She covered herself with the stiff blanket and fell into deep sleep as into a well.

Chapter Two

Mercy wound the wooden bucket up from the well. Full of water it was heavy, and she was small for eleven years old. She lugged it to the whitewashed frame house that was home and set it on the rough bench by the door. Some of the water spilled onto her linen apron.

The man she called Father, though her own was long dead, had stood and watched her struggle with the bucket. Now he reproved her sharply for the spill and roughly pulled her apron off. "It is time we went. Tidy yourself. At least look like a decent girl."

She smoothed the skirt of her old grey wool dress and tied her cap more firmly to her head, not because her stepfather had ordered it but because she was anxious to go. He had said they would see her mother and she had not seen Mother for weeks. Mother had been taken away and terrible things said about her.

They walked to the town square along the cobbled street. It was summer, and warm. But other folk who took the same way went close by the house walls as if for shelter. Mercy knew they evaded her stepfather and her. And yet only last year they had been friends.

At the edge of the green grassed square Isaiah Burdick pulled her to a halt with a hard hand on her shoulder. In the centre of the square, by the stocks, loomed a roughly built gallows. Two people stood on its wooden platform, a hooded man with a thick rope in his hands and a white-faced woman with bound wrists. The man set the noose around the woman's neck like a horse-collar.

Mercy opened her mouth to scream *Mother,* though only a whisper left her lips. She tried to run to the gallows but her stepfather held her back. She flailed her arms to escape him. He seized them and pinned them to her sides.

17

Someone muttered to him to take the child away. He did not answer, nor did he move.

The woman cried out something in a voice of despair. The words were lost among the crowd. Then she screamed more loudly, *"Mercy!"* The next moment the trapdoor in the platform suddenly opened and the woman - decently attired in a plain Puritan gown though she no longer wore her white cap and her fair hair was roughly piled high to bare her neck—dropped through it, swiftly, down. The rope tightened into a straight line...

Mercy shrieked, but the sound stuck deep in her throat and emerged as a bubbling groan...

She sat bolt upright. There was darkness around her instead of daylight. She pulled frantically at whatever it was that covered her. A coarse blanket. Her hands were tied! *Where was she?*

Moonlight glimmered through high windows and made shadows in a strange place. A tiny flame burned in a lantern overhead. It was not the town in Massachusetts Bay Province, nor was it her neat bedchamber in the farmhouse outside Williamsburg. *A ship...* She had left Virginia. Uncle Jonathan had died and Anne had married the most handsome of her young suitors. The ship had been sunk—*pirates!* She groaned again.

A man's voice, startled, cursed. "God A'mighty!" She heard bare feet strike the wooden deck, then a dark body in a light shirt strode toward her, stood and looked down, face in shadow. She crowded back against the bulkhead, dream terror flying before a real fear.

"For the love of heaven, girl, take me at my word! I'll not harm you." The captain sat on his heels beside the pallet, his shirt-tail falling between lean muscular thighs. "So, you can make sound of a sort. I thought I was caged in with a strangling bear."

The lights of moon and candle revealed his brown eyes, still unguarded from sleep. Mercy swallowed, then slowly eased her shoulders off the cabin wall. Yet she shivered in the warm night air.

"Bad dream? Well, you've borne enough today to warrant it. Settle now. It's passed." The voice was merely irritated.

She bit her soft underlip and shook her head before

she knew she did it.

"There's more there than fear of me." The dark eyes were unfathomable. "Dream like that a deal, do you?"

Mercy shook her head again, sharply. She did not dream it often any more. The terrors of the day must have brought it back, as he had said.

"Oh, don't be proud, girl. We all have nightmares. But some of us live them instead of dreaming them."

She stared at the pirate, surprised by the words. Fear had sunk to the bottom of her mind. Her throat, however, was dry with the aftermath of terror. She coughed.

He laughed shortly and stood. He went to the table and poured something from a brass pitcher into his pewter tankard and brought it to her. He held it within reach of her lips and when she turned her face away his irritation returned. "Oh, drink! It's only water. There's likely a few drops of wine left but you didn't cavil at half the mug-full, earlier."

She took the tankard into her tied hands and held it by the base so she did not touch his fingers. She drank and handed the cup back with a nod of thanks.

He ordered curtly, "Go back to sleep."

Mercy lay cautiously along the pallet. She kept her eyes on the man to see what he would do.

He turned away, strode to the stern locker and took out the wine bottle. He poured a half measure and sat at the table, sipping slowly, staring at the ship's hull as if he could see through it. He was still there, a dark and light figure among the night shadows and the candle flame and the diffused moonlight, when her eyelids fell.

****

When Mercy woke the next morning she knew where she was. Pale light seeped in through the stern windows, water lapped softly beyond the bulkheads and the ship rocked gently, at anchor. She lifted her arms to stretch and they were pulled up short by the rope.

She glanced quickly at the bunk. The captain was not there. She slipped off the pallet and used, with difficulty, the chamber pot. She felt cramped and fusty and wished she could walk and wash. All she could do, however, was to run her fingers, tied together, through her hair.

19

Jedediah came in with a bucket and refilled the brass pitcher with water. He set another platter and cup on the table then felt in the pallet until he found the others. She would have liked to keep them, though the need for weapons was past. He untied her rope from the ring, led her to one of the chairs and fastened it again. She held out her wrists in silent plea. They had begun to chafe. He looked at them and shook his head.

"They might be smartin', lassie, but I ain't givin' you no leeway to do 'im harm."

He drew something from his capacious waistcoat pocket. It was her white linen cap, still intact though crushed and marked by a boot heel. "He said for you to put this on. The less they see of that yeller hair the better, he said." He laid it on the table, went out and locked the door behind him.

She examined the rope that tied her to the chair and found it tight with intricate seamen's knots. If she picked at it for long enough she could probably undo them, though then she could do nothing but walk about the cabin. The door was locked and beyond it was the ship full of men. No. She was better off here, with the captain.

She broke her fast with dry bread and fresh cooked fish. The mug held coffee and she drank it without hesitation. It would be good to be on land again, to have milk... *Would it happen?* Would the captain really take her to safety? After she had eaten, she bent her head and prayed. She thanked God in her mind for saving her thus far, asked Him to keep her safe and committed to heaven the poor lost souls of yesterday.

Then she looked at her rope again and decided to unpick it so she could at least walk a little. The captain would not like it, but was she to sit here leashed all day?

As if the thought had conjured him up, the captain strode in through the door. He did not look at her. He went to his sea chest, pulled off his cambric shirt and drew on a stout dark one like a workman's. It was the first time she had seen him in clear light and with a mind unclouded by terror and tiredness.

He was not young, near to thirty years old. His features were neat and regular, unremarkable except for the gold-brown eyes. It was a face that would look well if its owner smiled...

He took two long steps to the table and braced his hands on it to look down at her where she sat. Both his eyes and his voice were cool. "The ship needs some repairs and we're cutting wood on shore. You'll stay here. The less they see of you, the less they'll think of your value. I know you're not comfortable, but there's no help for that."

Mercy nodded. She could still unpick her leash.

"Jedediah has claimed two trunks of women's clothes as his share of the booty. The larger one holds blankets and linen, a Psalm Book, a sewing box, three plain gowns, Puritan collars and caps, a grey cloak, two shawls, shoes, petticoats, shifts, stockings. Those are yours?"

She nodded again, felt her face flush at this impersonal account of her personal possessions and bit her lip.

He stood straight again. "You can likely get those ropes off if you work at them. Then you could brain Jedediah or I with the pitcher when next we come in. But that, little one, would leave you at the mercy of Gorman and the others. I advise against it."

Mercy's head jerked up. She stared at him.

"I see you've thought of it." For a moment the dark eyes sparked as if he was amused. "I think you're a sensible woman. Do what you're bid and you'll be out of this with a whole skin." He turned away to lift a leather jerkin from a peg and pull it on. "I'll find you something to write on, later."

Then he was gone, as quickly as he had come in. Mercy's cheeks flamed all over again. But it was not the blush of a maid whose underthings had been looked on by men. It was triumph, and she smiled.

Her money from Uncle Jonathan and that meant for Nathaniel were not all in English coins. *Specie* was hard come by in the Colonies and her inheritance consisted less of English guineas than Spanish pieces-of-eight and *reales*, Portuguese silver and even French *louis*. It had seemed only a moderate precaution to hide them, more from the crew of the *Jesselin* than possible pirates or French raiders. She had sewn them into the hems of her gowns.

And they had not been discovered. She had won a

small victory over her captors.

****

Mercy jumped to her feet at the first sounds of timber breaking. The noise continued, accompanied by loud voices. She recalled what the captain had said about repairs and guessed that some of the ship's planking was being removed.

The pirate had not, then, escaped unscarred from the fight with the *Jesselin*. However, she found little satisfaction in the knowledge, and when curses punctuated the work she closed her ears and turned her mind to keeping boredom at bay.

The captive of pirates, and bored! It amused her a little. Yet it was truth. She pressed the creases from her skirt with her bound hands, wiped her face with water from the pitcher, used more water to remove the boot mark from her cap and struggled to braid her hair. Then she had nothing to do but sit and repeat Bible verses and psalms in her head. At least these were a comfort.

The cabin grew stuffy as the sun rose higher and she drank water from the pitcher, pouring clumsily. She had barely set the cup down when she was startled again, by footsteps, then voices, outside the door. One was the captain's, the other was guttural and surly.

The captain strode in and picked a black tricorne hat from his sea chest. Behind him his lieutenant, Gorman, swaggered up to Mercy's chair and leered at her.

"It don't look much damaged." Gorman's tone was insolent in a manner that would not be tolerated aboard a normal ship. "Still got its dress on."

The captain said coolly, "I don't need her dress to be off."

"Jus' the skirt up, eh? I'd want it stripped, meself." The mate ran a red tongue over his thick bottom lip. "Mebbe I can kiss it, now it's used goods."

"She's my woman and not for you to meddle with. Get out."

Gorman took no notice. His greenish eyes stripped Mercy bare. The captain stepped to her side, dropped his hat on the table and slipped an arm round her shoulders. Mercy stood rigidly under his touch and saw the heat of Gorman's stare. She turned her face away, looked up at

22

the captain. His brown eyes were cold as ever, but she was less afraid of the man who had not yet hurt her than the man who would if given the chance.

The captain suddenly wound his free arm hard about her waist and pulled her against his chest. She gasped, tried to lift her bound hands to push him away and found them pinned between their two bodies. Before she knew what was happening, he bent his head and pressed his mouth onto hers, hard. She was frightened, then angry. She tried to struggle. His deceptively slim arms held her helpless.

When he raised his head his expression had not so much as changed. He said to the other man, without looking at him, "Leave me some privacy."

The mate guffawed. Mercy heard him stomp out and the cabin door slam. Gorman, however, no longer mattered. She had begun to trust the Captain and he had proved himself not trustworthy. She turned her face away from his and felt tears of humiliation and fury sting behind her eyes. No, she would not cry! Nor would she let him see she was afraid. She began to squirm, thinking to kick at his legs.

"Stop it!" His voice was low. "I'll still not harm you. But Gorman's the kind who doesn't believe anything he cannot see, so I had to provide him with some evidence." However he did not release her, instead turned her chin in his hard hand again to make her face him. "By heaven, you're angry! If you could talk, I'd receive the rough edge of your tongue, wouldn't I?"

Mercy glared at him. She believed what he had said, yet relief was tempered by outrage and she was troubled by the closeness of his body. She still wanted to hit him, even though she knew it would be foolish.

Once again he seemed amused. "I agree, little one, that it was a rough kiss, not the kind to be a maid's first. And it was, wasn't it?" When she neither nodded nor shook her head he smiled faintly and suddenly was good looking, with eyes like amber. "No doubt you've been told that kisses are only for marriage. Well, I'd meant to let you go with untouched lips as well as body but there's no taking it back now."

Mercy was confused by his warmth and wished he

would let her go. She forced her tied hands up, pressed them against his dark shirt and tried to lever herself out of his arms.

"Stand still!"

Surprised, she did. Then his face came near again. This time his lips touched hers very lightly and only for a moment. Then again. And again. The kisses were so unexpected, so soft and gentle, that she found herself quite unable to move.

He spoke quietly. "You're a tender armful, little one. And it's many a long year since I held an innocent. Those small kisses were for you, since the first one was for Gorman. The trouble is, I'm tempted now to take one for myself." Suddenly the amber light left his eyes and he released her, so abruptly she had to seize the chair to keep her balance. His voice hardened. "I've come to fetch you ashore. It's Gorman's watch on board and as you saw he's not to be trusted near a woman."

He untied her rope from the chair, his strong fingers loosing in a minute the knots that would have taken her half the morning. "Put your cap on."

Mercy was confused and wanted to hide her face. Instead she bit her lip and held up her bound hands.

"I see, you can't. Well, I won't free you yet. But that hair must be covered." He took the cap himself, set it over her loose braids and reached behind her neck to pull the drawstrings tight. With his arms around her like that he was again too close. Mercy felt her cheeks flush, though she tried to meet his eyes steadily.

"You're pretty, little one. Like a rose." He dropped his hands and actually laughed, quietly and genuinely. For a single moment his grim, lean face was different, alive and mischievous. "Your husband will be a fortunate man."

He really did intend to free her, then, if he spoke of her future. However she shook her head.

"Now what does that mean? Surely you hope for a husband?"

She shook her head again, emphatically.

"Don't want to wed. Why not?"

She jabbed a stiff small finger at her lips, knowing that what she hinted was half a lie.

"Ah, yes, you're dumb. Don't give up on that account.

24

Some men would count it a blessing to have a wife who couldn't talk."

That might be true, though the real reason was the other thing, what she was. Yet he had kissed her and given her an inkling of what marriage could be like. And he still stood too near. She held her body rigid and dropped her gaze from his to stare past his arm. Her cheeks cooled.

"Aye," he said harshly, "it's a matter for shame, maid or decent wife, that a pirate has robbed you of a kiss. Come out of here." He took her elbow and pulled her with him from the cabin.

The deck was quiet, almost deserted and newly scrubbed. It was totally different from the crowded, noisy, terrifying place it had been the day before. The ship rode calmly at anchor in a brown deep creek mouth, by a shore thick with trees and undergrowth above a narrow beach.

Mercy saw, a quarter mile eastward beyond a promontory of sand and low weathered trees, the blue line and sunlit flash of the sea. She turned her gaze to the beach and saw a party of men working around low fires. Below her feet she heard desultory hammering.

By the forecastle Gorman lazily watched two men clean the bore of a small cannon. One of them was the young gunner's mate from the *Jesselin*. He was pale, though he flushed when he saw Mercy and bent his head to the work.

The captain drew her over to the ship's rail and pointed downward. A dinghy bobbed on the water below, tied to webbed ratlines hung over the side. But the sight did not seem to please him. He frowned and called sharply to Gorman.

"I ordered a ladder for the woman. Where is it?"

The mate took his time to turn his head then grinned unpleasantly. "Nay got around to findin' one yet. Cap'n." He spoke the last word like an afterthought.

"You disobeyed deliberately," the captain said flatly. "Be careful, Gorman. There are things that are worth my fighting you and things that are not. I know the difference and you don't." He turned his back on his lieutenant and spoke to Mercy. "If I untie you, can you climb down? Don't say yes if you can't."

Mercy glanced at the square-set lines and nodded. As her mother's hoyden child she had climbed trees, a shocking pastime for a girl.

"I go first, you next." He pulled the tricorne hat out from under his arm and jammed it down on his head, then loosed her bonds and dropped the cord overside to fall into the dinghy. He swung his legs over the bulwark, slipped down the ratlines with sure hands and set his feet into the little boat so easily it barely rocked.

Mercy watched him, rubbing absently at her sore wrists. She had been hauled up the ship's side yesterday like a sack of onions. It had taken all her will power, then, not to beat with her hands on the back of the brute who carried her, and she had not noticed how he climbed.

Now she hitched herself up onto the rail, turned and slowly let herself down. She needed both hands, and there was no hope of holding her skirt and petticoat modestly about her while she used her feet to feel for the next rope. Her shoes were an impediment. It would have been easier in her stockings.

She felt her right shoe touch the rowboat's gunwale, then the captain's hands grasped her waist, firmly and impersonally, steadied her and guided her to the stern seat. She sat and clasped her hands together in her lap. The pirate took the middle seat and gripped the oars.

"That was well done. Like the veriest lady. I barely glimpsed your ankles."

Mercy looked straight ahead and would not blush. He said no more, merely pushed the dinghy away from the ship with one oar then rowed across to the beach. Where its bow struck sand, large Jedediah waited. He seized the gunwale and pulled the boat in sideways. She was able to climb out without so much as wetting her feet. She looked around and saw they had landed at a spot a hundred yards upstream from the main body of men.

The captain jumped lightly down, his boots barely splashing the water. "Jedediah, stay here and guard her. Though I don't think any of them are fool enough to trouble her and I don't think she's fool enough to run away. If she tries, her bonds are here in the dinghy." He regarded her with appraising eyes. "You've been brave this far and may be brave enough to chance the wilds. So

I'll tell you the plain truth. There's naught for a hundred miles every way but forest and swamp, bears and wildcats, snakes and biting insects. And alligators, south." He waited for a response.

Mercy jerked her chin down in a nod.

He strode off then, to where the crewmen laboured with logs and saws by the slow fires.

Mercy trudged up the beach to a place where the sand was dry and there was a little shade from overhanging tree branches. Her limbs felt cramped from her confinement in the cabin. She shaped her lips carefully and mouthed at Jedediah, *May I walk?*

He planted his back against a tree trunk, folded his arms across his barrel of a chest and said loudly, "Sit ye down."

Mercy sighed faintly but did not press the issue, merely sat. Jedediah, like most people, obviously assumed that because she was dumb she was also deaf and stupid to boot. She rubbed her red wrists again and studied her surroundings. Behind Jedediah where he sat squinting in the half shade there was a tangle of low-growing forest. Before her the ship floated with furled sails on the brown water and downstream the pirates went about their work. The high blue dome of the sky arched over all.

The pirate crewmen were the only creatures that moved, so she watched them. They were a motley crowd, eighty or ninety men of all sizes and colours, including two Negroes and at least six or seven too brown or yellow to be called white. They wore costumes mixed of rags and captured finery and few troubled with periwigs, most wearing kerchiefs over shorn heads or raggedly cut hair. All carried weapons, from knives or bludgeons hung about their middles to cutlasses and pistols slung from baldrics.

Her lips tightened at the sight of them—murderers and freebooters. She turned her attention to what they did. Logs had been split lengthways and trimmed with adzes to rough planks. These were balanced on rocks over the three beds of coals to dry out, at least sufficiently for rough repairs. Occasionally the sap spat and sparked as it dripped from the wood.

However, unlike honest workmen the pirates dawdled over their tasks and many seemed downright unwilling. Perhaps they considered it labourers' work, perhaps they were simply lazy, or perhaps they had sore heads after drinking the night before.

Mercy caught sight of the captain's neat plain figure and watched him. He was the only one who moved at any pace, going among the others giving instructions and even a helping hand here and there. He seemed to know what was needed better than they did, though his words were obeyed sullenly and more than once his crew disagreed. At those times he stood, listened patiently and then discussed whatever point was at issue. He did not seem to give outright orders.

My word is not law, he had said to Jedediah last evening, *I'm their elected chief only so long as I'm useful.* She recalled a conversation Uncle Jonathan and Lewis Phipps had shared once, before the war began. The merchant had forgotten, as people often did, her presence. He had lost a small cargo from the Indies to sea-thieves but had taken the news philosophically enough, as if pirates were a hazard of nature like storm and shipwreck.

Pirate captains, he had said, lasted only short terms, a year or two at best. The crews accounted themselves a fraternity and were not amenable to discipline. A leader was hard put to exert authority over men who considered themselves his equals. Often they voted on matters in dispute with a show of hands and majority ruled unless the captain had some obvious advantage in his favour.

She wondered how long this man had commanded the *Thalia.* It was plain that many of the crew resented him and that his lieutenant barely tolerated him. She wondered how he had come to be what he was. He was not a ruffian like the others, though he would probably meet a violent end, in a ship fight or at the hands of his crew, or hanged...

Hanged...

She shuddered in the warm air, sought desperately for another line of thought and caught the memory of that talk between her uncle and Master Phipps in Williamsburg... The merchant had said that many pirates began as seamen out of work, signing 'on the account' for shares instead of wages, on a ship where no questions were asked. Later they would be required to swear to its

28

'Articles', on a hatchet if no Bible was to hand. Still, almost every pirate, when on trial, claimed to have joined up in order to save his own life.

It was true that captured sailors were seldom cast adrift with food and water as the *Jesselin's* crew had been. Most often it was to drown on their sinking ship, if not forced to choose between death and signing on. She remembered the young gunner's mate, given no choice at all. He seemed a decent lad. Perhaps the captain had been such a one—no, he had spoken to Jedediah of commanding another ship.

She must remember that whether he was a pirate by threat or his own free will, he had blood on his hands. It was to his credit that he intended to save her, yet her heart must not soften toward him merely because of the sweetness of his kisses...

It was difficult to keep her mind profitably occupied! Desperate for rescue from her thoughts, she wiped the sand smooth beside her and started printing Bible verses with her forefinger. Soon, however, there was a diversion. Another party of pirates emerged noisily from the woods, bearing with them twenty or so carcasses of large birds— wild geese, turkeys and ducks. They plucked, dressed and spitted these over fresh fires and in a short time the rich smell of cooking poultry filled the air.

The captain stood aside to examine these fires and Mercy wondered why. Then he tipped his head back to watch the rising smoke and she understood. The pirates could not risk that their presence be detected by passing ships, rare though these might be. These days that rare vessel might be a man-of-war. He knelt, removed some of the fuel from a cooking fire and after a few minutes the little smoke that was not absorbed by the birds' flesh drifted away lazily in the warm air.

He also kept an eye on the hotbeds where the planks lay, though these gave off no smoke. And more than once he glanced at the spit of sand across the creek mouth. Mercy, following his line of sight, saw two men on guard there with blunderbusses. They were careless, strolling about and talking, however they did look out to sea now and then and he let them be.

She wondered what it was like to live like that,

always on edge and alert every moment. And was surprised to find that because she was a prisoner she understood. And would live the same way if she ever reached New Exmouth, because there she would speculate whether people knew about her mother.

Quickly she turned her mind from that path. The present was worry enough. She cast a brief glance at Jedediah. He had lit a clay pipe and seemed content. He seemed an unimaginative person, though not a stupid or unkind one. Had he chosen piracy for profit, or had he merely followed his master?

It would be a game for her mind, to make up a past history for him. Yet she baulked at doing the same for the captain. About him, she would prefer to know the truth.

****

When the sun stood west of noon the birds were cooked and the pirates downed their tools to gather at the fires. They drank water from a barrel and sat and lay about, talking and laughing much as any group of men would do. Some of them looked her way. They gazed in other directions when the captain strode away from them toward her and Jedediah.

He sat down a few feet away, drew his knees up and dropped his arms across them. He wiped sweat from his brow and neck with a clean kerchief and watched the ship for some moments. Then he turned and inspected her with unfathomable dark eyes.

"Feeling the sun, are you?" His voice was curt. "Jedediah, put up a bit of canvas to give her shade before that fair skin burns." He spoke more like one protecting a fragile possession than a person. Jedediah grunted and trudged off and the captain pushed his hat toward her. "In the meantime, here."

It was true she was hot and she knew her face must be flushed, however Mercy let the black tricorne sit on the sand. She did not want to wear male apparel.

"Oh, show some sense. It might be a pirate's hat, but pride runs a poor second to sunburn."

Pride, again. Mercy considered, then placed the hat on her head, over her cap. It felt heavy and too warm and a circle of perspiration wet the rim, however it did shade her face.

30

"I meant to bring you a piece of plank to write on. Or did I? Maybe it's better not to know what you think." His tone mocked himself.

Mercy smoothed her hand over the last Bible verse she had written in the sand and erased it. She printed with her finger, THANK YOU. She raised her eyebrows at him in inquiry.

"Yes, I can read. I was raised respectable. 'Thank you' for what? The hat?"

She brushed the words away and wrote again. YES. AND FOR HAVING MERCY ON ME.

He shrugged. "What's your name?"

MERCY.

His look was measuring. "I suspected there was a wit under that yellow hair. Do you have a last name?"

She hesitated, but what could he know of her mother? PENHALL.

"Well met, Mistress Penhall. I'm Edmund Gramercy. So if we were wed, you'd be Mercy Gramercy." He saw startled colour rush to her cheeks and added impatiently, "I but made a bad joke, girl! Gramercy's not the name I was born with." He turned away from her again.

For some minutes he watched his men strip meat off the spits then his gaze ranged further, to the lookouts at the creek mouth. When he spoke it was evidently to himself. "I've taught them that much, at least. The guards aren't running back for their food until they're relieved." His glance flickered suddenly back to her and he frowned.

Mercy, from long experience, knew the look. Because she was silent, he had temporarily forgotten her presence. She took the opportunity however and printed, WHAT WILL HAPPEN TO THE LONGBOAT?

His voice was low, but angry. "By heaven, you try my charity!"

She met his eyes, folded her hands quickly in her lap and clenched her fingers tightly together. She had presumed too far.

"Very well. If they are any kind of seamen, they'll make shore or survive 'til they meet a ship." His tone was dangerous, for all its quiet. "Why? Do you have a friend among them?"

She shook her head.

31

His voice cooled, though it remained angry, which made his next words the more surprising. "The old woman on board, the one the second trunk belonged to—there was no mark on her body, they said. Was she kin to you?"

Mercy shook her head again, and bit her lip. She printed hurriedly, so that he would not see her finger tremble, SHE DIED OF FRIGHT. She had wanted to ask him what became of other women from captured ships. Now she did not dare.

He stared at her silently, eyes dark and cold and unreadable. She had noticed before that when he was distant as now his eyes were all brown, and when he was approachable the gold lights appeared in them. She thought there must be the remnant at least of a warmer person beneath the cold outer one.

He turned his head away. By chance his face presented the same aspect she had seen in the cabin yesterday evening, the line of forehead and cheek and the long lashes outlined. She had thought then that he grieved. Was it possible that he regretted the death of an old lady and the fate of the sailors in the longboat?

How was it possible for a man to regret the deaths of others and yet remain a pirate?

Chapter Three

Silence stretched between Mercy and the pirate like a string that needed but a touch to hum. Yet neither made a sound. She could hear only their breathing, the lap of water on the shore, the more distant beat of the sea, the background murmur of the men's voices and birds' calls from the woods...

Then Jedediah returned. He carried a roll of old sail and a bundle of long sticks under one thick arm. His other fist held the handle of a small cooking pot, from which rose fragrant steam. He set it on the sand between the two of them and spoke. The string broke...

"There's wild goose an' duck an' turkey, an' a bit of boiled corn, an' flat bread baked in the ashes." From beneath his deep armpit he produced a pewter flask. "Sweet water, from the spring yonder."

"That's for the girl, Jedediah," the captain told him sharply. "You know to bring wine or brandywine, for me."

The big man looked squarely at his master. "Water's better'n wine for keepin' sense in your head. Anyways, if they sees you drinkin' wine they'll want rum."

Gramercy scowled. "Since when has what they want mattered to me, unless it's life or death? Who gives the orders here? And who constituted you my nursemaid? I brought myself to this spot for a little peace. The girl at least can't talk." He included Mercy in the scowl, then turned his back on both of them and frowned deeply at the creek.

Jedediah made a sulky face and pushed the pot toward Mercy. She was unused to eating in the middle of the day, but picked out a duck's wing. She leaned over as she ate so the juices dripped onto the sand and not her gown.

The big man stood, pushed the sticks into the sand

behind her, lashed them together with twine and spread the canvas over them. It made an effective lean-to and she was pleased to have the shade. Jedediah sat heavily again, plucked a goose leg from the pot, looked at the captain's back and opened his mouth to speak.

Mercy moved quickly into his line of sight, pressed a finger to her lips and shook her head. Couldn't the man see that he would make his master angrier if he tried to coax him?

Jedediah's mouth fell open in surprise, then he scratched his head under the sweaty kerchief and began to eat the drumstick himself. Mercy selected a small corncob. When she had finished it she pointed to the pewter flask. Jedediah pushed it across to her and she rinsed her mouth and fingers. There was no cup, so she raised the flask with both hands and drank several mouthfuls, one at a time, careful not to let the water run down her chin.

When she re-stoppered it, the big man said with simple admiration, "My, you got pretty manners."

She smiled.

The captain turned with an abrupt movement and looked at her quizzically, though he said nothing.

She was a little unnerved by the look. To cover her confusion, she lifted the tricorne off her head, held it out to him and indicated with her left hand that she now had the canvas for shelter. He took the hat but dropped it indifferently on the sand.

Mercy frowned. She pantomimed with her hands the action of placing a hat on her head.

"By heaven, you can't talk but you nag as well as Jedediah! And I had thought your company would be restful because you can't speak!"

Mercy compressed her lips and folded her hands in her lap again, however she did not drop her gaze.

They stared at each other, then suddenly he asked, "Were you born mute?"

Her quick temper had roused, though common sense overruled it. She did not want to answer, yet her life depended on his goodwill. She smoothed another place in the sand and printed there a short word, NO.

"How long, then?" He seemed impatient, though no

longer angry.

TWELVE YEARS.

"You would have been a child. How old are you now?"

TWENTY THREE

The dark eyebrows rose. "Three and twenty! I guessed no more than eighteen. I see now why you consider you're unmarriageable. Haven't been able to talk half your life as well. Lost your voice in 1692. What happened? Were you sick?"

Mercy felt as if she froze in the warm air. She had given away too much. Surely all the world knew what had happened in New England in the summer of '92? But common sense told her that other things had happened that year—Port Royal in Jamaica had been destroyed by earthquake, for one. There was no reason why Edmund Gramercy should connect her with the year. And of course he assumed she was from Virginia.

She really had been ill, afterward. The shock to her spirit had left her weak and an inflammation of the chest and throat had infected her body. She had barely recovered when Uncle Jonathan took her to Virginia and the care of Mam Felice. No one in Virginia had suspected the truth either.

She wrote quickly, YES.

The captain's disconcerting eyes were fixed on her, though he said only, "Well, if you had a voice once it may return." He glanced over his shoulder. "Jedediah, pass me a turkey leg. And without a smirk, if you please."

Mercy turned her eyes away while he ate. She struggled to keep evidence of the old bad memory from her face and stared toward the *Thalia*. When her mind cleared she noticed the blocky figure of Gorman on the quarterdeck. He held a spyglass to his eye and it was obvious he trained it on the three of them.

Gramercy, as he tipped the flask to drink, saw the direction of her gaze. "Aye, he's watching us. Me, more than you or Jedediah. But if he suspects I plan to run off into the woods with a woman holding me back, he's a bigger fool than I think."

Mercy ignored the inference she would be a burden and raised her eyebrows at the puzzling statement. She jerked her head toward the ship and Gorman, then pointed toward the main body of men.

He understood that she asked a question. "Oh, yes, they watch me. I'm a sea-artist, a navigator. They can't afford to lose me, yet." He tossed the turkey bone into the creek. "Jedediah, go tell the camp they're to return to work and the watchmen are to be relieved. I want the repairs finished by nightfall, no matter how rough. The green timber will hold out until we meet—" he glanced at Mercy and finished dryly – "a better carpenter."

Jedediah rolled away, taking the pot with him. Gramercy did not follow at once and Mercy caught his attention while the chance was there.

She printed in the sand, WHY THALIA?

"Do you know what it means?"

IT IS THE GREEK MUSE OF COMEDY.

"You've had an uncommon education for a girl, to know that." The eyes assessed her, then darkened. "Don't try to be friends with me, little one, out of gratitude. And don't be curious. The less you know of me, the more healthful for you. The same goes the other way. When I set you ashore, it'll be with gold for your ship-fare home. But I don't want to know where that is, or any more about you."

She looked back at him, then wiped the words from the sand and returned her hands to her lap. She did not nod agreement, merely lifted her chin.

He shrugged. "Remember you are at my mercy, Mistress Mercy." He turned his back to her, yet still did not rise.

Mercy knew she had no right to expect more from the pirate than her life and virtue spared. She had made the mistake of behaving toward him, for a few minutes, as she had to her uncle. Jonathan Penhall had always treated her as a person worth consideration, not a mere indigent female relative. He had had his failings, a hot temper and a headlong impulsiveness, however he had spoiled her, she supposed. She still missed him...

The captain made a sudden move to rise. She reached out quickly to grasp his sleeve and held it firmly. He shook her hand off. "What do you want? I have work to do."

She thought wryly, *men always do,* and wrote swiftly

36

in the sand. I NEED TO WALK AND TO WASH. Then as
he frowned at it, ALSO TO—she would not use the bald
common word—GO TO PRIVY.

"You can't stroll alone, or near the men. We need
Jedediah's strength for a few minutes, then I'll send him
back to watchdog you while you exercise." He examined
her with momentary interest. "Do Puritans believe in
cleansing their skins, then? He can bring a pail of water
back, and there's the canvas for privacy. As for the other,
I'll escort you into the woods now. But let's give them a
show, while we're at it. Look out, little one, I'm going to be
rough with you."

He leapt up with ease from his sitting position,
reached down a hand and hauled her to her feet. He set
off for the green forest fringe with a long step, so that she
had to half run to keep up with him. Once in the shelter of
the trees he released her hand and turned his back.

"Don't worry, Mercy Penhall, I won't look."

The nearest trees were a kind of straggly pine and
their trunks were not wide. Mercy retreated behind the
widest she could find and inspected the ground for snakes
and insects before she lifted her skirt and petticoat. When
she had finished, she went back and stood an arm's length
from the captain's side.

He did not look at her but said, "Wait a little. Give
them time to think I might have run off, or am interfering
with you."

Mercy sighed and clasped her hands before her. She
was not patient by nature, though of necessity had
learned to practise the virtue. And she needed to be
patient with this man, when she must wholly rely on him.

After some minutes Gramercy spoke again. "To add
to your education, these trees are swamp oaks." He
turned toward her, leaned back on a sapling and folded
his arms. "You have gentle manners, Mistress, an
education and a preference to be clean. Is your family
wealthy?"

She stepped back a quick pace, away from him. She
had believed again she could trust him and again it
seemed he was not to be trusted. Had he decided to hold
her for ransom after all? She shook her head quickly.

"You mistake me," he told her dryly. "I thought, not

of gold, but your reputation. Don't tell your relatives that I kept you in my cabin. A maid you will remain, but your good name would not survive the truth. You must let them think you were locked away alone." He stood away from the tree, dropped his hands to hook his thumbs in his belt. "But I dare not do that. Gorman has an eye for you because you're pretty and he could reach you. Do you understand?"

She bit her lip and nodded sharply. She had reasoned out the last part of what he said this morning. As for the first, she was surprised by the decency of it. She mouthed carefully, *thank you.*

He frowned slightly. "It puzzles me that you are a spinster, even dumb." Then his manner became brisk. "I will tell you now, where there are no listening ears, that the only place I can put you ashore is Charles Town in Carolina Colony. That's two or three days' sailing. I'll smuggle you through the harbour and into the company of decent folk. Hopefully you'll find passage home." His words were businesslike, and he did not know that the dappled sunlight found the gold flecks in his eyes.

Mercy met his look and nodded once more, gently.

For a single moment their gazes meshed. Then with one of his quick movements he turned away. His voice was suddenly harsh. "A few of the men are getting restive and Gorman has his glass on this spot. Come now."

He seized her hand, and again walking too fast for her pulled her out onto the sand. At the lean-to he pushed her shoulder hard downward, so that she half fell into the patch of shade thrown by the canvas. He scooped the tricorne hat onto his head and strode off, without another word and without a backward glance.

Mercy drew herself up to sit. She dropped her chin, folded her hands and tried to play his game by seeming cowed. Her right hand, that he had held so hard, tingled strangely. She pressed it tightly within the other as if pressure would still the sensation.

Yes, best she be sent ashore, soon, away from him. She must not like him. For whatever reason, Edmund Gramercy was a pirate.

And who are you, mocked her conscience, *to despise a mere pirate?*

****

The raggedly repaired ship slipped out to sea with the tide the following dawn. For two days and nights it sailed south, slowly, in light airs. And for two days and nights Gramercy almost totally ignored her.

Mercy saw little of him, since he spent all the daylight hours on deck and did not return to the cabin until late each night. Jedediah made sure she was tied when his master slept, otherwise she was left unbound. She could walk about the cabin and that was all. Unused to being idle she slept much in the day and, therefore, little at night.

At those times she lay awake on the pallet, watched moonlight glimmer through the stern windows, heard the sounds of sea, ship and men, and Gramercy's deep breathing. More than once she guessed that he, too, was wakeful and sensed again the intangible string stretched between them as it had been on the beach. She would pray in her mind then, because it seemed wrong, evidence of the perversity of her mother's blood.

He spoke to her twice on the first day and once on the second.

On the first, he gave her a piece of thin smooth plank to write on and told her curtly that it was to be used only when necessary.

Mercy drew chalk from her bag at once and printed, MAY THE WINDOWS BE OPENED FOR COOL AIR?

"No. Can you swim?"

She shook her head sharply. Did he imagine she was such a fool as to try to escape that way? To drown?

"Oh, I don't think you're fool enough to leap overboard. But Gorman, or any sailor used to climbing rigging, could lower himself over the stern rail and come in through the windows, if they're open." His tone was at its most expressionless.

She believed him. She lowered her chin to nod and to write again. I NEED A CLEAN GOWN AND LINEN. The grey wool dress she had worn since boarding the *Jesselin* had become uncomfortable in the heat, its plain collar and cuffs grubby and limp. Her petticoat and shift were in the same state.

Gramercy showed a moment's sympathy at this.

"Aye, I know you're sweating. But I can't be seen to show you consideration. It's not for long." And with no other word he strode out.

She did not see him again until the evening, by which time she was near distracted with boredom. She asked, with her chalk, for something to do, something to read. DO YOU HAVE A BIBLE? She had seen books in the stern locker.

"No," was all he said. Nor did he offer any other book.

But when Jedediah brought her supper he handed her a sea-stained pack of cards. He also tied her hands, after she had eaten, so she had no chance to look at the pack by lantern light. She fell into a heat-drugged sleep.

On the second morning the captain was gone before she woke. She invented, since she had never before played cards, her own games. She was at the oak table, frowning at the suits, when Gramercy came unexpectedly below.

He took a book, a journal, from his sea chest, together with a quill and the bottle of ink from the brass stand in the table. Plainly he intended to write and not in her presence. He halted a moment though, to inspect the cards.

He asked abruptly, "Do you play chess? Though I believe Puritans do not approve of it."

She nodded, surprised. Uncle Jonathan had decided it was an exercise for the mind more than a game and had taught her.

"You've had a liberal upbringing." He frowned. "I have a small set, with ivory and ebony pieces. Not heavy enough," he added dryly, "to damage a man. I'll loan it to you later. You can play against yourself."

She inclined her head in thanks and waited for him to leave.

He stood where he was and looked down at her, so that she had to lift her face to see him. His voice remained curt and his eyes were dark, at odds with his words. "You aren't afraid of me now."

She met his gaze and felt the invisible cord pull tight. Her chalk and board lay to hand and on impulse she wrote, I TRUST YOU. And saw in time that this would not do and quickly added an R and WORD, so that it read, I TRUST YOUR WORD.

For a moment the unfathomable eyes burned into hers. She felt blood rise to her face. Then he shrugged and turned to go.

She seized his sleeve with one hand and printed hurriedly with the other, YOU DID NOT TELL ME, WHY THALIA? She knew in her heart it was merely a ruse to keep him there, but he could not see her heart.

Little flames leaped in the brown eyes. "It may have always been called that, so far as you know. Take your hand from my sleeve."

She did so slowly, and waited.

"But it so happens that I changed its name." He bent slightly closer, not seeming to know that he did. "Is not life a comic play, Mistress, in which things happen you'd never dream of?"

Mercy wrote no more on the board. She did not nod or shake her head, only met Gramercy's gaze, aware of her cheeks still warm. She felt as if something had twanged the cord and made it vibrate between them.

"Your silence is like quicksand," he said softly. "It traps a man before he knows it." He turned on his heel and strode from the cabin. She heard the key turn in the lock.

Her hands trembled. To stop them she wiped the board clean with vicious strokes. Then the cabin seemed too quiet and empty. And she felt lonely, as if she missed him.

****

On the third morning, the voice of the lookout, sudden and strident, cut through the quiet air. "A sail! Inshore. Off our starboard bow!"

Mercy had broken her fast and washed her face and hands. She was in the act of setting up the elegant little chess pieces on their sandalwood board. The captain had departed for his quarterdeck at sunrise. She had heard the swift movements of his dressing and had kept her eyes closed.

Now she clutched the ebony knight tightly in her fist. She felt her stomach tighten. Who was it? A French privateer? Or another victim? They must be close by Charles Town now. There might be ship traffic to, or from, England.

41

She listened intently to the following calls, but uproar had broken out on deck and it drowned them. Then the captain's voice shouted orders over the noise. The orders must have been to crowd on sail, for the *Thalia* after some minutes began to gain way. Mercy dropped the chess piece and clasped her hands together. She felt sick. Another attack–more death, more loot, more prisoners. And Gramercy would lead it...

The door slammed against the bulkhead and he strode into the cabin. Without a glance at her he drew the flat case from under his bunk, unlocked it and tipped both pistols onto the table beside the chessmen. Swiftly he primed and loaded them.

"Pack the set away, little one. *Thalia* might move fast and often." His voice was cold and curt. "There's a ship of the Queen's Navy patrolling north out of Charles Town and she's likely seen us." He jammed the pistols into his belt. "If you hear cannon shot, lie flat. That's all I can advise you."

She nodded and swallowed the lump of new fear.

He saw her white face and shook his head sharply. "We may outrun her. We are heading south and she'll lose time to turn. I've no wish to fight. She's bigger than we are."

There was a shout from the deck, Gorman's voice. "She's set up the forward guns for warnin' shot! Now she's..." His next word was lost in a sound like the bark of thunder, followed immediately by another. The naval ship's two forward cannon had fired.

Mercy trembled. *Not again, please God,* she prayed. Only three days ago she had sat helpless under a cannonade.

"I told you, lie flat!" Gramercy seized her arm across the table and dragged her down on the deck-boards with him. He pushed her head lower, flung himself across her body and pressed his face between her shoulders.

The sound of the shots shrieked high overhead and ended in a loud double splash. Mercy heard the men on deck shout relieved obscenities then heard the breath whistle from her own lungs. Only then did she notice the man's weight on her back. She lay immobile a moment, aware to her bones of his body, then wriggled frantically to try to get away.

Gramercy jerked to his knees and drew her up with him. "Our English flag's not deceived them. *Thalia's* known to the Navy. There'll be a fight. I must go." He snatched one of the pistols from his belt. "If I am killed, if you are left with Gorman, use this on yourself."

Her great blue eyes stared at him.

"Pull the hammer back first," he went on grimly, "then put the barrel in your mouth and squeeze the trigger. You'll feel nothing." He laid the pistol beside her.

No, she shaped with her lips. She shook her head violently, then seized his waistcoat with both small hands and held tight.

Edmund did not know whether her denial was for death by her own hand or the thought of his. "I have no time for this! Remember to lie flat as I said." He tore her hands loose then saw one tear roll from each of her eyes. It was too much. He seized her head and kissed her lips. He meant it to be hard and quick, but her softness was like solace and his mouth wanted to linger... *No time.* "That is farewell, if needed." He leaped to his feet and ran from the cabin, though he still took one second to lock the door.

****

"Ye nay had time to dally with the wench!" Gorman shouted at Gramercy when he reached the quarterdeck. It was plain the mate hid his fear with anger. "I've ordered we stay on course, pending your pleasure!"

Edmund did not trouble to answer, simply held out his hand for the spyglass. He trained it on the set of sails west of them. Gorman informed him bitterly, "It's a man'o'war an' nay mistake. *Tresadern*—the gunner's boy read her name through the glass. And we're a hawk to her eagle." He fell to swearing and describing luridly all he would do to the company of the Queen's ship if they captured her. At the same time he ordered the portside deck guns be rolled to starboard.

"Belay that order!" Gramercy shouted down to the deck. "More sail, quickly." As the crew scurried with unaccustomed speed to obey, he told Gorman harshly, "We'll lose our trim if the cannon are moved. She's too big for us to fight, but we have the advantage of the wind.

We'll outrun her."

"Damned fool! She'll be in place to let loose two, three broadsides afore she has to turn!"

"Yes!" On this ship the mate could call him a fool. "And we'll answer her shot. Once or twice only, if I can trust my eye. She'll think we want to fight. But by then we'll be ahead of her, too far for another discharge." *If the naval captain did not guess his intention.* "Order the starboard guns only run out."

Gorman relayed the order with a roar, then grinned like a feral beast. "Better pray their broadsides miss your cabin, Cap'n, or there'll be nay left o' your dainty piece but red meat."

Gramercy had seen among his gunners the pale face of the boy from the *Jesselin* and had spared no time for pity. But now his mind's eye saw the picture Gorman had just painted. The Puritan woman, her soft sweet body smashed by a cannonball... He snapped the glass closed. "We may all be in pieces. Stand ready for my orders."

Tresadern drew abreast of them, her bow pointed north and his south, still over a half-mile distant. She fired her first broadside. It was well-aimed and would have raked *Thalia's* length if she had been within range. The roar and splash of the shots fell mostly short, as he had known they would, except for one that ploughed down a bulwark and gouged the ship's side. It knocked a cannon's snout askew but struck no one.

Gramercy shouted immediately, "Fire!"

Their own smaller shot blasted raggedly across the water. Their fire was not as neatly timed as the naval ship's and of course would fall far short. He could imagine the Queen's men laughing at this. He hoped they did. While *Thalia's* guns were reloaded, he swiftly raised the spyglass and studied *Tresadern's* position. As he expected, she had drawn nearer and a little ahead. Her next broadside would strike his stern.

And down there, in the great cabin, Mercy Penhall lay helpless, her ears assaulted by the roar of the guns, her courage useless against iron shot...

He told Gorman, "This will be the last round she can get off! Then she'll have to haul around into the wind to pursue us. We'll catch no more than stray shots and those only at an angle."

"She's got more sail than us!" snarled the mate. "You can nay be sure we'll outrun her!"

"I'm sure of nothing, Gorman. I'll play each move as I see fit. You be sure of one thing only, to relay my orders quick and not to question them!" Edmund glanced up at the masts. The men had already put every sail to the wind and were climbing down. It could have been done better, though not by these. He looked to see if the helmsman was steady and saw behind him Jedediah, feet braced on the deck, ready to help with the wheel.

Gorman spat down the breeze. "Aye, we'll do what you say sailin', it's what you're good for! There now, she's fired again!"

The mate had heard the guns, but before that Edmund had seen through the glass the little smoke puffs along the warship's side. He measured their line with his eye and knew this time *Thalia* would not escape with a simple scratch.

He knew his face was the mask it always became in action, but his mind begged of God and the fates that they not be holed below the waterline, which would dim their speed. *And that no shot enter the great cabin.*

Most of the cannonballs fell in *Thalia's* wake. But three or four whistled across the half-deck—*Tresadern* must have raised the angle of her guns, hoping to cripple the masts. One slammed into the bulwark, another tore into the superstructure below it and another flew cleanly through the rigging before falling into the sea. But the last fell on the deck's edge. By the screams it caught two or three men... He heard the gun-captain curse and ran to the rail.

The starboard gun nearest the stern was cluttered horribly with bodies and blood. "Clear that cannon!" he shouted. He did not need to say, *Dead overboard!* The devils would do that themselves and throw off the wounded as well if they weren't shipmates. "Listen now! He can't shoot us again! We're ahead of his course and he must turn. All of you, fire when ready!"

Their ragged volley burst out again but he did not even look to see if any of it touched *Tresadern*. "Port watch! Up to the sails and lash them firmer! And a lookout in the crow's nest reporting to me!" Now they must run in earnest. *And he must stay on deck and not go to see what had happened to the girl.* It near unnerved him that in the midst of a sea fight he remembered her at all.

They raced before the breeze for one turn of the hourglass. The heavy warship had lost time coming about, however by virtue of her greater spread of sail stayed steadily in pursuit a mere mile behind them. Thank Providence, such damage as they'd suffered had not dulled *Thalia's* speed. It was morning still and he must run her all day, then hope to evade the bigger ship in the dark.

Tresadern had gradually worked across until dead astern of the pirate. She had fired twice from her forward guns but the shots had fallen short. *He hoped well short.*

Edmund became aware of Jedediah at his shoulder. "Yes?" he barked.

"I'll fetch ye some water, Cap'n," the big man said stolidly, "an' see the cabin ain't shot about."

Gorman sneered. "Aye, make sure the woman's nay dead." Though he was more concerned with his own skin. "You said we'd outrun her but she's keepin' close!"

"If she was able to catch us she'd have done it by now. We'll slip away after the sun's down." Edmund kept his hands still when he longed to smash the spyglass into the mate's face. Gorman should know him well enough now to understand that the angrier he became, the colder his voice.

Jedediah returned within minutes, with a bucket and a tin dipper. "Cabin's not damaged." His broad face was expressionless.

Gorman chortled briefly, however was more interested in keeping his eyes on the warship.

Another hour passed. Excepting for small gains and losses of distance that were caught up again by both crews, the respective positions of the ships did not change. If they ran all through the day they would bypass Charles Town... Edmund stood the men down one watch at a time to rest, eat, drink. They sat in the sails' shade and probably grumbled, yet did not disagree with him directly about their state of readiness. He thought bleakly that he might make a crew of them yet, if he survived.

Then the man in the crow's nest called excitedly. "Another sail! North and east of us, on our course!"

Gorman bared his teeth. "These waters been uncommon busy of late, for the Colonies." A thought struck him. "If it's a Frenchie, they'll fight the Navy an' we'll get clean away."

It might be a French warship. It might be a merchantman bound for Charles Town or the Caribbean. It might be another Navy ship. It might even be another pirate.

Edmund cupped his hands to shout up to the lookout. "Call me the colour of her hull when you see it for certain!" He waited tensely another quarter-turn of the sand in the hourglass.

The lookout's voice bawled down. It carried plainly in the light air and there was no doubt of its triumph. "Black! 'Tis the *Prospero!*"

Late for the rendezvous by half a week, but, as always, in the right place at the right time.

Within thirty minutes they were sure. *Prospero* bore down on *Tresadern* at full stretch and Edmund turned *Thalia* into the breeze. The naval ship was larger than either pirate but no match for both of them together. Still, she might choose to engage. No Queen's captain fancied to run before enemies.

Instead she crowded on every extra stitch of sail from her lockers and began to show her wake. Doubtless the captain would report himself attacked by a larger force, to save pride. It would be plain foolish of him to fight and probably lose his ship, yet there were always superior officers to placate. Naval captains might be the Queen's representatives in Carolina but the Proprietary Governor had the last word.

Prospero sent *Tresadern* on her way with two impudent volleys from her forward guns, then gradually came up with *Thalia*. When the pirate pair finally lay athwart each other on the water, all to be seen of the Queen's ship was a sail south and west of them, beating home to Charles Town's safe harbour. Gorman and the crew hurled lewd and bloody insults after her, just as if they'd run her off themselves.

Edmund ordered that they heave to and saw the black-hulled ship ease its own rigging. The Naval captain would gather reinforcements and come out to hunt for them, of course. But by the time they reached this position both pirates would be well gone.

The problem of the woman remained. First, however, he would see Richard.

Chapter Four

Mercy felt *Thalia* lose way, then ride the gentle swell like a great sea-bird come to rest. She breathed out her terror and with effort composed herself. The ship would not halt if in danger of attack. There would be no more cannon fire, then. She thanked God for that.

She heard the door-key turn then saw Gramercy stride briskly into the cabin. Some of the habitual grimness had vanished from his face. In fact, he seemed pleased. He unhitched his leather sword belt, lay one pistol in its case and held his hand toward her for the other.

"Unless, little one, you wish to shoot me." His manner was downright good-humoured.

Mercy, of course, like any woman, had never fired a pistol in her life. For one instant she wholeheartedly wanted to try it, to let a ball fly into the ship's timbers behind his head. *He had not asked how she was, when she had been so frightened!* Sense again prevented her from acting like a fool. She needed his good will and might lose it if she tried to keep the pistol. She bit her lips in frustration and sent it sliding across the floor, like a spoilt child giving up a forbidden toy.

"Ah." He smiled gently when he had retrieved it. "My suspicion was again correct. There's a spitfire behind those angel eyes."

He locked the gun away. Then he knelt by the sea chest and dug from its depths a coat, waistcoat and breeches all of crimson broadcloth. He laid them on his bunk along with clean cambric shirt and black stockings.

He looked her way. "We've been fortunate, little one. A ship we know has chanced along, bigger than we are. I will visit the captain and you will come with me. It is possible they may be able to put you ashore easier than I can." He saw her start of alarm and widened eyes, and added curtly, "There's no need to fear. I trust them. Turn your back, now. I'm stripping everything."

Mercy turned her face to the bulkhead and frowned at the import of his words. She found herself reluctant to leave *Thalia* and bent her head in shame. The sooner she left Edmund Gramercy behind her the better. However, would she feel so safe in another ship's company, even if they were his friends? Her thoughts were confusing and she prayed silently for calm.

Yet when he told her to look again, she quite forgot to be perturbed. He was dressed as splendidly as a nobleman. The long red coat and waistcoat, falling exactly to the hems of the breeches, were embroidered in black thread and bore gilded buttons. In the prevailing fashion only one of these held the coat closed, at the waist. The wide cuffs revealed two layers of ivory lace at his wrists, and the muslin *cravate* round his neck was richly embroidered and also trimmed with lace. His stockings were rolled over the breeches at the knees and instead of boots he wore black shoes fastened across their long tongues by gold rosettes.

In the act of running the horn comb through his hair he saw her look. "You approve the costume, Mistress? Even if stolen?" His voice mocked himself.

Mercy schooled her face to a prim expression and decided she could nod an affirmative. He did look almost handsome.

He slung a dress sword from his shoulder by a gold silk baldric and lifted to his head a wide-brimmed hat pinned up one side with a crimson feather. "Come, then." He opened the cabin door and waited for her to pass through.

From the open deck she saw, perhaps two hundred yards off *Thalia's* port side, a large ship painted black with two great stripes of gold running boldly above its gun-ports. With sails half-furled it too seemed an exotic bird, swooped down to float on the blue sea. Like the *Thalia* it flew the combined crosses of Britain. Mercy had no doubt that, also like *Thalia,* it could lower that flag in a trice and run up a black one.

Gramercy spoke brief orders to Jedediah and to

Gorman, then climbed over the side by the rope ladder, this time down into the longboat with a crew of six at the oars. Mercy, however, did not descend the same way. Gramercy had ordered a canvas sling rigged for her and she was lowered sitting in that. He indicated the stern seat and sat there by her but neither touched nor spoke to her. He gazed ahead at the newcomer until they were under its lee side.

A carved and painted figurehead of a bearded man decorated the bowsprit and the word *Prospero* was painted boldly in gold on the ship's side. The longboat clunked alongside until it touched amidships and then was lashed fast. The oarsmen clambered up a rope ladder. Gramercy held it firmly and nodded at Mercy to climb.

She did not know what she would find at the top of it and looked the question at him.

He said, "Don't be afraid."

She took a deep breath and went up, not troubling to hold her skirt. He had seen her ankles before.

Above the bulwark, the ladder was held firm by a thin man with a black moustache, a black kerchief on his head and gold rings in his ears. He looked at her curiously but did not manhandle her.

Behind him a lazy voice drawled, "Go forward, Mr. Turner. I'll take care of the lady." The other obeyed without argument. A tall, fair-skinned, well-fleshed man dressed in peacock blue and silver helped her gain her footing. In an English voice he asked with a chuckle, "Well, what have we here? Edmund turned Puritan?"

It did not occur to Mercy for a moment to be afraid. The stranger seemed to be of Gramercy's age, with a hawkish profile and keen hazel eyes relieved by well-fed cheeks and the creases and glints of easy humour. His head boasted a startling blond periwig and a blue-dyed hat trimmed with silver lace. This hat he swept off then bowed to her as elegantly as a courtier.

"At your service, ma'am, nonetheless."

Mercy had seen from the corner of her eye the longboat crew received noisily before the forecastle. Now she saw Gramercy drop lightly from the bulwark to her side.

"She can't talk, Richard. But she's no fool and your

charms won't wash with her. Mistress Mercy Penhall, Captain Richard Collyer."

All the manners ever taught her had not included proper response to formal introduction to a pirate. She simply inclined her head.

Gramercy added, too softly to be heard, "I'm sending her in to Charles Town."

"One of your charities, I presume." Captain Collyer's sharp eyes showed only merriment. "Well, tell me all above."

He led them up the steep companionway to the poop deck, where a striped awning was spread above a table and two chairs of carved mahogany. He sent a hovering servant to fetch another chair and "refreshments for the lady."

"Where do you want her to sit, Edmund?" He grinned at Mercy. "Begging your pardon, Mistress, to talk about you to your face. But I never met a dumb woman before."

"Sit her over the other side of the deck," Gramercy told him. "Her hearing's sharp and she can read and write. My name and face are known, but she'll doubtless be questioned. We should be east of the harbour bar this evening." He glanced at the other man in direct inquiry. "Unless you've business there and can take her with you."

"I've paid my visit to Monsieur and Madame, under my other name. This good claret is a gift from Monsieur and he's particular about his wine." Collyer lifted a bottle from the table and poured two measures into silver goblets. "They'd deem it strange if they hear of me in the city again so soon."

Edmund frowned. "You must do nothing to arouse suspicion."

Collyer pushed a silver bowl of raisins across the table. "It'd be less risky to let her loose east of the Indies, where Her Majesty's ships aren't so thick on the water."

"I don't wish to keep her aboard longer than I must. I'll get Jedediah to take her in." Gramercy took a mouthful of the wine.

Collyer cast him a keen look though he said only, "You know your own business best." He shrugged. "But if she's so astute, maybe you should've left her aboard the *Thalia* instead of giving her more to see." He winked at

Mercy.

Edmund made a wry face. "I can't trust Gorman. Jedediah would guard her but if it's a choice of risks, it's easier to keep her under my eye." He picked out a couple of raisins, then smiled faintly. "You take your own risks, running into Charles Town."

Collyer grinned his sharp grin. "'Tis worth them, to talk of learning with Monsieur and ask what books I can bring him next time I unload goods. After all, bringing books and Burgundy wine into port is how I made his acquaintance. And, he thinks, Madame's. All the while I talk I pretend to have no interest in Madame. 'Tis an excellent game." He turned to share the grin with Mercy. "How long since you captured the lass?"

The servant returned with a small chair for Mercy and Gramercy did not answer. The chair was set by the opposite rail, a tankard of watered wine and a dish of raisins were handed to her, then the man left for the lower deck.

Mercy now heard the voices of the two captains as murmurs only. She struggled briefly with her conscience then decided to read their lips. It was possible their conversation contained clues to her own immediate fate. However, she wanted to know more about Edmund Gramercy.

It was Collyer whose words she shaped first. "—after you transferred your own load to the sloop, then. But they told me you'd sailed south."

Gramercy had laid his fine hat on the dark tabletop. His face was plain to see and it was set in stern lines. "I'd already persuaded them to head for Brazil. But Gorman's greedy for pickings and sways the others. I was out-voted. Nor did I believe that little ship would fight, out-gunned. Well, it's done now. But I'd rather prey on French, Portagees and Spanishers than my own countrymen."

"With the righteous reason that England's at war with France now because of Spain."

"And Spain's colonies on the Main are now better defended. We're too late to be buccaneers, by some six or seven years, even with dregs of them in our crews." Gramercy took a good mouthful of the wine.

"Yet you had the luck to be with Sir George Rooke,

year before last, when he and the Dutch cornered the Spanish treasure fleet in Vigo Bay. There's a sight I'd like to have seen!" Collyer's face shone pink, though that might have been the heat of the day.

Gramercy smiled slightly. "I can't imagine you there if it meant being under orders of the Navy, even as a privateer!" The smile vanished. "Aye, it was a great sight, but I'd had enough by then. I went along for adventure and got a bellyful of it. I was almost pleased to get the message that Father was sick and needed me to captain the *Teign Swan* to the Indies." Mercy heard across the deck his short laugh, not amused but bitter.

It did not trouble Collyer. He had kept his fine hat on, and lounged in his chair three-quarter face to Mercy. "An honest merchant venturer, you said at the time, was all you now wanted to be." He lifted his goblet in mock salute. "Whereas my family sent me with you hoping I'd make something of myself in Jamaica—and to save me from the Excisemen. Glad to see the back of me, they were. But you should write to yours, Edmund, and let them know you're still alive."

"They'd rather me dead, than a pirate."

"Still bothering your head about it, are you? We had no choice, when the *Swan* was taken. Better a live pirate, I say, than a dead merchant - and richer."

"Faith, I wish I had your free and easy conscience! Gold is cold comfort, bought with blood."

Collyer shrugged like a drake sliding water off its back and helped himself to a fistful of raisins. "Gorman's still the thorn in your side, then?"

"If those rats have any loyalty, it's to him. Their old captain took them round Africa when the war began, swore they'd find great booty up to India and could careen in safety north of Madagascar. But they found no nabob's barges, and St. Mary's Isle when they got there was deserted. It was Gorman led the vote to sail back to the Caribbean." He smiled again, if faintly. "Your case is different. You landed on your feet when they sold you to *Prospero*."

Collyer nodded carelessly, as if good luck and bad were the same to him. "But don't their numbers thin out, in ship fights?"

Edmund downed another deep mouthful of wine. "Their old crew's still near intact, except of course for the captain the *Swan* blew off his quarterdeck. It's only the new hands who seem to be killed. Fiendish bad luck, for me. With different men, I might prevail to some extent. As it is they fret under the little discipline I have instilled."

Collyer spat a seed from a raisin. "Tell you what, Edmund. You're here and the woman's here. I'll blow your command out of the water for ye."

Gramercy stared across the sea at *Thalia*. "God help me, I'm tempted." Then he looked back to the other with the same odd smile. "I thank you, but Jedediah's on board. Gorman knows he's safe, with either one of us for hostage."

"Some men'd count it cheap, to buy their freedom with another's life."

"No." Gramercy shook his head. "I don't know why he latched on to me in the first place. Perhaps it was a whipping I was able to spare him, on the *Swan*. But I owe him my life twice now, and I won't take his."

"Then there's no hope for you!" Collyer shrugged again, laughed, and drank deeply of the claret. "Well, 'tis short lives we'll have, mayhap. But for me I'll make it a merry one and drain it to the dregs."

"'Tis a comedy that will end, no doubt of that." Edmund also drank again, then raised the goblet a moment to watch the light shine on the silver. "I can but act the part."

"Ah, yes, *Thalia*. And your crew never thinking it anything but a woman's name."

"The little one there, she knew." Gramercy glanced across at Mercy where she sat quietly sipping her drink. He frowned slightly when he saw her blue eyes upon them.

Collyer raised his eyebrows. They were dark, which looked odd on his light skin and under the blond wig. "A scholar? Girls ain't sent to grammar schools. What's her history?"

"I know not and I don't ask. At least she's quieter company than her predecessors. That lovely fool I returned to Kingston town and the bondservant I sent on to New York, both near wore me out with tears and pleadings. I suspect that, even dumb, Mistress Mercy is made of sterner stuff."

"Best is to be like *Prospero,* make out your Articles to disallow meddling with women on board. Only place we have truck with females is ashore."

"Gorman won't hear of changing ours. Thank God women are rarely ship's passengers! I have a battle with him, every time, to get them shoved off with the other survivors. It's unfair in his eyes that I keep one now and then for myself. It may yet be the death of..." In midsentence he suddenly stood and crossed the deck swiftly to where Mercy sat. He bent to examine her face, balancing himself with one hand on each arm of her chair. His eyes were dark with anger.

"You can read mouths." It was not a question.

He had moved so quickly that she'd had no time to lower her eyes. It was useless to deny the charge. She nodded. Her cheeks flushed hotly, though she returned his stare. She clenched her hands tightly in her lap, crushing in her fist two sticky raisins.

His voice was as cold as the ice on a New England pond in winter and as cutting. "That is a betrayal of trust, Mistress. You may believe you owe no honour to a pirate. But if you're as clever as I credit you, you'd see your spying gives you knowledge that's a danger to yourself as well as to Captain Collyer and I. I'll thank you to turn your back. Now." He straightened and swung away from her without another word.

Mercy bit her lip and turned her gaze to the sea. She heard the sound of shoes on the deck behind her and judged that the two men had moved to stand at the stern rail. However by a quirk of the air their voices now carried around to her ears. She fought again with her sense of right and wrong and again lost. It was anger that moved her this time. *How dared he speak to her like that!* She peeled the raisins off her palm, threw them overside, wiped her hands on her grubby kerchief and listened.

Gramercy's stern words were the first she heard. "— knife in the back, cannon fire, or noose, that's the only question."

"You've forgot the sea!" Collyer was irrepressible.

"But since we're both uncommon sailor-men and can swim, maybe it don't count. Yet you've become a black minded soul this past year, Edmund. There's no knowing the future. Who's to say you won't grow old and rear a pack of brats? There's always the amnesty."

"Oh, aye. Give up piracy by a certain date and you're pardoned. But the Brotherhood spoil that for themselves. As soon as their money runs out, or the Queen's officers turn their backs, they are at the trade again. No one takes it seriously, now."

"But, speaking legal, it still stands."

"And, speaking legally, the laws become harder, these years. There'll arrive a day, not too far distant, when pirating won't be so easy. The buccaneers plundered only Spaniards. Henry Morgan, God rest the old rascal's soul, did it in the law and was knighted. But we are nothing but sea-going thieves. Merchants who used to wink at us for the trade are beginning to look sideways. It'll soon not be worth the risk of fines or prison for them, to pay less than thirteen pence the pound for sugar and thirteen shillings the gallon for brandy."

"True enough." Collyer sounded almost thoughtful. "The tide turned three years ago, when they hanged William Kidd, privateer and respectable citizen of New York, in London. But there's still time enough to make one's pile."

"Speaking of which..." There was a clinking sound. Gramercy's tone turned to self-mockery. "My share of coin, since last I saw you, is in this bag. Keep it for me."

"Ain't it better under your own eye? I've as much chance to be sunk tomorrow as you have."

Gramercy seemed amused. "Now who looks at the black side!" His tone altered to indifference. "I care little what becomes of it. But it's too much trouble, for Jedediah and I, to constantly guard it."

Mercy's temper had cooled and she willed her ears closed to any more of their speech. Surely it was foolish to know too much of their dealings. Then against her will she heard Gramercy add, "It's better away. If they touch anything of mine it's blood-letting and they know it."

She shifted forward in the chair and stared at the bright sea and high sky. Her changed position took her from the path of the vagrant breeze that had blown the men's words to her ears. Though the world before her eyes was real enough, she felt in a strange dream. In her mind she pictured the two brilliantly clad figures and thought, this cannot be I, Mercy Penhall, Puritan spinster, listening to two personable pirates discuss their trade. Even though they were both surely exceptional and most of their kind brutes like Gorman...

Gorman was real, unpleasantly so. Her mind fell back sharply into focus and strangely presented another picture, that of the young gunner's mate from the *Jesselin*. He had been given no chance to choose, then had elected to stay a pirate to save his life. Were she a man, given the choice between such a life and death, what would she do?

She was a woman and had believed she would be dishonoured yet had chosen to live. Even now, threatened with ravishment or death, how would she choose? She wanted to believe she would be noble and prefer death, but would she? And if Edmund Gramercy chose to take her, it would not be ravishment, because she would be willing... The shattering knowledge stained her cheeks with shame. She shifted her chair around completely so that her face could not be seen.

Half the hour later, with the blush mercifully faded, Mercy heard Gramercy's cool voice directly behind her. "It is time to go, Mistress." As she stood and turned, she found she could not look at him. Instead her lowered eyes fixed on his arm with the crimson coat thrown over it. Certainly the day grew warm enough to shed outer garments, though Collyer had elected to remain grand in his coat, albeit with a reddening face.

"Been a pleasure to make your acquaintance, ma'am." He actually took her hand and kissed the wrist, as if she were a lady. When she smiled, amused, he grinned.

"I cannot help but wonder. What do you think of me?"

Mercy took up the board and chalk from her waist and printed without hesitation, YOU ARE A ROGUE, SIR.

He chuckled, delighted. "No doubt. And what is Edmund?"

HE HAS BEEN KIND TO ME.

"'Tis not what I asked, lass," Collyer teased.

Mercy looked at Gramercy and saw his frown and unsmiling eyes. She wrote deliberately, ONE OF NATURE'S GENTLEMEN.

Collyer laughed, and Gramercy said bitingly, "You've no need to flatter me, Mistress, to make up for your spying." He turned to the other man and his tone changed. "Farewell for now, Richard. We'll meet again. Perhaps."

"Perhaps," shrugged Collyer. "Tomorrow, a se'ennight, next year, or never."

****

The *Prospero* unfurled its sails as the longboat pulled away. They had begun to swell in the breeze when the rowers drew in to *Thalia's* side.

Gramercy had laid his coat and hat on the seat between himself and Mercy, as if he wanted her at a distance. She could not blame him. It was true she had repaid his forbearance poorly. At the same time she did not regret what she had learned about him. Even so, when next he was in the great cabin, she would apologise. She could not write such words here with the sailors close by at their oars, though it was unlikely any of them could read.

Their looks at her were lewd and inquisitive, as had been those of the pirates on *Prospero*. All but Collyer and Jedediah believed Gramercy was bedding her, though that in itself was not enough to earn their stares. It was the irony of seeing a Puritan in such a pass that put the slyness in their eyes and the sniggers behind their whiskers.

The longboat's gunwale bumped the planking and two of the rowers caught the overside ropes and fastened them for the craft to be drawn up. Gramercy called for the sling. When it was sent down he did not assist Mercy into it but left her to settle herself. Nor did he watch it rise, instead turned his head to see the slow departure of Collyer's ship.

Mercy also watched *Prospero* and at first did not notice that the sling had slipped a little. Then she heard a hoarse cry from the deck—Jedediah's voice. Before she

knew what happened the sling plunged downwards. It
missed the longboat's stern by inches. Her mouth opened
in a soundless scream, then she swallowed salt water and
could neither scream nor see.

Her body was engulfed by wetness yet her mind
instantly transformed itself into a cold analytical thing
that worked separately. *Even angry, he will not let me
drown. But I must help myself.* Unable to swim, she tried
to climb upward with her hands.

Her wool gown grew weighty with water. She felt the
canvas and rope of the sling, wrapped around her. She felt
herself sink down and down... *I must not panic.* She
closed her mouth on the choking water and held her
breath. Still she dropped down, down, even while she
flailed toward the misty light above... There was a dark
wall beside her, which must be the ship's hull...

Terror welled. Her mind remembered the razor sharp
barnacles on ships' bottoms... She imagined shark and
octopus... She felt the sling drift away like a great
jellyfish...

But when she felt her hair pulled then a body beside
her own and something winding about her waist, she
knew it was no sea monster and let herself be borne
upward. It was a struggle and she did not know if her
reaching arms were help or hindrance. After a time which
seemed agonisingly slow her head broke surface into air.

They were close in by the high oaken wall of *Thalia's*
side and his dark wet head had surfaced beside hers. He
gulped a breath, braced one long brown hand against the
hull, spat out water and shouted up for a ladder.

Mercy breathed, choked, breathed again. His free
arm supported her and she was so heavy that without it
she would sink and sink... She saw the longboat, now a
short distance away. The men in it had barely risen from
their oars, to stare and shout... Crimson dye from his
clothing pooled slowly around them both, like blood. A
rope ladder snaked down into the red water.

He set her hands on the rungs and held her body
there with the weight of his own while they were drawn
up. They fell over the rail, Mercy to her knees on the
planking and Gramercy onto his wet stockinged feet,
instantly balanced, like a cat. He knelt quickly before her,

his breath harsh, and gripped both her shoulders. She had not swallowed much, and was able to nod at him within moments that she was all right. She leaned her head back on the bulwark and opened her stinging eyes wider.

She saw Edmund's brown eyes as hot as amber in fire, under the water drops on his brows and within the smooth dark frame of his wet hair. He rose abruptly and she lifted her gaze, still clearing her throat behind one hand. She saw now a group of bodies and faces. Jedediah's and Gorman's stood out, the one open-mouthed and anxious, the other sneering.

Gramercy's voice was cold, heavy with anger but cold as that New England pond. "By God, Gorman, that was deliberate."

"Nay, Cap'n." The mate smiled in his whiskers like a beast, yet smugly. "Couple of the lads lost their grip on the rope, was all. A wettin' never hurt nobody."

"It near drowned her and it was no accident. The woman is mine and I'm your elected captain. You have flouted my authority again." Gramercy stood quite still, hands strangely loose at his sides, like a tiger ready to loose its claws. "You know I won't challenge you to fight now, when if I lose both she and Jedediah are in your hands. But I warn you, Gorman. One day I'll be angry enough not to count the cost, if it'll rid me of you."

Mercy saw the group of motley bodies stir uneasily and heard, dimly because of the moisture in her ears, two or three voices growl in response.

"Aye, you know." Gramercy spoke to them without taking his eyes from the mate. "Navigators aren't easy come by, and I've brought you luck with booty and dodging warships until today." He raised his voice. "All of you have a vote! Do you risk Gorman killing me, on the chance you'll find another captain tomorrow?"

Mercy lifted her head, saw some of the faces sullen and some rebellious. Some looked guilty, like schoolboys caught in mischief. Gorman was unmoved. His greenish eyes glinted and he hissed through his bad teeth.

"Why, Cap'n, if you'd happened to have drowned, accidental, we'd of got Cap'n Collyer to take us with 'im. Make a two-ship squadron."

"Fool! Have you ever seen two ships of the brotherhood work together without argument over prizes and blood running after? Collyer's my friend, but I don't sail with him for that reason." He flung out an arm toward *Prospero*, which sailed slowly, parallel with them. "And since he's my friend, he'll have had his spyglass on us to see what the commotion was. He's not so nice in his mercies as I. If I'd drowned he'd have blown you out of existence."

Gorman sneered still, though with less certainty.

Mercy struggled to her feet. It was evident that the sling had fallen by design and the mate had used her to contrive another confrontation with the captain. Whether she had lived or died in the process was immaterial to him. Then he saw her move, and smirked.

"Well, there's nay harm done. And your woman's still fit for enjoyment."

Something broke in her. All the fears of the last days melted together and channelled into fury. She dragged from her head her sodden cap where it clung to her wet hair, crushed it into a ball and threw it in Gorman's face.

Of course it did no more than startle him. He brushed it aside and stared at her ludicrously, as if she were a fluffy kitten that had swatted him. Then an ugly grimace twisted his features and he started toward her. Mercy's breath rasped in her throat, however, she staggered forward a pace in the dragging skirt, perfectly ready to scratch his eyes out.

Gramercy stepped between them. "That is enough!" To the crewmen he flung an order. "Return to your duties, all of you!"

"The little vixen!" ranted the mate. "I'll..."

"You'll do nothing to her, Gorman. And nothing to me. *Prospero* is abreast of us. Cut my throat now and you're not only leaderless but sunk. You'll have to wait a better chance." His eyes burned at the shuffling sailors. "Get the longboat up and the sails set! We still head south." He added with biting sarcasm, "Or do you wish to wait while the Queen's ship brings friends out to chase us?"

The men began to disperse, slowly at first and then running, grumbling all the way but going. Gorman stood alone, Jedediah behind him like a watchdog awaiting orders to attack. And also, Mercy saw with surprise, the boy from the *Jesselin,* studiously inspecting the lashings of a gun.

Gramercy turned his back on them, seized Mercy's arm and pulled her with him to the port side rail.

Thalia's midships were in line with *Prospero's* quarterdeck. Mercy saw on it a long patch of bright blue— Collyer. Gramercy lifted one arm high, then waved it forward. A narrow black line, a spyglass, was lowered. A blue dot fluttered; Richard Collyer's hat, waved to the red figure on the smaller ship.

Gramercy watched his friend's craft with darkened eyes for a minute of time. Then he whipped around and strode toward the stern, still dragging Mercy with him. She had to hop, since her right shoe had fallen off, but he did not stop for it. Over his shoulder he ordered Jedediah to find dry clothes for the woman. For the rest he said he would be on deck again when he changed and he expected to find the ship under way.

Gorman was already under the mainmast, bellowing orders.

****

Edmund slammed the cabin door shut behind them and shoved Mercy toward her pallet. "Cool your temper, little spit-fire!"

He hauled off his sodden waistcoat and dropped it to the deck. The crimson dye from it and from his breeches ran down his body and puddled at his feet. It stained with red the white shirt, the neckcloth and the fine laces. He pulled angrily at the shirt's water-tightened drawstrings.

Mercy's anger had drained away as quickly as it had risen. She turned her back without being asked, less from modesty than from the need to hide her face. Delayed terror from the near drowning had caught up with her. She longed for Gramercy to be changed and gone so she could spill her welling tears in private. She began to tremble, and hugged her arms over her breasts to stop it.

A muffled exclamation sounded behind her and the blanket from his bunk was thrown over her shoulders. "Jedediah will be along soon with your clothes!"

She had not expected the blanket and could not catch

63

hold of it. It slipped to the deck.

"Curse it!" He strode over and snatched it up, then pressed it hard around her neck. His hands felt the shaking of her shoulders and he pulled her around to face him.

Mercy desperately did not want him to see her cry. She tried to wrench herself free and the strong hands held her more tightly. She saw the anger in his face give way to concern and her emotions broke. Her eyes let loose the tears and she mouthed through them, *I am sorry, I am so sorry.* She wished passionately that she still possessed a voice, to tell him she bitterly regretted she had betrayed his trust to eavesdrop on the *Prospero,* that she had been the cause of his quarrel with Gorman.

"Sorry! You?" His face darkened with a passion of his own. "I've had the audacity to be angry with you. But I forfeited all rights to civilised consideration when I became what I am! God in heaven, little one, why should it be you who weeps? Weeps without a sound!" He shook her. "You fell into the sea in silence—I would not have known if the others had not shouted. Then I saw the splash! For a moment I thought you lost." His voice was thick, his eyes the colour of burned honey. "Of all the women on earth, why is it you? A speechless Puritan!"

Chapter Five

Edmund was bare above the waist and Mercy saw and felt that his whole body trembled even more than hers. Without thinking she lifted her hands to his brown shoulders, to steady him.

He groaned like a man tortured beyond endurance. In one swift movement he swept her to him and bent his head to her lips in a fierce kiss.

Mercy stood for one moment stiff with shock. But in the next she felt something within her surge toward him. It was as if the tight cord that had stretched between them for days had rolled up inside their wet bodies, leaving no space between. They were together, as they should be. She was safe. She sighed deeply under his mouth and felt his lips slip inside hers. Her arms, of their own volition, wound around his neck.

He groaned again, into her mouth. His arms crushed her closer. He tore his lips away but only to kiss her throat, her face, her wet hair, her wet eyes...

Mercy, mindless, lifted her head higher so he could reach her face more easily. She wanted more of him, needed him... She had been all water, now she melted into wax and wine and fire... Time and the world were all forgotten. Nothing existed but this moment, his lips that devoured her. She had never been alive before, had never felt anything before.

His mouth seized hers again, sank into it. His hand held her throat, then slid down to cover her breast. The clinging gown was just another skin, not a covering. She buried her fingers in his hair, pulled his head down and pressed her body closer into his...

From a very great distance she heard sounds, a voice and thumps on the door. They did not matter. But his caressing hands stilled, then suddenly gripped her upper arms and thrust her aside. Her feet tripped on the pallet and she fell against the bulkhead. She threw out her hands only by instinct to save herself from a fall.

Jedediah came in and dropped a grey bundle on the pallet. "There's your things, liddle girl." Then he scolded his master, "I'll get your coat and hat and shoes out of the longboat - ain't you changed yet?" He inspected the captain with large lips pursed. "That suit's ruint."

"Get dry things out for me." Edmund's voice was thick and harsh. As the big man turned away he shook his head grimly at Mercy. Then he flung cool water from the pitcher over his face and chest. He leaned on the table a few moments, breathing deeply. He began to unfasten his wet breeches.

She slowly moved her head so that she faced away, leaned her trembling hands on the bulkhead and bowed her head onto them. As if from a distance she heard him speak to Jedediah again.

"What happened up there with the sling?" His voice was rough, though under control. "I'd told you to be on one of the draw lines."

"I were. Here's yore dry clothes." Jedediah's voice rose anxiously. "Mebbe I can soak the shirt in fresh water, get the dye out."

"Jedediah, I'll steal more shirts! *What happened?*"

"All I seen was that them on the other rope seemed to lose their grip, like Gorman says." Jedediah was sulky, obviously in a fret over the spoiled suit. "I held to mine hard as I could, but the weight were too much and it was skitterin' through me hands afore I proper knew what were happenin'."

"It was not your fault. It's plain enough the others did what Gorman told them. Never mind, he knows I know he was behind it. We must keep a closer eye on the lass, that is all." His tone was quite cool, now. "Leave her to change, but stay outside the door. I'll go up to see they get *Thalia* moving aright."

Mercy did not turn her head at the sound of his steps, nor when he halted by her for a moment. He was dressed in black breeches and indigo shirt again, like a Puritan... He ran a hand through his wet hair. His eyes were dark.

"It was a desperate way to bathe, Mistress, and get

yourself a clean gown." Then he was gone.

Mercy turned to face into the cabin again. Jedediah had gathered up the soaked waistcoat and breeches and now mopped with the red-streaked shirt at the pool of dye. He muttered, "That Gorman, he'd kill us both if he didden need the Cap'n." He wrinkled his wide forehead at her. "Least we'll be rid of you, lassie. Ship'll be off Charles Town this night."

Mercy clenched her fists in the wet skirt to hide her trembling hands. Her mind whirled around his words. Would Gramercy put her ashore, now? She stared at Jedediah as if he could answer the question.

"Big eyes you got. Sometimes I can near see in them what you're thinkin'." He went past her to the door, and brought in a bucket of water he had left there when his hands were full. He refilled the brass pitcher, dumped the red clothes in the pail and shook his head. "Meself, I say it'd be safer to let you off in the Indies. That Queen's Navy captain, he'll rouse the town, tell 'em there's pirates near about."

She had forgotten the *Tresadern,* forgotten the sea fight. She lifted her hands to hold her head. Edmund Gramercy could not risk standing off Charles Town. He would take her with him. In this cabin, with him... With the last sense left to her she pointed to her bundle of dry clothing, shook her head at him and indicated the door.

"Oh, aye, you want t' change. An' I want t' get his hat and shoes afore one o' them thieves does." He went out. Mercy heard him growl to himself on the way up the passage.

She stumbled to the table and fell into one of the chairs. Her wet dress and underthings were uncomfortable, yet she had no strength to strip them off. She held her head in her hands and tried to think.

For twelve years her dumbness had set her apart from others. She had seen their lives from aside and seen their lives were disorderly. She had loved only two people, Uncle Jonathan and Mam Felice, and even they had seldom touched her physically. She had been able to rule her existence with her mind.

Now she had behaved like a creature without a mind. Her face and arms and breasts were warm, as if they remembered the man's body of their own accord. How could a thing that had felt so lovely be wicked? But it really was wicked. Such intimacies were only for marriage.

That, then, was what the stern ministers had meant when they said the body was a deceiver, a lustful thing separate from the soul. It could make one do wrong in spite of oneself. She had been able to disregard his other kisses because he had taken them without her leave. This time she had given herself, as willing as a loose woman. If Jedediah had not interrupted, she would have let Edmund Gramercy take her like a whore, here on the bare deck.

Mercy's hands fisted and dug into her forehead. She wanted to pray and could not for shame. What would happen now? He would expect to have her, would not believe she did not want him. Her body wanted him. What hope had she to tell him otherwise? Her mind circled the inevitable. She was a prisoner in his cabin, and would remain so because he could not now send her in to Charles Town. What could she do?

Dull common sense at last surfaced through her turmoil. At this moment, all she could do was to dress.

She went to the corner of the cabin next to the pallet, furthest from sight of anyone who came through the door. She peeled off every stitch she wore and rinsed the sticky salt from her skin and hair with the water in the pitcher. Her body was refreshed, though she felt exposed and sinful to be naked. She quickly drew on the clean linen shift and petticoat and dropped the grey linen gown, creased from the trunk, over her head. It fell heavily - there were coins sewn into the hem.

She laced the bodice, pressed the collar into decorum and folded back the cuffs. Jedediah had even brought clean stockings and cap—had he acted maid to other women?

She began to roll her wet things into a bundle and saw then the skirt of her wool gown. It was stained red from the waist down with dye from Gramercy's breeches where they had clung together... She felt her indrawn breath sharp as a knife. It was a fitting badge of shame. She wrapped it inside her soaked petticoat into a tight wet parcel on the pallet, then set her board and chalk bag to dry on the table. What else to do, before she must think again?

Ah yes, her shoe. She had heard Jedediah return as she dressed, could hear him mutter to himself in the passage. She beat on the door and he opened it, looking sour, and with Gramercy's crimson coat, feathered hat and rosette-buckled shoes in one hand. She held up her single wet black leather shoe with its plain steel buckle.

"I c'n see. Well, he says I'm not to leave here 'til he comes back. You'll 'ave to walk in your stockin's." He took his master's things into the cabin and set them carefully in the sea chest, then glared moodily at her bundle. "You want I should dry those for you?"

Mercy felt blood rush to her face at the thought of that incriminating skirt hung in the rigging... She shook her head emphatically and mimed a throwing motion with her hands.

Jedediah took the bundle from her and flung it in the bucket with Gramercy's ruined suiting and shirt. "All of it thrown overboard - waste o' good clothes," he said sulkily. He left, and shut the door.

Mercy stared at the back of it and felt hysteria rise in her throat. If only she could be like Jedediah, and consider spoiled garments the worst part of this day! She sank onto the chair and searched amongst her sticks of chalk laid out on the table. She broke open three until she found one dry in the middle. Her board was still too wet to write on, but she could use the surface of the table. What to say?

Everything that entered her mind seemed ridiculous in plain words. *Do not ravish me? I beg you not to touch me? I was mad when I returned your kisses?* She pressed her hand to her mouth to stifle hysteria again. At last she settled for, I BEHAVED LIKE A WANTON. I ASK YOUR PARDON.

Then she could only wait, and she did not know for how long. She felt very much alone.

****

Thalia had sailed for a full turn of the hour-glass when Edmund returned. Mercy heard him speak sharply to Jedediah outside the door, heard the big man's surly answer and then his footsteps clumping away. She braced herself for whatever might come.

He entered the cabin with the quick stride she now knew as his natural step. He leaned against the bunk post and crossed his arms on his chest. His face was set in the hard lines of their first encounter, the eyes as dark and cold as they had been then.

She twisted in the chair to face him and clasped her hands tightly under the table. Her heart beat a little faster. She recognised the look he wore. It was his armour, but she had not expected to see it, not now.

He spoke calmly and without inflection. "You have an admirable nerve, Mistress. I had thought to find you in hysterics, or ready to kill me."

He took the blame upon himself. Mercy sat stricken, cowardly glad to be dumb.

"What occurred before was madness on my part and foolishness on yours," his voice continued without expression. "Learn from it. Never offer comfort to a man whose blood is up. We are all the same, and will abuse your kindness."

Slowly she moved her hand to point to the words she had written on the table.

It took him only a second to read it, but much longer to answer. "Any woman's passion can be stirred if a man handles her as I did you. It was only your body, lass, that behaved so. Your soul is pure."

It was so near what the ministers had said and yet it came from a pirate... She had blushed often in the last days, but now felt the blood leave her face.

"But if you stay in my cabin I will seduce you." He said it flatly, as if he talked of something commonplace. "Therefore Jedediah will sleep in here as well, as chaperon. In a few days, perhaps a week, we will be in the Indies. Then I can pretend to take you to a slave market." He shrugged in a manner worthy of Richard Collyer. "Of course, I will escort you to a decent household instead, where you can await passage home."

Mercy reached for her chalk then. CAN I BE SENT IN TO CHARLES TOWN? She knew what the answer must be, but it was a straw she grasped at.

"You are so desperate to be away from me?" His voice

sank colder. "No, you must be patient and wait. We can take no risk of going there, however disguised. The Queen's ship will be out on the morrow looking for both *Thalia* and *Prospero,* likely with another Navy vessel in company. It is hard to enter Charles Town at any time - it is a walled city. With news of pirates beyond the harbour, it will be impossible."

Mercy reached for her chalk, then let it lie. It was plain that nothing she could say would convince him to change his mind. Nor could she tell him that it was not him she did not trust, but herself. Her pride had been sorely tried by all that had happened since her capture, and that last humiliation she would not let him know. She clasped her hands again in her lap, met his darkling eyes for one charged moment and bowed her head.

"Aye, there's no more to be said between you and I." His tone was bitter, self-mocking. He stood straight, then strode past her and out the door.

Mercy remained in the cabin alone all afternoon, and spent much of that time asleep on the pallet. She was as tired as if she had lived through weeks in that one day, and her heart was heavy, as if all of it had been grief to her.

In the evening she unpacked the little chess set and began a half-hearted game against herself. She did not feel like doing anything, however she must keep her mind occupied so that it did not dwell on Edmund Gramercy and his kisses... When the shadows of twilight deepened, she found the flint and steel and lit the candle in the lantern. She had to climb on a chair to reach it down from its hook, and did not trouble to climb back up but left it on the table.

When she heard the key turn in the door lock she did not look around. It would be Jedediah with her supper.

The man who came into the great cabin was not, however, Jedediah. From the corner of her eye she saw a shape not large enough and for one moment was afraid it was Gorman, then when she looked again saw it was not the mate at all. It was the gunner's boy from the *Jesselin.*

"Beg your pardon, Mistress, but Jedediah's busied, an' I'm the only one he knew would do you no harm." The boy set platter and mug before her, took off his shapeless

71

cloth hat and stood turning it in his hands. His hair was brown, thick and untidy, and his eyes blue. A few pox scars marked one cheek, yet otherwise he was comely enough and well shaped. He was perhaps seventeen or eighteen years old.

Mercy waited for him to leave. However he merely stood, shifting from one foot to the other. She reached for her writing board. WHAT IS YOUR NAME? And then wondered if he could read.

"Ben Heslett, ma'am," he answered. "I can read, if a bit slow." He blurted, "Mistress, is you fond of the captain?"

Mercy slashed her chalk across the board. NO.

"Then you'd not care if you left the ship tonight?" The boy's fingers tightened on his hat.

I WOULD BE GLAD. BUT HOW? Mercy's heart suddenly thumped hard against her ribs. What was happening?

The boy looked around him, as if fearful of listeners hiding in the cabin, and lowered his voice. "Jedediah, ma'am, believes you're a danger to the captain as long as you're aboard. He told me to tell you, that he'll take part of the first night watch and lower the dinghy overside when no one's looking. Then he'll give me his key to this cabin and I'll come fetch you." His cheeks flushed red. "That is, if the captain's asleep, and you're—you're able to come."

Mercy stared at him, surprised almost out of her wits, yet found herself, instead of weighing the chances of escape, being pulled in two by indecision. It was a chance to get away, as one half of her longed to do. The other half, the sinful half, whispered that if she did she would be parted forever from Edmund Gramercy, and sooner than she had thought.

She wrote with care, HE DOES NOT BED ME. I SLEEP ON THE PALLET. BUT HE SLEEPS LIGHT.

The boy stared at her as if he could not believe what he read. "He has spared you? The crew all believe otherwise. Ah, Mistress, the things they say about you in the forecastle…" He went red again, then continued hastily, "Jedediah says he'll put a little mast and sail in the dinghy, with the oars. That's why he asked me, ma'am. I could handle it like a lady could not. He said, take it into Charles Town harbour, tell folk you was both cast adrift from the *Jesselin* and say naught about being on *Thalia*."

This was uncommonly cunning of Jedediah. She would not have believed him so clever, though for his master's sake he seemed capable of anything. She rubbed the board clean and wrote again. THE RISKS? Her heart still pounded unevenly.

The boy went to the door and peered through the keyhole. "Beg pardon, Mistress, but if any of them hear me, we're done for." He whispered now. "The captain told everyone the Navy ship is sure to come out tomorrow to search for us and for Captain Collyer, with another ship or two along with it. If I row due west in the dinghy we're like to be picked up by them. Then it's safe you'll be, and I can work passage home to Norfolk town."

She shook her head. I UNDERSTAND THAT, BUT WHAT DANGER TO GET AWAY FROM THIS SHIP?

Ben wrinkled his forehead to read. "They keep a careless watch at night, ma'am, them that's up on deck drink and talk with the helmsman. Sometimes Mr. Gorman or the captain comes up, and if it's needed they order a sail trimmed or such. But in this fair weather, that should not be needful."

She wiped the board. HOW WILL THEY NOT SEE US, GETTING DOWN INTO THE DINGHY?

Ben seemed to find the need to read so much a strain. After a minute he whispered in answer, "They have only one lantern, for the helmsman to see by, up near the wheel. Rest of the ship's black dark at night, and tonight there'll be but a sickle moon. And Jedediah said he'd give them extra rum to boot." His hands twisted his hat. "Please, Mistress, I know it's risky still. But it's best for you to get away soon as you can, and me—I don't want to be hanged for a pirate." His whisper had become hoarse.

Mercy laid her hand on his arm in quick sympathy, and nodded. YES, I WILL GO. I WILL BE AWAKE WHEN YOU COME.

The young face lit up. "Yes, ma'am. Thank you." Then he left the cabin swiftly and did not forget to lock the door.

She sat and stared at the platter of salt beef and corn. She must eat, even though her stomach churned with fear and excitement. Yet her soul felt something different, which strangely resembled regret...

****

Mercy's trepidation was wasted. The escape was as easy as a game of hide-and-seek.

Gramercy had come below two hours after sunset. He had glanced briefly in her direction and said only, coolly, "Jedediah's on watch and will be here later. But you've no need to fear tonight. I'm too weary for a woman."

She did not know whether to shake her head or nod it, so merely lay still.

He snuffed the candle in the lantern, took off only his boots, and dropped into his bunk.

Mercy closed her eyes, and then had trouble not to really fall asleep. She risked lifting her lids a little, and between being able to see and feeling her limbs tighten with suspense, was no longer in danger of slumber. However she had no means of knowing time. No bells rang the watches on this ship.

From under her eyelashes she watched and listened. She saw only the large glimmer of light that was the stern windows, and the dark shapes of the sea chest, the table, and the man in the bunk. She heard only the soft lap of water against the hull, the ever-present creaking of ship's timbers, the mutter of voices on deck and Gramercy's even breathing.

In the space of so few days, it had all become familiar. She discovered herself reluctant to leave it, and not only because of Edmund. She tried to reason her way out of such folly. It was because it was a kind of dream, she told herself, an unreal link between her past life in Virginia and the unknown future in New England with Nathaniel and his family. No, she must be honest. Only the presence of Edmund Gramercy made this place tolerable, even safe. Therefore it was for his sake as well as her own that she must leave it.

She wrestled with her troubled thoughts and her body's efforts to doze, until at last she heard the key turn in the lock. The door opened quietly and she saw Ben's shape crouched beyond it, beckoning. She glanced at the dark quiet figure on the bunk. He did not move, but it seemed to Mercy that the taut invisible cord stretched from him to her once more. Though it was only a trick of her mind, it held her for a moment as immobile as a real bond of rope...

She wrenched her head toward the boy and slowly sat up. She crawled out the door on hands and knees with her shoes pushed into her worsted belt, careful that her breath did not quicken, her skirt rustle too much, or the writing board strike the planking. In the passage she rose to her feet while Ben turned the key again. The lock made little noise, but then Jedediah kept it oiled.

The boy, unthinking, had placed a finger to his lips for silence. Even in the darkness Mercy saw him flush as he realised the gesture was not needed, to a woman with no voice. He turned and walked very softly, in stockinged feet as she was, to the end of the passage, and she followed.

Outside she saw the night-darkened deck, the long black cannon, the pale sails above. And the dark lump that was Jedediah, whistling tunelessly as he cleaned fish beside the mainmast.

Mercy stood behind Ben, who watched the other man and seemed to wait for something. Her nerves were stretched taut. She could hear voices growling on the half and poop decks above them, but she was more conscious of the captain in his cabin behind her than the crew, or his servant, or the boy, who were all closer...

The tune of Jedediah's whistle changed and that seemed a signal, because Ben eased out of the passage. He pressed his back against the shadowed starboard bulkhead. She did not need his gesturing hand to do the same. He inched along to the starboard rail. When Mercy gained his side she saw Jedediah move to the port rail and throw the fish guts overboard. He stayed there, picking scales off his waistcoat and muttering to himself. Again she marvelled at his planning. Any sound she and Ben made would be attributed to the big man.

That was not all Jedediah did. He dropped the cleaned fish into a pot, left it there and climbed the companionway to the upper deck. They heard his voice, then raucous laughter from the men on watch. Jedediah began to sing, very badly but very loudly. It was a seamen's ballad of some sort, and was greeted with more cackles. Such words as Mercy heard were ribald.

The song drowned out any noise she and Ben made when they climbed overside to the dinghy. She thanked heaven that she had done it before, climbing down to Gramercy... *No, do not think that!* She sat in the stern seat and the boy took the oars. They had been muffled with cloth, and the rowlocks were thick with grease, so that when Ben began slowly to row there was no sound but the tiniest susurration of wood through water.

She looked back over her shoulder after some minutes and saw the *Thalia* a black shape under the crescent moon. The white sails seemed like ghosts of clouds, and the speck of light on the rear deck a fallen star. She could still hear the crew singing discordantly along with Jedediah's booming tuneless voice.

They were a bare hundred yards from the ship, although Ben strained hard at the oars. It seemed to her then that it was foolish for the boy to exert himself while she did nothing, a useless passenger. She moved cautiously to sit beside him and held out her hands for one of the oars. His brows rose and eyes widened in surprise, then after a moment he relinquished the one on his left.

It was not as easy to do as it looked, though she understood that she must keep time with Ben and pull as hard as he did. After a little she fell into the rhythm of it, and looked back at the ship. It did not seem that the dinghy moved, more as if *Thalia* fell away slowly and was swallowed by the night and the dark sea.

She saw the silhouette of the high deck and stern, and knew precisely where, beneath them, Edmund Gramercy slept in the great cabin. She felt no triumph of escape. Instead she felt like a traitor, deserting him.

****

It was not the Navy ships that picked them up in the middle of the next morning, but a trio of stinking fishing boats. The fishermen's master, surly at the interruption to his work, made them wait alongside until the nets were in.

Mercy shaded her eyes from the sun and its glare off

the water, and was interested enough to watch. Ben
fretted at the delay. He had put up the sail after dawn,
and although the north-east breeze was light it had
helped them in the right direction. Mercy was glad they
rowed no more. Though she had wrapped kerchiefs
around her hands, the blisters on them from the oars
were still painful.

She was fortunate to have the kerchiefs at all.
Jedediah had wrapped all the goods from her trunk in
canvas bundles and presumably dropped them into the
dinghy. If she had not been so weary she would have
wondered anew at his foresight.

The fishermen towed the dinghy behind them into
Charles Town's great calm harbour. Behind the sandy
palm-grown shores that faced the ocean were wide
marshes, and in the harbour itself several islands. Pilot
boats stood off one of these, though the shallow keeled
fishing boats needed no guide and picked their way with
care through a navigable channel. Mercy saw the palm
trees clearly as they sailed by, rough serrated trunks and
fronds like fans. There were also great cypresses and the
ubiquitous swamp oaks.

The harbour was so big that it took long to traverse,
yet so flat they did not see the city itself until they were
almost upon it. Its earthen ramparts above the grey
waters made it seem merely another island.

Charles Town occupied one side of the promontory
between two rivers with deltas so mighty she could not
see the far banks of either. They had been named Ashley
and Cooper, after the English Earl of Shaftesbury,
Anthony Ashley Cooper, one of the English Lords
Proprietors of Carolina Colony. The fishing boats sailed
slowly northward into the grey waters of the Cooper, and
above it, they told Ben, yet another wide river, the
Wando, poured its waters into the Cooper.

They passed a muddy point, saw an open creek with
a little palisaded island, then a triangular bastion with
walls of earth. At its foot rainwater had collected and the
mud could be smelled even from the smelly fishing boat.

Along the river the walls were of brick. A great wharf
of wood jutted out from them, another triangular bastion
then one half-rounded, with a watch-tower on it and

cannon at its embrasures. Beyond that was a smaller wharf, and the masts of ships like bare tree trunks. One of those might be the warship *Tresadern*.

The fisher leader claimed the dinghy as his fee for rescue and would not allow them ashore until they agreed. Then he hustled them up a ladder onto the first wharf—he called it a 'bridge'—and bawled the story to the guards who lined the wharf's gap in the wall. These would not allow them through until satisfied they spoke English and not French. And upon inquiry where they could seek shelter the guards advised the English church.

Perhaps four thousand souls lived within the walls and on the farms around, and many religious faiths all together, but the Governor did not allow any church to be open in this time of war but the Church of England. There were congregations of Quakers, Anabaptists, the French Protestants called Huguenots, even Roman Catholics, and, incredibly, Jews. All existed side by side in apparent amity.

The Church of England congregation took care of Ben, and Mercy gave him a coin snipped from her hem to buy new clothes. As for herself she was directed to the members of the Independent Church of Charles Town in Meeting Street and was taken into the home of a childless couple of Puritan Dissenters called Hutcher.

The story she and Ben told was believed. Indeed, the sunburn Mercy had acquired during their morning sail and Ben's haggard look bore them out. They were informed solemnly that the pirate that had sunk the *Jesselin* must be one of the two that had attacked the Queen's ship *Tresadern* only two days before. *Tresadern* and *Creda* had sailed that very morning in pursuit of them, and the Hutchers hoped piously the pirates would be caught and sunk.

Fortunately Mercy, being dumb, was not expected to answer on her board to every remark. She did not believe they would catch either *Thalia* or *Prospero*, because Edmund Gramercy had said so. Therefore he would live a little longer, even if bedevilled by Gorman and his own crew. She prayed God to have mercy on his soul. She should then have put him from her mind. But it was too soon yet to forget and he remained there, an unsettling, aching presence.

She had asked of the Hutchers, by her board, about passage to Massachusetts Bay Province. She was told that most ships that sailed from the colony were bound for England. This was the case also, of course, in Virginia, New England, New York, Catholic Maryland and Quaker Pennsylvania, but sometimes a trader like the *Jesselin* picked up cargoes from the Caribbean and along the eastern coast. Mercy must wait for one of these.

She felt that again she lingered in a dream before she could settle into the life of a spinster in her stepbrother's household in New Exmouth. She saw little enough of Charles Town while she waited, since Mistress Hutcher took her from their narrow house only when she needed help with the market baskets.

She saw then the streets of sand and the footways paved with brick only in the principal thoroughfares. The largest of these was called, confusingly, The Bay, and ran alongside the brick Cooper-side wall. The wall was kept clear and opposite it were commercial premises and inns and the houses of the Naval captains. She saw the inner and outer earthen walls with three-sided bastions at intervals in each and the ditch between, she saw the covered fort also called Half Moon that dominated the inland western wall and protected the Gatehouse and drawbridge at Broad and Meeting Streets. Once she saw the Governor, Nathaniel Johnson, carried in a sedan chair to inspect the small fortified trading posts outside the walls.

At the time of the summer solstice she was informed that a ship would be sailing within the week with cargoes for England. It would call in to Virginia to take on tobacco, and agreed to let Ben off near Norfolk town. After that, bypassing New York, it would sail into Boston.

One of the French Huguenot citizens of Charles Town,the elderly Monsieur de Vaugeret, had paid passages for himself and his handsome young wife to New England. He was, they said, a scholar who wished to write a history of the American Colonies, and found it necessary to visit the Puritans of New England to receive a correct picture of their experience. The Governor had given permission, since Monsieur was known to be harmless and, it was gossipped privately, if he did not return one less Huguenot would be no loss...

Mistress Hutcher sniffed at this peculiarity of travelling in order to write, but since there would be no other passage for her guest for no one knew how long, most captains being in fear of French privateers, could hardly disdain it. She did warn Mercy to keep to herself. Madame de Vaugeret, she hinted, was not quite proper, could not act as a chaperone and should not be spoken to. When Mercy asked WHY, by her board, no one would tell her.

Ben would also sail on this ship, working his passage and therefore not permitted to speak to the passengers. It would be a lonely voyage.

So Mercy, late in June, with the weather still fine, set foot on a ship for the fourth time in a month. As it cleared Charles Town's harbour and set course north, she turned her face southward and prayed again for Edmund Gramercy.

Her pride was no longer so rigid as it had been, but she yet had her determination. After the prayer she closed her mind against the pirate and set her gaze northward, toward New England.

Chapter Six

It was early October and the leaves were turning. Mercy had always loved their colours, yellow and orange and red. Though in New England, even more vividly than Virginia, they warned of winter.

She remembered from childhood the short days, the snow and bleak winds, the icy storms and penetrating cold. At least as a child her heart had been warm with Mother's love and she had not minded the season. But Mother was gone forever. Now she must also forbid herself to yearn for the big farmstead built outside Williamsburg when the town had been Middle Plantation. She must forbid remembrance of Uncle Jonathan's ruddy face as he sat reading by the great fireplace in the parlour, of Mam Felice teaching her to roast apples in the warm kitchen, or of the pile of quilts on her bed and the warming pan between the sheets...

She would spend this winter and every other of her life in Nathaniel and Hephzipah's small drab house in New Exmouth. It was what she herself had chosen out of pride, must be grateful for after her brush with death. And she had no other place to go. Anne would never welcome her back to Virginia, nor did Mercy ever want to see Anne and her husband again.

Mercy lifted her chin in the chill breeze and continued what she did, packing crab apple windfalls into a basket. The trees grew on common land off the road that ran beside the Exe River up to the grist mill, and the apples had been shaken down by last night's squall.

Hephzibah had intended that thirteen-year-old Sarah go with Mercy to gather them, but Sarah had woken with a cold. A cold was no reason, in Hephzibah's book, for her daughter to shirk chores. Mercy, however, had hinted by her board that there was no profit in making the girl worse. Therefore Sarah remained at home peeling vegetables for pickling and swallowing sniffles, and Mercy was blessedly alone. She was never alone in Nathaniel's house.

Here no other human being was in sight. Mercy had not kept her own company since her stay in Edmund Gramercy's cabin... Even at night she shared a tiny room with Sarah, upstairs in the little house between the boys' room and that of their parents. Yet today she found solitude a mixed blessing, since her mind wandered away from New Exmouth to warmer Carolina, and even now the gold-brown leaves reminded her of his eyes...

She shook her head sharply, lifted the basket over her arm and began to walk back through the damp grass toward the road. To be busy all day was better after all. It was bad enough that her mind tried to wander during the nights.

It would be different if she had books to read. But the only volumes in the Burdicks' house were Nathaniel's big Bible, Hephzibah's New Testament, the Bay Psalm Book and a few tracts, all ensconced on their own high shelf of the cupboard beneath the stairs. Jedediah had not included her own Bible and Psalter in the bundles of her belongings stowed in the dinghy, perhaps judging them too heavy...

There, she thought of the pirate ship again! How long would it take to free her mind of what had passed? Mercy turned onto the rocky verge of the road and quickened her step. The cold breeze pulled at the hood of her cloak, and she drew it closer. It had been July and still fair weather when she had arrived in Boston, and almost the first piece of news they had heard was of a pirate hanged there, Captain John Quelch...

She stood still and berated herself. Where was her good sense? Only time would dim her memories, but she had time, a lifetime. It did not matter that she remembered Edmund Gramercy and the *Thalia*, because she would never see either of them again. It was not as if she dreamed of him... She halted in mid-step and shuddered.

She had dreamed, once, the old dream of the fair woman hanged. It had been worse, because another gallows had materialised beside it, bearing a dark-haired man in a red suit and a white shirt stained red... She had woken Sarah with the same bubbling moan that had once disturbed Gramercy, and the girl had tried awkwardly to comfort her... *No, do not dwell on that either.*

Instead she recalled busy Boston, which she had last seen as a sick child in company with Uncle Jonathan. The hosts of the Huguenot de Vaugerets, two merchant brothers named Plummer, had searched out for her Patience Hallam, the eldest of Nathaniel's three sisters. Patience had arranged her passage to New Exmouth in a fishing boat, and Mercy had paid for it with another coin unstitched from her gowns.

Look ahead, Mercy, not backward. She needed to walk only a quarter mile to reach the stout timber wharves where New Exmouth's fishing boats tied up, and then three hundred yards to the town. Today most of the boats, including Nathaniel's, were at sea; the breeze was brisk though the autumn storms were not yet severe. The only larger craft that came here were those that carried goods to the warehouse of the merchant William Chase. The sloop she saw anchored in mid-stream must be such a one.

It must become a matter of pride, then, to keep her mind engaged with such mundane matters rather than the thoughts that beset it when she was alone. She watched the dark dot of Rocknest Island in the river's mouth with its teeming flocks of terns and gulls, watched the blue-grey sky and the scudding clouds. The town itself, closer now to her right hand, gave no rest to her eyes.

New Exmouth boasted a rough palisade, grey and weathered like its unpainted houses. Each dwelling was much like every other, a two-storey frame with plank walls, wooden shutters and shingle roofs. In some a few small fixed windows gave the appearance of blank eyes.

The only colours in the town were the leaves of the few trees left unfelled when it had been built sixty years before. A handful of maples had been spared for their sweet sap and a mighty beech left in front of the smithy for summer shade. Some fruit trees had been planted because they were useful.

Mercy turned her eyes from the sweep of the foreshore with a sigh and started down the road to the town. Above the wharves the road was rutted deeply with the tracks of the carts that had been dragged up it to the grist mill with corn, barley and rye to be ground, though here it was merely stony. She walked with her eyes fixed on the scarlet of the maple leaves, and did not see the group of men before William Chase's warehouse until she was almost opposite them.

They were talking and did not notice her. A tall stranger stood among them, his back to her. He must be the master or owner of the sloop in the estuary, to judge by his clothes. He wore russet-brown breeches and a fashionable coat of dark blue with lace falling over his wrists below the wide cuffs. His lace-edged hat sat atop a long periwig of white hair and was pinned up on one side with a silver brooch; his high-heeled shoes were fastened with silver buckles. It was a moderate costume but plainly not that of a Puritan.

Visitors were rare in New Exmouth and Mercy glanced at the man as she passed by. She could not discern his features from the road, but the loud voice of William Chase she could not help but hear.

"—news! I confess it gives me reason for disquiet. The War Of The Spanish Succession"—everyone else called it Queen Anne's War—"is far from us fought in Europe, but we border on French lands north and west of New England, and none of the towns there have lain quiet after the massacre at Deerfield. Acadia and Newfoundland are in dispute, and also the land between here and Hudson's Bay. We'd have felt safer if the raid against Port Royal in Acadia had been successful, two years ago."

The tall man answered lightly, "But ye're secure enough here, by the sea."

Mercy frowned slightly and slowed her steps.

William Chase, everyone knew, lived in constant fear of French raiders sailing up-river and sacking his warehouse. However he continued portentously, "Yes, if the French of the Americas don't seek revenge for the loss of this battle in Bavaria. Where was it, did you say?"

"Blenheim, on the Danube River below the city of

Ulm. They say the Duke of Marlborough and the Prince of Savoy routed them utterly. Middle of August, that was. I know not what's happened since, but by now the armies'll be seeking winter quarters. I daresay we'll hear no more of any import 'til after the spring campaigns, next year." The stranger spoke carelessly, as if battles and wars were of no importance to him, and tweaked the lace at his wrist.

Mercy had heard the voice only once before, yet she recognised it. She had never expected to hear it again, in New Exmouth least of all places in the world. She walked no further, instead turned toward the stranger where he stood with the three local citizens. As a person with an impediment, she was allowed her quirks.

Master Barnard the blacksmith, huge as a horse in his leather apron, frowned heavily to see a woman watching them, then when he recognised her merely shrugged.

"'Tis the dumb woman, though I don't know why she stares."

"Dumb?" The stranger turned to look, casually as if not really interested. Only Mercy heard the sudden sharp intake of his breath.

It was Richard Collyer.

She stared a moment, then set her basket on the ground and dropped her cloak hood to her shoulders. The chill breeze caught at her linen cap but she did not notice. She saw the man's face turn blank with astonishment, then the hazel eyes flickered and narrowed as he watched her. She did not lift her board and chalk from her belt. She stood still and met his gaze.

He rubbed his smooth chin thoughtfully, an unspoken question in his face, though no fear. "Why, I do believe it is Mistress Penhall."

William Chase was surprised. "You know her? From Virginia, I presume?"

"Why, no. From Carolina Colony, just this last summer. I passed through Charles Town and recall the lady arriving there in amazin' circumstances." He strolled over to her, held out his hand and winked one eye. Mercy gave him her fingers and he squeezed them hard for an instant before releasing them. "Well met, Mistress. I never thought to see ye again."

She did not miss the meaning of his words. Their meeting, then, was an accident. He had not sought her out. She nodded, took up her writing board and slipped a piece of chalk from its bag. YOU ARE WELL, SIR? It was not, of course, Collyer she really wanted to inquire after. Her mind worked quickly enough, though her heart beat faster.

He grinned approvingly. "In rude health, ma'am, I thank you." He turned back to the other men and bowed. "I wonder if it would be deemed proper of me to escort the lady home? Master Chase has driven a hard bargain for my poor goods, and these gentlemen have all politely heard such scraps of news I've been able to bring of the war."

Mercy bit her lips so they would not twitch.

William Chase, of course, had to be pompous. His presence was the most influential at the Town Meeting, after John Hanson the minister's. "Why, sir, if you've met previous, and keep in plain sight, I see no harm."

Master Reuben Carey the shoemaker, a prim little man, added his two-pence worth. "Nathaniel Burdick is fishing today and his sons are at school, but his wife and daughters are at home. You must introduce yourself to them, since Mistress Penhall cannot."

"She seems to do well enough with her chalk. But I thank you for your advice." Collyer's face was solemn. "I'd not like to endanger a lady's reputation."

Mercy felt an indignant giggle rise in her throat, though thankfully it could not escape. How correctly he behaved, and how shocked they would be if they knew what he was!

Thomas Barnard demanded, "There was no other news then, Captain?"

"No, sir. But allow me to end our conversation with mine own opinion. When this war is over and ships of the Navies laid up and seamen laid off, I very much fear our trade routes will be afflicted with more scum turned to piracy for a living." He doffed his hat and bowed again. "Good day, gentlemen."

If Mercy had owned a voice she would have choked. But her indignation at Collyer's effrontery did not affect

her observant eye. She saw William Chase frown while
the others mumbled good-days and wondered if the
merchant was aware of Collyer's true occupation. Chase
was wealthy, and more than one Colonial merchant had
dealt with pirates in the good cause of profit. If that was
the case, Collyer's words were over bold.

However their dealings were no concern of hers. She
drew the hood back over her head and bent to lift her
basket.

"Allow me, ma'am." Collyer took charge of the apples,
and his eyes laughed at her. "Do lead the way."

She nodded to the other men and walked off, keeping
the chalk in her hand. Within fifty yards they had
reached the space between the warehouse and the town
where the maple trees shed scarlet leaves, and were out of
earshot.

He asked calmly, "You don't intend to betray me,
Mistress?"

She shook her head.

"Why not?"

She halted to use the board. YOU WERE KIND TO
ME. And added, BUT I OWE YOU FOR NO MORE
THAN THAT.

He chuckled. "One thing I'll say for you. Having to
write your thoughts, you don't mince matters. Still think
I'm a rogue?"

She had heard what he said to the three respectable
Puritans. MORE THAN EVER. She saw from the corner
of her eye the blacksmith striding up behind them. She
rubbed the words off and continued along the road.

Barnard passed them with heavy steps and a
sidelong glance. Collyer tipped his hat affably and said no
more until the smith entered the square. The pirate had
slowed his long stride to match Mercy's smaller one, just
like a gentleman.

"I am known as Captain Stephen Alexander, here.
You'll address me by that name, Mistress, I trust."

She merely nodded. She had heard him clearly, but
her mind was elsewhere. How to broach the subject
nearest her heart, which a short time before she had
believed would cease to trouble her as time passed? Well,
she thought, why not directly? She had a right to ask

after the man who had been far kinder to her than this one.

But was it God or the devil who had sent Collyer to cross her path? She said a prayer in her mind, lifted the board again and printed, I WILL CALL YOU THAT. The chalk hovered a moment, then quickly moved on. AND HOW DOES CAPTAIN GRAMERCY?

"Alive, Mistress, when last I saw him, and well save for a sword cut across the ribs, which was healing. That was a month since, in the Bahamas."

He had told her nothing she could pass on with any profit, yet she was grateful. Her heartbeat speeded again, she nodded and printed no more. There were times when it was an advantage to have no voice.

They approached the houses before the square. Collyer said no more but sauntered alongside her with the apple basket on his arm, as guileless as a gallant squiring a lady. He looked about him as if he found the plain dwellings of a Puritan town as exotic as the grass huts of the Indies. Part way across the square, he stopped by the old weathered stocks and bent to inspect them.

"Are they still used, Mistress?" His hazel eyes glanced back and forth. He saw the blacksmith enter a house beside the church, though he did not know, as Mercy did, that it was not Barnard's own but the minister's. Reuben Carey trotted up behind them and veered toward the workshop under his own home. Chase had disappeared from view, and the only other person in sight was a girl driving geese into a laneway.

NOT FOR MANY YEARS. The minister refused to have them pulled down, but that was not worth writing. AND I AM TOLD THE DUCKING STOOL IS NO MORE.

He straightened and did not bother to comment. "You had a kindness for Edmund, I think, and he for you. He's no intention of coming further north than Florida again, he told me." He seemed amused. "Adding two and two together, I guessed he took no chance of meeting you again."

She met his twinkling eyes, then wrote, HE TOLD YOU I ESCAPED? Of course he must have, because Collyer had mentioned something to William Chase of how she had arrived in Charles Town. However she had relived the escape since in her mind, and come to certain conclusions.

He picked a crab apple from the basket and inspected it. "Fit only for cider. You believe it was Jedediah arranged for you and the lad to get away so easy?" The hazel eyes were sharp, now.

He had confirmed her suspicions. HE IS NOT SO CLEVER. CAPT. GRAMERCY PLANNED IT?

"Aye," Collyer said unblinking. "Mostly to get you to safety quicker. But also because of that kindness I told you of, not wishing to do you any harm." His tone was indifferent. "Edmund's a noble-minded soul. Too much so for his own good." He squinted at another apple, an examination that also served to note they were still alone.

Here was the one person she could ask the fearful question. YES. BUT HOW MUCH LONGER WILL HE LIVE?

"There's no knowing that in our trade, Mistress."

WHAT OF GORMAN?

"The rat seems stuck to him with glue. Made himself unpleasant, only days before they met me, over some booty they'd won off a Portagee ship by Brazil. Edmund challenged him to an open fight for the captaincy." He grinned. "Gorman backed down, saving his face by claiming he'd counted wrong. The men were in high gig with the good haul, you see, and voted on Edmund's side." He dropped the apples back into the basket and shrugged. "In the long run, it makes no difference who we sail with, when we're known to be pirates."

Mercy slowly wiped her board. Her thoughts were desolate. She wondered if she would ever know what happened to Edmund Gramercy. And she wished that Collyer had not come to New Exmouth.

****

It was almost worthwhile, though, to see Hephzibah's face when she arrived at the house with a stranger, and a personable and well-dressed one at that. Hephzibah was testy at first, busy with cauldrons of pickles and preserves simmering both in the open fireplace and on the iron stove whose chimney served to heat the upper floor.

Mercy's sister-in-law was thirty-four, middle-aged, with no grey as yet in the brown hair under her cap and a

89

countenance only slightly lined. Mercy sometimes thought she might still be a pretty woman, if she would ever smile.

Richard Collyer had her smiling within minutes. He swept off his hat with a flourish, bowed deeply, and introduced himself by his assumed name—"a merchant, ma'am, of Barbados." He repeated his tale of having met Mistress Mercy in Charles Town, and begged Mistress Burdick's pardon for calling at her house so unexpectedly. Mercy was both annoyed by his impertinence and entertained by his deliberate exercise of charm.

He continued to Hephzibah, eyes twinkling, "And I beg your pardon also that I interrupt when you are so occupied. My word, Mistress, how delicious a kitchen smells when the preserves are being put up! It quite puts me in mind of my boyhood in England, when I was scolded constantly for begging a taste of everything! And here are your apples—no, allow me to put them on the table. The basket's really too heavy for a lady." The implication was that Hephzibah, not Mercy, was the 'lady' concerned.

He was diffidently offered warm pickles, a slice of yesterday's bread and a mug of buttermilk. Naturally he needed to sit to eat and drink, and then of course one of the beechwood table's drop-leaves needed to be raised to fit him in.

He smiled at Sarah as she served him, big-eyed and holding back her sniffles, and at little Martha in her crib. He complimented Hephzibah on her pretty daughters. "Take after their mama, I see." He inquired after the other children, and once Obed, Samuel and James had been described with prim pride, asked how her husband did. When informed that Nathaniel was not expected home until the evening, he lamented that he himself must soon leave and would miss meeting him.

The cosy scene was disturbed by an imperative knock at the door, and Hephzibah opened it to John Hanson. The warm air around the stove chilled as he brought the breeze in with him. The housewife fluttered around her minister but he introduced himself, not troubling to pretend he was interested in anyone but Collyer. "Master Barnard told me you had a visitor, Mistress Penhall. Captain Alexander, is it not?"

"Aye." Collyer did not rise, merely inclined his head.

"And you met Mistress Penhall in Charles Town?" The minister's pale gaze flicked to Mercy for an instant. "But I understood that she stayed quietly with members of the Congregationalist church?"

"I had business with one of the flock and was invited to supper there one evening," Collyer lied without a blink. "Do you disapprove the acquaintance, sir? I'm not a heathen. I was brought up in the Church of England, though my attendance has fallen off somewhat in recent years." He cocked an eyebrow at Mercy, who had spluttered into her buttermilk. "I hear there's Church of England congregations in your Province these days. And Baptist, and even some Quakers."

Hanson's lips thinned. Perhaps he knew he was being baited, since he did not fall into his customary diatribe against these incursions into what had once been purely Puritan territory. He merely observed shortly, "That may be so, Captain, but it means only that those of us who hold fast to unsullied forms of worship must be vigilant. We cannot allow our churches to be contaminated or our standards lowered."

Collyer rubbed his chin. "But I thought," he remarked innocently, "that you'd already done that yourselves, with the Half-Way Covenant?" He added, "I've a scholar friend with knowledge of Puritan history, who instructs me." And if the reference to the Covenant was also a bait, the fish this time rose to it. Collyer listened with half-closed eyes to the minister's brittle account as to why the ruling of 1662, allowing the children of the original saints to be baptised, was a necessity that maintained membership in the Congregational Churches.

Collyer looked at the pulse that beat in Hanson's bony temple and thanked him gravely for explaining the matter. "But then, I heard that in 1691..."

Mercy's hand jerked and knocked the stoneware pickle jar off the table. In the ensuing confusion, while she, Hephzibah and Sarah all tried to clean the floorboards at once, the two men seemed to lose the thread of their conversation. Hanson asked with frosty politeness how long Captain Alexander intended to stay in New Exmouth, and was informed lazily that it depended on "circumstances."

The talk again lapsed and in the silence the minister gave Mercy a hard look. However he shortly took his leave, clapping his black hat on his white-haired head with undisguised ill-humour. Hephzibah saw him anxiously to the threshold, and a puff of cold air swept in again as he swept out. She shut the door softly then snapped at Sarah to put another faggot in the stove.

Mercy rose to check the pots in the hearth. She felt her cheeks to be pale in spite of being near the heat, and saw that Hephzibah noticed it. Her sister-in-law did not like to be reminded about Mercy's mother. And the process that had hanged her had begun late in '91... Hephzibah addressed Collyer briskly.

"It is best not to tease John Hanson on some subjects, sir. There are matters that he and others of the old clergy are offended by. Such as the requirement that every voter be a church member being abolished in 1691." She untied and re-tied her apron strings and thus avoided his eyes.

Whether or not he knew what had occurred the year after, Collyer was immediately contrite. "I had no right to pick at your minister under your own roof, ma'am. I beg you'll forgive me. 'Tis a boyish sense of mischief which mine own mother, alas, said I'd never grow out of! Also forgive me for keeping you from your chores, when you've a winter to prepare for."

Hephzibah crossed her hands on her apron. "I could not expect you to know the—the convictions—of a church-man you'd never met, sir."

"Thank you for your forbearance, ma'am." Collyer rose and returned the beechwood chair to its place with as much care as if it was a fine piece in a palace. "But may I beseech you to stretch it a very little more? I should like to talk to Mistress Penhall a few minutes. In your back garden, perhaps? I can assure you that she will be safe with me."

He waited humbly while Hephzibah considered. He turned aside only once to wink again at Mercy, who longed to throw a pot at his head and another at her sister-in-law's. She was three and twenty, yet because she was a spinster must be treated like a child! And an addled one at that.

Hephzibah agreed to his request with the stern rider that they remain in the garden. He thanked her as warmly as if she'd given him gold and bowed once more. He included Sarah in the bow, trod softly past the sleeping Martha and followed Mercy out the rear door.

The back garden at this season was mostly fallow soil. The outbuildings—a privy, a hen coop, a byre for the house cow, a shed for firewood—had already been boarded up against cold winds.

Mercy led him to the weathered plank bench beside the sweet potato patch. When they were seated she took up her board and wrote, YOU ARE A SHAMELESS FLATTERER.

The place could not have been more private if he had chosen it with his own strategic eye. Nathaniel's home had been built only twelve years, on the edge of town, and the palisade had been erected beyond its garden. Nor were there any other houses nearby. They were in plain sight, which had the equal advantage of being in a position to see anyone approach.

"I admit it was a challenge I could not resist, to cozen a Puritan dame of such lemon countenance. By the by, your name is Penhall and your brother's Burdick. How is that?"

NATHANIEL IS MY STEPBROTHER. BOTH HIS PARENTS AND MINE ARE DEAD.

"You've no closer relative? But your ship sailed from Virginia."

I LIVED THERE WITH MY UNCLE UNTIL HE DIED. HE HAD NO CHILDREN. She wiped the board with her rag. WHY ASK? YOU CANNOT CARE.

"True, I don't. But Edmund might."

I FORBID YOU TO TELL HIM WHERE I AM.

"Ah. I see." His tone was strangely satisfied. "Well, Mistress, I'll make no promises either way." He saw her begin to write again and held up a hand. "Wait. If and when I see him again, I would be the one to do the telling. Even knowing I've traded north, to Virginia as well as New England, he wouldn't ask. After he told me of your—escape—he mentioned you no more."

She tried to write once more and he reached over, neatly flicked the chalk out of her hand and caught it in his. "Edmund saying nothing on a subject means a deal more than other men talking it to death." He politely handed back her chalk.

Mercy seethed at his impudence and printed with slashing strokes, HE WILL NOT SEEK ME. YOU SAID SO YOURSELF.

"The thing is, Mistress, when he told me of your escape, I had the feeling he found solace in thinking you safe among family and friends."

SO I AM. DO NOT TAKE MY CHALK AGAIN.

He crossed his russet-clad legs and grinned with maddening complacency. "Mistress Mercy, I'll be like yourself and not mince words. This is a miserable little place for a lass of your spirit to spend her life."

She chose to misunderstand. IT IS NOT SO LITTLE. THERE ARE SIXTY HOUSEHOLDS, ENOUGH TO MAINTAIN AN ELEMENTARY SCHOOL.

"You're a clever woman, for all you're mute. And I would say also used to a better life." His sharp hazel eyes measured the empty kitchen garden with its sparse soil and a stubby peach tree, almost bare-branched already, huddled by the house wall. "And yon black-garbed minister watches you like a crow does the growing corn. Why?"

HE CONSIDERS MY UPBRINGING TO HAVE BEEN NOT STRICT ENOUGH, IS ALL. HE TROUBLES ME NOT. That was almost a lie, and she scrubbed it from the board. NONE OF MY LIFE, SIR, IS ANY CONCERN OF YOURS.

"And yet chance, or fate, or God—you can choose which—led me here. And I'm a man who takes opportunities when they come my way." His eyes were hooded for a moment, and the smile had slipped. For the first time Mercy saw the ruthless face of the pirate beneath the mask of genial charm. "Come away with me, Mistress, and I'll take you to Edmund."

Mercy's breath was taken away and if she had possessed a voice that would have been as well. She could only stare.

"It's not a dishonourable proposition, Mistress. My scholar friend told me once—he does like to instruct one—that your folk consider only baptism and communion to be sacraments, and marriage a civil matter. It needs only statements in the presence of witnesses and both parties' consent, followed by living together, to be legal. So I don't suggest you be Edmund's mistress, but his common-law wife. He could set you up some place safe for him in the Indies, in a fine house, with servants, and a maid for companion."

Mercy's hands shook on the writing board. She printed furiously in large letters, NO.

"That's your church speaking, Mistress, not your heart. Why not?"

BECAUSE IT IS WRONG.

"You've not had enough time to think on it yet," he told her equably.

She wiped the board with an angry stroke of her rag. 'TIS YOU WHO DOES NOT THINK. WHAT WOULD BECOME OF ME IF HE WERE KILLED?

"Why, ma'am, if that happened, I'd look out for you. And if you wanted no part of me—and to tell the truth I've no wish to tie myself to you—I'd give you passage back here, or to wherever you chose to go. You'd be a respectable widow, and a wealthy one. I've salted Edmund's money away safe for him and he'd see you well provided for from the first." He laced his fingers together complacently across his waistcoat, as if the matter was settled.

She wrote brutally, BUT YOU TOO ARE HEADED FOR THE HANGMAN.

He remained placid. "You've a temper, haven't you? All up in arms and not listening. If you're a decent widow, and one of means, you won't need me to take care of you. You'd be able to pay your own way."

Her fingers clenched around the chalk. YOU ARE A DEVIL, TRYING TO TEMPT ME. A PIRATE'S WIFE— DECENT?

He gave her a hard look, then brushed a blown leaf off his coat. "A Puritan after all. I merely offer you the chance to be a comfort to him."

HE WOULD NOT ACCEPT IT.

"Edmund's a man, not an angel. If I presented him with your person, and you stood firm, I believe he would." He lolled on the seat and rested one hand on his knee. "I'll

not argue any more, Mistress. But I'll delay takin' the
sloop to sea 'til tomorrow morning, to give you that time
to think. I'll order a man to stay by the dinghy with a
lantern, on shore by the wharf, all night. If you change
your mind, slip away, and he'll row you to the *Dart*."

NO. LEAVE TODAY. WHERE IS PROSPERO?

"Ah, I don't trust you so far as to tell you that, not
until you're on it." His gaze slipped sideways and then he
cocked an eyebrow. "The worthy Mistress Burdick is
frowning through her shutters. School your face out of
fury, Mistress Mercy. I'll talk to you of inanities 'til your
ire settles." He smiled sweetly.

Mercy knew she should run inside, away from him.
Though then Hephzibah would want to know why she was
angry. She gripped her board hard and turned her eyes
from Collyer to the depleted corn patch behind them. A
scarecrow hanging on sticks among the plundered
cornstalks suddenly seemed a ragged corpse...

The stalks were scraggy like all New England crops,
unlike the lush yields of Virginia. It was true she would
lead a barren life, here. Her anger faded and a terrible
temptation took its place. To go away from here forever—
to be with Edmund...

"Edmund's folk were—are—shipowners, of Bideford
in Devon, and honest ones, which is rare," the tempter
continued calmly. "Prided themselves on making a
moderate livin' out of their two craft, instead of getting
rich by pushing ships and men, paying low wages and
feeding the crew on slops. Edmund inherited their active
consciences. But they didn't want him to go to sea with all
its dangers, sent him to a grammar school to learn Greek
and Latin instead. But he was young, and mad for the salt
water and the wind." Collyer removed his hat and
brushed breeze-blown dust from the crown.

Mercy wrote nothing, and kept her face averted.

"He persuaded them to let him learn a trade on the
ships. He voyaged the ports of Europe while I learned my
ropes, ah, differently. When the war broke out with
France, they leased one ship to the Navy as a privateer
with Edmund in command. The rest I think you heard,
Mistress, on *Prospero's* deck." He re-settled the hat over
his periwig and continued affably, "All good trainin', for a

pirate. He don't like it, and you don't like it, but that's what he is, Mistress, and there's no changing it."

Mercy heard the words. His tale did not alter by one jot the impossibility of his offer, though at least she was no longer angry. She returned her eyes to his face, though she kept her hands clasped firmly on the board.

He nodded. "Aye, your temper sinks down as quick as it rises. In fact I'd say that mostly you have a cool head. Have you seen the reason, yet, of what I ask?"

She met his eyes steadily, and shook her head.

He stood, looked about casually to make certain they had no accidental audience, then back at her. "I'll wait until dawn. Women often change their minds."

She used her board then. I WILL NOT. BUT WILL YOU ABDUCT ME FORCIBLY?

"Ah, no, not from a town. I've more regard for my hide than that." He shrugged. "And there's no point, if you don't come willing."

Mercy stood and walked quickly back into the house. He strolled after her and closed the rear door gently behind them. She took her canvas apron from its peg, tied it on, and watched Collyer bid Hephzibah a fulsome good-day. Then he held out his hand to her, and she could not refuse to shake it. He grinned at her behind Hephzibah's back.

Both women accompanied him to the door. Hephzibah blushed when he kissed her hand and Sarah's eyes grew big. Mercy did no more than incline her head in farewell. He strolled off, coat swinging. She tried to shut the door with no more than necessary force.

She returned to the table and began to sort the crab apples into three piles, one for fruit good enough to last the winter in the root cellar, another for the ones suitable for stewing and the third for those fit only to be pressed for cider. Hephzibah checked the stove then drifted to Mercy's side to inspect the apples herself. She held her wooden stirring spoon upright as a sceptre, and spoke primly.

"Well, Captain Alexander may be Church of England, and fallen away some, but he seems a pleasant man, Mercy."

This was high praise from her sister-in-law and

Mercy was tempted to shake her head. However she nodded briefly instead, then cut a bad piece from one apple with a vicious stroke of the paring knife. At least she could take out her feelings on the fruit. A residue of anger remained in her mind like the last coal of a fire.

Hephzibah told Sarah to make some mush for Martha and returned to her pots. Mercy saw her face flushed over the stove and smiled to herself in spite of her annoyance.

What would Hephzibah think if she knew that the man of whom she so approved, and had entertained beneath her own roof, was an unregenerate pirate?

Chapter Seven

Mercy did not sleep well after the candle was snuffed. She could hear no sounds except the night cries of the watchmen and sniffles from Sarah, yet she remained wakeful.

Her bed was a trundle from under Sarah's, so neither of them usually disturbed the other. Though there had already been a few nights chill enough for them to be glad to snuggle together in one. Nathaniel did not allow hot bricks until the first snow, his daughter had told her.

On those nights Mercy had watched the innocent young face with an aching heart. Sarah had been born before Mercy's mother died, in that other town, and as a child herself she had delighted to nurse the baby. And, she now knew, she would never hold a child of her own.

There was her own determination not to wed, but nor would any man of New Exmouth ever offer for her. For that she had the minister to thank. John Hanson had known her mother's history, had heard of it from relatives in Boston. He had told it to his congregation - out of duty, he had said, to welcome Jemimah Penhall Burdick's orphan child into their town. He had not said the reason outright. He had simply mouthed pretend sorrow at her trial and hanging.

For two months afterward the children of New Exmouth had peeked at Mercy as if she had two heads. Their parents had avoided her. The townspeople's suspicions had eased gradually when they saw that the dumb woman behaved quietly and that her stepbrother's family had taken no harm. However, Nathaniel's boys remained a little wary of her, and Martha of course was only a baby.

Sarah had not seemed to share others' concerns. Shy at first, she had soon warmed to her pretty and friendly, though mute, step-aunt. This evening the girl had asked, as they donned their flannel smocks and nightcaps, if Captain Alexander had come courting. Mercy shook her head, and Sarah whispered that it was a pity, he would make a fine husband. Sarah could not have said such a thing to her mother, however she knew she could trust Mercy with her confidences. Mercy smiled and wrote on her board that the Captain was just the kind of man of whom young women should be wary.

Now in the quiet night, Mercy could no longer deny that her mind and soul were disturbed. The things Collyer had said took on a dreadful logic. If she went to Edmund, a short happiness might compensate for bitter grief afterward... Uncle Jonathan had said once that temptation always seemed logical, whereas the guidance of God often made no sense. She was not certain if there was any Biblical foundation for this statement, or whether it was one of the opinions, reasonable in his own eyes, that had kept her uncle at odds with the minister of every church he'd ever attended.

One of the Watch-men called midnight and Mercy abandoned the attempt to sleep. She sat up in bed, hugged her arms around her knees and tried to think through her situation. She could not marry for life because of what she was. Edmund was her only chance of love. Yet what if Edmund survived, and found himself cursed because of her?

She could not sit here all night, battling with herself! She rose, wrapped the duck-down quilt she had brought from Virginia around her, and took the rag rug with her feet to the little window. The shutter was fastened with a hook, and she unlatched it and pushed it open a fraction. It let in a little of the chilly air. The breeze had died and there would be heavy frost in the morning.

There was some illumination outside. The moon was at three-quarters and stars pricked the black sky. Two bobbing lights were the lanterns of the Watch-men, and here and there shone bright pinpoints in dark shadows, the candles of citizens late abed in their homes. Between the town and the sky, the estuary glimmered pale silver. On it the shape of a ship was etched sharply as a brooch, its lamps like tiny diamonds at bow and stern. Collyer's sloop, the *Dart,* where he undoubtedly slept like a babe.

A fallen star winked on the stony shore below it, the lantern by the dinghy that waited for her. The way was still open for her to go to Edmund.

Her mind swam with confusion. She turned quickly away from the window and left the room barefoot, went softly downstairs to the parlour and looked for Hephzibah's New Testament on the shelf. It was missing - Hephzibah must have taken it to bed. Nathaniel's big Bible had been his father's, Mercy's stepfather's, and she shrank from it. So she reached down the Bay Psalm Book, and took it to the table.

On the table top lay the Primer from which young James had recited his letters that evening, from *In Adam's fall, We sinned all,* to *Zaccheus he, Did climb a tree, His Lord to see.* Beside the book stood the tallow candle he had read it by, and Mercy lit it on a coal in the stove, wrinkling her nose at its rank smell. Her uncle had used beeswax candles... She added more wood to the fire, because the stout homespun clothes that Nathaniel wore on the boat were hung before it drying, and he would need them again tomorrow.

Her stepbrother had come in with the last of the light, too soaked and weary to be much interested in the news of Mercy's visitor. He had been more concerned with getting his catch of cod in barrels up to the house. The women would be busy tomorrow, salting it down.

Mercy looked around her before she opened the Psalter. She needed guidance, she needed to pray, she needed peace. Why were these harder come by here in Nathaniel's little kitchen-sitting room than in Uncle Jonathan's parlour, three times larger, in Virginia? Surely she was not so worldly as that, that a poor place could make a difference to her spirit?

She lifted her eyes to pray and saw the low ceiling that also served as floors in the bedchambers above. Jonathan Penhall's walls had been higher. Here, tall Richard Collyer had needed to duck his head, not to hit it on the door lintels. She tried not to think that it was a pity he had not.

And there were the sins of pride and anger, rearing their heads again! She closed her eyes and dropped her head into her hands. Her fingers trembled, not with shame but with rebellion—another sin. She had swallowed her pride to act the modest maid before the town and she felt as if she could swallow it no more. *Help me, God,* her lips shaped into her palm, and she opened the Psalm book.

She had no chance to read a word. From her left Nathaniel's voice cut through the darkness.

"Mercy! What are you doing out of bed?" He strode over and stood before her. His black hair, greying in swatches, fell uncombed about his thick features, though he had pulled on waistcoat and breeches over his sleep-crumpled shirt. "I thought a thief had come for the fish." Nathaniel was in no danger of striking his big head on his own roof beams, being but five and a half feet tall, though heavily built.

Mercy felt her face flush with anger. With great care she closed the Psalter, then stood and looked him in the eye. Not for the first time she was glad that she was dumb.

Nathaniel's thick cheeks reddened too. "Cover your feet, girl! If you wished to look into God's word, you should have dressed first!"

Mercy dropped a corner of the quilt over her feet, but inside it clenched her fists. She must live her whole future life under such strictures. A spinster was the whipping boy of a household.

"I daresay you meant no harm." Nathaniel gripped his square hands behind his back and frowned less fiercely. "I lay your faults at your uncle's door. He brought you up too loosely. But you have been a good girl since you came here, giving yourself no airs, and willing to work." He cleared his throat, perhaps embarrassed to speak so much praise.

Mercy saw that his eyes, cloudy grey as his father's had been, were red with weariness. Her temper abated. Nathaniel had spoken harshly because he was tired. She nodded.

He changed the subject abruptly. "I confess I did not listen carefully when my wife told me of your caller. But when I saw this light from under my door I remembered. Tell me, sister, is he likely to ask for your hand?"

She shook her head decisively, and did not smile at the richness of the joke. Poor Nathaniel would be apoplectic if he knew exactly what it was Richard Collyer had asked of her.

"Well, that is unfortunate." His broad forehead wrinkled, and he paced a few steps away from the table. "As my wife described him, he does not seem the kind of man a Puritan woman should wed. But you are three and twenty, and unlike to find a husband in the Province." He faced her abruptly. "That, of course, can be blamed on your affliction, and your mother." Nathaniel had never referred to Jemimah as 'my stepmother'. "Hephzibah said he was not troubled that you are mute."

Mercy did not have her board and chalk and could not answer. She bit her lip, not caring if he saw. Was he so eager for her to leave his house? She did not know. She had never known Nathaniel very well. He had been a young man when she was a child.

The stove smoked and he lifted the iron lid and stirred the fire fretfully with a poker. "I am mindful that the money your step-aunt sent with you, and the work of your hands, will earn your keep in this house. But Hephzibah and I are older than you and old maids live long. If we go to our reward before you do, I hope I have brought up my children to know their duty, that one of them will provide a roof over your head." He fussed with the fire a little longer, and a few pieces of charcoal fell out onto the floor.

He did not know she had an inheritance of her own. Mercy knew that some of the fifteen Pounds from Anne had paid for new tackle for the boat, and that the remainder was locked in an iron box under his bed. That was Nathaniel's due. It was his words that hurt. In her uncle's house she had been treated like a precious daughter. In this one she would always be a dependant.

Nathaniel put the poker away and cleared his throat of smoke. "It is always best for a woman to be wed. But for you, Mercy, there exists the problem that if you are asked, you must tell the man who your mother was." He looked at her with red and puffy eyes. "I must ask, while we are private, if there has been any sign in you of her—propensities."

Mercy stared at him a moment, felt anger well inside her. Then she clutched the quilt more tightly about her and bent to pick up a piece of charcoal with the stove rag. She wrote in large letters on the fir-wood floor, NO.

"That is good. I do not believe you would lie." His face was red from the fire. "You understand that we cannot risk any evil in the house. John Hanson reminded me that the Bible says the sins of the parents are visited upon the children. But I myself think that the loss of your voice was punishment enough." He looked uncomfortable, and finished brusquely, "You may go back to bed. But first clean the floor and return the Psalm Book to its place."

She did not move for a moment. But then she moved quickly, and Jonathan Penhall could have told her stepbrother that it meant she was angry. She wiped the NO away with a shaking hand and threw the rag into the wood-box. Then she ran to the front door, unbolted it and flung it open.

"Close the door! Have you run mad?"

She wanted to run, run in the still cold air until she felt free! The house was too small, New Exmouth was too small. She was a prisoner, belittled and constricted. All her life here she would be watched. Any behaviour not normal, not able to be blamed on her uncle's spoiling, would be attributed to the heritage of her blood. All her life she must conduct herself more modestly, more obediently, more industriously than any other unmarried woman, because of whose daughter she was.

"I said to shut the door!"

She heard the thick voice from a distance. Before her the moon's half-light shone on the houses and the bare earth. The road to the foreshore was silver with it... There was a place she could go! She could run down to Collyer's dinghy and go away with him, go to Edmund!

But not now, when Nathaniel could see her. *Later*

Mercy closed the door firmly and strode to the shelf to put the book in its place. She did not look at Nathaniel, but went quickly up the stairs.

She heard him blow out the candle and then tread after her, muttering bad temperedly to himself. She closed the door to Sarah's room and leaned against it, breathing fast, until she heard her stepbrother pass by to his own chamber.

She thought, I will roll my clothes in a blanket and wait a little until he sleeps again. Then I will go down to the boat and be away from here. Away from this barren life, to another that may bring shame and grief, but will also bring me Edmund...

She saw then that Sarah was awake. The girl stood by the window. Obviously she had looked out, as Mercy had earlier, on the tiny jewel of the ship on the magically moonlit estuary. Now she gaped at her step-aunt who had so suddenly reappeared. In the poor light Mercy saw her blush.

"I could not sleep for my cold, Aunt Mercy," she said in a voice of guilt, and produced a sniff.

Mercy stood, still and wild, in the darkness outside of the moon's light. She knew, without knowing how that Sarah had been dreaming of the handsome gentleman from the sloop.

If Mercy ran away, she would set an example her niece would not forget. If ever the chance came Sarah's way, and her heart desired it, it would be allowable to go off with a fine-looking man in fine clothes, because Aunt Mercy had done the same...

Her anger drained away. She went to the window and hugged the girl close, protectively. She heard Sarah gasp with surprise. In her experience people did not so plainly show their feelings, however she squeezed her aunt timidly in return. Mercy stroked the girl's head, then gently pushed her down onto her bed, drew her blankets around her shoulders and kissed her forehead. Sarah's eyes widened, and Mercy smiled a wry little smile at her.

She firmly closed the shutter and lowered herself to the pallet on her trundle. She rubbed her cold feet, and said farewell to love.

What was love? Only passion after all, and there was no sense in passion. There was an example in Uncle Jonathan, a sensible man and lifetime bachelor. Late in life he had fallen in love with the lovely Anne, behaved as foolishly as a boy half his age and married her. But at least it had been a respectable marriage, the right thing to do. The surrender to passion that Mercy had contemplated would have been wrong, a sin.

She would stay in New Exmouth and make the best future here that she could. Her adventure with the pirate was over just as the soft years with Uncle Jonathan were over. When she left Virginia she had not expected anything better than this, the same kind of life she had known as a child in Salem...

A knock sounded heavily on the door, and Nathaniel's voice carried through the boards. She had not heard his step. He must have taken his shoes off ready for bed again.

He said, "Mercy, I have decided to purchase a Bible for you, from your step-aunt's money." He said no more, waited for no answer, and shuffled back to his room.

It was unexpected kindness from Nathaniel. But a Bible would complete the picture - Mercy Penhall, virtuous Puritan spinster, of New Exmouth in Massachusetts Bay Province.

She smiled strangely into the night, and fell asleep.

****

William Chase the merchant subscribed to the newspaper first published in Boston in April, the *News-Letter*. Nathaniel, not normally astute, considered he did so only to show everyone he could afford it. The news it contained they had usually heard well beforehand from the crews of boats come down from Boston. This October they had heard it from 'Captain Alexander', tidings of the great battle won at Blenheim in Bavaria.

Three weeks after the *Dart* had departed, Chase finally condescended to pass the paper to Nathaniel. It had already been loaned to John Hanson, Thomas Barnard and Reuben Carey, then the schoolmaster, the constable, the miller, the tanner and the sail-and-cord maker. Nathaniel read the thin sheets that night after supper to Hephzibah and Mercy.

The children were in bed and the hearth and the iron stove stoked for the night. Nathaniel sat in one of the beechwood chairs and the two women on the bench, both of them sewing. Hephzibah stitched the beginnings of a quilt for Martha, and Mercy darned one of Samuel's wool stockings.

Mercy listened because it was the only occupation available for her mind. There would be physical work in plenty to do during the approaching winter. There was wool to be drawn into thread on the spinning wheel and woven to homespun on Hephzibah's small loom, clothes to be sewn and stockings knitted for the year ahead, soap and candles made. A thousand tasks filled a woman's life when she had no servants.

Mercy knew she must not begrudge it, boring though it would be. There had been work also as a matter of course at Jonathan Penhall's. But she missed the challenge of chalk-written conversations with her uncle and communication by sign and shaped words with Mam Felice. Here there was nothing of interest for her brain to dwell on except the past. And that she had forbidden herself.

Nathaniel finished the news of Blenheim on the first page and rattled the paper sheets irritably. He had spent the day repairing nets, which always tried his composure. Though all of them were on edge to some degree. Today, Tuesday, was the Thirty-first of October. On Wednesday, which was All Hallows Day to the old Church, John Hanson had declared a day of prayer.

Tonight, however, without anything being said, each household had hung a lantern by the front door and inside burned thriftless numbers of candles. Even Nathaniel read by the light of two, and the women had two to work by instead of sharing one between them.

Mercy's hard-won patience had been tried all day by people who looked at her sidelong as if they expected her to fly away on a broom. She did not herself believe in ghosts. Now, however, the cold breeze from the sea made the boards creak and the shutters rattle, and the thin branches of the peach tree tapped like skeleton fingers on the rear wall... Yet she disliked the sounds only because they were lonely, almost desolate. She deliberately paid more attention to Nathaniel's voice.

He was repeating something William Chase had said.

Since Master Chase, while a shrewd man for trade, never entertained an original idea, Mercy rather thought the opinion had come second or third hand—possibly even from the spurious Stephen Alexander.

"The Grand Alliance fights the French for the rights of the Spanish succession. It must be grief to Her Majesty

107

that she has no living child to carry on the English. The Queen is the last of the Stuarts, after all. When she passes to her reward they say the son of the Elector of Hanover is next in line for the throne. His mother the Electress was the daughter of the Queen of Bohemia, who was herself a daughter of James the First. Of Stuart blood also, then."

There was a little silence. To say any more would be to approach sedition, even in his home. A tiny smile tugged at Mercy's lips and she compressed them. Nathaniel's inference was clear to she and Hephzibah, who knew him. All those Queens—what had been wrong with the Stuart Kings, who had seemed unable to beget healthy legitimate sons? The only surviving male of the bloodline was Queen Anne's half-brother, the Catholic Pretender.

"Ah," murmured Hephzibah. "They say that the Queen, poor lady, has increased very many times, but miscarried and bore stillborns and babes that lived only shortly." Her tone was smug. Hephzibah had borne six children and never miscarried, and only one had died, a girl child between James and Martha.

Nathaniel's forehead smoothed. He had three fine sons, so he was in that respect superior to the Kings of England and the consorts of the Queens. He continued his reading in a more equable tone.

"It says here that King Louis the Fourteenth when he received word of the battle could hardly believe it, since the armies of France had not been defeated in two generations. He heard it at the new palace he is building at Versailles. And he calls himself the Sun King also. The Lord has punished his pride." He began to read the next sheet.

Political news from England did not hold Mercy's interest. Besides, Nathaniel's voice was so toneless it could flatten even splendid passages of Scripture. Her mind wandered once more. Her thoughts wanted to dwell on Queen Anne and Hephzibah and child-bearing, that common lot of all women, which would never be hers... There was no point in that either.

Then Nathaniel's voice was suddenly surprised. "Why, here is an item from the Colonies!" Local news was never world-shaking and seldom reached the pages of the *News-Letter* unless the printer needed to fill a space. "From Carolina Colony, Charles Town in fact. Listen. 'On the fifteenth of September, Her Majesty's Ship *Tresadern,* two hundred tons and eighteen guns, in convoy with *Creda,* seventy tons and eight guns, surprised and sank the infamous pirate craft *Thalia.*"

He glanced up at Mercy's sharp intake of breath, and saw she had prodded her finger with the needle. "Take more care, sister!" He went on. "'During the battle the pirates resisted with great savagery, and from a complement of a hundred men only nine of its brutish crew retained their lives. These were taken aboard the *Tresadern.* They shall be tried at the Common Law Court in Charles Town at the end of November, when the incumbent Magistrate shall have returned from leave in England.'"

He held the sheet up higher to the candle to read the smaller print that wound up the paragraph. "'It is a regrettable fact that many pirates have been looked upon with tacit approval because of the trade they bring. But we say, may all such scum as these be swept from the Seas and make them safe for honest men! It is good fortune that the pirate captain was one of those saved. We trust justice will be served and Edmund Gramercy condemned to be hung as a common thief.' *What* - !"

Mercy had risen suddenly to her feet. Her workbasket tumbled from her lap and spilled its threads and pins and iron scissors down her skirt and over the floorboards. Nathaniel saw her white face and rebuked her crossly. "You still dislike hearing of anyone hanged? You must forget the past, Mercy! Now, pick up your things and sit still!" He turned to the last page of newsprint.

She dropped, almost fell, to her hands and knees and scrabbled blindly over the boards, tossing precious steel needles, brass pins and reels of linen thread willy-nilly into her basket. She heard Hephzibah's cluck of annoyance, saw her shoes scrape out of the way.

But all she really saw was the slim dark-haired man, all she could hear was the steady beat of his heart under her head. And all she could feel was his wet skin and his

living mouth on hers... In the patch of darkness under the
bench she felt her eyes sting and fought back the tears.
Her determination to forget was itself forgotten.

"Sister, come out!" That was Hephzibah. "You are
like one of the children, playing on the floor!"

Mercy had a terrible impulse to tip up the bench and
slide Hephzibah off it. She was appalled enough by the
thought to clamber back to her feet. She stood staring at
Nathaniel as he droned over the *News-Letter*. He finished
a paragraph and looked up at her in annoyance. And the
look on her face gave him pause.

"What is it now, Mercy? A spilt basket is not a matter
to overset your nerves."

She reached for her writing board, the board Edmund
had had made for her, and printed without thinking first.
THALIA IS THE PIRATE SHIP THAT SANK THE
JESSELIN.

Nathaniel craned his neck to read it. "Ah! Then you
must be glad it is sunk."

Only barely did Mercy prevent herself from shaking
her head. Her mind was in turmoil and she could not
think clearly. She tried to recall exactly the tale she had
told, in Charles Town and here. THE CAPTAIN DID
SPARE MOST OF THOSE ABOARD, BY CASTING US
OFF. It was true enough, if a lie of omission. She wished
wildly that she could throw sense to the lonely wind and
tell the honest tale.

Hephzibah had leaned forward to look at the board
and read its message to her husband. "But after all, he is
a pirate. Well, Mercy, this will be the end of him." She
turned the quilt on her lap to stitch the other side.

Nathaniel still watched her. Mercy could tell he was
not yet suspicious, simply believed she had been startled
by the news. Yet if she remained in this room she would
become even more agitated. She wrote, I WILL GO TO
BED, and held the board briefly for them to see.

"Finish the stocking first," Hephzibah chided her.
"Samuel must wear it tomorrow. And tidy your basket."

Disobedience would invite disapproval and questions.
Mercy dropped onto the bench again. She found enough
wit to seat herself so that the candlelight fell upon her
hands and not her face. Even so her hands trembled as

she stuck needles and pins back into the linen scraps that lined their little boxes. Hurriedly she completed the darning to the sonorous accompaniment of Nathaniel's voice, then rolled the stocking with its mate, took her candlestick and went up the stairs. She wanted to run, and dared not.

Once inside her own little bedchamber she blew out the candle with a shaky breath and leaned back against the closed door. Sarah, thankfully, was deeply asleep.

Edmund Gramercy was to be tried and hung.

She tried to breathe more deeply, to calm herself. But calmness was impossible. Her nightmare would be made real and she could do nothing to prevent it. Charles Town in Carolina was seven or eight hundred miles away. And she was one woman, not an army.

She kicked off her shoes, ran to the tiny window and threw the shutter open. She did not know what she sought, but the room was too small to contain her frenzy. Before her eyes the candle-lit windows of other houses glowed in numbers she had never yet seen in New Exmouth. Everyone, of course, waited out the spirits abroad on All Hallows' Eve, an old superstition discouraged by the church and not spoken of aloud.

The moon shone on the estuary. Only weeks before Richard Collyer's sloop had floated there...

Collyer! He had not known of his friend's fate. Where was he? Long gone, surely! But he was the only person except herself who could, or would, help Edmund.

Perhaps William Chase knew where to find him. She must ask, and if the merchant knew Collyer's whereabouts she must somehow send a message to the pirate.

She heard Sarah's soft breathing, the moan of the wind and the tap-tap-tap of the peach tree's branches on the wall. She felt the cold floorboards through her stockings. She saw, strung on a line near the house, a square of canvas that flapped in the wind. It was a sail from Nathaniel's boat that had been patched, though in her mind's eye it became *Thalia's* rigging full with the breeze... But Edmund Gramercy's ship was at the bottom of the sea.

She wondered detachedly if Jedediah Bullen had

survived, or First Mate Elias Gorman. They did not matter to her. Only Edmund did. She must go to William Chase. But she could do nothing until Thursday, the day after the church service. John Hanson's ideas of prayer were, she had gathered, more like grim acceptance, yet she could not draw attention to herself by being absent. William Chase would also be there. She must exercise all her hard-learned patience, and use the time to plan what she would say to him.

She lay wakeful long hours before falling into troubled sleep.

****

On Thursday morning after the children had been sent to school, Mercy packed two salted cod into her basket and walked to John Hanson's house. One of the fish was for him. By her board she asked leave of Hephzibah to trade the other to William Chase for a pair of cloth shears.

Hephzibah sometimes reminded Mercy that as mistress of the house she had first say in such matters. "But you may borrow mine, Mercy, if ever you need to make a gown. You need only your thread scissors, and certainly no more pins or needles to judge by the contents of your work basket." She added, "Ask him for peppercorns instead."

Mercy nodded and went out. She smiled tightly behind the hood of her cloak. It did not matter what the errand, she simply needed an excuse to see the merchant.

Her smile faded as she crossed the square. It had been Nathaniel's idea, the night before as he prepared his boat to go out, that she take a cod to the minister. Her stepbrother did not request in so many words that she ask Hanson to pray for his safety on the sea. John Hanson's reply to that would have been that Nathaniel was well able to pray for himself, that he as a Puritan minister was no Papist to bless boats, and God's will would be done in any case. No, the fish was sent more in hope to be remembered in the minister's prayers than in payment for them.Mercy and Hephzibah and the children had prayed sincerely anyway. The wind had decreased to little gusts in the town, and at sea it would be stronger. The storms of autumn and winter had held off for weeks but would soon

112

begin. None wanted Nathaniel to lose his life, and none wanted the hard existence of the widow and orphan. For Mercy, however, it meant she must visit John Hanson.

She was afraid of no one, she would have said once. This representative of the old order of the Puritan clergy was the exception. Although officially the minister did not have the powers that would have been his fifty years before, his word carried a disproportionate weight in New Exmouth. So much so that no one cared to miss church attendance on the Sabbath, just as if he could still fine those who stayed away, or even whip any parishioner foolish enough to behave badly on the Sabbath.

It was not the stern force of his personality that troubled Mercy. It was the fact that his sort had sent her mother to trial and seen her condemned to death. Ever since Mercy's arrival in the town he had watched her, waiting like a gull over a herring for her to slip, to make a mistake, to show that she was like her parent.

Mercy had never dared, here, to use the lore of plants and herbs taught to her in childhood. In August, when a sore on young Obed's leg had suppurated, she had bitten her tongue not to suggest it be bathed in seawater and bandaged with a compress of boiled comfrey leaves. Mistress Carey had busily recommended the comfrey and received no word of censure, only thanks when the sore healed.

Yet if Mercy had done the same it would have brought frowns and suspicion her way, from John Hanson in particular. The minister was so strict he had even had the church steeple shortened, considering a high one vainglorious. He had it cut down even though it had been the only place available to hang a light for the guidance of late-homing fishermen. He had not even made the excuse it might guide French raiders also.

And so, once again as she had on the *Thalia,* she must face her fear. She lifted her chin as she passed the weathered stocks in the centre of the square, and when she knocked on the door of the Hansons' unpainted house beside the church she voiced in her mind, *he is only a man, after all.* But she had dreamed a new nightmare last night, of her mother and Edmund both hanged, with the horrible addition of John Hanson waiting piously under the gallows to catch a body in each hand...

Mistress Hanson answered Mercy's knock on the door. She was a faded creature, seeming to have no will of her own. She had only one surviving child, an equally colourless daughter married to a Boston lawyer's clerk. It was no secret that Hanson blamed his wife for the deaths of their four infant sons. Mercy often felt sorry for her, and now offered the cloth-wrapped fish with a smile. The woman's dull face lightened a little.

"Do come in, Mistress Penhall. Master Hanson will wish to thank you." The shadowed look returned to her face. "He is in the parlour, writing a sermon, but has always said to bring you—a visitor—in."

Mercy's smile faded. She would have infinitely preferred to discharge her errand only to Mistress Hanson. However there was no avoiding it. She inclined her head and stepped inside.

The minister's house was larger than most in New Exmouth, and boasted the luxury of a wall between parlour and kitchen. John Hanson sat in a straight high-backed chair at his ponderous oak table, his huge Bible before him and paper and ink beside it. Obviously he took notes for his Sunday sermon, and by the thickness of the Book's pages Mercy saw it was open at the Old Testament, not the New.

He looked up. "Be seated, Mistress Penhall." He returned to his writing for a few moments, then put his quill aside. He saw his wife about to leave for the kitchen and ordered, "Be seated also, Mistress."

Mistress Hanson sat as reluctantly as Mercy had, cradling the fish awkwardly on one arm. By her fidgeting Mercy guessed she had left a task unfinished and would rather return to it. Mercy herself would rather be almost anywhere else, though she wondered why the minister asked his wife to remain. Naturally he held the opinion that female intellect was inferior to men's, and also of course considered his reputation above reproach.

Hanson told Mercy to thank her brother for the fish, and after she inclined her head fixed her with his pale eye. "I wish to ask you some questions. I have requested my wife's presence so that my words will not be misconstrued."

The hint was that Mercy might lie. Mercy could guess the direction of his questions and set her teeth. And against her will she was afraid. She gripped the handle of the basket tightly, and waited.

He made her wait one more minute, seeming suddenly to remember a note he had forgotten to make from the Word. He looked up again when Mercy wrote a mundane housewife's inquiry on her board and passed it to Mistress Hanson. His wife stopped speaking in mid-sentence, and Hanson lay aside his papers with great deliberation.

"This is a matter of importance, Mistress Penhall, therefore you must answer truthfully." He steepled his fingers beneath his chin and lowered his voice to a heavier tone. "Have you noticed in yourself any inclination to the evil talents which were evident in your mother?"

Mercy longed to write on her board, as she had longed to write to Nathaniel, that no evil had been evident in her mother until hysterical neighbours had pointed accusing fingers at her herb-lore. That was what Uncle Jonathan had told her. But her heart trembled within her. People recalled only the cause of death of lovely Jemimah! She shook her head as firmly as she was able and tried to meet the minister's cold gaze.

"You are not lying, are you, Mistress? That is as much a road to perdition as the sin of witchcraft."

He had said the word. Mercy drew back as if she had been slapped. However she shook her head again, lifted her board and wrote cowardly words on it. SIR, I HAVE ANOTHER ERRAND TO DISCHARGE FOR MY SISTER IN LAW. NOW I HAVE ANSWERED, I WILL TAKE MY LEAVE.

He waited, allowing the worm to squirm on the hook, then said coldly, "Good day, then."

Mistress Hanson saw her out silently, whispered "Good day," and retreated to her kitchen with the fish clutched to her bosom. Hanson himself came and shut the door with a bang. His eyes reminded Mercy of those of the dead cod...

She walked several paces and forced herself to breathe deeply. She knew the minister had deliberately set out to unnerve her, and was angry that he had succeeded. A cold gust of wind struck her face and she pulled up her hood. How could she live in this place for all her life, with the congregation aware of her history and the minister outright suspicious because of it?

A wild thought entered her head. She halted beside the weathered wooden wall of the church, where no one could see her. *Could she possibly go to Charles Town herself?* Her mind sought a reason and discovered it. If she found a way to go, she could at the least testify at Edmund's trial that he had spared her.

She could not remain in New Exmouth in safety, tortured by waiting, as the days rolled inexorably to the month's end, the Court, the hangman! She *must* go to Charles Town. She *must* find Richard Collyer.

And need she ever return to New Exmouth even if Edmund was not freed? *No, she need not.* She would take her inheritance and leave, and whatever the future held, she would leave forever.

Her mind quieted as she made the decision. She stepped out from the cold shadow of John Hanson's church and into the cold breeze that scythed through the square.

Chapter Eight

As Mercy strode away from the minister's house she saw there were now people in the square. Half a dozen young men, who had volunteered as militia, drilled under the bleary eye of old Roger Tyler, who had in his own youth fought the Indians.

She had asked Uncle Jonathan once about the red men who had killed her mother's family. He had said it was not to be wondered at that the poor heathens fought, when the old clergy hanged and burned them for not being like Puritans.

She left the square to Master Tyler and his youths, and walked around its perimeter. She passed the smithy, where the blue-grey bark of the bare beech tree trunk seemed like the single pillar of an ancient ruin. Master Thomas Barnard the blacksmith, huge and red-faced, stared at her a moment over the glowing metal on his anvil. Points of red reflected in his eyes.

She nodded quickly and kept on. She passed the school-house, from which the voices of children chanted obedient numbers, and the shops of the tradesmen on the first floors of their homes. A few wives swept dead leaves from their stoops. Most took no notice of her, though two or three wished her good-day and at those she smiled and nodded. But there was freedom in the thought she might never see any of them again.

She passed through the avenue of maple trees, whose leaves were now the deep crimson of dried blood. At the warehouse, she knocked at the small door of the room Chase used as his counting house. The merchant himself opened it, grumbled that his clerk had not yet arrived and told her to come in.

The room was warmed by a small iron stove, set in a corner behind Chase's imposing mahogany table. This table was piled importantly with papers and account books and the merchant held a quill in his fat hand. His half-bald head was bare and his rotund belly strained against the brass buttons of his brown velvet coat. He regarded her warily. His manner toward her had been constrained ever since Richard Collyer's visit.

He asked stiffly, "How may I be of service, Mistress Penhall?"

She printed, IF YOUR CLERK COMES, I AM HERE TO TRADE FOR PEPPERCORNS. She laid the wrapped cod on the table, then wiped her board. DO YOU KNOW WHERE CAPT. ALEXANDER IS?

Chase almost stepped back a pace. "Ah. I understand he spends his winters—ah—trading—I know not where." His tone turned pugnacious. "Why do you wish to know?"

I KNOW WHAT HE IS. When his stunned expression told her he had read the words, she rubbed them away. DO YOU STILL NOT KNOW HIS WHEREABOUTS?

"No!" The merchant wiped a sudden bead of chilly sweat from his forehead then seemed to gather his wits. "How do you know, ah, what he is, Mistress?"

IT WAS WELL KNOWN IN CHARLES TOWN. Mercy knew she now entered deep waters. She waited for the inevitable query.

The merchant looked at her keenly. "Why did you tell no one here, then?"

IT DID NOT THEN SUIT MY PURPOSE.

Chase rubbed his chin. "Be careful, Mistress. If it suits your—purpose—to hold this over my head, you may find yourself confounded. My word will always be taken before yours."

I DO NOT INTEND TO HOLD YOU TO RANSOM. I REQUIRE YOU DO ONLY ONE THING FOR ME. Mercy wiped the board. I MUST LEAVE NEW EXMOUTH WITHOUT BEING SEEN. I HAVE MONEY.

The merchant's thick mouth fell open. "I cannot connive at such a thing! But why do you want to run away?"

IF I DO NOT TELL YOU, YOU CAN PLEAD IGNORANCE. BUT I INTEND TO RETURN. This lie she added as a sop to Chase's conscience, not her own, but prayed in her mind to be forgiven it. Ever since she first met Edmund Gramercy, she had needed to lie. DID CAPT. ALEXANDER TAKE HIS SHIP TO BOSTON? This question was a calculated risk, but she could see no other way to send herself to Carolina Colony.

"It is possible. The *Dart* sailed north." The merchant opened his door, looked about and saw no one within hearing. He shut the door and said in a low rumble, "There are Huguenots, a man and his wife, visiting Boston from Carolina, who are his friends. That is all else I know about him, Mistress."

She bent her head so that he could not see her relief. ARRANGE FOR ME TO GO TO THEM IN BOSTON. I WILL ASK AFTER HIM THERE.

He stared at her with narrowed eyes. Mercy could almost see his thought, that perhaps it would be a good thing if she left New Exmouth and took her knowledge with her.

He spoke slowly. "The de Vaugerets will leave for Charles Town soon, before winter. They are staying with acquaintances of mine in Boston, the Plummer brothers. But to get you there—I cannot send you on a local boat, when they all know your brother. Fishermen from other ports still put in, though." He thumped his foot and frowned. It was plain he was less uneasy, now he had a practical matter to consider.

CONTRIVE WHAT YOU WILL, BUT I MUST LEAVE UNDETECTED. She scrubbed the board. DO NOT PLAY ME FALSE, OR I WILL TELL THE CONSTABLE YOU DEAL IN PIRATE BOOTY.

"No need for that, Mistress!" He was downright testy. "I will send you word by my clerk that the fabric you wanted has been found. When you hear that, you must come as soon as you can. But do not bring anything with you which cannot be concealed under your cloak." He inspected her narrowly. "I also warn you not to implicate me if you are caught. I shall deny all we have said."

What a fine pair of Puritans we are, Mercy thought, plotting and lying and making threats. On her board she wrote I SWEAR I WILL NOT.

"Very well. You have passage money, you say? No, I don't wish to know where it came from! And I will pay your way to Boston." He looked at her with active dislike, yet confirmed, "We now have a contract, Mistress Penhall. I will honour my part of it, if you will yours."

Honour, Mercy thought bleakly, played little part in the matter.

****

When Mercy reached home her head seethed with plans. Also she tried to estimate how much money she would need.

At the house, through the back door left ajar, she saw Hephzibah and Sarah in the back garden, pulling up the last of the root crops. Inside there was only Martha, asleep in her cradle near the stove.

Mercy stood still a moment. The sums in her head had not been adequate, and for now she was alone in the house. A wicked thought entered her head. She did not flinch from it and in the next moment acted on it.

She went to the cupboard under the stairs, the one that held the Bibles and the Psalm Book, knelt, searched with her fingers behind its stout front leg and found the key hidden there. She had heard Nathaniel's voice, discussing its hiding-place with Hephzibah, one night when she had lain awake. *I would carry it in my pocket,* he had said. But he went often to sea and there was the chance it would be lost...

Mercy ran upstairs before she could think, into Nathaniel and Hephzibah's cramped bedchamber, and dragged the small iron box from under the bed. Quickly she unlocked it and emptied the coins into her apron pocket. At the last moment, stabbed by guilt, she replaced two of them. That left in her hand the equivalent of twelve Pounds, in the form of English gold guineas, Spanish *reales* and pieces-of-eight. The remainder of the coins her step-aunt Anne had sent to Jonathan for her bed and board.

She sat smitten by guilt for one second. She could not make the excuse, even to herself, that the money was rightfully hers. The hard truth was that she stole it. And by stealing it she had deprived Nathaniel's family of their surety against time of need –for the sake of a pirate.

There was no time for the luxury of a stricken conscience. She ran to her own room and flung up the lid of the wooden box Nathaniel had made for her clothes.

Her inheritance from Uncle Jonathan, picked from her gowns, she kept in a leather bag at the bottom of the box. She added the stolen money, careful not to clink the coins together.

While the trunk was open she rolled up her grey linen gown, a petticoat, a shift and a pair of stockings, into a shawl and around the bag of money; she could carry the bundle under her cloak. When the summons came from William Chase she would tell Hephzibah that she must fetch coins to buy the fabric. Then, alone in the room, she must swiftly don another shift and petticoat and her black gown, wear them under the dark blue.

She had already, quite unknowing, paved the way. She had told Hephzibah only last week she needed a length of grey woven wool to sew another winter gown, to replace the one spoiled by the sea... She remembered what Richard Collyer had said. *God, the devil or fate has brought me to this place.*

Her head whirled a moment, and she dropped it onto her hands. What am I doing? Where am I going? She felt like one of the autumn leaves, tossed by the winds of the world. After she left New Exmouth she had no knowledge of what would happen to her. The world was no longer the safe place it had seemed during her life in Virginia.

She looked into her own soul and found foreboding. Yet she also found the excitement of adventure, of boundless possibilities. Anything could happen when one cast oneself to the winds of circumstance.

The real wind blew outside the little window and she heard the branches of the peach tree tap on the wall, like someone knocking at the door... The winds of circumstance blew strangely, without direction, plucking up human beings and dropping them down. Edmund Gramercy had not wanted to be a pirate, and had showed kindness when he could. But the forces of law would try to hang him. William Chase, whose kind made piracy possible, would in all likelihood never be punished. And John Hanson, who deliberately tormented her, was considered a good man.

And she, Mercy Penhall, had become a thief. How had she dared consider William Chase a hypocrite?

"Aunt Mercy!" Sarah's young voice called up from the

kitchen. "The cow has got out of her byre! And Mother says it is your fault, you did not shut the gate proper after you milked her, you were in such a taking to leave the house this morning! Oh come, we must chase her back in!"

Sarah. Mercy had been so proud of her own integrity, when she had refused Richard's invitation to join Edmund, three weeks before. What would Sarah think when she left now?

"Aunt Mercy? Are you there?"

She ran out to the stair, waved both hands at her niece and nodded emphatically. The girl ran outside again, and in a few seconds she heard her niece's voice loudly shooing the cow.

She ran down the stairs, and pushed the key back behind the cupboard leg. Then she rushed out into the garden, her heart suddenly lighter.

I am not a wind-blown leaf. I choose my own way.

That night while the house slept she wrote two letters, one to Nathaniel and one to Sarah. She wrote to the girl, *I know it is wrong to leave like this. But something drives me.* John Hanson would tell Sarah it was Mercy's bad blood. *Pray for me, and pray forgive me.*

The wind still blew in gusts and the peach tree branches still rapped on the wall. But All Hallows Eve was past and it was not ghosts that knocked. It was a summons to Edmund's help, and a new life.

****

Madame Soulange de Vaugeret had never before journeyed out of Carolina, and had been intrigued upon arrival in Boston to learn that the village across the river was also called Charles Town, after the English king. This Boston town was also situated on a promontory, between the Charles and Mystic Rivers, like the Carolina settlement which lay between the Cooper and the Ashley.

In all she had been happy to travel so far, to see a new place, and to meet people who knew nothing about her save that she was the scholar's wife. But she was not happy, now they were ready to sail, with the letter delivered through their hosts. It was from one William Chase, who requested that they be so kind as to allow a Puritan spinster accompany them on the voyage home.

Soulange knew the woman, the mute who had

travelled on the same ship as they to Boston in July. This fact piqued her curiosity. Why did Mercy Penhall wish to return to Carolina? And it was Soulange who must decide the matter. The letter, of course, had been given to her husband, and Paul, equally of course, had not been interested and had asked his wife to deal with the girl.

Soulange had not seen the Puritan at close quarters on that first journey. Therefore she was surprised by the small person she interviewed in a corner of the Plummers' parlour in their good house in Beacon Street. Soulange had of necessity long ago learned to be a good judge of character, and saw quickly that the woman was far from being the vapid creature she had looked from a distance on shipboard.

The Puritan rose when Madame swept into the room, not with the alacrity of the socially inferior, simply out of good manners. She was some five or six inches shorter than Soulange, yet carried herself straight and with dignity. Most would agree she was pretty, with fair skin and rounded features and blue eyes, and see no more than that.

But Soulange saw determination in the soft chin, firmness in the line of the rose-lipped mouth, and more than a little sadness behind her intelligent bright eyes.

Soulange had known sadness, and unbent a fraction. She invited the Puritan to sit again on the wooden settle. She thought, she would look exceptional if she were dressed in better than that sober dark-blue gown and plain white cap. Soulange lowered herself to the other end of the seat and arranged her skirts like a velvet wall. She would have taken a separate chair, however in time remembered the woman's need to communicate by writing. She folded her long hands in her lap.

"Mistress Penhall," she announced coolly, "you will understand that I do not know you except by sight, and must talk a little to form an opinion. I will be frank. If we agree to take you with us, it will be an imposition. My husband has his body servant and secretary and I my tire-woman, and we are all of quiet disposition." Her English was perfect, though lilting, she had once been told, with the French accent that was all she had left of her father.

The Puritan smiled faintly. She lifted a thin black-painted board that hung from a loop on a belt of plaited worsted at her waist, and chalk from a small bag beside it. She printed quickly in a clear hand. I AM NOTHING IF NOT QUIET, MADAME.

Soulange, accustomed to her husband's manuscripts, could read quickly in both French and English. She lifted her chin. "I am not so bad mannered, mademoiselle, that I refer to your lack of a voice. I mean that we keep our own company and would provide poor entertainment."

I WOULD NOT TROUBLE YOU IN ANY WAY NOR EXPECT YOU TO AMUSE ME. She brought a square-folded cloth out of the bag and wiped these words off the board. I NEED ONLY TO BE CHAPERONED TO CHARLES TOWN.

"And is no member of your family, or a friend, able to go with you?"

NO. MY BROTHER CANNOT LEAVE HIS WORK, OR HIS WIFE THEIR CHILDREN. Soulange noted that the woman said nothing of friends.

"But surely you are under age?"

I AM TWENTY THREE.

"You look younger than that, mademoiselle. I myself have twenty-five years but am considered nearer thirty."

The Puritan smiled slightly. BUT YOU HAVE A FACE THAT WILL CHANGE LITTLE. She regarded Soulange candidly for some moments. YOU ARE VERY BEAUTIFUL.

Soulange frowned. Her beauty had been a mixed blessing. Still, she preferred that this straightforward young woman see only her exterior. The thick black hair dressed high on her head with a Spanish comb and a wisp of lace, the translucent olive skin and exotic features, and the large black eyes which her own mirror told her gave away nothing of her mind and soul.

"You think to flatter me, mademoiselle, and thus assist your case?" Soulange unconsciously smoothed her skirt. Today she wore the russet velvet gown with blond lace set in the bodice, the same lace falling along her forearms from the cuffs of the sleeves, the rounded skirt looped back with gold ribbons to show the yellow satin under-skirt, and her russet velvet slippers. "Or perhaps it is my costume you admire?"

NO, MADAME. IT IS A PLAIN FACT.

Soulange met the direct blue gaze. No, this one flattered nobody. She smiled wryly. "Our conversation has diverted itself. I must ask you, why do you journey to Carolina? It is a great distance." At the beginning of October, all Boston had talked of the feat of one Madam Sarah Knight, who had ridden with a kinsman two hundred miles to New Haven. And here was this small person desiring to travel much further.

I AM NEEDED AS A WITNESS IN A LAW COURT.

"And you will come home after you have done this?"

The woman nodded, unsmiling.

Soulange kept her errant mouth from twitching. It could not be a welcome prospect to return to this cold and barren New England. "You understand, mademoiselle, that if you come with us we cannot be responsible for you in any way after your arrival in Charles Town? That is, beyond the common courtesy of conducting you to your destination." She knew the Puritan had stayed previously with members of the Independent Church. "Which is where, may I inquire?"

THE HOUSE OF MASTER HUTCHER THE WOOL MERCHANT AND HIS WIFE. DO YOU KNOW THEM?

"You can show us its location, Mistress Penhall." Soulange tapped her long foot in its soft slipper. "We ourselves are Huguenots. You know that?"

YES. AND I KNOW THAT PROTESTANTS WERE MUCH PERSECUTED IN FRANCE. The determination on the pretty face softened. This descendant of England, well grounded in the history of the persecution suffered by Puritans, understood that of others.

"My husband fled France with his family more than twenty years since, and settled on land on the Santee River." Soulange wondered how much to explain, though at least the woman did not condemn outright anyone not Puritan. "My father was also from the town of Vaugeret. He was driven away even earlier by the edicts of King Louis, and went to the first village, on the Ashley River." She needed no caution against speaking too much of herself. "You have a right to know something of us, if you seek to entrust yourself to our care. Are you aware of the reason we came to Boston?"

BUT VAGUELY, MADAME.

"My husband is a scholar. He read a copy of Master Cotton Mather's '*Magnalia Christi Americana*', oh, before last year. He decided that he himself would author a work on the Huguenot presence in the Colonies as Master Mather and Governor William Bradford did on the Puritan experience. He has completed that volume, but decided that in all justice he must add chapters about the Massachusetts Bay Colony. To gather correct information we sailed here." She respected Paul's motives though she thought him foolish to travel so far to fulfil them. But if they had not sailed she would not have seen Boston.

The fair woman listened with apparent interest, and Soulange continued. "Next summer, if his health permits, we will travel up the Delaware and Susquhanna valleys to the Penn colony, so that he may write of the Quakers there." She carefully did not allow her voice to dry at the prospect of a sick man undertaking more journeys. "He already has accumulated knowledge of the Dutch who settled New York, and of course the English in Virginia." She said nothing of Catholic Maryland. Paul himself had not decided.

Mistress Penhall's expressive countenance assumed a look of real respect. MADAME, THAT IS A MOST COMMENDABLE AMBITION.

"*Oui*—yes, mademoiselle," she frowned. "However, it is difficult for him. Monsieur is thirty years older than I and his health was ruined by the many fevers of the Santee. He remains poorly, which is why we must be quiet. The voyage home, at this season, will tire him greatly. You understand now why it is a grave consideration to add to our company?"

YES. MADAME, I ALSO WILL BE HONEST. IF I CAN HELP YOU IN ANY WAY ON BOARD SHIP, I WOULD BE GLAD TO DO SO. She rubbed the words away and wrote others. I NEED TO WORK PART OF MY PASSAGE. I HAVE MONEY, BUT FEAR THAT IF I USE SOME TO PAY SHIP FARE I WILL HAVE TOO LITTLE LEFT.

Soulange pursed her full lips and looked hard at Mistress Penhall. "And what will you do, mademoiselle, if

I refuse to take you with us on those terms?"

The Puritan sat with her back straight, hands clasped tight on her board, blue eyes directly meeting the other woman's dark ones. Her features had set into stubbornness and she dropped her gaze only to write. IF YOU DO NOT TAKE ME, MADAME, I WILL FIND ANOTHER WAY. CAN YOU TELL ME IF CAPT. STEPHEN ALEXANDER IS STILL IN BOSTON?

Soulange's spine stiffened. She answered carefully, "How do you know that we are acquainted with Captain Alexander, mademoiselle?"

FROM HIMSELF, MADAME. HE CHANCED TO COME TO NEW EXMOUTH, AND CALLED ON ME THERE. She wiped the words, and added, I MET HIM IN CHARLES TOWN BEFORE I TOOK SHIP NORTH.

Soulange knew this was not right. Richard had visited them in Charles Town twenty days or more before the little Puritan had arrived there. Paul had told him at that time about the voyage they planned to Massachusetts Bay. She said coldly, "I think you lie to me, mademoiselle."

Mistress Penhall looked back at her unblinking. And then she wrote, MADAME, I GO TO CHARLES TOWN TO TESTIFY ON BEHALF OF EDMUND GRAMERCY, THE PIRATE. CAPT. ALEXANDER KNOWS HIM. The moment she saw by Soulange's startled look she had read the words, she wiped them clean.

Soulange thought, *No fool, the little Penhall.* None of her conversation could be sworn to, since it could not be overheard and it all disappeared. Soulange regained her composure quickly, and looked around her. No other person was in sight, though there were sounds of servants working from the kitchen and the chambers above stairs. She rose, smoothed her skirts, and strolled to the window of leaded glass panes that looked down onto the cobbled street. She beckoned the Puritan to join her.

Mistress Penhall did so calmly, and with eyebrows raised in inquiry.

Soulange spoke in a low voice, which would carry less than a whisper. "I do not know of Edmund Gramercy except that he is known to—Captain Alexander. He – Stephen—is our friend, and came north in September

127

with the intent to escort us home. He was—trading—in Boston and other towns, but he suddenly departed and sailed south again." Soulange considered her next words. "There was an account in the Boston *News-Letter* which I think you also have seen."

The Puritan nodded, twice. Then she asked through her board, DO YOU KNOW CAPT. ALEXANDER BY ANOTHER NAME?

If Richard had not told Soulange the tale of his friend and the Puritan woman, knowing he could trust her tongue, she would have denied the question. But with Mistress Penhall, she knew with a certain relief, she could be truthful. "Richard Collyer." She pronounced it *Ric'ard Coll-ee-ar*. She looked the other directly in the eyes. "I am not his mistress, mademoiselle." She could not say to this Puritan, *but I knew him, before I was wed.*

Mistress Penhall studied Madame de Vaugeret's dark, proud face. Bright blue eyes met velvety black in a moment that challenged both women. And each drew back from it. They had met only minutes before. It was not possible for either to believe that the other knew their hearts had been given to men they should not love...

The moment passed. The Puritan dropped her board to hang from her belt, not even asking by it how Madame knew Collyer's true name. She clasped her hands at the front of her dark blue skirt and did not lower her eyes. She simply waited.

Soulange drew a deep breath. "You may come with us to Charles Town, mademoiselle, and pay no fare. Monsieur will make no complaint. We leave the day after tomorrow, on a ship seeking to join others for trade in the Caribbean. You have a place to reside until then?"

THANK YOU. However Mistress Penhall shook her head slowly. MY STEPBROTHER'S SISTER LIVES IN BOSTON BUT IT WOULD BE UNWISE TO ASK BOARD OF HER. I WILL GO TO AN INN.

Soulange, on impulse, lay an elegant dark hand on Mistress Penhall's sleeve. "You cannot stay unescorted at an inn. Our hosts are of the most genial, and are bachelors, so have no families to fill the house. If I ask, I am certain they will allow you to remain here."

The Puritan smiled, and printed, MERCI, MADAME.

"Ah, you know at least the French word for *thank you*. And, if I am not mistaken, you play on words." Soulange, now she had made the decision, was calm. "Merci is near enough to your own name, Mercy." Soulange pronounced it *Mercie*. She shrugged in Gallic gesture and her eyes narrowed keenly. "As for thanks, those will be due to the brothers Plummer. As for *moi, myself,* I choose to aid you for Ric'ard's sake. I trust neither of us will ever regret that I have done so, mademoiselle."

****

Mercy had never had a close woman friend. Her nurse Mam Felice in Virginia had been more like another mother. As a child in Salem she had played normally with girls her own age, then after her mother's trial and execution these had not been permitted to speak to her. Indeed when she had fallen ill Uncle Jonathan had taken her away so quickly that the cut-off from their company had been complete. In Virginia her mute state had kept her from attending school, and her uncle had educated her at home.

Even later, her dumbness had kept her apart from other girls. With a few, the daughters of tobacco planters and merchants, she had been on good terms without being close. None of them had patience, in their teens, to be constantly reading her slate, instead of chattering as they could to others. And by eighteen or twenty they were mostly married.

It had been a similar case in New Exmouth. Young women her own age were married and mothers, and all of them knew about Jemimah. A few braver souls had been friendly, after time and in a fashion. These, however, had not attempted closer acquaintance.

Soulange de Vaugeret, by the time their ship reached Charles Town, was a friend.

One thing that was evident to Mercy from the first was that the marriage of Soulange and Paul de Vaugeret was such in name only. In Boston and also on board ship they maintained separate quarters. Soulange visited her husband twice a day and usually read to him, complimented his first drafts of manuscript, saw that he was comfortable and inquired whether he had any requests to make of her. Quite often she merely asked after his health.

His health was certainly poor, and the pitching of the ship in the rough autumn seas did not improve it. They had sailed later than they originally intended, since Monsieur would not leave New England until he was satisfied he had gathered all the facts needed for his book. Their departure from Carolina had also been later than he wished. He had suffered the recurrence of an old fever in May, and had been unable to leave until June.

At that time, of course, they had taken ship aboard the same vessel as Mercy. She could not help but find it strange that they travelled together again. Though before she could wonder if, in Richard Collyer's words, it was God or fate that had ordained matters so, her common sense came to her rescue. Few people travelled between the Colonies, especially in these days when they risked meeting French privateers. It was simply the fact of them taking a passage at the same time that set them in each other's company.

Paul de Vaugeret was a small man in his late fifties. He had thick grey hair, a deeply lined sallow-skinned face and faded brown eyes whose expression was at the same time intelligent and distant. He had been introduced to Mercy in the Plummers' house, however his eyesight was weak and he was irritated by the need to read her board. Madame had read it for him.

He had asked information from Mercy about daily life in New Exmouth, about the Separatist church she and her uncle had attended in Virginia, and then apparently lost interest in her. He seemed to be not even curious that his wife had engaged the mute as her companion for the voyage.

Soulange explained this on the mildly tossing deck some days out of Boston. At dinner, a reasonable meal of cold beef and cabbage, Monsieur had roused himself to ask about New Exmouth's defences against the French. Mercy had hesitated to write of the militia and the two beacons standing ready to be lit as alarms. He had snapped at her reluctance. King Louis had exiled him, he said, and Madame had been born in the Colony, and did the Puritan think they were spies?

On the deck Soulagne spoke plainly. "You must not be hurt by Monsieur's temper, Ma'm'selle *Mercie,* or his indifference. His health is so bad that he saves all his strength for his writing."

Mercy shook her head, smiled, and braced her small body against the bulkhead of the half deck. She took up her board and managed to write on it. I AM NOT. MY CONCERN IS THAT IF I CANNOT HELP YOUR HUSBAND, AND YOUR MAID DOES SO WELL FOR YOU—she wiped the words off to make space for more— THAT I DO NOT EARN MY PASSAGE AFTER ALL.

Soulange told her firmly, "But you do, as company for me." She drew her green velvet cloak closer against the damp and chill of the open deck. "Sapra is excellent in her way, but has not your"—her lips twitched — "conversation."

Sapra was Soulange's tall, dignified and almost silent maid. There was nothing wrong with her voice, she simply did not speak unless it was necessary. Her looks were unusual, and Soulange had explained that to Mercy only the day before. The maid had been a slave, and when Soulange had freed her she had told her mistress of her origins. Her Negro mother had been raped by one of her Arab captors in Africa, and Sapra had been born of this cruel union.

Soulange had said in a hard voice, "The world is not kind to any woman, *petite,* but to the black it is wholly callous."

Soulange's hardness seemed deep-rooted, yet though she used the word 'conversation', neither she nor Mercy had communicated to the other anything of importance from their past lives. It was as if Soulange also carried a burden she could not speak of. Though Mercy allowed that particular thought might be her own imagination, and Soulange's occasional brittle humours simply part of her character.

They stood a little apart and watched the grey-green swell of the sea. Their silences until now had been companionable, but a slight unease pervaded this one. Both had said all they safely could. To trust each other further was to step onto unknown, and perhaps shifting, ground.

Mercy heard a lonely call from overhead. She recognised it for the honking of wild geese, and looked up to see a great flock of the birds crowding the sky to landward. She touched Soulange's cloak-clad arm and pointed to them.

"Ah, yes. They head for warmer quarters, they. New England and the northern lands in summer, and the Caribbean and Brazil for the winter."

Mercy printed, with a little difficulty on the sloping deck, LIKE RICHARD COLLYER. She glanced up at the other woman.

"Perhaps." Soulange's expression was severe, though not resistant. Madame had admitted to knowing 'Stephen Alexander's' true name, however had said no more except that Monsieur did not know it and she would be grateful if *Mercie* did not write it in her husband's presence.

Mercy added, IF YOU CAN GUESS WHERE HE MIGHT BE, I BEG THAT YOU WILL TELL ME. The ship dipped its bows into a narrow trough and the chalk skittered across the board. She grasped a stanchion for balance.

"I think..." Two sailors approached them, struggling with a wet line. Soulange looked at them, at the rough sea, at the dark cloud of flying birds, and at the Puritan's face. The blue eyes within the grey cloak hood gazed directly into her own. "Come, ma'm'selle, we will go below, and find for you some mittens."

On deck the air had at least been clean. In the cabins it was thick and stuffy. Soulange and Sapra shared a small one opposite the larger area allotted to Monsieur and his two minions. Next to it was the narrow space, no wider than a cupboard, occupied by Mercy. They were borne into Madame's cabin by the wind blowing down the cramped passageway. In there Sapra sat on a wooden trunk, feet planted firmly on the moving deck while she patiently mended a tear in one of her mistress's gowns, timing the rise and fall of her needle to that of the ship.

Soulange asked her courteously to take her work to Ma'm'selle Penhall's cabin, and the woman did so without surprise or complaint. Soulange gestured for Mercy to sit where the maid had and lowered herself beside her, graceful in spite of the need of both to brace their feet on the floor. She gazed at Mercy from keen dark eyes.

"*Mercie*, do you hope that Ric'ard will somehow be able to rescue Edmund Gramercy?"

Mercy's relief at the candid question was real. However the past had taught her not to trust too soon, and she had known this woman but a short time. She gently withdrew her hands and wrote warily on her board, I DO NOT KNOW YET WHAT TO HOPE. EXCEPT THAT I MAY BE ALLOWED TO GIVE EVIDENCE. CAPT. GRAMERCY WAS KIND TO ME. She wiped the board. PERHAPS IT MAY MOVE THE COURT TO A MILDER SENTENCE.

The dark eyes searched hers. "Forgive me that I say it so baldly, but I think you know that will not happen." Soulange watched the blue eyes, and they barely flinched. She rose, put off her cloak, and stood with her hands behind her holding the bunk post. "I comprehend, *Mercie*. You feel I would not give you any information that might lead Captain Collyer into danger. *Petite,* I have no influence over him. He regards only his own counsel. Nor do I know where he may be found."

SURELY HE CANNOT BE FAR AHEAD OF THIS SHIP! Mercy swallowed a sudden dryness in her mouth. HE MAY BE IN CHARLES TOWN ALREADY. HAS HE NOT TOLD YOU WHEN HE WILL NEXT VISIT? She held the board for Soulange to see.

Soulange slowly shook her head. "He is like those birds, *Mercie*. He winters in the seas and islands of the south. And he is like the wind, blowing where it will. We never know he comes to call until he knocks upon our door."

This was a blow, though Mercy did not lose hope. BUT HE MUST HAVE LEFT BOSTON BECAUSE HE SAW THE NEWS PAPER.

"I understand that you hope that is so." Soulange shook her head slightly. "But we do not know if he saw it at all. He may have departed for his own reasons." She added slowly, "You hope he left to rescue Captain Gramercy. If he knows he will do all he can, but I know not what that could be. Charles Town is a walled city, and though the Watch-house lies beyond the walls it cannot easily be reached."

Mercy would have written, *I have money, perhaps I can bribe a guard to free Edmund.* However she did not yet know how far she could trust the French-woman. Even if she could write such words to her, it would be better if Soulange had no knowledge of such a plan, if only for her own sake. She bit her lip and lowered her gaze.

"I see. You, also, would keep your own counsel. You need friends, and help, but do not know in whom to confide. You can trust me, *petite,* but you have no proof of that." Soulange compressed her dark red lips for some moments and examined Mercy like a merchant judging the quality of goods to buy. "I can offer you proof, and my own trust. I will tell you a thing about myself, *Mercie,* which you will any way hear gossiped in Charles Town. And by the telling I will risk losing your friendship before I have gained it."

Mercy lifted her gaze again, blue eyes wide with questions, though she wrote nothing.

Soulange took a deep breath. "My father had a small farm in France, and was partly a tenant of the de Vaugerets. He was a Huguenot like they, and was forced to leave his home, his wife and children, to escape prison. He came to Carolina as one of the first white men there, to the first settlement on the bank of the Ashley River. This was seven years before the de Vaugerets arrived on the Santee. *Mon pere,* my father, set up as a trader in deerskins with the Indians." She made a strange sound. "I do not know how to tell you the next thing."

Mercy frowned and printed, DO NOT TELL ME ANYTHING THAT DISTRESSES YOU. She lost her balance as the ship pitched and fell back against the bulkhead. Her instincts told her, *danger,* but not danger from the sea. Here was the challenge, the plunge into intimacy she had feared.

"It is too late. I have decided." Soulange spoke on with a tone of bitterness, and her eyes flashed. "Listen. My father took from among the Yemassee a woman who was half Indian and half Spanish, to share his life. She was his wife in their eyes, but not of course in the eyes of white men. She bore him three children, two of whom died when young. I was the one who lived, mademoiselle. I am a bastard, and one-quarter Indian."

Mercy was astonished, yet shamefully relieved it was no worse. She wrote quickly, THAT IS WHY YOU ARE SO BEAUTIFUL, THEN. And also, out of her relief, piously, YOUR PARENTS' SIN IS NOT YOURS.

"Mon Dieu, that does not turn you away? But that is not all. I will tell it quickly, because it pains me."

Mercy shook her head slowly. She sensed keenly the pain Soulange spoke of, and perhaps feared the 'all'.

Soulange braced herself more stiffly against the bunk post, as if to meet a blow. "My *maman* died when I had fourteen years. My father took no other wife, and I kept his house for him, and received my education from him. In all ways, mademoiselle, he raised me as if we had been in France and I the daughter of a small land-holder of good lineage. He died of a fever when I had sixteen years." She bent her head a moment, then lifted it.

Mercy wrote slowly, MY FATHER DIED WHEN I WAS A BABE.

"Then you understand a little." Soulange bit her lip, then continued in a strange thick voice. "He left no money, only our cabin, which was sold for debts. I was penniless and an orphan. The Yemassee did not help me, because I was too much white. The citizens of Charles Town did not help me, because I was too much Indian." She seemed overcome for a moment, then lifted her proud head. "Understand this, *Mercie.* I could have been sold on the slave block."

CRUEL AND WICKED! SOULANGE, WHAT DID YOU DO?

"That is the first time you have used my given name. *Merci,* thank you. Perhaps you are my friend. I go on. I became a whore, mademoiselle."

Mercy sprang to her feet, forgetting all else, and grasped the other woman's shoulders. Her face, had she but known it, plainly reflected her baffled horror. How had she ever dared to feel sorry for her own case? She at least had not been left alone for the world to prey on, at sixteen.

"You touch me? Then listen to more," whispered Soulange. "I had a thing to be thankful for, which I had enough wit to grasp. Because I have beauty, I priced myself high. I was beyond the purses of common men. I was kept by traders, merchants, ship's officers, men such as those. I will not sully your ears with the next eight years, but tell you of Monsieur. Please be seated once more."

Mercy felt tears sting behind her eyes, though she did as she was asked.

"The de Vaugerets had made a house and farm by the Santee River, and although I heard of it I attached no importance to it. They were but a name to me, and the Santee was forty miles north through the swamps and great forests. Oh, one could go by sea, but I believed I would be unacceptable to them. Two years since, Monsieur's wife died. He gave his land to his two daughters—all who remained of their six children—and their husbands. He was worn down after many fevers, and wished only to live quietly in Charles Town, following the scholar's pursuits which life had denied him." She was silent for a moment, and smiled a tiny, enigmatic smile.

Mercy heard the sounds of the sea and the ship and the wind, and those were as lonely as the cries of the wild geese and the tapping of the peach tree on the wall in New Exmouth. She waited for Soulange's deep warm voice to bring life back into the stuffy cabin.

"He had a cottage built and lived there while he had timber milled for his house. He had time, then, to search for *mon pere.* Monsieur had sorrowful news to pass to him. His wife in France had died, his children had returned to the Catholic fold and his land seized by the King. Instead he found *moi,* me."

Still Mercy did not write on her board, and still she looked at Soulange with great eyes, taking it all in, seeming to understand...

"He was horrified, *Mercie,* that he had not known what became of us. He married me, not so much for my own sake but to fulfil his duty to his former tenant, *noblesse oblige.* He did it also to spite his daughters, who live in fear that I will give him a male heir and thus lose them the right to his land on the Santee."

Mercy wrote at last, YOU HAVE A CHILD, MADAME? But she believed she knew the answer.

"*Non,* no. I have not borne a babe to Paul, nor will I. We made a bargain, you see. He does not touch my body, but gives me his name, a home, the needs of life and some of its elegancies. In return I manage his household, keep disturbances from him, and do nothing to dishonour his name." She paused, bit her lip and sat down again by Mercy.

MONSIEUR HAS BEEN KIND TO YOU.

"Yes. He did not need to wed me. He could have given me employment in his household, or made me his pensioner, or his mistress. Therefore, I also am under *oblige*, to honour my part of the agreement." She took a deep, shuddering breath, but then her voice firmed. "I do not tell you all this to seek your pity. I have left the past behind me. But I tell you so that you can know you may trust me with your own tale."

Mercy's eyes swam in tears and she needed to wipe them before she could write. SOULANGE, HOW DID YOU BEAR IT?

Soulange seemed tired, as from the unloading of a burden. She knew what Mercy meant, and shrugged. "One separates the mind and soul from the body, *Mercie*. And one looks upon the occupation of the body as merely work that keeps one fed and clothed and housed. Older whores taught me that, when I was still young. Yes, some of them are bawds. But kindness dwells sometimes in strange places. You must know why women are driven to sell their bodies! They are widowed, or orphaned like I, and have no kin to take them in. The choice is between that life and starving. It is seldom wickedness." Her voice was hard, though not bitter.

Mercy had known this as a fact of life for poor women as beggary was for men, yet had never considered it consciously. Humbly she wrote, FORGIVE ME.

"You did not mean harm." Madame sighed wearily. "So, I learned to think as they advised. Otherwise, I might have gone mad, or become a cheap thing all through instead of only in part." Her lips pressed together and her eyebrows straightened in a frown. She was the only person Mercy had ever met whose face could not be marred by a frown. "You—you are a Puritan. I did not expect you to understand."

WHEN I WAS CAPTURED BY THE PIRATES, I THOUGHT I WOULD BE RAVISHED, OR SOLD FOR A

SLAVE. I THOUGHT I WOULD RATHER DIE. She cleaned the board swiftly. BUT I FOUND THAT I WANTED TO LIVE, AND DECIDED THAT I WOULD, WHATEVER BEFELL.

"Aah," Soulange sighed at length. "And Captain Gramercy spared you that. You also found kindness where you did not expect it." Her beautiful dark eyes regarded the other woman steadily. "*Mercie*, it is more than gratitude that has brought you so far. Your heart is involved." She held up one hand. "But that is between you and he only. Between you and I, you seek to help him if you can."

YES. Mercy's mind skirted around the words *your heart is involved*. She concentrated on the fact that she could not be less than honest with Soulange, after her revelations. I DO NOT YET KNOW HOW, BUT FIRST I WILL TRY TO TESTIFY ON HIS BEHALF IN THE COURT.

"*Petite*, allow me to be blunt. I am not sure that even so much is wise." She laid her long hand firmly on Mercy's plain sleeve. "It will seem—particular—that you sailed from New England to do so."

Mercy printed, her hand firm on the chalk, I BELIEVE I WOULD HAVE DONE IT FOR CONSCIENCE'S SAKE EVEN IF I DID NOT—the chalk slipped away in a crooked line. Mercy stared at it, stunned at the knowledge that the next words she would have written would have been - *love him.* She had deluded herself all along as to her reasons for making this long journey. She had chosen to be convinced she must repay Edmund for sparing her on the *Thalia*. With great care she wiped the untidy line from her board. Her hands trembled. She bit her lips together, and looked up at Soulange.

"Yes," said that wiser woman, softly. "You have a passion for him."

Mercy blushed. Nor did she know what to write, what to do. This trust of another person was new to her, since Uncle Jonathan's death. She drew a deep breath, and entered the deep waters. YES. I MUST DO FOR HIM WHAT I CAN.

"And you will do it, no matter what others say?" But

Soulange frowned again. "I would help you in the only way I am able, ask you to be a guest in our house. But Monsieur must have, *absolutement,* a quiet life. And it may be that your mission will disturb that."

Mercy had not looked forward to staying with the Hutchers again. They too would prefer a quiet life, and were quite capable of forbidding her to go out into the town. The only alternative was an inn, and a decent woman could not stay alone at an inn. I WOULD BE GRATEFUL TO STAY WITH YOU. I WILL PROMISE ON THE BIBLE THAT I WILL LEAVE IF I CAUSE ANY TROUBLE.

Soulange had followed the chalk with her eyes, and was now thoughtful. "Monsieur finds your company unexceptional, though I would need to ask his permission. I am sure he will agree to what he thinks I want. Can you learn not to mind his ways? You would see him little."

YES. Soulange had not asked her to swear on the Bible, which determined Mercy to keep the unasked for promise. THANK YOU, FROM THE BOTTOM OF MY HEART.

Soulange smiled. If she was beautiful unsmiling, she was dazzling now, and Mercy understood why Richard Collyer was drawn to her. "It is I who will be thankful that I can keep your companionship. The ladies of Charles Town do not speak to me. I am still barely able to credit, *cherie,* that you do." The full rich lips laughed. "*Speak* may not be the correct word, but your board says more, and kinder, things, than the tongues of other women. And men."

Mercy dropped her board and touched the other woman's hand, though lightly. She was ashamed, and felt a coward, because she was afraid of losing this new friend. She could not tell Soulange the complete truth about her own background. She herself accepted Madame's history. She could see that the French-woman had been more sinned against than sinning.

Yet she had no doubt that Soulange would recoil in horror from the daughter of a condemned witch. Soulange might be soiled in the body, but her soul was untouched. Mercy's was the worse case. Her body was clean and her soul was accursed.

Chapter Nine

For three days Mercy waited opposite the dingy
Watch-house on the marshland by the Ashley River. She
felt her face pale and her spirits low. It was now her ninth
day in Charles Town. She had first waited three days
outside the quarters of the Royal Governor and then three
more before the house of the provost marshal.

Soulange had told her truthfully, "Sir Nathaniel
Johnson will not interest himself in you, *petite*. He cares
only for the collection of monies for the English Lords
Proprietors, and for keeping the city secure against the
French. And alas, I cannot help you!" Soulange did not
dare flout the terms of her marriage agreement to
accompany Mercy while her friend waited. But she did
send Sapra.

On the third day there a guard had fetched her into
the presence of the Governor's lowest-ranking aide, a
sulky young Englishman in periwig and fashionable
finery.

"Sir Nathaniel wearies of your presence, woman," he
stated loudly, as if she were deaf. "State your business, if
you please!"

I WISH TO TESTIFY AT THE TRIAL OF CAPTAIN
EDMUND GRAMERY. Mercy printed her words swiftly,
concerned the young man would not convey her message.
I WOULD ASK THE GOVERNOR'S PERMISSION.

"Then it ain't the Governer you need to see." The
young man was clearly relieved. "I'll give ye a note for the
magistrate's clerk." He dipped a quill in his inkpot and
began to scribble.

SIR, I ALSO WISH PERMISSION TO VISIT
CAPT.GRAMERCY IN THE WATCH-HOUSE.

The quill hovered in mid-air. The aide was clearly
taken aback. "Decent women do not visit gaols!" He stared

at the diminutive Puritan in her plain dark blue gown, grey cloak and simple cap. "Particularly young unwed women without male escort." He glanced at the tall silent maid-servant in mustard-yellow dress and magenta turban, and clearly found such escort inadequate.

Mercy wiped off her board and lifted her chalk again, however the aide added hastily. "I will write you a note to the provost marshal as well. He has charge of the prison."

He had not deigned to show them out, yet Mercy had been pleased enough with the two notes. They were a beginning to her mission to help Edmund.

The magistrate's clerk had seen her after only an hour's wait. However he had told her immediately, "Your evidence can make no difference to the pirate."

HE CAST ME OFF, SIR, WITH THE SAILOR LAD FROM THE JESSELIN, TO SPARE OUR LIVES.

"He still plundered the ship, madam." He regarded her curiously. "Why travel so far in a useless cause?"

AT THE BIDDING OF MY CONSCIENCE, SIR.

The clerk scratched his ear under his modest wig. "A Puritan one, far too active." He shrugged. "It is possible that the magistrate will allow you to speak, if he rules you to be of sound mind despite your impediment."

Mercy had understood he said this not to seem too unkind. He had not really believed it would happen.

She had waited for another three days outside the provost marshal's house. And when he had finally consented to see her he had proved more difficult than the aide and the clerk.

"No!" he had said, shocked by her request to visit the prisoner. And continued, annoyed, "Gramercy is in reasonably good fettle, for all he attempted escape three weeks ago and was flogged for it."

Mercy blinked, bit her lips and bowed her head quickly to write on her board. MAY I GIVE A HALF-GUINEA TO PROVIDE HIM EXTRA FOOD AND ANY OTHER NEEDS?

"If you insist, ma'am!"

He had accepted it to get rid of her, though for the next three mornings he saw her just the same. When he arrived at the Watch-house to unlock the thick entry door, she was there ready with her request printed on her board. He refused her entry each time and with increasing testiness.

"You waste your time, Mistress!"

Mercy had to hire a boat each day to reach the Watch-house. The filthy and forbidding building did not cheer her soul, nor did its surrounds. She was tired of the smelly flat marshland, the two great sluggish rivers, and the sandbank called White Point where hangings took place...

She was weary of worry that her doings might reach the ears of Paul de Vaugeret, of the hope each evening that Richard Collyer would bang the brass knocker on the door. She wearied of the stares of the colourful inhabitants as she walked the sand streets of Charles Town, and of the sniggers of the guards at the opening to the wharf along The Bay. She was even tired of reading her book.

"A book of sermons?" Soulange had queried, with a smile.

IT PASSES THE TIME.

Soulange had rolled her eyes a little. "At least let me give you a stool to sit on while you read."

AND ONE FOR SAPRA?

"Sapra prefers to stand. It looks better that way, *Mercie.*"

I AM GLAD OF HER COMPANY. IT IS NOT A PLACE TO BE BORNE ALONE. Mercy did not add, *not when I know Edmund is confined there.*

They had waited, she on her stool and Sapra on her feet, under a great Sea Island oak tree festooned with the grey growth called Aaron's beard in Virginia and New England but here Spanish Moss. Mercy's hard-won patience had begun to run short. She must not become anxious, yet it was difficult to keep her spirits up in this place and in these circumstances.

TOMORROW IS THE SABBATH, she had written for Soulange that ninth morning.

Madame had nodded her understanding. "And the Independent Church was closed, like the Huguenot, at the beginning of the war. Only the Church of England remains open."

THE PURITANS HERE WILL EXPECT ME TO

VISIT THE HUTCHERS' AT LEAST FOR PRAYERS. She wiped the board almost angrily. BUT IF NECESSARY I WILL GO TO THE WATCH HOUSE AGAIN, TO WAIT FOR THE PROVOST MARSHAL.

Soulange had touched her hand, dark eyes soft. "And on Monday the pirates' trial begins."

YES.

Soulange had nodded gravely and said nothing. Later, however, when they broke their fast she said that Monsieur's secretary, the pallid Dupuis, had informed her that he and Monsieur would soon join them for dinner in the evenings. "Dupuis, *Mercie,* does not like your presence in the house. That is nothing, though now that Paul has recovered from the voyage, I am anxious he not be troubled." She smiled. "You will not trouble him, but Dupuis will say what he can against you. He does not like me, either!"

Soulange's voice was light, yet Mercy wrote soberly, I MUST DO NOTHING TO DAMAGE YOUR RELATIONSHIP WITH YOUR HUSBAND, MY DEAR FRIEND. She wiped the board. IF NECESSARY I WILL GO TO THE HUTCHERS' OR TO AN INN.

"It will not be necessary, *Mercie!* I but tell you how the case stands, so that you may be at your most charming with them both." Madame had laughed gaily.

Opposite the Watch-house, Mercy rose from her stool and stood with folded hands. She could see only the tall masts of ships that wintered in Charles Town's harbour, and the ever- present birds. Herons, brown pelicans, gulls and terns hunted along the rivers' shores, ibis and egrets crowded the branches of cypress trees and swamp oaks, little yellow wrens sheltered in the palmetto trees and ospreys glided overhead like eagles. And also, around the town's markets, ugly red-throated turkey buzzards waited for rubbish and carrion... Harbingers of death...

Just as Mercy shook her head free of the unpleasant thought, the provost marshal arrived on a flat barge. With some ceremony the heavy main door of the prison was unlocked. Mercy walked quickly forward, her board already prepared with her usual request. But the officer frowned and strode over to her.

He looked angry and uneasy. She knew that he, like

many other people, found her silence unnerving. Yet he
was also the subject of her persistence, and she wondered
if that morning he intended to drive her away by force.

Instead he announced sharply, "You may see the
pirate, Mistress, for all he don't want to see you! He said
to tell you to go away and cease to plague him and
Charles Town both. But it is I you plague!" He slapped his
broad hat on his knee. "I've told the turnkey to take you to
the courtyard and stay there with you durin' the
interview. And don't think you can persuade Wickes to do
anythin' not his duty - he can't read."

Mercy's heartbeat quickened unbearably, though she
retained enough presence of mind to merely nod her
thanks, and not to smile.

The marshal squinted up at the sun. "You're allowed
a half-turn of the hour glass. Take your woman in with
you for decency's sake. And when you leave, don't come
back! I ever see you here again, I'll order you escorted
away." He grunted. "The prisoners will be kept in the
Guard House by the Court during the trial. You cannot
visit there!" He did not wait for an answer and turned
away.

Mercy gripped her book of sermons tightly, lowered
her chin and walked as sedately as she could to the big
iron-hinged door. The turnkey, a large ruffian with a dirty
periwig, wore a dirt-creased coat and breeches that copied
the fashions of his betters. He waited for her, small eyes
peering like a pig's. He carried his ring of keys in one fist,
a truncheon in the other, and a long dirk was thrust into
a wide belt around his belly. Behind him were two guards
who bore muskets with short bayonets.

"It's a mute, and a-going to talk with the pirate," the
turnkey observed with a snigger. He let the women
through then crashed the door shut behind them.

Mercy swallowed a sudden lump in her throat. It
would be easy to be frightened. However she looked at
Wickes with a mild expression.

He had not moved. "Mebbe we ought to search 'em for
weapons."

Mercy understood, and from her pocket gave out a
florin and two sixpenny pieces. The two-shilling coin of
course went to the turnkey, and the sixpences to the

guards.

Wickes chuckled unpleasantly, but turned and led the way through the guardroom. He opened a thick-planked door at its rear with one of his large keys, and entered the gaol itself. Sapra followed Mercy, the guards fell in at the rear, and this door also was locked behind them.

They walked down a narrow corridor with a dirty wooden floor. The walls were rough yellow pine, stained and unwashed, on an earthen base, with doors set in at regular intervals. Small iron grilles were set at eye height in each door. Through these she heard pacing feet, groans and curses, though mostly silence. She shut her mind to the sounds. Most prisoners were undoubtedly criminals, but even if merely unfortunate she could do nothing for them.

The gaol stink had assailed Mercy's nostrils from the first moment. It seemed compounded of every human odour atop the reek of the swamps and tidal mud on which the town and Watch-house were built. She wanted to hold to her nose the perfume-sprinkled kerchief Soulange had pressed on her each day. She did not, however. If Edmund must bear this, so would she. Yet she remembered how he had preferred to be clean...

The turnkey clumped to the far end of the passage and she followed him. He stopped before another thickly braced door. Through its grille pale sunlight fell in small stripes on the filthy floor of the corridor.

Wickes stuck his face against the opening and bawled through it, "Stay where you is, pirate, an' no tricks. I got two guns a-hind me. 'Ere's yore pretty visitor, but you cain't 'ave 'er to yourself. I'm to watch ye." Into the door went another key, turned with one fist while the truncheon was held in the other. The door squawked on unoiled hinges as it opened. Mercy was shoved ungently through and Sapra calmly followed. The guards remained in the passage and this door also was re-locked.

"This part's to be built into more cells," Wickes announced, as proud as the master of a manor.

It was an area perhaps thirty feet by forty and its hard trodden ground supported not so much as a weed. Its wall was a palisade of fourteen-foot logs with iron spikes set at irregular intervals. Mercy felt she was in the bottom of a box that needed only a giant lid to seal it off from the pale blue sky. There was no bench, no stool, nothing.

Except the man in dark shirt and breeches who stood in the shadow of the furthest wall, stood straight with his feet apart and hands thrust into his pockets. He did not move. But Mercy would have known he was there if it was darkest night, or the midst of a storm.

In the past weeks and the long recent days she had known moments of doubt, when she hardly believed she was doing what she did, all for a chance-met man to whom she had been inexplicably drawn. But misgivings vanished in the presence of the living Edmund Gramercy. Once again she felt the unseen cord stretch between them...

She allowed herself to feel no more than that, or to think. She walked across to him and wrote swiftly on her board. She slipped a silver Spanish *reale* out of her cuff onto it, and held it to him flat, like a tray.

WILL WICKES BE BLIND AND DEAF FOR THIS?

He took his hands from his pockets without haste and held up the coin so it caught the pale sunlight. "Oh yes. Wickes, you will see and hear nothing."

Edmund tossed the piece through the air and the turnkey caught it in one thick hand, tested the metal with his teeth, then grunted and leaned on the doorpost a few yards from the imperturbable figure of Sapra. He even turned his back, thick as a log itself.

Gramercy's eyes moved to Mercy, then. They were dark and cold, his face was without expression and his voice was indifferent.

"It is hardly worth the spending, Mistress. I recall you, but barely. They've allowed you here against my wishes, but now I have your ear I tell you that you're a fool and on a fool's errand."

Mercy recognised the armour of the pirate captain. She had not expected he would behave any other way, that he would try to save her from herself. Nevertheless she filled her gaze with him, not pretending otherwise.

He was thinner. His hair was longer and obviously combed only by his own fingers. The lines around his mouth and eyes were deeper and his left cheek was grazed and beginning to scab. He wore the dark breeches, indigo-dyed shirt and plain neck-cloth he worked and fought in. Seen close, the garments were torn and threadbare. His black stockings had holes in them and he wore unbuckled shoes a size too large. Perhaps he had sold his boots for food or water. And yet, shabby as he was, he still gave the impression of neatness. He was cleaner than she had imagined, but not, she knew, as clean as he liked.

She took a deep breath, hardly noticed the stink that infiltrated even this space, and bent to lay her book on the ground so that her hands would be free for the board. I KNOW WHAT YOU ARE DOING. DO NOT WASTE TIME. I AM HERE TO HELP YOU. I WILL TESTIFY TO THE COURT THAT YOU SPARED ME.

"Your evidence will make no difference to the outcome. Your generous impulse is most Christian, Mistress, but useless." Prison had altered nothing of his bearing or his coolness and the tone of the words was cold. He knew, as well as she did, that the coin to Wickes would not stop the turnkey's ears.

I KNOW IN ALL SENSE THAT MY WORD ON YOUR BEHALF WILL NOT SAVE YOU. She wiped the board. CAN THE TURNKEY, ANYONE, BE BRIBED TO FREE YOU, RESCUE YOU? I HAVE MONEY.

"From where?" he asked sharply.

She smiled a little. IT IS MINE, AN INHERITANCE. IT WAS SEWN INSIDE MY CLOTHING. YOU WERE POOR PIRATES, NOT TO FIND IT.

He spoke carefully. "Who would have expected it, of a Puritan?" For a moment she thought he would smile, but he did not. "Well, Mistress, now you have seen I'm in health, you may go. I have no need of money. The shillings you sent will provide better than prison fare until the trial's end. Our friend Wickes there can do no more than see to that. To act otherwise would be to put himself at peril."

His eyes remained dark. She looked into them deeply, tried to penetrate his armour. IF YOU KNEW DIFFERENT YOU WOULD NOT TELL ME, TO SAVE ME FROM TROUBLE. BUT I MUST KNOW. TELL ME

THE TRUTH.

"It's true, Mistress, that I'll hang."

She bit her lip against sudden nausea. YOU GIVE UP EASILY! WHAT OF RICHARD COLLYER?

He shrugged. "I do not know."

I SAW HIM IN NEW ENGLAND. HE VANISHED AFTER YOUR PLIGHT WAS KNOWN.

He frowned. "If I had any friends in the world, woman, what could they do? Lay siege to Charles Town?" His voice was sarcastic.

He was determined not to involve her. However, she knew his Achilles heel. WHAT OF JEDEDIAH? IS HE HERE ALSO?

For a moment she saw a flicker of light, deep in his eyes. "Yes. But my first mate is dead."

He had let her know he was rid of Gorman, though that no longer mattered. I OWE MY LIFE TO YOU AND JEDEDIAH. IF YOU WILL NOT INSTRUCT ME, I WILL ACT ON MY OWN.

The invisible cord between them drew slowly tighter. Then he said, "Pass me your board." He took it by one end so that he would not touch her fingers, and looked at it hard. "It is the same one."

She nodded and risked a smile; her back was to Wickes. Even in this place, in these circumstances, she was glad simply to see him so near. The empty corner of her heart that had filled in those minutes in his arms on the *Thalia* was filled again.He held out his hand for the chalk. She pressed it into his palm and deliberately used the movement to briefly clasp his fingers. The physical contact sent heat up her arm, and she saw that Edmund also felt that fiery strand of love. His eyes met hers and they were warm and golden brown. Gently he pushed her hand away then wrote quickly.

Mercy, do nothing, place yourself in no danger. My life was destined for this end when I took up piracy.

She took another piece of chalk from her bag and printed under the words. NO. WHAT OF THE AMNESTY?

"But yes, Mistress." His tone was implacable. He cleaned the board with his sleeve. *The amnesty is for those who surrender, not the captured. I beg you, leave this place. You have lost reputation simply by coming here.* His gaze was grave, his eyes still warm.

And all avenues of hope seemed to be closing. She touched his hands, his long warm brown hands, to take her board again. The piece of plank, and memory, were they all she would have left of him? She wrote unreasonable words, I DO NOT CARE FOR MY REPUTATION.

"But I do." He spoke coolly and wrote warmly. *The provost marshal told me how you arrived, with whom you are staying. Richard has said she is a good woman. I trust she will take care of you.* He wiped the board impatiently. *Did you come with your family's permission?*

I TOLD THEM I MUST ACT ON MY CONSCIENCE.

"That is no answer, Mistress. Write 'yea' or 'nay'," he said sternly. He wrote, *Set my mind at rest. Can you return home? Be safe there?*

She met his eyes and nodded. Certainly she could return to New Exmouth –if she wished. And she would be safe enough, if she did. But she would not!

You will marry someday.

NO!

"Don't be so sure, woman." To Wickes' ears, the words would sound as a threat. The board said, *There must be an honest man somewhere to value you, who will not care about your voice. I pray he finds you.*

Her eyes stung. She held her lower lip in her top teeth until she had felt the tears recede. HE DID FIND ME.

"You will forget." His tone mocked. His eyes, however, were flecked with gold.

She shook her head until her brain reeled.

He took the board from her. *Stubborn—if you'll not act for your own sake, do so for mine. For my sanity, go home before the executions.* He wiped the board clean, pressed it firmly into her right hand and brushed the chalk dust from his torn sleeve. Aloud he said, "Time you left, Mistress. It has been a profitless visit. And your notion of appearing in court is equally profitless."

He glanced once at the turnkey's back and once at Sapra who gazed unblinking at the palisade. He took Mercy's left hand and kissed it, then turned it and kissed the palm. If the other two saw the first, it had been formal enough, and the second he hid with her body. But Mercy felt the pressure of his strong fingers, the fervour of his lips on her skin.

He whispered, "I did that in spite of myself. Mercy, go home." Then he released her abruptly and stepped back a pace, unsmiling. He did not know that his eyes were like amber in firelight. "Wickes! Take her away. Faith, I should make you return that *reale*. You haven't earned it."

Mercy stood motionless and stared at him, hugging the board to her breast. She saw his eyes darken and his face stiffen into Captain Gramercy's. Then she felt the bear-like presence of the turnkey behind her, turned on her heel and went. She walked quickly and felt that her heart dragged reluctantly after her body. She passed through the doorway and Sapra fell in silently behind her.

Wickes banged it closed. He shouted through the grille to Gramercy that he'd see him back to his cell when the mute was gone. When his key grated in the lock its sound was as final as a clod of earth dropping on a coffin...

Mercy never remembered walking the stink-filled corridor again. When they had quit the gaol she stared at the live oak, which seemed to weep streamers of grey tears. Slowly she tied her board to its loop on her belt. She tried to calm her spirit. The boat trip back to the town would not be long enough, for that.

She had been in possession of her own soul until she met Edmund Gramercy. Even so she did not resent that they were bound together, though the bond was painful, though her heart would bleed if he died... But he was not yet tried or condemned! There was always hope.

She hoped he still loved life enough to fight for it. She hoped he had found the book of sermons she had left behind. She hoped it would be useful to him. She had cut into the middle pages, hollowed them into a box, and in the hollow lay every last coin she possessed. She was now dependent on the charity of Soulange, and her stepbrother and his family had no buffer against hard times.

She was a thief and hoped to aid a pirate. And tomorrow was the Sabbath, when she must pray piously with her fellow Puritans.

****

Edmund, alone in his dank cell, leaned against the wall to think. He had forgotten his back, still lacerated from the whip, and winced. Thank God Mercy had not asked about it.

The interview had shaken him deeply. He had known since the days on the *Thalia* that he cared for her, but had placed her in the past, a vivid, precious, private memory. To see her in the flesh again—tiny, pretty, direct, silent and utterly valiant—had been torture. He had been a fool to kiss her hand, when above all things she must remain unsuspected of anything but Puritan charity.

He wrenched his mind away from hopeless longings. He had learned one thing – Richard probably knew what had happened. Richard was not a fool, and would not throw his life away taking useless risks. Yet if anything could be done, Richard would do it. Then again, Richard might not know...

He touched the book where he had dropped it carelessly onto his pallet. Some of the coins were under the dirty straw, and others in his pockets and shoes. He had showed the volume to Wickes and read to him the title page. The turnkey had chortled at the notion of the Puritan bringing the prisoner a book of sermons, but had not otherwise been interested. If Edmund used the money, Wickes would not know where it had come from.

He had asked the turnkey a month ago his price for such small help as he dared to give. The price was twenty pounds for himself, and fifteen for Jedediah. And here were thirty-eight, by the hand of his little one. All she had in the world, most likely, and her heart as well.

The price was too high.

****

Soulange took one look at Mercy's white face and drew her upstairs to her own boudoir. She sent Sapra to make an infusion of sage for her to drink.

Mercy told her by her board what had occurred, and then appalled herself by bursting into copious, if silent, tears. However, her friend's soothing voice, and the herb tisane, as well as the emotional release of weeping, helped her to recover.

But she wrote, I DESPISE TEARS! I MUST BE STRONG.

"You ask of yourself not only that you not be a woman, but not be human! *Cherie,* you have drained your strength with anxiety. You need to recover your spirits." She smiled, rose to her feet and went to her carved walnut armoire. "This is for you, *Mercie.* Oh, do try it on!"

Her arms were filled with the gown of pink silk brocade, worked in silver thread and trimmed with silver lace, that she and Sapra had sewn all the past week. Mercy had wondered once, vaguely, why Soulange made a dress so unsuited to her colouring. Now she understood. But as she lifted her board to write a protest, Soulange stopped her hand.

"I know Puritans consider pretty clothes to be not necessary. But wear it here among ourselves, to please me, and because you need distraction. Ah, men call us vain, and forget it is they who judge us by our appearance! Even they know that to look well lifts the soul." She lay the gown across her day bed. "Come, let us put our griefs aside for just a little and be silly schoolgirls! Try it on, *petite.*"

It was amazing, but Soulange was right. At first Mercy did as she was bid only to please and with a heart still heavy. Behind a painted screen she stripped to the skin, drew on a fine linen chemise, silk stockings and a full-skirted petticoat of ruffled cambric and lace. She felt a stirring of pleasure at the luxurious feel of these on her body. She emerged shyly.

Soulange laughed at her and with Sapra's help dropped the rustling folds of the gown over her head, then smoothed it into place and laced it up. Then they made her sit on a damask-covered stool and unplaited her braids.

Soulange exclaimed as the soft blonde curls fell to Mercy's shoulders, "So lovely! But hair worn so is for the bedchamber, for a husband or lover." Almost before Mercy could blush or feel any hurt for what would never be, her hair was brushed with a boars'-bristle brush and made to shine. Then it was piled on top of her head, pinned in place with a curl that escaped charmingly here and there, and decorated with a silver-backed comb and a froth of lace.

Sapra slipped onto her feet little kid-soled slippers, made of silk brocade and tied across the long tongues with pink satin bows. Then they stood her up before the mirror.

Mercy had seen herself in a full-length glass only twice before, in Virginia in the house of Uncle Jonathan's friend Lewis Phipps. She stared at the little lady before her, a fashionable stranger in a shimmering pink gown. It was trimmed with pink bow-knots, which outlined the V-shape of the bodice and looped the overskirt back so that it looked like a scalloped shell. Impossible not to wonder what Edmund would think of her in this costume...

She turned quickly to Soulange, eyes brimming, and reached for the board to thank her. Then she remembered the board was with her own clothes. Indeed, it would look strange to tie her belt of dark plaited worsted and her chalk-bag over the waist of such an elegant *toilette.*

Soulange said softly, "You would pass anywhere as a lady of quality. A little pale, perhaps. Pinch your cheeks, *cherie,* and bite your lips, put some colour into them." She added in mischievous threat, "Or I will use rouge on your face, and carmine on your mouth!"

Mercy did so, tried to enter into the spirit of the game. Strangely, it was not difficult. Was she worldly at heart, as well as wicked? No, she would not let such thoughts trouble her now, not when Soulange was so kind. She also recognised that Soulange was enjoying herself, she whose existence had changed so suddenly from a courtesan's to that of wife of an old man.

Madame clasped around her friend's throat a delicate necklace of small pearls and tiny sapphires, and Mercy touched it with some awe. So valuable, and they gleamed so prettily. The sapphires drew attention to her eyes and made them seem more blue. Then into her hand was pressed a fan of embroidered pink silk on ivory sticks, and a mantle of embroidered silk was draped about her shoulders.

Soulange inspected this last with a critical eye, then took it away. "It is too much. You are so little, the simple style suits you best."

Mercy went behind the screen and fetched her board

and chalk. The silk skirt swirled and whispered around her and distracted her mind. She wrote, SOULANGE, I CANNOT KEEP THESE.

"You do not know that for certain, *petite*. I will store them here until the day comes that I can give it all to you. But ah, I should so like to see you at a grand ball! The gentlemen would surround you."

Mercy looked at her gravely, then smiled. MERCI AND THANK YOU. BUT WHAT NOW? I MAY NEVER WEAR THESE LOVELY THINGS AGAIN.

"Now, Mercie, since you are dressed for a ball, we shall teach you to dance a little. Oh, do not stare so! I know that your people do not sing or dance, but those are not sins! And we are private. Sapra, clap your hands for the music. I shall be the gentleman."

And so Mercy learned some of the complicated steps of the *minuet*, and movements of the *polonaise*. Soulange pretended to be a most stern dancing master, and Sapra provided melody with a throaty hum added to the gentle rhythm of her palms...

After an hour Soulange sent the maid for cool drinks and collapsed onto her day bed, laughing. Mercy had known all the while that her friend worked to keep her mind from the ordeal of the days ahead. Now she knelt before her in a billow of pink skirts, took both Madame's hands in her own and pressed them tightly.

Soulange looked into the other woman's face, saw the gravity of her small smile and gratitude plain to read on her expressive countenance. She smiled back.

"Ah, yes, we understand each other."

****

Later, however, she saw the Puritan watch with a pensive face from the parlour window as the sun sank into the wild lands behind Charles Town in colours of gold and fire and blood. She left her to her thoughts; there was only so much one person could do for another.

They shared a silent, formal supper with a heavy-eyed Monsieur and his surly secretary. When the meal finished these two immediately retired to Paul's rooms, and not long after that Mercy begged by her board Soulange's pardon, she was tired and would retire early.

Soulange smiled and wished her *bon nuit*. Then after

an hour she tiptoed into the guest chamber and stood looking down at the pale pretty face and tumbled curls on the pillow of the four-posted bed. The fine wool blankets had slipped from Mercy's white shoulders and exposed her plain flannel shift.

Soulange drew the covers up, tucked them around the other woman's soft throat, and smoothed the counterpane. She wished Mercie had accepted the loan of one of her own lace-trimmed linen smocks to sleep in, yet understood her friend's reluctance to be completely beholden to her.

Her heart was heavy with sadness. *Mercie* had told her much, but beyond that was a wall which no one, not even her new friend, was allowed to penetrate. The Puritan trusted her, yet Soulange wished she could trust her more.

After all, what could conceivably be wrong in her, she who looked like an angel flown down to earth? What could be worse than the history of Soulange de Vaugeret?

Chapter Ten

Paul de Vaugeret awoke two mornings later to the news that the mute guest in his house had become a *cause celebre.*

Until then he had barely noticed her presence. He had rested in his chamber to recover from the voyage and fretted to begin his work once more. He had been vaguely aware that the woman's company had pleased Madame, and was kind enough to think, as an abstract notion, that as such it was good they had given the wench bed and board. The little person had been no trouble.

Now Dupuis, his secretary informed him with disapproval that all Charles Town talked of the Puritan spinster who had testified at the pirates' trial. Paul was astonished and angry. So much so that instead of beginning on the new volume, he sent for Madame to come to his book room. He requested Dupuis to wait outside while he spoke with his wife.

Soulange's gold-skinned cheeks had hollowed a little, though she answered Monsieur's questions readily and quietly. *Oui,* the court had ruled that Ma'm'selle Penhall was of sound mind even though dumb and allowed her to write her evidence on her board. Sapra, in attendance, had told her mistress that the bailiff had then read her words aloud, and the citizens in the public area had hushed to hear of this strange pirate who spared innocent females.

The Puritan told Soulange by her board that she had also written in court that Captain Gramercy's servant, Jedediah Bullen, had told her of two others thus spared. She had testified that Bullen also had treated her with consideration. The court had already heard that Gramercy spared the crews of plundered ships when he could, and that the other survivors of the *Jesselin* had been rescued months earlier near Cape Hatteras.

Paul was not interested in the details. "And now that the trial is over, Ma'm'selle Penhall will return to New England?" At least she would soon leave his house.

"Monsieur, the trial is not over until today when the prisoners are sentenced. *Mercie* insists that she will attend, and that she will not leave Carolina until after the executions. I do not know why she punishes herself so, but I believe that she hopes against all hope that somehow Captain Gramercy will be spared."

"He will be hanged at White Point with the rest of them! Madame, the woman is our guest, but I did not expect this gossip, this furore, which surrounds her! It reflects upon ourselves! Is it not enough that we must be wary, because we are *Francais* and England is at war with King Louis?"

Soulange clasped her hands across the skirt of of rich yellow brocade. "I know it, Monsieur. Above all things, I desire that you not be distressed. But neither myself, nor Mademoiselle Penhall, expected that she, and the trial, would catch the town's fancy as they have." The citizens were also morbidly interested in the fate of the dignified Captain Gramercy, though she did not say so. Paul was already irritated. However Soulange knew how to cope with her husband. She met his eyes, meekly and without challenge.

He paced the floor and ran a frustrated hand through his grey hair. Paul had no patience with fashion and did not shave his head to wear a periwig. "And will you pay her fare, when she does sail home? The treasure I smuggled into this savage country melts away! I pay quit-rent in lieu of service to the Colony so that we will be left in peace. My sons-in-law torment me to buy slaves, to drain the swamps and build dykes so that they can grow more rice. It will be years before there is a profit to show!"

Soulange showed a face of concern. "Monsieur, I could direct the household with more economy. For myself, I need no more gowns, and could sell some of the jewels." She did not remind him, this day, that most of her clothing and jewellery she had brought with her to the marriage.

Paul pulled fretfully at the plain white *cravate*

around his thin throat. "Never let it be said that I cannot keep my wife, or my house, in comfort. But Madame, I cannot have these distractions! I need my energy, and time, to work now on the Puritan chapters. And next year I must find strength to travel to the Penn colony, for the volume on the Quakers." He added pettishly, half to himself, "They make it difficult, now they have a separate legislature for the Delaware section. And the name offends the ear. Their King Charles called it *Sylvania* and they add Monsieur Penn's name to it. Penn-Sylvania—*faugh!*"

Monsieur had distracted himself, though Soulange soothed him nevertheless. "I beg your pardon, Paul, that I have, unwitting, caused you this upset. But I believe I have not neglected you in favour of our guest."

"*Non, non.* But she must leave this house, go to one of the members of the Independent Church."

Soulange spoke gently. "It would look bad, Paul, if we turned her out at this time."

"I care not. The woman presumes too much on my hospitality!"

"If she knew that she troubled your mind, I think she would go of her own will." Soulange took a deep breath then a step closer. "Monsieur, she plans to attend the execution of Captain Gramercy. I cannot allow her to do so alone, even with Sapra as escort. I would ask that you permit me to bear her company."

Paul stared at her in disbelief. "You would defy the terms of our arrangement, for this foolish Puritan?"

"Monsieur, I have thought on it long and hard. You have been only good to me and I remain most deeply grateful. But I cannot let Ma'm'selle *Mercie* endure such a thing without the company of a friend. If it means that you must expel me from your house, and your protection—then I must accept that."

"And you would return to your former way of life, to earn your bread?" he asked harshly. "You are a fool, Madame!" When Soulange merely nodded, he pulled petulantly at his ear. "I do not need this drain on my vigour! I am too unwell."

"Monsieur, I need not have said anything to you. I could accompany Mercie without having asked your leave, and could depart from your house also without having spoken. It seemed that to consult you was the least thing I could do."

"Leave my protection! You are my wife, Madame! And I have become accustomed to your presence here! You run the house smoothly, you do not allow me to be disturbed."

"Good servants could do the same, Monsieur."

"Servants cannot do everything! Your looks—the fashion of your dress—your circumspect behaviour—all do me credit. And keep my harpies of daughters to circumspect behaviour also. Madame, your request amounts to coercion!"

His wife did not answer. She bit her rich red lower lip and turned her face away. However this movement presented to Monsieur's gaze her left profile, which was the most beautiful aspect of her face. Her eyelids fluttered uncertainly and he saw a single tear in the corner of her dark eye. Monsieur was quite aware that Madame's former life had taught her to be something of an actress, but surely no one could weep at will. And sunlight through the one diamond-shaped pane of glass in the window turned to gold the topaz earrings which had been his bridal gift to her. The light transformed the gown, his favourite, into a garment of gold.

It occurred to Paul, not for the first time, that his wife was beautiful and comparatively young. He had abstained from a physical relationship not because he was unable, but from fear of using his small store of strength. The knowledge that she had sold her body to other men was of little importance to him, and the fact of her mixed blood not at all. His was the detachment of the true scholar.

Indeed, now that he considered it, her old profession should have taught her how to make love with little exertion on the part of the man... Monsieur turned his head away, a little ashamed. After all, his part of their agreement was the understanding that he would not possess her body. But—if she broke part of her promise, might not he also break part of his?

The morning lengthened, and he must begin the Puritan volume. "Madame, if as you say our guest has made a favourable impression on the fickle public—well, then, we would be seen as poor hosts, not to help her. I myself will accompany both of you to the pirate's hanging. But you and I must go in the coach." This entirely unfitting name he gave to the vehicle, on a sledge instead of wheels, that carried him over the sand streets of Charles Town. "Allow Mademoiselle to watch as she wills."

It was more than Soulange had hoped for. She turned toward him again, seemingly impulsive, smiled beautifully and clasped her hands to her breasts in a most becoming gesture. "Ah, Monsieur, you of all men are the kindest I have ever known! Thank you! *Merci!*" She hesitated, then added softly, "I know that it grieves you to lose time on your work, and I know that I have reneged a little on the agreement between us. If—if there is anything I can do to repay you, please tell me, I beg of you." She looked at him through her eyelashes and then lowered them. She produced a tremble of the lips.

Paul was relieved to hear her hint so strongly at what he was too embarrassed to say himself. "For now, I must begin my work. We can discuss—what you have said—at some other time. Perhaps if I come to your boudoir on a night after supper?"

"*Oui.* Yes, Monsieur," she agreed quietly.

Paul smiled for the first time in many months, kissed Madame's hand and escorted her to the door. He bowed her through it with a brief formal bob of his upper body. Dupuis, huffing impatiently in the outer room, went in and shut Madame out with a slam.

Soulange closed her eyes and leaned back against the polished panelling. She pictured in her mind the fair skin and twinkling hazel eyes of Richard Collyer. He had known her body when she was a whore, as her husband had not—yet.

Absurdly, she felt she was unfaithful to Richard. She smiled wryly in the empty room. There was more than one way to prostitute oneself.

****

Edmund Gramercy had not looked at Mercy during her short time in court, nor had she expected that he would. To the end, she knew, he would try to protect her.

His demeanour had been cool and calm, his appearance neat. Soulange had sent to the Watch-house, with a coin for Wickes, an old brown waistcoat and coat of Monsieur's, black stockings, a plain white stock for the neck and plain white bands for the shirt cuffs, and Mercy had enclosed her own bone comb.

She remembered how she had thought him sober as a Puritan when she first saw him. In this dark and undecorated attire he looked more than ever a modest, decent man, nothing like a pirate. Except for the shackles that confined his wrists, which he ignored.

In the dock he had listened to the evidence as if it concerned someone else. Jedediah, not as big as he had been, his skin pale instead of ruddy and tanned, stood stolidly beside him.

Edmund, when questioned, did not defend himself. Indeed it was the magistrate who had asked if his excuse was the usual one that he had become a pirate to save his life. The answer was a bare '*Yes.*' However he did ask clemency for Jedediah Bullen, who had followed him out of loyalty.

Mercy's heart had turned slowly colder as she watched him. His bearing was that of a man meeting his fate with dignity and courage, not of one who hoped to cheat the executioner. When she gave her testimony at the end of the second day, his countenance did not alter. When she left the court she had tried to match his dignity, had held her chin high and her eyes steady.

Then at the door she had heard one of the crowd ask another if he thought the dumb woman's evidence would make any difference. The second onlooker had whispered his opinion, not having any notion that Mercy could lip-read. He said that perhaps the judge might order the hanged pirate be cut down immediately he was dead instead of allowing the body to remain exposed on the gibbet, but that would be all...

Mercy had needed to lean on the door and fight nausea. And yet these men were not the rabble who normally attended court proceedings but solid citizens. From the first the crowd in the courtroom had been enlarged by groups of well-dressed and prosperous townspeople. The city had gossiped of the little Puritan, and was now curious.

Among their colourful costumes her plain gown and white cap were like a seagull's feathers amidst the plumes of parrots, and her muteness the silent eye in a storm of chatter. She saw men look aside at her and wondered if they believed her tale. Perhaps, being men, they could not believe that the pirate had let her be. She saw also women who regarded Edmund from under their lashes—did they speculate what it would be like to be at a pirate's mercy?

She woke on the morning of the third day, when the sentences were to be given down, to rising fear. The nightmare approached nearer with each hour. But her courage must be alive, to show him a brave face. She berated herself fiercely. If it was hard on her, a witness, how must it be for the man who would suffer? Though such thinking was of no help, and she was close to despair.

She joined Soulange in the parlour for breakfast. They were alone, since Monsieur every morning took a light meal in his bedchamber. However she was unable to eat. Carolinians fed largely and, faced with buttered hominy, eggs, ham and shrimp, she could only pick at a single egg.

Soulange poured with her own hands a tankard of coffee and set it before her. "Drink, *petite*, if you cannot eat. And, though I know it will be of no help but to have company, Monsieur has given me permission to go with you to the court. In the sledge—coach—no less." She did not tell Mercy that Paul would accompany them to White Point for the executions. One day's sorrow at a time was all that any soul could bear. Instead she smiled. "He thinks it hides us from the public, forgetting everyone in Charles Town knows that Monsieur dislikes sedan chairs and it is his!"

Mercy was barely able to twitch her lips in response. However she tried to fall in with Soulange's attempt to lift her spirits, and wrote, NOT EVEN THE GOVERNOR HERE HAS A COACH. THE GOVERNOR OF VIRGINIA DID, AND A FEW WEALTHY FOLK IN WILLIAMSBURG. She wiped the board automatically. I WILL THANK MONSIEUR.

"I will do that for you, *Mercie.*" Soulange reached

across the table and squeezed the other woman's hand.

At the heavy entry door to the street, Sapra, wordless as usual, helped her mistress into the green velvet cloak. Mercy donned her old grey one, and thought, *Soulange looks tired this morning. Am I such a worry to her?* Madame's eyes were smudged beneath with shadows, and her smooth golden cheeks were drawn. Yet she wore her gown of russet velvet and looked no less lovely than always.

Mercy knew that she herself was pale, and her dark blue woollen gown with its white collar and cuffs emphasised the pallor. However her grey linen was with the washerwoman and her only other choice was the black gown that she had worn under the blue when she left New Exmouth. And she would not wear black, the colour of mourning, today, for Edmund to see...

They walked out under the little porch and stepped down onto the brick flag-way. Monsieur de Vaugeret's house was built of cedar and yellow-pine, and behind it stood the cottage of logs where Paul had lived while the main dwelling was constructed. This now served as quarters for the cook and housemaids. There were three small outhouses and one large, the stable and carriage barn with a room above for Tobias the coachman. Dupuis, Sapra, and Monsieur's body-servant Henrique slept in the main house.

The coach-sled waited at the front gate and Tobias held the heads of the two sturdy brown horses that drew it. Tobias was the man-of-all-work and merely doubled as coachman when necessary. He was short and wide and a white servant, not a slave, and therefore did not hesitate to address Madame directly.

"The priest is waiting inside, Madame."

Mercy looked at Soulange surprised. Her friend merely nodded at Tobias as if the information was expected. The coachman opened the door and the three women climbed in. The so-called carriage, made by a boat-builder to Monsieur's specifications and nailed onto the sled, was smaller than a French coach, therefore the tall man in a black soutane seated in one corner took up a good deal of the space.

Soulange seated herself opposite him with a careful

arranging of skirts and Sapra sat beside her mistress. Mercy therefore had to squeeze herself in next to the priest, as well as step over a cloth bundle on the narrow floor. The interior of the sledge was stuffy with the smells of leather and horsehair and dim as well, since all the leather curtains were pulled across the little horn windows. The priest looked out through a chink beside one of them. Mercy raised her eyebrows at Soulange, who simply smiled and extended a hand toward the stranger.

"Look more closely, *Mercie*."

The man turned his head to face the Puritan and grinned, not at all like a man of the cloth. He wore a flat-brimmed low-crowned hat over a dull brown periwig, his face was half covered with a short brown beard and moustache and his skin was also brown. However there was no mistaking the hazel eyes. Mercy, unable to cry out her surprise, seized his arm.

Richard Collyer laughed very low. "Aye, Mistress, it's myself under all this berry juice and hair. I waylaid Sapra last evening with a note for Madame. And I thank Providence that Monsieur owns this useless conveyance in a city where other folk walk. I'll talk low and solemn now, so the coachman won't think I'm any but a Church of England parson. You've seen Edmund in the Watch-house. How ready is he for an escape?"

Mercy's heart had leaped out of its despair, yet the first thing she wrote on her board was, YOU CANNOT INVOLVE SOULANGE.

Richard squinted at the words in the poor light. "Madame's assistance involves no more than use of this carriage for a short time. She is willing for that."

Soulange leaned forward. "*Mercie*, I see no danger to myself. Do not fear. Ric'ard has an excellent plan."

AND IF IT GOES WRONG?

Collyer frowned, though that might have been because he had to peer so closely at the board. "Then, if Monsieur can't take care of his wife, I will. Quick now, what did Edmund say?"

Mercy glanced at Soulange's lowered eyes and knew at once why Madame took the risk. Not for Mercy, not for Edmund, but because Richard asked it. She hesitated no longer. She really had no choice. HE TOLD ME

NOTHING. BUT I LEFT HIM NEAR FORTY POUNDS.

His eyes narrowed, though he asked no questions. "He has money, then. He'll know if he can use it, and how. I will be at the Guard House shortly, to pray over a dyin' man..."

"How do you know, Ric'ard, about the dying man?"

"The gossip of the port, Madame. I will see Edmund if I can." He saw Mercy's widened eyes, Soulange's pursed lips. "Don't look so shocked, ladies. The sick man won't know no difference, and God must hear prayers even if they're from the likes of me. Listen, now. *Prospero* is out at sea, but the *Dart* is in the harbour. You remember her from New England, Mistress Mercy?"

Mercy nodded, barely able to contain her excitement. She wrote with an unsteady hand, HOW WILL YOU SAVE HIM?

"Won't be difficult. The prisoners are escorted to and from the Guard House by constables and a few soldiers. Today they'll be sent back to the Watch House because it's nearest White Point. I thought to waylay the guard outside the walls, but we'd be seen from two of the bastions. No, my men have come up one by one from the sloop, let into the city as common crewmen, and are ready to act. There are others left hidden on the boat to sail her..."

"*Mais*... but—how to rescue your friend, Ric'ard?"

"Simple, Madame, we'll attack the prisoners' escort in the Court of Guard. Surprise will work in our favour. 'Tis a large space and there'll be a crowd we can hide among until we're ready. Rescue ain't so difficult. To get them out of a walled city when there'll be hue and cry after them is the hard part. That is where Madame and her maid assist us. They know their parts. Now you, Mistress, listen for yours."

****

The coach-sled halted before the brick paving of The Bay, that strange name for a street. It faced the Cooper River and its length was filled with inns, warehouses, merchants' quarters and the homes of the influential, including the Navy captains. Mercy and Sapra alighted and passed by the gate-house unchallenged. Here the city wall was of brick, but the soldiers on guard were there to prevent the French coming in, not the citizens going out. It was a serious duty requiring several soldiers; the wharfs created the only gaps in the city's defences.

The women walked onto the wharf, called a 'bridge' because the other city gates had drawbridges, which jutted out into the flat grey waters of the great harbour. The estuaries of the Ashley and Cooper Rivers combined to make that harbour and it could have held fifty times more ships than it did.

Mercy looked for one ship only and knew where to find it. Nevertheless she first walked up and down, with Sapra behind her, and asked by her board and sometimes the maid's seldom used voice, about passages to New England.

She met the man Richard had described. She remembered Ned Turner, the *Prospero's* first mate, though he wore a hat instead of a kerchief, had removed his gold earrings and shaved off his moustache. With him she pretended to arrange passage on the *Dart,* not only for herself but Sapra. The sloop, he told her with a solemn wink, departed on the noon tide for New York and Boston. In winter they were unlikely to meet French privateers.

He spoke loudly, as if he thought her deaf as well as dumb. Every soldier, sailor-man and labourer within earshot could hear that the Puritan would leave Charles Town this day. Mercy had never dreamed herself capable of play-acting, but managed to show a resigned face. Some of these witnesses might have seen her outside the Governor's house or in the Court. Her heart beat fast, not because she was afraid but because at last something was to be done for Edmund.

The arrangements made, the women returned across The Bay to the coach. Sapra laid a restraining hand on Mercy's arm and after a moment Mercy understood. Richard and Soulange were in it alone. She dropped her board on the brick footway and took a minute to retrieve it. When she opened the door and climbed in Richard cocked a knowing eyebrow at her. He and Soulange still sat opposite each other, knees unavoidably touching in the cramped interior. Soulange had pulled the curtain aside a little, and stared out the window.

Richard asked in a low voice, "Done, Mademoiselle?"

Mercy nodded firmly, she and Sapra took their places and Soulange pulled on the string that would signal Tobias to move off.

To move was easier ordered than done, since the streets near the 'bridges' and The Bay were busy, although not so crowded as in summer. Porters, sailors, merchants and beggars all vied for space with loads of goods dragged along on open wooden sledges to the warehouses. The coachman shouted and grumbled at them, but guided the awkward vehicle through it all. When clear of the port area they drove Richard to the wide Court of Guard.

Richard swiftly kissed Madame's hand, grinned at Mercy and Sapra, and left the coach. Mercy appreciated that at least he treated them like intelligent beings and did not assume they would forget their roles merely because they were women. She lifted the shade of the nearest window to see if he parted from them safely.

The coach-sledge was moving forward again but she saw him step into a doorway and emerge a minute later to mingle with the passers-by. He walked briskly to the Guard House. She dropped the curtain, and her heart beat a little fast again. It had begun, and there was no knowing what the day's end would bring.

She looked across at Soulange, saw her black eyes unnaturally bright, slid into Richard's vacated seat and reached for her hands. They understood each other perfectly without needing to speak. In a few hours their loves could be either dead, or free men.

Soulange held her fingers tightly for a moment before she found a husky voice. "We must pray." She loosed one of Mercy's small hands to take Sapra's larger one in her own, and Mercy grasped the maid's free hand. The woman looked from her mistress to the Puritan, who both chose to touch her like an equal.

Soulange said softly, "You also take risks. By my order, yes, but also for love of me." She closed her eyes, her lips moved, and then aloud she said, "Ah, *bon Dieu*, we ask for help, for safety, and for your blessings."

There seemed nothing else to say. Mercy asked in her mind for Edmund's life, and for forgiveness that they transgressed the laws of men. And then they sat silent while the sledge bumped unevenly over the sand, three different women born long leagues apart, but each drawing comfort and strength from the other two.

****

Mercy had to sit still in the Court, listen when Edmund was condemned to death, and show nothing more than disappointment.

That was for the eyes on the onlookers. For herself she felt sick in the stomach and the old terror began to tighten her chest. She told herself fiercely, *he will not die.*

Soulange had inspected Captain Gramercy with cool curiosity. Now she took out her perfumed kerchief and said in a low voice from its folds, "Courage."

Mercy lifted her chin. *He would not die, would not, would not...* Not like her mother had, not any other way.

The magistrate passed the same sentence on Jedediah, who made a face but otherwise seemed not to care. Then he sentenced their five fellow prisoners. There had been seven but one had died of wounds and another lay dying of gaol fever—the wretch whom Richard had pretended to pray for. Mercy did not remember their faces, except vaguely as some of the cut-throats who had supported Elias Gorman. Every person in the court hushed to hear the words of death.

Edmund's eyes, dark and cool, examined the audience while their attention was on the bench. Across their heads, through spaces between periwigs and hats and sleeves, his gaze for a single instant met Mercy's. She saw light in it, low as a candle flame yet bright. He lowered his chin for one second, a gesture that could not be construed as a nod except by someone who looked for it. Then his glance passed on, measuring, unhurried, icily calm.

Her heartbeat reached up into her throat. He knew. Richard had somehow spoken to him. He was ready.

She tore her eyes away from the dark, stern figure. She must not draw attention to either of them. She looked at Jedediah. He seemed restless now, shifting from one foot to the other. And he was uncommonly bulky, under his torn shirt and stained waistcoat, as if he had eaten heavily and lost his prison thinness... Bulky as Sapra was this morning...

She turned her gaze away from him, stared blindly at the five other pirates, heard the voice from the bench that spoke over and over the words, *hanged by the neck until dead.*

She fisted her trembling hand and touched Soulange's velvet elbow. The other woman understood the plea in her face, and moved quietly with her toward the door. They needed to push here and there and Soulange said crisply, "*pardon - if you please - thank you.*" Sapra had stood outside with other attendants, and fell in behind her mistress. All three walked with normal tread, silently, to the coach-sled drawn up fifty yards away.

As they passed the corner of the court building, Mercy saw near its side entrance the militiamen who acted as part of the pirates' escort—the constables were in the court. These men had been sitting but now began to stand, ready to take the prisoners back to the Watch-house. From there, at the given time, they would escort them again, to White Point and the hangman. Or so they expected.

A sergeant growled at them to make formation. They responded slowly, seeming bored. One, who must have been half-asleep in the pale winter sun, yawned. Mercy shuddered and passed on.

Soulange ordered Tobias to take them to a street behind The Bay, to one of the taverns, to find a certain wine that Monsieur liked. He grumbled that once there he would need to go on foot, that it would take him half an hour or more, and that it would be better to do it after they had taken Mistress Penhall to the ship. Soulange insisted firmly that he drive there now, since the sloop did not depart until noon.

Sulkily he climbed up to his seat, and once the women were inside took out his ill humour on the horses. At the head of a certain alley his mistress ordered him to stop, and he tied the horses' reins to a post and left on his errand, stomping bad temperedly over the sand surface.

When they could no longer hear his step, Soulange said to Mercy, "Your captain is a brave man, *cherie.* But I think there is more to him than that. He does not fit the part life has cast for him."

Mercy shook her head, tight-lipped. Her nerves were

stretched and her ears strained with listening. After a moment she saw that Soulange listened also. Sapra—Sapra merely began to take off her outer garments. Mercy watched the alley, chosen for its comparatively deserted state, from a slit beside the curtain. Soulange helped her maid to disrobe in the awkward confines of the carriage.

Within minutes Sapra's plain brown hooded cloak, her equally plain woollen gown and her stuff petticoat were piled on the seat. She unwound her dark red linen turban, and Soulange fetched from under the carriage bolster another cloak of similar brown. Sapra drew it on around her dress of mustard and maroon that she had worn beneath the other, and sat back, as calmly as if she did this every day of her life.

They had nothing to do then but wait. The suspense and inactivity tried Mercy's hard-learned patience. To steady her nerve she took up her board and began to write, even as she listened, the words of a psalm she knew by heart. Soulange raised her eyebrows in inquiry, and Mercy passed the board to her.

THE LORD IS MY SHEPHERD. I SHALL NOT WANT. HE MAKETH ME TO LIE DOWN IN GREEN PASTURES. HE LEADETH ME BESIDE THE STILL WATERS.

Soulange smiled faintly and gave the board to Sapra, who read it with knotted brow and handed it back to Mercy. Thus the twenty-third song of David King of Israel went back and forth between the Huguenot, the Puritan and the Arab-African while they waited and listened.

Then, over-riding the murmur of town sounds, they heard sharp reports in the distance and a clamour of shouting. All three tensed and Mercy's fingers clamped on the board. She reckoned time in her head, how long Tobias had been away, how long before the man they waited for could get to the coach.

If he could, if he could... Mercy willed fiercely that he would. That he be unharmed. That he and Tobias would not arrive at the same moment, that Soulange could deal with Tobias if he did. She knew Madame had another errand planned for the servant if the other man did not come on time. But they could not wait for too long.

Once then twice she peeped out through the slit by

the curtain. The entrance of the alley where the coach waited was a quiet place, however people did traverse it now and again, going about their business. Only one or two spared a glance for the odd-looking sledge. It was known in the wharf area of course, and known to come on just such errands as Tobias ran now. No one seemed to hear the distant sounds the women heard, or if they did they attached no importance to them.

A man rounded the corner, a slim man in a brown coat, dark-haired and hatless. He walked at a normal pace. The only other people in sight were a Negress with a babe on her back and a porter bent under his load. The man walked past the coach whistling, through his teeth, a sailors' shanty Mercy had heard on the *Thalia.* Though she did not need that, to know him.

The Negress disappeared in the direction of the market, the porter to the warehouses. The slim man doubled back, still at walking pace. Through the curtain she saw his face, deeply flushed beneath its tan and the scabbed cheek. He had stopped whistling. She leaned forward and set the door ajar a fraction. Her heart felt risen in her dormant throat, choking it. She made herself swallow.

The door was opened without urgency, the man pulled himself in as casually as if the coach was his own then closed it carefully behind him.

Edmund Gramercy had escaped, at least this far.

Chapter Eleven

Edmund sank onto the seat beside Mercy and released air from his chest with a barely suppressed groan. Then he bent forward, his hair falling beside his face, and breathed in harsh gasps. Mercy reached her hand toward him, then drew it back when she saw he needed fresh air for his lungs before anything else.

Soulange began to speak, to cover the sound, but lost nerve and trembled, unable to think of any words. Mercy passed her the board, on which was written, appropriately, YEA, THOUGH I WALK THROUGH THE VALLEY OF THE SHADOW OF DEATH, I WILL FEAR NO EVIL, FOR THOU ART WITH ME.

Soulange read it aloud in a voice that shook, then added more calmly. "Where is Tobias? You watch also, Sapra, from your side." She looked out by the curtain.

Mercy lifted the pile of Sapra's clothing from the opposite seat and set it in her lap. Within a minute Edmund's breathing was less laboured and she touched his wrist. At first she had wanted only to throw herself into his arms, then realised there was no time for such transports. Neither he nor they were yet out of danger though she was calmer, now he was with them.

He turned toward her and his face was the grim mask she had first seen on the deck of *Thalia*. For a moment his eyes were all darkness. In the next he began to drag off his coat, waistcoat and shirt. It was impossible for him to stand, in the coach, and he struggled to draw the petticoat and gown over his head. Mercy helped as best she could, then straightened the garments and fastened the laces. He left his breeches, stockings and shoes on, and certainly they could not be seen beneath the skirts.

Soulange whispered, "Here is Tobias. Sit back in the

corner a moment, monsieur."

She alighted quickly and as quickly shut the door behind her. Just before she closed it, Mercy heard more plainly the distant bedlam of sound. She heard Tobias's alarmed voice, then Madame's brisk tone as she told him it was probably some drunken sailors or gangs of apprentices fighting. *Non,* no, that could not possibly be musket shots he heard, but fire-works.

"Let me see the wine bottle. Yes, that is the one. Come, we must take Ma'm'selle Penhall to her ship, now."

They felt the carriage lurch as Tobias took his seat. Soulange climbed in, skirts bunched under her arms, and almost fell into her place. She sank back into the corner and held a shaking hand over her eyes. When she lowered it, the coach was moving. She saw Mercy reach up and wind Sapra's turban around the man's head.

Sapra took a small brown bottle of berry stain from her pocket and applied it diffidently to his face and hands. Mercy could not do it; the juice would show like paint on her white fingers. Soulange took a deep breath then. That much was accomplished. He would do.

He was of medium height for a man, Sapra tall for a woman. The hem of the gown might be an inch shorter when he stood, that was all. The colouring was now near perfect, the man being tanned for a European and Sapra brown rather than black. Her resembled her not at all in the face, but Sapra's features were strong by way of her Arab father, and no white person looked closely at a black servant.

Edmund sat with hands spread on the skirt to dry, not one whit less a man for the female attire. His breathing was deep, under control. The carriage creaked and clattered and under cover of the sound he spoke to Soulange, voice low and unshaken.

"Madame, I have no right to endanger you, all three. Offered a chance of life I took it, even knowing what it might cost." His tone was tinged with bitterness, though his voice softened to add, "I will thank you now. But I pray that none of you suffer for this day's work."

"I do not know you, Captain. I do it for *Mercie,* who is my friend, and for Ric'ard, who is also my friend. The risk is small."

He turned his stern countenance to the servant woman. "I thank you also, for your garments." Sapra merely blinked.

Mercy touched his arm, then handed him Sapra's cloak. He pulled it around his shoulders and she inspected him carefully, then frowned. She lay her small hands flat on his chest, shook her head, took them away and without a blush indicated her own small round breasts. They all understood and searched about them for something to give him a woman's shape. They ended by tearing open one of the carriage cushions and rolling some of its horsehair filling into rounded pads. He pushed these down the front of the gown.

He asked quietly then, "Will you look around us?" and Soulange and Sapra peeked through the curtains. There was nothing unusual in the street. A few passers-by glanced idly back toward the now faint sounds from the centre of the town.

Soulange turned back to nod at him and he smiled faintly. He twisted on the seat to look at Mercy, a long unsmiling look. Yet the Puritan found something in it to please her, smiled warmly at him and reached forward with both hands. He gripped them hard in his own. Soulange held her breath a moment. They had forgotten the world, the coach, herself and her maid. But it was only for a moment. Mercy touched her fingertips to the red marks of the shackles on his wrists and raised her eyebrows.

He answered her obvious question in a steady voice. "That is part of what your gift bought, little one. The key that unlocked the chains." He kissed her hands then gently released them.

He picked up Monsieur's old brown coat and waistcoat, and his own threadbare shirt, from the floor. He hung them over his left arm, under the cloak. Mercy made a gesture of taking them herself but he said in the same soft voice, "No. If anyone is discovered with a man's apparel, it will be me."

She lifted the bundle on the floor into her lap, and raised her board to give instructions.

He shook his head at her. "I know, Mercy. I am the servant and carry the goods. Is it your own clothes?"

Soulange answered. "No, those remain at my house. These are rags, monsieur, with a few kerchiefs on the top." She saw Mercy smile again at the man, her pretty face tender and determined together and could only admire her self-possession. Her own soul seemed turned to water. She felt pain for both of them, and for herself. She asked in a low voice, "Can you tell us what happened, sir?"

"It will be common knowledge soon enough, but take care not to speak before you hear the tale. The escort was attacked by perhaps thirty men dressed like common sailors, and most of the prisoners were snatched away. Soon more military will be called out and messengers sent to warn the bastions and the gatehouses on the Cooper. The attackers, since I know the planner, will have their own escape arranged. Do not fear for him, Madame. I have known him all my life and he is like a cat, always landing on his feet, and with as many lives."

Mercy wondered what had happened to Jedediah, then realised Edmund would tell Soulange as little as possible, for her safety's sake.

Perhaps Soulange guessed that. She looked at him gravely, turned her head and gazed out from the crack by the curtain. "I see the bridge."

The coach slowed and its wheels clattered less noisily. Edmund leaned close to Mercy and breathed by her ear, "Keep your nerve, little one. You are only a Puritan traveller, with an attendant." He looked an inquiry at Madame.

"I must come out, to say farewell to my guest and to give instructions to my maid." Her voice was very low, but Soulange was once again in command of herself. "But I will not be able to say this there. *Le bon Dieu* go with you. And I charge you, take care of *Mercie*."

If Mercy had possessed a voice she would have told Edmund that she had no intention of losing nerve, and Soulange that she could take care of herself. But they were concerned for her and she did not write the words.

Tobias growled *whoa* at the horses, and Edmund answered Soulange, "With my life." He kissed her hand, turned to Sapra and took hers to shake it like a comrade's. He smiled a little as her eyes widened in surprise.

The carriage jerked to a stop. Before Tobias could descend to open the door, Soulange let herself out, followed by Edmund and Mercy. She shut it sharply on Sapra in the dark corner and turned to meet an approaching guard. The wall and the bridge were guarded against the French, not the townspeople.

Soulange told him calmly, "I take my friend to her ship."

The man swept her an exaggerated bow and said with a leer, "Yes indeed, Madame de Vaugeret."

Mercy felt Edmund's arm stiffen and pinched it in warning. This was the first time she herself had seen what Soulange must endure, mockery from those who knew of her past. She was angry herself and would have liked to slap the guard. But they must ignore him.

Soulange had flushed darkly along her cheekbones, however she lifted her head and spoke firmly to Tobias. "I am hurried, now. I have been absent from Monsieur too long. I will return the moment I have said farewell to Mademoiselle." Tobias rolled his eyes at the whims of women and climbed down to hold the horses. Soulange added for his benefit, and the guard's, "Mademoiselle, when you have met this other woman passenger and are comfortable, send Sapra back by the pilot boat."

Mercy glanced suddenly at Edmund. She had forgotten that of course Tobias knew Sapra. But Edmund had thought of it himself. His back was turned to the coachman and he had drawn the hood of the cloak over his head.

Soulange moved her hand to touch Mercy's but suddenly dropped it, her eyes uncertain. Mercy firmly laid her own hand on her friend's velvet sleeve. Why should Madame feel unworthy of her friendship because a common soldier knew what she had been? Soulange smiled then.

They walked across the brick paving and Edmund fell in behind them, shortening his step to keep the same pace. Out on the wharf—bridge—where piles made of mighty tree trunks penetrated the grey waters, a dinghy manned by two sailors floated below a ladder. The thin man waited for them with a show of impatience. His eyes slid sidelong to the figure in the cloak, then he nodded and addressed Mercy.

"We need to linger a little for one o' the crew. He better not be drunk in some tavern."

Soulange told him haughtily, "I trust this is a decent vessel. I expect that both you and your captain will see my friend safe home." She turned to Mercy and kissed her on both cheeks. "Farewell, *Mercie*. You know you may always return to me."

Mercy's eyes suddenly stung. She stood on her toes a moment to kiss the smooth dark gold cheek, and nodded. The plan was that she return to the de Vaugerets' with some excuse as soon as Edmund was safe away, but there was no certainty about what would happen.

Soulange said to Edmund, "You know what to do." Edmund inclined his head and Soulange swept gracefully away, holding her russet skirts clear of the dirty timbers. At the end of the wharf she dropped a few coins among three or four beggars who sat there.

Ned Turner announced in a bored voice that he could not give the tardy sailor much more time, or they would miss the tide. Edmund's face tightened.

Mercy knew then it was Jedediah they waited for. She gazed at Edmund with what she hoped was encouragement, and looked town-wards herself for the remembered bulky figure. She saw beyond the gate the back of Monsieur's coach as the sled slid away over the brick-paved street.

She saw also the beggars inspecting their booty. One of them, his face hideous with puckered scars and with a crutch under one arm, held up his coin and cackled with triumph. His voice was distorted, as if his throat also had been damaged by whatever had caused his injuries.

He called to Mercy, jeering, "Nay waitin' to see the hangin', Puritan?"

She lifted her chin then turned her face away. Had she become such a public figure that the very beggars knew her? She glanced at Edmund's cloaked figure for reassurance, and saw him frown.

It was not at the beggar but at a big man who had run, stumbling, onto the wharf. It was the turnkey, Wickes! She reached to touch Edmund's arm in warning.

Turner said coolly, "Here he is."

She looked again, and saw that the face under Wickes' dirty periwig was Jedediah's. Not surprising then, that he had seemed so large in the court. He had worn the turnkey's bribe-bought clothing under his own. He walked unsteadily toward them and she saw a bloodied bruise on his forehead.

Turner pointed at this with disgust. "Been fightin', have ye? Down to the dinghy then. I'll not trust you with an oar, but stay clear of the passengers."

Jedediah peered at Mercy, then at Edmund, bared his teeth in what was meant to be a grin and swung awkwardly onto the ladder. He descended slowly and flopped into the bottom of the little craft.

Edmund went next, and caught Mercy by the waist as her feet felt for the gunwale. A servant might do that, yet Mercy had a vivid momentary sense of time repeating itself. She moved aside as Turner dropped easily beside them and stopped to speak to Edmund in a low voice.

"Captain said, you for sure, Bullen 'cos you won't come without him, but what's left o' Gorman's rats could sink or swim."

Jedediah, chest heaving, told them hoarsely, "Two of 'em at least's been cut down or shot. And three or four of the guards, an' a couple of Collyer's men too." He wiped a hand across his mouth.

Edmund's voice was bleak. "I know. Keep your voice down."

Turner pulled Jedediah with him to the dinghy's bow, and the men at the oars began to row. Mercy felt Edmund's tension through his skirt-clad leg beside hers, though the hood hid his face.

Moments later, when the little boat was perhaps ten yards from the wharf, she felt something else, a prickling, burning sensation in the back of her head that was not physical. She turned her head to search behind them.

The beggar with the scarred face stood by the ladder and stared after them. Perhaps it was his twisted features that unnerved her but she shivered at the look. Then again she felt that time had doubled on itself, that she had seen the face before, that she should know it...

She grasped Edmund's arm and jerked her head

backward. She hoped he would understand without the necessity of her taking time to write on her board.

He too swung his head around, keeping his face within the hood. Then he said shortly, "I thought you meant we were pursued. Do not let him distress you. The world is full of them."

Mercy's nerves were stretched and she was angry for a moment that he had not comprehended her meaning. Though after all Edmund could not read her mind. She looked again, and the beggar's back was to her as he shambled back along the wharf. She told herself it was her own tension that deceived her, and gazed ahead. The *Dart* became visible, moored at a distance from the other ships in the harbour, and she forgot both her annoyance and the beggar.

****

The human wreck that had once been Elias Gorman shuffled along hurriedly on his crutch, stumbling in his eagerness.

He had survived the destruction of the *Thalia* by holding to a floating spar, and had been plucked from the sea by a fishing boat a whole day after the ship sank. The fishermen had dumped him ashore to fend for himself. He had been sick for a long time, nursed by other beggars who used him to stir the pity of passers-by for money. His brain no longer worked well but he had recognised the Puritan woman two days earlier, outside the court.

That recognition had seemed to open a closed path toward others. The big one—Bullen, Bullen with a wig. Turner, yes, Turner, even with no moustache. And Collyer, he had heard the big one say. And the servant in the brown cloak—the way she stood, something about her. He might remember in time.

But Bullen should hang, along with his precious captain. Gorman hitched himself on his crutch toward the guards at the head of the bridge, furious, cursing. He must find someone who would listen, anyone who would listen...

****

Mercy helped Jedediah into the first of the sloop's two tiny cabins. Edmund stopped to give orders to Turner.

"It's near the tide, but don't hurry to set sail. It will

179

draw attention to us. And you have few men. Richard's crew must be spread thin, among *Dart, Prospero,* and the rescue party."

"Aye, and *Prospero's* longboat crew to pick them up. There's a gale brewing as well, west, beyond the city. But it should not strike before nightfall."

"With luck it will confuse the pursuit. Richard told me where we will rendezvous, so until we reach the place run close inshore. I'd say take the channels down behind the Sea Islands but we'd run aground or become lost. I'll be on deck to help you as soon as I've seen to Jedediah."

Turner nodded briskly and went to pass on the orders.

Edmund strode forward. In the cabin, barely wide enough to fit one person beside a double tier of slat beds, he found that Mercy had assisted Jedediah onto the pallet in the lower one. Jedediah protested incoherently and she shushed him with a firm finger to her lips and a shake of the head. She pulled Wickes's periwig from his head and dropped it on the deck, where it lay like a dead dog. Then she unknotted his filthy kerchief and inspected a vicious cut across his scalp.

She looked around when Edmund entered, and for one moment smiled at him. Then she wrote imperatively on her board, WATER.

Edmund smiled back at her and fetched some in a stoppered pitcher from the main cabin. Fortunately he knew the sloop well. He watched bemused as she wiped blood from the cut with a rag from her bundle, then tied one of her own kerchiefs around Jedediah's head. The big man muttered all the while, and with her free hand she gestured for him to drink.

Edmund held Jedediah up while Mercy coaxed water into his mouth. He drank thirstily and they laid him back down, where he seemed to fall into a half sleep. Mercy drew a grubby blanket around him and lifted her eyebrows at his captain.

"He'll do," he said softly. "That's his only hurt, though he's had gaol fever. But it'll take more than that to kill Jedediah." He lifted the pitcher and drank deeply himself, then sighed. "Fresh water." He stood, and helped Mercy to her feet. "I must go on deck to help them set sail."

She shook her head vehemently.

Edmund smiled again. "No, not in this guise." He lifted Monsieur's old clothes from where he had dropped them and took Mercy's hand in his free one. "Come help me change. Bring your bundle."

He drew her into the captain's cabin, only twice as large as the one where Jedediah lay. It boasted a wider pair of bunks, a pine table fastened to the bulkhead and a sea chest. He released her hand, dropped the clothing on the table and pulled off Sapra's cloak. He wrenched at the lacing of the dress with brown fingers.

"Help me with these things. I feel I'm trapped in a fish net!"

She smiled and went to his aid. When the dress and petticoat were off and the horsehair padding dropped, she reached for his shirt on the table. He stopped her hands and seized them hard in his own. She looked up into his face, saw his mask had slipped and that there were twin flames in his eyes.

"Mercy," he said urgently.

It was a declaration of need. She went to him and pressed her hands to the bare skin and smooth hair of his chest. He drew her hard against him, enclosed her tightly within the strong circle of his arms and lowered his head hungrily to her mouth. The kiss was hard, desperate, and greedy, like the first taste of food to a starving man.

It had been five long months since Mercy had touched him so closely, and she was overwhelmed, forgot all else. Her arms closed hard round his waist, and danger and the rest of the world ceased to exist. For a moment in the coach they had felt so. Now they were alone together, and once again in a ship's cabin.

To Mercy it seemed that in those five months she had not been alive. She opened her mouth for him to drink of her, as if she was wine and he thirsted for her as much as he hungered...

He released her mouth to look at her face. His eyes were hot coals. "If I had not escaped, you would have stayed to see me hang and hoped to the last for a miracle. Is that so?"

She nodded, though it no longer mattered. He lived.

"I did not escape to spare you pain, Mercy, but to save my skin." His look was both hunted and haunted, his voice bitter. "And I have bought my own life with other men's, again."

She shook her head at him. She longed for a voice, to give comfort. What else could he have done? No matter what path one chose in life, no matter how strong one believed oneself to be, the winds of the world tossed people like small ships in a great sea, taking no care that other craft might be on collision courses. She lifted her hands to hold his face, and touched tenderly the scabbed cheek.

Pressed close against him she could feel his ribs under the thin layer of his flesh, could see the long scar across them that Richard had described in New Exmouth. But his heart beat strongly. He was alive, and, right or wrong, nothing else mattered to her.

He unfastened her cloak and pushed it away, pulled off her cap and buried his fingers among her fair braids. "I've dreamed of you, wanted you!" His voice turned savage, though the savagery was directed at himself. "And I risk you too, to save my damned hide!"

There was no answer but life. She drew his head down once more until his hot mouth found hers again. The kiss, fierce at first as a caress between hawks, slowly became less urgent, just as deep but lasting for longer... She wrapped her arms more tightly around his body, felt his shoulder blades sharp under her hands, felt the thin welts of the whip.

She felt his hands on her own body. They stroked down her back, came to rest on her hips, drew her even closer into him. She felt all of him then, chest, hard belly, male parts and thighs, until her breasts and loins tingled and sent melting heat throughout the rest of her... If she had owned a voice, she would have asked him why he was the only man whose touch she longed for, the only man who had ever reached her heart.

He held her away, with a sigh so deep it was a groan. He lifted his hands to hold her face and looked deeply into her eyes. "Virgin's eyes." He smiled, kissed her forehead, and lost the smile. "Sweet life, you cannot come with me. I am more than ever a wanted man. Nor will I endanger you any further. As soon as it's safe, I must send you back to Madame." He dropped his hands to her shoulders and shook her gently. "Mercy, did you hear?"

She stared at him. Her joy had fled. The rushing warmth left her body, as if a cold sea had closed over her. She remembered her determination in New Exmouth to leave the place forever. That had been born of anger and pride. She could not go with him. Not because she feared danger, but because of what she was, who her mother was... It must always be enough that he was alive. She blinked, and bit her lip so she would not cry.

His hands held her shoulders. "Don't look like that, little one. I'm not gone from you yet." He kissed her again, lightly. "It's of no use, Mercy, to wish I had found you while I was yet a decent man." He smiled gravely. "I will talk sense, before I forget it. Little one, I used all your money to bribe that dog Wickes. But I swear I'll get it back to you."

Mercy shook her head hard. She did not care. She lifted her face to his again and smoothed her hands along the skin of his arms. She knew she behaved with sinful abandon, just as she had done on the *Thalia*. Yet what did it matter, when they had so little time together, when they must part again? She felt his hands behind her neck, his lips moving on hers as softly as a warm breeze on a rose. From far away she heard sounds that were echoes of that other time, that other ship...

His mouth tasted her cheek, then his warm breath on her face was a sigh. "The anchor's up. Love, I must go on deck, they're short-handed. I need only to look like a common sailor, and the berry juice is a start. Come, help me, quickly." He loosed her and stepped back a pace.

She saw that the haunted look had left his face, had been replaced by the exhilaration of freedom regained. He drew on his worn indigo shirt, and for his sake she smiled a little and considered his appearance.

The turban had fallen loose when the gown came over his head. With an imperative gesture of her hands she made him bend, and plaited his dark brown hair swiftly into a rough pigtail. She tied the end with a strip of rag, delved into her bundle again for a kerchief and tied that around his head.

Edmund turned the waistcoat inside out so that the black lining faced outwards, drew it on, and wound Sapra's turban piece around his waist for a sash. Mercy nodded quickly. He did not now resemble the grim, sober gentleman of the courtroom. He looked like a pirate, no less.

He grinned and kissed her ear. "I shall be back when we've passed the bar. Take care of Jedediah." He strode out.

She stood still a second, half bereft, half bemused. How much time did they have? Until they found a pilot boat, or fishing vessel, that would take her back to Charles Town. Soulange had told her Richard had suggested she pretend to whomever it was that she had taken suddenly sick, and needed to return to the port and the de Vaugerets' house.

It might be an hour, or it might be half the day, and then she would truly see Edmund no more. She swallowed a sudden lump in her throat, but refused to think further ahead and walked slowly back to the smaller cabin.

Jedediah tossed uncomfortably in fitful sleep, muttering words she could not hear. She felt his forehead. It was over-warm and she wiped his face with the rag and water. When his skin had cooled he settled into more natural rest. She found another blanket on the top bunk, folded it and sat on it for a cushion on the deck boards.

She felt the sloop getting under way, heard its timbers creak. She closed her eyes in sudden weariness, folded her arms on her knees and rested her head there. She felt she had lived seven days since she woke that morning. Her mind circled with profitless thoughts, and to distract herself she raised her head to look at Jedediah again. He had begun to snore.

She wondered where he had been born, whether a mother or a sweetheart waited hopelessly for him in England. As Soulange had said, the world was hard for women.

But nor was it easy for men. Honest sailors were forced into lives outside the law. Others, doing their duty, were killed in the doing. Monsieur, wasted with fevers, struggled to complete a worthy task before he died. Nathaniel Burdick worked like a very slave to keep his family. Uncle Jonathan had cut himself off from all he had known, to build a new life in Virginia.

She remembered the comfort she had just now given to Edmund. After a few minutes of loving he had left her a different man from the nerve-stretched escapee who had drawn her into the bigger cabin. Was it truly wicked to take hold of such happiness as came her way, with both hands and all of her heart? No. She would take it. She was willing to pay, later, whatever it would cost.

****

Edmund came in softly when the sloop had begun to move with the breeze and tide. He bent over Jedediah, felt his head, and nodded. Then he took both Mercy's hands and pulled her up beside him.

"Come into the other cabin, Mercy. There are things I must say to you, and I don't know how much time we have. We look innocent enough, but we must pass by the bastions and their guns. Half Moon at least is now behind us. The pilot boats wait for custom at the bar, and we will be there too soon, for me."

Without hesitation Mercy went with him and did not care when he closed the door. He looked weary. She kissed his fingers then reclaimed her right hand to write on her board. YOU NEED TO EAT.

He smiled a little. "Ever practical. We will soon. For now I've had a swig of rum, to keep me going. My mouth reeks of it, so it's as well I kissed you before." He drew her into his arms and said with feeling, "I need to be doused in sea water, to get the gaol stink off me."

She stood on her toes and kissed his cheek, then wound her arms around him and leaned her head on his shoulder. He did not smell sea clean as he had on the *Thalia*, but it did not matter.

He stroked her cheek. His chin rested on her hair, and she felt his jaw move when he spoke. His voice was grave. "You don't believe I do not love you, or you would not have journeyed to Charles Town for my sake. Do you still believe it was Jedediah who sent you off the *Thalia?*"

She shook her head on his chest.

"Mercy, this time it is I who must leave you. But don't waste your life pining for me. A heart that has loved once can love again."

185

She looked up at him then with indignation, and reached for her board. He took her hand away from it, held her fingers fast in his own and laughed softly.

"Oh no, little termagant. I will have my say, and you will listen. For once I'm glad you cannot talk." He took her face in his hands and held it firmly, so that she must look into his eyes. His gaze was golden warm and the sorrow she had seen there earlier was gone. He was in command of himself again.

She pursed her lips at him, then smiled. She could not help it.

"I loved you on the *Thalia* for your courage. When you stood among the captives on that murder-riven deck, you were the only creature there who was still and quiet. My own heart was in a pit of despair and you drew me like true north draws a compass needle." He smiled back at her. "And when we left the beach where we had repaired the ship, I wanted what I could not have, to keep you with me. Your presence after was freshness and hope to my soul. I had to send you away, for your own sake."

She shook her head within his hands and wished for her board, to tell him that on that deck she had been too frightened and too proud to move. And that after the beach she too had wanted him.

"You can write your thoughts later." He drew his fingertips lightly down the line of her brow, nose, lips and chin. "When I looked past your pretty face, I found strength. You are a woman that any man of sense would take to wife and prize for all his days. And I lust for your sweet body, but it is not for me. You will go to your husband a virgin."

Her mind absorbed the sweet words and stored them away like treasure, yet at the same time her soul despaired. He had taken her heart by surprise, and in a way it was fortunate he was pursued and must leave her. Even if it were possible for her to love another she could never allow it. But they had so little time, and he wasted it.

Edmund saw emotion and shadows of thoughts flit across her face, though he could not know their meaning. He smiled. "Besides, Mercy, you have a quick, hot temper and I a slow, cold one. We would clash, and quarrel."

She pulled her hand out of his, snatched up her board and wrote, NOT NOW. Then she dropped it and drew his head down and kissed him ardently. She did not care that she was shameless, she only wanted the moment, whatever she could have of him.

He received the kiss, wrapped his arms tightly around her and then took charge of it. He did things with lips and tongue to her mouth she had never dreamed of, until she was dizzy and clung to him. Only when he lifted his head did she notice the slight taste and smell of rum.

"Little distraction! I hope we are able to send you off before tonight. I do not dare share quarters with you again." He pressed her head firmly back onto his shoulder. "Now, listen. I must return to the deck, soon. They need every pair of hands, and eyes. With luck, it may be some time before the naval captains think to send ships after us. Charles Town will be closed and in uproar, looking for men on foot. Richard had his own plans to get his crew away. The less you know the safer for you."

All of this meant they would part. She closed her eyes, felt his body, and listened obediently to his words. She did not want him distressed on her account.

"If *Dart* is stopped by Navy ships, you must act the part of enforced hostage. Or, if we meet a boat that can take you back, the part of a sick woman. Agreed?" The question was stern, and he touched her chin until he felt her nod. "If sick, you must look the part. We will find something in the galley, flour and fat, to paint your face a bad colour. But you must make certain you are taken to Madame, and not to the pest-house. Write her direction on the back of your board." His voice lowered to huskiness. "Soon."

They stood quietly together for long minutes, until a sailor banged on the door. He brought food, cold salt beef and dark bread, grunted to Edmund that Mr. Turner asked for him and left.

Edmund smiled, kissed her hands and cheeks, stuffed food into his pockets, and returned to the deck.

Mercy looked in on Jedediah, who still slept and still snored, and returned to the main cabin. She would have preferred to be on deck, where she could see Edmund and breathe clean air. Here she could do nothing but wait.

****

The day passed, and the only boats they saw were fishing craft with such rough crews that Edmund would not trust them to take Mercy back unharmed. No pilot boats had stood at the bar. They were few at this season and those few had seen the storm brewing and returned to the harbour.

She could tell he worried about involving her further in his escape. But he said that to let her go with those they met was as good as having her ravished or murdered. It was true, though Mercy could not be sorry at it.

They slipped slowly south off the coasts of the Sea Islands south of Charles Town, sailing within spyglass sight of the sandy seaward beaches of the Islands. The ocean ran in a long swell and a great bank of clouds piled up to the west, but the sloop now needed the tending of fewer men.

Edmund came below and talked to Jedediah, now awake, who insisted on going up on deck to clear his head. Then he told Mercy they would soon steer into a channel he and Richard knew, to reach the rendezvous, though he would not tell her where this was.

She persuaded him to rest a little, and in the bigger cabin he sat on the sea chest and pulled her down onto his lap. For Mercy this was a new and sensual feeling, and she was now troubled by her body's responses to his. She asked by her board, AM I A WANTON?

His strong fingers plucked gently at her braids, to loosen them. "No, Mercy. You are a woman who loves. Why should you not enjoy lovemaking? It means much to a man, to know he can stir his woman to passion." He combed his fingers through her blonde curls and added quietly, "Any man you love, can make you feel the same way."

YOU STILL TRY TO CONVINCE ME I WILL FIND SOMEONE ELSE.

"Yes, I do. I know you do not believe me, now. We will speak no more of it. I ask only that you remember." He filled his hands with her hair and held her face before his own. "I have also waited for you to ask, *why can't we sail away to the ends of the Earth, where no one knows*

Edmund Gramercy? And the answer is, the world is wide and full of peril, and no fit place for a woman to wander in."

She was indignant for one moment that he thought she could not bear hardship. Then in the next she lifted her hand to his scabbed cheek and looked at him with sadness. She would have asked that, and she would have gone with him, if she did not carry a curse within herself that she must spare him. Instead she wrote, WHAT WILL YOU DO? SAIL WITH RICHARD?

"I don't know yet, little one. One day's evils at a time. First we must survive today's."

She understood that even if he had made plans, he would not tell her of them. And she understood his reason, that he wanted to protect her. She could not be angry, so she sighed and snuggled into him. She had made him take off Monsieur's musty waistcoat, and before he had come into the cabin he had washed himself in a bucket of cold seawater. His dark damp shirt and the clean smell of the sea were an integral part of him in her memory.

His hand stroked through her hair, down the satiny line of her throat, over the white collar on her shoulder, her arm clad in dark blue wool, along the back of her small hand, and captured her fingers. "Do you realise, my Puritan, that all I know about you is what I heard in court? I do not know who your family are, where in New England you live." He pressed her lips with two fingers, as if she could speak and he would prevent it. "Nor do I want to know. One day in a moment of madness, I might search for you."

She was startled to recall that what he said was true. In court, she had written that her home was Massachusetts Bay Province, Colony of New England. The judge, impatient that she must write her answers, had not inquired further. And in the Guard-house, when Richard had bribed speech with him, there would not have been time for Collyer to tell him of New Exmouth. He might, when the two met again. But even then Edmund would not seek her out. He feared too much for her safety.

And she feared too much for his, if he kept her with

him always, tied to a witch. So she frowned, and wrote nothing.

"Come, my lass, smile. It's no use to be sorrowful, when this time is all we will have." He kissed the corners of her mouth, and repeated softly, "Smile, Mercy."

She was closer to tears, but for his sake plumbed her soul for courage, and smiled. She traced a finger over his smooth chin, then wrote, WHAT DID YOU PAY IN PRISON, TO BE SHAVED?

He smiled, eyes golden warm. "Brave girl. I gave a coin from a hoard always hidden in my boot heels. It seemed as important as food. Then I sold my boots and stole these clumsy shoes from a man who died." For a moment his eyes hardened. "Do you have any other questions, Mistress Puritan?"

YES. I HAVE WONDERED OFTEN, HOW DO YOU KNOW A VIRGIN BY HER EYES? She laughed soundlessly at the look on his face.

"So, you can tease. I have suspected more than once, my lady, that you have the makings of a minx." He lifted her chin with one brown finger. "The answer's not to my credit."

TELL ME.

"Very well." He settled her in the crook of his arm, his chin on her fair curls. "When I was sixteen I was enamoured of a maid, a cowman's daughter, who was fourteen. She let me see that she liked me as well. Chance presented us with a barn in the midst of a rain squall, and we tumbled in the hay." He paused and bent his head to look into her eyes. Mercy did not write any censure, simply waited for him to go on. "I was sorry the next day, because her eyes—I forget their colour—had changed, all innocence gone from them. I thought everyone must see it, yet no one did. We spent an anxious week until we knew she had not conceived."

She tipped her head back to look at him with bright eyes, picked up her board to encourage him. GO ON. She was not shocked. Fornication, it seemed, was a normal activity of most men.

"You are tolerant." He smiled faintly. "But I had learned my lesson, and swore I would deflower no other maiden without wedding her first." He brushed a

190

thoughtful finger over her rosy mouth. "But I watched, after, and saw new brides with the same look. My own sister one of them, when she returned from her wedding journey."

WILL YOU EVER GO BACK TO YOUR FAMILY?

His eyes darkened a little. "Even if I was by some miracle pardoned, it would spoil their joy at my return, to know what I have become. Best not."

IF THEY LOVE YOU, THEY WILL BE HAPPY THAT YOU LIVE.

"The 'ifs' are too many." He took the board firmly from her hand, unlooped it from her belt and set it aside. "Who wastes our time now, with past and future but not this present?"

For answer she combed her small fingers through his clean, damp hair, received his mouth on hers again and kissed him back like a wanton.

Chapter Twelve

Acting upon information received, if from an unreliable source, Her Majesty's warship *Tresadern* and the small frigate *Belfort* sailed out from Charles Town in pursuit of escaped pirates on the sloop *Dart*.

The sloop was listed in the records of the Collector-of-Customs as being the property of one Stephen Alexander, merchant, of Barbados. Captain Alexander was known to trade in Charles Town, but had not been seen since the vessel entered port. Senior officers considered that this possibly proved that the *Dart* had indeed been captured by some of the escaped pirates and their rescuers.

The informant had insisted that the sloop would sail north, to New England, therefore the *Tresadern* investigated in that direction. *Belfort* merely went south to cover all contingencies. Major Cuthbert, commander of the frigate, discussed this with his first officer.

"Why would pirates sail to New England at the beginning of winter? It is more logical that they head for the Caribbean, where they've the better chance of evading capture." The captain of the *Tresadern* was his senior and had ordered him south, and with luck might yet be mortified if it was Cuthbert who seized the sloop instead. However he could hardly say so to Lieutenant Morven, no matter how long they had served together.

"I trust, sir, that if we discover the escapees, the crew will be fit to deal with them." Morven said it diffidently, knowing his superior to be touchy on that subject at present.

"Aye." Cuthbert's voice was harsh. "A pity most were on shore leave." He clasped his hands behind his splendid dress coat. "To be hauled out of taverns and whorehouses and driven to their duty with ropes' ends, has not rendered them as alert as they need to be." The crew had been forced into obedience, but were surly and not in good fettle for action. "By God, any of the rascals not do his work fitly I'll render him sorry."

"They seem to manage the sailing for now, sir."

"Well enough," grunted the Major. "Considering none of us yet know this coastline." *Belfort* had arrived on Carolina Station to relieve *Creda* a mere two months before. Probably only the Red Indians were familiar with the jumble of islands and inlets that stretched down to Spanish Florida. "Sweep those beaches with your spyglass, Morven. I shall search ahead for a sail." He frowned at the towers of cloud that gathered off the starboard stern. "A storm may render the pursuit impossible."

Some time later Morven reported with some excitement, "A sail! Just off the southern-most beach of that island!"

The Major swung his telescope landward and watched intently for some minutes. "Yes! And the craft has the lines of a sloop!" He bared his well cared-for teeth. "There cannot be many sloops abroad in this region and at this season. Order we turn closer in. We must investigate."

"Yes, sir!" Morven roared the orders and *Belfort* slowly tacked and turned.

Cuthbert cast a critical eye over his ship's handling, but the men were doing well enough, flailed by the shouts of junior officers and the rope of the boatswain. He allowed himself some private excitement, though it must be tempered with caution. "It will be impossible to take the ship too far into the channel below the beach," he told Morven. He had heard that these channels deteriorated into shallow water and marshes.

But minutes later Morven announced as a matter of unwelcome fact, "The sloop's heading into the channel, sir!"

"Aye, damn them! Though if we'd arrived even ten minutes later we'd not have seen her." He congratulated himself on the speed of his frigate. "That is, if it is indeed the *Dart*."

Belfort bore down on the little ship, and Morven at last reported, "It is the *Dart*, sir! I can read the name."

"You've younger eyes than mine." Cuthbert would have preferred Morven to allow his captain that discovery. "But now you can use your loud voice. Order the guns run out."

The Major watched the crew with a sharp eye, and noted with anger that this piece of work was performed sluggishly. "By God, Morven, for that alone I promise them whippings back in Charles Town!"

Morven roared to the deck for speedier gun work, and the ropes' ends snapped as they struck flesh. However they must catch the sloop before they could fire the cannon.

Belfort, even if not well manned, was more than a match for a smaller craft that carried only two light deck guns. "Morven, we are in position! Order a broadside! And by heaven, if the cannon don't fire together, I'll arrest the gun-captains!"

The first broadside was fired, and only Cuthbert's experienced ears detected the slightest split-second differences in the explosions. The cannon-shot fell short of the sloop by mere yards. He told Morven tightly, "Aim higher!"

The order was relayed, and the second salvo carried away the sloop's largest mast. "Got her!" shouted Morven. "Signal surrender!" The Major fought strictly by the rules. Also he would prefer live prisoners to be returned in triumph. He waited for the white flag. When after some minutes the near helpless little ship did not run one up, he said in a low voice, "Damn them!"

Morven glanced up at their straining sails. "Sir, the wind."

"I see it, Lieutenant," Cuthbert told him testily. The wind had sprung up ahead of the storm. It whipped the sea into surf that carried the crippled vessel like flotsam.

"Two small boats putting off from her side, sir." Morven was excited yet had the tact to add, "You can see them," as a statement, not a question.

The Major held his glass on the boats behind the wrecked sloop. "Look, by God!" One was swamped before it made landfall. Four or five figures from this struggled through the waves to join the other dinghy on the beach. Two of them appeared to aid one who might be wounded.

"That one to the right of the injured man—'tis a woman!"

"So it is, sir! I see the skirt."

"The information was that there were two women on board." Cuthbert's feet were braced on the deck, his hands and eyes steady with the telescope. "Though one was only a Negro maidservant."

"I do not see her." Morven squinted hard into his spyglass. "The maid must have either been killed or left on board while the pirates took the other with them as a hostage."

"Watch! We'll soon not be able to take the ship closer." The Major saw the people who waded ashore join the crew of the dinghy on the beach. Both groups dispersed rapidly. He would have liked to put another salvo amongst them but held fire because of the woman. If he killed a female hostage there would be unknown repercussions... *Annoying!* He heard the fathoms called and ordered the ship hold position. He snapped his spyglass closed. "Morven! Send two parties of men to deal with them, one in the longboat and another in the jolly boat."

He watched the boats lowered with a critical eye. But the men seemed downright eager for action. *Good.* They rowed with enthusiasm to the shore, then after that he could not see, even with his spyglass, what happened. "They'll catch a few refugees held back by a woman with no trouble." He squinted at the sky. The storm came over at speed and nightfall was also close at hand. "Did they take lanterns? And who is in charge?"

"Senior Midshipman Bayliss, sir. I doubt they thought of lanterns."

Cuthbert cursed. "They should have!" He would not have considered them himself, but if the pirates escaped he could always accuse Bayliss of insufficient planning. Though the lad was usually efficient. His spyglass was glued to his eye, though he could see nothing except the broken sloop and *Belfort's* boats drawn up on the beach. The low tangled woods beyond the sand were as dark as if they'd never seen a human.

The hourglass had half run out when the lookout cried, "A sail! Astern!"

Morven and he both swung their spyglasses to

seaward. The strange craft, carried by the running swell and stiff breeze, closed on them rapidly. It was a big, black ship with two gun-decks. "A Frenchie?" Then, "By God, no! It's a black flag! A pirate!" This arrival smacked of a premeditated rendezvous. Cuthbert snapped, "Signal the shore parties to return!" *And, by heaven, Bayliss had better have left a man to watch for signals.*

He had, but the boat crews were barely aboard *Belfort* when the stranger fired a challenge from its forward guns.

"Send the crews to the cannon!" Cuthbert was not pleased when he saw their performance was still ragged. Morven did not dare point out that men who had just rowed out from shore after pursuing a party of fugitives were unlikely to have energy to spare.

A salvo from the frigate's guns was answered with a hefty broadside from the black ship, then another. The shot from this raked his portside deck. The Major heard screams and grimly hoped some of his crew had received their just desserts. Angrily he told Morven, "We'll have to run for it!" A galling truth–his smaller vessel had no chance against the larger. Discretion would be wiser than futile valour. "Order all our sail up!"

One watch of tired men left the guns and climbed to set extra sail. The *Belfort* ran south before the breaking storm. Cuthbert's eye socket felt stuck in his spyglass as he tried to fathom by the big ship's movement whether it pursued them.

Lieutenant Morven, his younger eyes trained on its quarterdeck, swore to the Major, "Damme! That ship's commanded by a priest! I can see his black soutane."

"Nonsense, man!" But Cuthbert, turning to a better vantage point sternward, saw the black figure himself. Then "He's breaking off the engagement!" He did not admit relief, even to himself. And before they lost sight of the pirate in the gathering darkness, they saw it heave to off the beach and send boats of its own ashore. "Morven, did Bayliss capture the survivors from the sloop?" This was important. It would stand to his credit in Charles Town. And he needed credit, after avoiding a fight...

"I shall have him report to you at once, sir."

"In the great cabin. Take charge here."

A ray of bloody sunset slid sideways through the horn windows as the young officer knocked. His face was pale, his periwig askew and his clothing dishevelled, though he spoke steadily enough. Major Cuthbert demanded first if he had all the sloop crew aboard—and the woman, he added as an afterthought.

"I am sorry, sir, but no. Only the woman, and she is screaming. I've had her locked in the midshipmans' berth for now. There's no getting near her." The Midshipman wiped sweat from his brow. "Two of the pirates were killed, sir. The others lost themselves in the woods."

Cuthbert's face crimsoned. "That is a poor effort, Bayliss!" He clasped his hands tightly behind his coat. It did not do to let junior officers see one lose control. "Very well, report what happened, and be quick about it."

"Sir..." Bayliss drew himself straight. "Gramercy was in the swamped dinghy. He stayed behind the others as rearguard to fight off our shore parties. He is a skilled swordsman. It took a little time to surround and disarm him. Some of our men shouted that he had been condemned to death. I ordered silence, told off three sailors to guard him, and with the remainder of our party attempted pursuit of the others." Bayliss's Adam's apple bobbed painfully. "The woman came running back, sir, and ran at Gramercy, doubtless to attack him. She was restrained and I told the guard to watch her. Then we pursued the sloop's crew. One was down already with a shattered arm." At this point the young man pulled at his neckcloth uneasily.

"Continue!" barked Cuthbert.

"They had scattered in the woods behind the dunes, and with the storm imminent I ordered the chase abandoned and we returned to the beach. The sight that met my eyes there I hardly believed." Bayliss's expression was wooden, his eyes stared straight ahead. "Gramercy's guards had seized a length of cloth from round his waist, thrown it over the high branch of a swamp oak and hung him themselves."

For two seconds even the Major was speechless. "Dead?"

"I believe so, sir. I had no time to examine the body. The woman did not seem to recognise our party as rescuers. She turned on us scratching and kicking until two sailors forcibly pinned her arms to her sides." The Midshipman's voice was hoarse. "She had groaned and shrieked, they said, and when the pirate's body fell from the branch had collapsed on the sand in a swoon. The guard saw *Belfort's* signal then and we put off in the boats. We threw the woman in the longboat."

There was a deadly silence. Bayliss waited, chin clenched, for blame. But Cuthbert had already attached it.

"Very well. You will now find the men who hanged the pirate and put them in the brig." He scowled. "You are dismissed!"

Bayliss bowed and marched from the cabin, a relieved young man, and followed his orders.

The *Belfort* rode out the storm in the lee of the next island south, which was large and heavily forested. The Major then had time to consider what to do with the woman. He ordered her locked in the Senior Midshipmen's cabin and Bayliss and his mate to doss with the junior midshipmen.

Cuthbert was puzzled by her. According to the informant, the white woman on the sloop had been the Puritan mute who had testified at Gramercy's trial. But this woman had a voice. She screamed hoarsely over and over, *"No, no!"*

"Plainly she was taken hostage when the sloop was captured," he observed to Morven. "She has probably been mistreated, maybe even ravished. Her face and hands are scratched, her gown torn and wet. There is blood on her skirt." One of her shoes was missing also, he had seen. "She is out of her mind."

"She is to be pitied, sir." Morven decided on diplomacy. "At least, though the crew have made a sorry mess of the enterprise, you have rescued her."

The Major grunted. He could claim that much.

The next morning *Belfort* beat her way back to Charles Town against the wind. The *Tresadern* was already there. She had of course found no trace of pirates and had sheltered from the storm in the Santee River delta. The captains of both ships met ashore with their fellow Navy officers in the Governor's house, and pieced together the tale of what may have happened.

"The attackers of the pirates' guards in the town, and the two prisoners they rescued, somehow tricked their way on board the *Dart* and took it over." The senior captain rubbed his chin. "The sloop belongs—belonged—to a respectable merchant and was cleared to sail for Boston and New York."

"Plainly," Cuthbert said stiffly, "its captors attempted a rendezvous with the black ship." He reminded them, "But they were discovered by myself on the *Belfort.*"

"That is obviously the way of it." The senior captain did not like Cuthbert. "There is a minor matter, the absence of the maidservant, whom you believed dead on the *Dart.* I have searched out the truth there, and 'tis easily explained. The woman was sent by her mistress to accompany the Puritan out of the harbour. She had already returned home on a pilot boat before you—er—found the sloop, Major."

"I had more on my mind than a Negro servant, sir!"

"Just so." The senior captain was annoyed, and he had the ear of the Royal Governor. He would take down this Indies upstart a peg or two.

The upshot of the affair was that Major Cuthbert was reprimanded. Not, however, his senior informed him kindly, because he had fled from the larger ship. "After all, Cuthbert, if you had stood your ground and fought you would have been sunk and the Queen's Navy would have lost a frigate, if a small one."

The reprimand was for the official reason that he had not held his crew in better control. The Major accepted it with frozen dignity that hid fury and wounded vanity.

The sailors of the *Belfort* suffered for the displeasure of their captain. Those who had taken part in the illicit hanging were thoroughly flogged. The whole crew were put on short rations and forbidden shore leave. It was an uncomfortable time to be confined to shipboard. The rough weather continued for two days after the storm and was felt even in the great harbour. But by the third day the sea returned to calm, a brief lull before the true violence of winter finally set in.

As for the Puritan woman, she was taken to the house of the Huguenot de Vaugerets in Broad Street. She

was known to have been a guest there during the pirates'
trial. And since she was alternately unconscious and
raving incomprehensibly, the Navy was glad to wash its
hands of her.

****

Soulange and Sapra nursed Mercy like a baby for
three days. On the fourth, when the Puritan seemed
recovered, at least physically, Soulange sent the maid out
of the bedchamber and spoke to her friend alone.

First Soulange made her rise and dress and the other
woman obeyed like an automaton, indifferent that she
was naked for the first moments. She drew on the shift
and petticoat that were handed to her, Madame helped
her with the grey linen gown and wrapped a warm shawl
around her shoulders.

Soulange deemed it unwise to let Mercy wear the
black dress, and the blue had been ruined. She and Sapra
had sewed, while they sat with her, a plain new gown
from woven wool, lighter blue, with white Puritan style
collar and cuffs. But now was not the time to present that.
The Huguenot brushed and braided the fair hair in
silence, then led her friend to a tapestry-covered chair by
the window.

She herself sat opposite on the matching stool, and
took Mercy's small white hands in her own. The fingers
were cold, and the blue eyes lifeless but no longer a crazy
woman's. Soulange had feared, on the first day that the
little Puritan would end in a madhouse.

"*Mercie*, you have been ill with grief. You grieve still,
but I will not permit you to drown in it. You will now
begin to take up the threads of life again." Soulange knew
her words were brutal, but if all her experience had
taught her anything, it was that it was of no use to allow
the past to drag one down. "And you have an instrument
that will aid you. The shock has given you back your
voice. We heard it, in your delirium, but could detect no
words. Then you lay in that bed like a doll, and made no
sound. Today you must learn to speak again." She took a
deep breath. "*Petite,* say my name."

Mercy looked at her without comprehension. She
reached automatically for her board, and discovered it
was not at her waist. Neither was her bag of chalk, or

even her belt of plaited worsted.

"I have taken them away, *cherie*. You will not need them again. Now, say 'Soulange'."

Mercy remembered that her voice had come back when Edmund died. She did not care. She shook her head.

"*Mercie*, in all bad things there is something, however small, that is good. Just as in all good things there can be found the worm of something bad. Edmund Gramercy has died, but by the grace of God your speech has returned to you. You must use it, exercise it, or you may lose it once more." She shook the little hands that lay so still in hers.

Mercy stared at the wall and would not answer.

Soulange said softly, "Coward! I liked you from the first because courage shone from you like a light. If you lose that, you lose all. Listen! It is over. He is dead. Nothing you can do and no amount of sorrow can restore him to life. But you are still alive, and must live to the end of your days. Will you do so in defeat, or bravery?"

The words struck home. Tears stung like hot needles behind Mercy's eyes, and a painful lump rose into her throat like a bucket being drawn up a well. A small sound escaped her mouth, an echo of the strangling groan she had used to utter in nightmares. Her eyes met those of her friend, and were wild. She tried to jerk her hands free.

Soulange held them very hard. "If I must be cruel to you to make you speak, to make you want to live again, *Mercie*, I will do it. I love you enough to make you hate me for it. But I cannot be brave for you and I cannot speak for you. In the name of God I charge you, *say my name!*"

The bucket was close to the lip of the well, and Mercy knew she could make the lump rise to her tongue if she tried. She looked into the dark eyes of her friend, and found that she wanted to try. "S-Sou-Sou-lange." The voice was like rusty hinges on an old door. "Sou-lange." And then she burst into tears.

Soulange rose swiftly, put her arms around the other woman's shoulders and held her while she cried with terrible rusty sobs. When she was quiet again, Soulange dried her eyes and cheeks with a linen kerchief and made her drink a little water. Then she instructed gently, "Say it again. I wish to hear my name from your lips, *petite*."

"Sou-lange." It was a whisper but this time the sound came a little easier, as if the long disused hinges hadbeen oiled by the tears.

Soulange sat again on the stool, clasped her hands in the lap of her skirt and smiled gravely. "It is a blessing, a gift."

Mercy swallowed, to moisten her throat. She had to think about how to shape her lips, how to work her tongue. "The price"—she coughed—"was too high."

"Yes, *ma cherie*. The prices we pay for everything we gain in life are always too high. We can but accept that it is so, and use to the full what has been bought."

****

The next day they sat by the parlour window, warmed by a fire in the grate behind them, and watched through the diamond-leaded panes the world as it went by on the brick flag-way and the street of sand.

Charles Town went about its everyday business. Slaves ran or lazed on errands, the colourful populace walked and talked, an occasional horseman trotted past, a lone sledge of pelts clattered toward the warehouses. Some of these people had probably attended Edmund Gramercy's trial.

The whole city had been agog, Soulange said, with the story of the rescue and escape. Charles Town, gossiping inordinately, had also discovered that the pirate had died after all. A few of the passers-by looked sidelong at the de Vaugerets' handsome house and wondered what had become of the dumb Puritan who had been taken hostage. It was said she had been ravished and lost her reason. All of this conjecture reached Soulange's ears by way of the house slaves, who heard it in the markets.

"Do not mind what people say, *petite*. They will talk it to pieces and forget it when the next event of interest happens along. In time no one will remember what is true and what is not." Soulange sat on a fringed cushion in a carved mahogany chair, embroidering on a tambour.

She sewed much and read much, she had told Mercy only ten days ago, to pass the time. At present, they could speak freely. Paul and Dupuis were closeted in the library, with Henrique in attendance on Monsieur. The cook and maids were busy in the kitchen-cottage and

Tobias groomed the horses. Only Sapra was in the house.

"I hope you are right," Mercy said slowly. She was seated in the twin of Soulange's chair, slowly hemming the new sky-blue gown. Her hands were mostly steady.

Master and Mistress Hutcher had called that morning despite their prejudice against Madame, out of duty and probable curiosity, to ask after her health. They had been astonished to find her on her feet, in her right mind and with a voice, though shaky on all counts. They had hinted to hear of her ordeal, but Soulange had previously advised her to say nothing. Mercy could protest she had not been harmed, but that would raise questions about her role in the affair.

Soulange must also have thought of the Hutchers, just then. "Your visitors had no doubt you were an innocent victim. Let them all think that."

Mercy nodded. Sometimes she forgot she could speak. It did not matter any longer what people thought, but the blood on her skirt had not been her own. It was Jedediah's, whose arm had been wounded in the second broadside from *Belfort*. She did not know whether he still lived, or what had happened after *Prospero* ran the frigate off. She lifted a hand to touch the healing scratches on her cheek, caused by flying splinters and now beginning to heal.

She remembered to speak, then. "I was not in possession of all my senses when they were here." She cleared her throat, which she still found necessary after each few words. "I might have betrayed myself. And it seems I must yet live." Her grief had been violent and she may have spent the worst of it, but much remained. Mostly it took the forms of sadness and an aching heart. She supposed both might heal in the course of time, though at present such healing seemed impossible... She found the ghost of a smile. "You speak wisely. You are a great lady."

"*Moi*? I?" Soulange was startled and dropped her needle. "*Non, Mercie*. I am a trollop of mixed blood who has lived enough to learn the ways of the world."

"No. It is in your heart, what you are." She needed to rest her voice a moment. "You have survived more and worse than I. You give me heart to go on. I shall go home, and try to live."

"Go home?" Soulange pressed her lips together, retrieved the needle and set it hard in the stiff cloth. "What is there for you in New England, *Mercie*? Punishment for running away, a life of hard work, people who are not your family by blood." She dropped the tambour onto the elegant work-stand beside her chair and clasped her hands tightly across the lace at her waist. "I have asked Monsieur and he is agreeable. I now ask you. Remain here as our guest." For this she had seduced her husband.

"I cannot." Mercy looked at her friend's eyes, and then outwards to the street. She knew Soulange was often lonely. "Not here, where he died." He, and others. The two ruffians of the *Thalia's* crew who had been recaptured had been hanged, Soulange had told her, on schedule.

"Wherever we live, someone we love has died."

"Forgive me, Soulange. I have not forgotten your mother and father." However what she had said was horribly true. Edmund had died in Carolina, Uncle Jonathan in Virginia and her mother in New England. Mercy wet her lips. "It is not only that." She rested her voice, and also practiced how to transfer thoughts from mind to mouth. Now she spoke those thoughts in a rush. "It is as if I am cursed. Everyone I love has died. Not you too."

"That is nonsense!" Was this superstition the secret she let no one know? "I thought you a woman of sense! You told me you were but a babe when your papa died, and your uncle lived by you eleven years. The Mam Felice yet lives in Virginia and your niece Sarah in New Exmouth." She added deliberately, though softly, "And you told me that Edmund Gramercy knew his end would be hard."

Mercy flinched, but went on. "Never-the-less"—large words had to be broken up so that they did not leave her breathless—"I must return." She waited for the cough, but it did not come this time. "Soulange, I would like nothing more on earth than to stay with you. But"—she did cough, now, and laid a clenched white fist on her chest—"I feel in here, as a certainty, that I must go back."

Soulange regarded her steadily before she spoke.

"When I was—what I was—I met strange people. Some could not find fulfilment unless they inflicted pain upon others, and some when they inflicted pain upon themselves. You are sometimes like these last, *Mercie*. Why are you so cruel to yourself?"

How to answer her? With anything but the truth—yet perhaps a different truth would do. "Nathaniel gave me a home. I must repay him." She saw then that this could be turned around. "I know that I owe you much too, Soulange. But"—she drew a deep breath—"your husband is wealthy. Nathaniel is not." She rested her voice and gazed out the window, turning her eyes up to the sky that was pale blue and no longer filled with clouds. "I can help in his household." No need to burden her friend with the knowledge that she had stolen money from Nathaniel.

Soulange was silent for some minutes. The look in her beautiful eyes was deeply thoughtful. At last she asked, "And will you, in New England, build a shrine in your heart to Edmund Gramercy?"

Mercy kept her eyes on the street. A Negro boy passed by, wheeling a barrow market-ward. By his lips, he sang. "Why not, Soulange?" For the first time she allowed herself bitterness. "While he lived, we had no hope to be together. I can at least remember him."

Soulange's brilliant gaze remained fixed on her friend. "Do not, not in the way you say. It will turn you inward, and life is outward." She saw Mercy's chin set stubbornly. "You remember your uncle with affection but no longer grieve for him. In time Edmund Gramercy will be the same to you."

"It is not the same!" The blue gown had been piled, forgotten, in her lap. Now Mercy sprang to her feet and the dress tumbled to the Turkish carpet on the floor. She struck her small clenched fists together. "He did not run for his life, to save himself! He left me to bear the burden of knowing he tried to the last to protect me!" The words were too many, and she choked.

Soulange stood also. "Good! You are angry with him. We are permitted to be, when we grieve. My mother's people knew that." Her eyes flashed. "There was nothing else your Edmund could have done, but yes, be angry with him. Your grief must run its full course."

Mercy stared at her friend and her anger faded. "I see that now." She swallowed, found her throat dry, and reached for the water kept by her these last days. She drank a mouthful, set the beaker down. "But, Soulange, knowing so in one's mind does not ease the pain."

"No." Soulange sighed. "But no matter how painful, it is better to talk of it." She compressed her lips. *Mercie* would recover, in time. However it was too soon to say to her that she was but three-and-twenty, which was not young but nor was it old. Life had not yet passed her by. She found a smile. "Be grateful, *petite,* that you are able to talk."

Mercy shook her head wearily. "I am grateful. Perhaps it will make life easier." She seated herself again and lifted the blue gown from the floor. "For now, I will live in the present, and sew."

"So also will I." Soulange brushed her skirts under her to sit down, then frowned at the tambour and her embroidery. "I am yet learning it myself. I too have much to be grateful for, but I confess that I become bored with the sewing."

Mercy's lips twitched in the first hint of a smile. "Perhaps Richard will come calling."

Soulange snapped her fingers, annoyed. "That one! He does not so much as send a message that he is alive." Yet she did know he was alive. Mercy had remembered talk on the *Belfort* of the 'priest' on the deck of the black ship. "*Mais non,* but no, I am unjust, a little. Ric'ard's light manner protects his heart like armour." She lifted her needle and stabbed it into the tambour. "You think he makes love to me when we are alone? No. He flirts, he makes jokes. In the coach, when you and Sapra were on the wharf, he said to me, 'Faith, Madame, you now have two silent women about you, instead of one!'"

"Sapra—how did you keep Tobias and the household from seeing her?" It was a good thing to speak, if only because it kept the mind occupied.

"*Pouf,* it was easy. I sent Tobias on another errand when we returned home. He was much annoyed! Then I took her up to my bedchamber to hide for half the day. At sunset she slipped out and around, and as I did instruct, walked into the house again saying she had come from the wharf and the pilot boat."

Mercy recalled something. "Her gown and cloak were destroyed." She winced. They had been on the *Dart*.

"Clothes can be replaced, *cherie*." She reached over to feel the material of the blue dress, and sighed. "If you insist upon returning to cold New England, you also must have a new cloak."

"You cannot give me more." Mercy bit off the linen thread with sharp small teeth. "I will manage with shawls."

"Shawls will not be enough, in the snow." Soulange shrugged. "Let me do this for you, since I can do naught else, it seems." A touch of bitterness crept into her voice.

Mercy dropped the gown again, unmindful of creases, and knelt by her friend's chair. "I cannot repay you in any way, not even with my friendship, when we will be so far apart." She swallowed to clear her throat. "And you will yet pay my passage home."

"Do not speak of repayment. It is unwise to loan to one's friends, to keep accounts with them. Better to give." She set two stitches and pushed the embroidery aside. "But I say this to you, which at this time you will not like, but now it seems I may have no other time with you." She frowned into the blue eyes, which were wide and bright as ever, though also more sad. "You believe you will be a spinster all your days. But if chance brings a husband to you, remember that it is better to have one's own household than to be a poor relative in another."

Mercy laid a hand on Soulange's skirt of emerald green. "I cannot think so far ahead yet. Forgive me." She could not bear the thought of any man but Edmund touching her, and there was also the old secret. For the same reason that she could not stay with her friend, she could not marry.

"Forgive me also. I did not intend to speak of it." Soulange's frown remained. "Let us speak sense instead. It is winter, not a time for voyages. The ships now in the harbour will pass the winter here, and I do not think you will find one to give you passage. You could write a letter to New Exmouth, then keep us company until next summer when we go to the Penn colony. We can send you home from there." She added sternly, "That is not a requirement for the repayment of favours. It is a suggestion only. You must decide in your own mind if you wish to do that."

Mercy smiled faintly. "Visit Quakers? My minister would drop of apoplexy if he heard of it!" She cleared her throat again. "I would like to travel with you, Soulange, but I know I must go home. Shall we wait and see? If I find no passage I must stay here until spring at least." She laid her head on the velvet lap. "But when I do go, I will miss you terribly."

"I will miss you also, *ma cherie*. But if God wills it, you will stay here. If not, we shall meet again." She turned one of the other woman's fair braids around her graceful dark fingers, thoughtful again. Why did *Mercie* wish to return to New England in winter, rather than the summer when travel was easier? She recalled her friend's strangely superstitious words, *Everyone I loved has died.* She sighed. "Do not twist your heart with regret. You had only a little time of love, but what you had is yours forever."

Mercy lifted her face, and this time her blue eyes were wet. "Soulange, if I had known he was going to die, I would have gladly given him my body."

"No! There is nothing will ruin a woman's life more certainly than the loss of her virtue! It is unfair, yes. But life, and men, who judge us, are unfair."

Mercy slowly wiped her eyes, and found no more tears in them. She was tired to her soul, tired with grief and also tired with the effort of speech. "It was sinful of me, to think it."

Soulange stroked her head, and her voice gentled. "That I do not know. Sin is for God to judge, not men and women. But I do know that women, when they love, long to give of themselves." She sought for words of comfort, for herself as well as Mercy. The man whom she desired to love, she could not. "Think also this. You might have borne a bastard child and been utterly cast out from your own people. It is better you did not follow your heart."

"Soulange..." Mercy hesitated. Then she said quietly, "I wish to ask an impertinent question. Do not answer me unless you wish." She saw her friend's eyes, dark and waiting. "How, how not... When you lived as you did, how did you not conceive?" Perhaps her mind was yet unhinged. Before Edmund died, she would not have dreamed of asking.

"Yes, you are impertinent." The Huguenot's eyes now glittered. "But I will tell you. If you ever marry, you do not want to die young of too many children." Her eyebrows arched. "Half of a lemon, *Mercie*, inside oneself."

Mercy blushed. "I am sorry if I have recalled the past to you."

Soulange sighed, then. "Yes, it is all past. I pray our friendship at least will endure. Write to me sometimes, and I will pray for the safety of the ships that carry your letters."

Mercy nodded, silent because her new-found voice was for the present exhausted. But she stayed where she was, with her head on the rich soft material of the skirt, comforted by the other woman's touch. She would have liked to experience this friendship for a longer time, just as she would have liked to stay with Edmund if he had lived. Yet the world had given her all she would ever have of both of them.

In the end it was the same for Soulange as it would have been for Edmund. She could not afflict her, as she could not have afflicted him, with herself. She remembered wearily her angry decision, before she left New Exmouth, never to go back. But that was before Edmund died.

She must return to New England. In New Exmouth, at least, there was no need for secrecy. They knew what she was, there.

****

As it happened, it was a Quaker ship's captain, Thomas Coleman from the island of Nantucket, who gave Mercy passage home.

His dour wife Maria, being childless, had taken the unheard of step of accompanying him on his voyage to the Bahamas and Carolina. The de Vaugerets' cook had heard gossip when she bought fish at the wharves, that the Colemans' crew said it was because Captain Thomas had once roistered amongst the black and Indian women of the islands, and his wife now guarded him.

That may or may not have been the truth. Maria

Coleman was certainly a stern woman and not friendly, though at least she was another female presence among the sailormen. Her husband did not speak to Mercy at all. Perhaps the Colemans were wary of her. They had converted only two years before, and they knew, and she knew, that the Puritans of Massachusetts Bay had hanged Quakers in the past.

However she had no mind, even if she had been so inclined, to preach to them. It was not only because her spirits were low, but because the passage was rough. Although they did not experience any snowstorms, the ship at one stage needed to heave-to before a westerly gale. Mercy, usually strong stomached for travel, was seasick for several days. The remainder of their journey north was beset by more storms, though no more as severe.

The Colemans might not have been kind, but they did their Christian duty toward their passenger. They let her ashore at the town of New Bedford on the shore of Buzzard's Bay and waited three days while she sought out means to travel northward. This, eventually, was overland, with a family moving up to Boston town with all their goods and children in two crowded ox-drawn carts. The Colemans ascertained the folk were decent then set sail for Nantucket with the briefest of goodbyes.

The family travelled slowly along the New York post road, taking three days to cover the fifty miles to Boston. The first night they put up at a little inn and the second slept nervously under the carts. After they reached Boston their goodbyes to Mercy were warmer than the Colemans', as were hers to them, especially the children.

She went to Nathaniel's sister's house. Patience Hallam was astounded by Mercy's second unexpected arrival on her doorstep, however once again sent her down to New Exmouth with respectable fishermen. The weather was now bitterly cold, though at least not stormy. Mercy's enduring image of Boston this time was Patience's goggle-eyed surprise at hearing her stepsister speak for the first time in twelve years.

From the small deck of the fishing boat, under grey skies and across grey sea, she saw Rocknest Island come into view. She hugged her thick new cloak around her.

And even the cloak brought back a memory of Edmund...

She had worn her old cloak, and taken Sapra's up to the deck of the *Dart* for him, when he took a turn at the helm. He had tucked her little figure between himself and the wheel, his arms reaching to its spokes around her on both sides, his living body at her back. The dark sea had been empty, but he had made her keep her hood drawn forward and her body close in to his, so that a man with a spyglass on another ship would have seen only a stout man in a cloak working the helm.

His mouth had been by her ear when he told her this. He had kissed it and his lips and breath had been warm...

She wrenched her mind back to the present before she could weep. How cold it was! She had no idea what kind of reception awaited her in New Exmouth. It depended largely on whether Nathaniel had told anyone of the theft of the money... It had been easier to be brave in the milder winter of Carolina Colony, in the de Vaugerets' house warmed for Monsieur's health by fires in every room.

She remembered Soulange, a darkly glowing figure in yellow brocade gown and chocolate-brown mantle, lifting her hand in farewell at the wharf outside the walls, and Sapra behind her in tan and red. An easier memory, because although it had been painful to part with Soulange, her friend at least still lived.

Edmund was dead. She did not even know what had happened to his body. *Oh God,* she prayed for the hundredth time, *forgive him his deeds in life, have mercy on his soul.*

When the little boat moored in the Exe estuary she saw New Exmouth again, huddled small and grey in the chill air like a hibernating opossum. *God help me also*, was her new prayer. Edmund had met his death fighting. She hoped that she could meet life, whatever it might hold, with courage worthy of him.

Chapter Thirteen

Mercy was sure that John Hanson had planned exactly how to punish her, if and when she ever returned. But the fact of her restored voice threw him completely off balance.

However he viewed the matter as devil's work, not a miracle. Though a long discussion with his elders proved them to hold the majority opinion that the devil took away, but did not restore.

She told New Exmouth only the bare facts of her journey. She had gone away to do her Christian duty by that Captain Gramercy who had cast her off in a dinghy from the *Jesselin*. She had been chaperoned by the Huguenot guests of the Plummer brothers. She had testified in court of the pirate's clemency, but the captain had been hanged anyway. She lied by omission.

It helped the opinions in her favour that she told her tale directly, even that she obviously regretted the man's fate. It helped the minister's opinion against her that she had regained her voice when the pirate died, just as she had lost it when her mother did. However this fact swayed other church members to goodwill.

John Hanson held it wrong that she had stayed in the de Vaugerets' Huguenot household and not the Hutchers' Puritan one, though few others did. John Hanson deeply disapproved that Charles Town was also populated by Quakers, Church of England, Catholics and heaven knew what heathens. Most of the town thought Mercy had shown sterling character not to be converted by any of them.

But the minister insisted that she publicly apologise in church, the following Sabbath, for the sin of running away without her family's knowledge. She did this quietly and firmly, admitting her guilt, and therefore everyone was disposed to forgive her. The church had filled just to hear her new voice. John Hanson saw that fact too late, and could in no way deride it since she had simply obeyed him.

He also insisted that she rise each morning at first cock-crow to pray on her knees, and that she read the Scriptures an hour each night when her chores were done. He would liked to have had her whipped, and in the old days of the Colony undoubtedly would have. But for punishment he left her to Nathaniel, making it plain that he expected her stepbrother to be severe.

She had been surprised by her reception from Nathaniel. He did admonish her sternly for leaving of her own accord, however he seemed to think that the minister's strictures were punishment enough. He was obviously relieved that she had survived two long sea voyages, one of them in winter weather, and that she had also remained safe and unmolested. Taken together with her regained speech, he was inclined to view it as a matter of God showing grace for her act of conscience.

It helped also, he said, that in the letters she had left for him and for Sarah, she made no excuses but admitted her clandestine departure was wrong.

He did not speak of the money before Hephzibah, nor had he told his wife or anyone else of its loss. To discuss it, he took Mercy outside into the penetrating cold of the bare garden. He did not sit on the wooden bench, but stood with his hands clasped behind his back.

"Certainly it was wrong of you, Mercy. And though I have wrestled and wrestled with my conscience over this, I cannot bring myself to charge you with thievery. It would mean the gallows or prison, or at the least the whip. In the end the money was not mine, but yours. Your aunt's letter with it informed me that it was not only for your keep, but also for your use if need arose. And as your nearest relative I was bound to provide your keep in any case."

"You have been kind, Nathaniel," Mercy replied quietly, and meant it. Her impatient self had rebelled against his former admonitions. Now she understood that he had always spoken them in the context of his duty toward her.

He cleared his throat noisily. "Indeed, I did not expect you to return, for fear of chastisement alone. I thanked God when I saw you." He frowned ferociously past the deep blue of her cloaked shoulder, plainly embarrassed, and angry to be embarrassed.

"You have also been merciful, Nathaniel." She did not look directly at his eyes, since that would make him uncomfortable. "More forbearing than I deserve." That was true. He simply assumed that the money had been eaten up by ship's fares and other necessities. He would not be kind at all if he knew that all of it, and more, had gone into the pocket of a turnkey in Charles Town.

"Well, we will say no more about it. But, Mercy, if anything of the like ever happens again, if your conduct is ever again so hoydenish—I will not forgive you so easily."

"I do not foresee that any such occasion will arise." She hoped he was too unused to her voice to find its dryness unnatural. It hurt her pride, to seem so amenable and spiritless. However any show of pride, defiance or anger would bring down on her head the punishments she had so far avoided. And she must live in the Burdicks' house, a decent maiden lady, for the rest of her life.

Nathaniel pulled his wide hat further down on his head and his short homespun cloak closer around him. "I must speak to you on another matter. It is not impossible, Mercy, that you may wed sometime. Most folk seem to believe that God would not be so kind to the daughter of a witch"—he did not seem to notice that she flinched—"as to return her voice. I have seen one or two unmarried men look your way already. And Master Barnard."

The blacksmith's wife had been one of winter's early casualties, succumbing to a congestion of the lungs some three weeks earlier. It was well known that his elderly aunt found the care of his house and children a burden, and that Master Barnard sought a second spouse.

Mercy's pride and anger had to be fought down. "Am I to marry, then, anyone who asks for me?" The thought of the huge blacksmith, compared to Edmund's physical elegance, sickened her.

"If any man asks, of course I must be applied to, as your only male relative." Nathaniel grew increasingly peevish at this converse in the cold. "But you are of age.

Surely, Mercy, you desire a husband and home of your own, and children? That is the lot God ordained for females and it may now be within your reach."

"I have no desire to be wed, Nathaniel." She could not imagine sharing her body and her life with anyone but Edmund, and Edmund was gone. Yet she had for so long been accustomed to thinking herself unable to marry that she was confused. "But would not any man here be wary of—of what I might be?" She pressed a cold hand to her cold brow. She had spoken her fear aloud only twice in her whole life.

"There has been no evidence of it yet." Nathaniel was merely impatient. "Time enough, if you are courted. Come inside! It will snow again, tonight." He strode to the half door by the bare peach tree without waiting to see if she followed.

She whispered, in her new voice that was huskier than the one she had had as a child, "Then I'll not be courted."

Nathaniel did not hear her. She slowly went in after him, and closed the door.

****

Mercy was unsettled all that dark grey afternoon. She helped Hephzibah prepare supper, and since her mind was preoccupied she wondered but little why it was such an elaborate meal.

She had been home several days, and they had eaten mostly fish stew. Now, however, they cooked a whole turkey hen, a big pot of corncobs, a sweet potato pie, and stewed some dried apples as well. When they sat to table, Nathaniel said grace and for the first time gravely rendered thanks for his sister's safe return. Hephzibah announced briskly that since Mercy had been absent for the thanksgiving harvest dinner she might as well have it now.

Mercy looked at Hephzibah, startled, and then around the table. Sarah smiled shyly. The boys, all in clean collars, nodded solemnly, and little Martha had already been lifted to her mother's knee to suck gravy from a spoon. She forgot her pride in a new humility. Certainly she had been taken into this household out of Nathaniel's sense of duty, but they must have been concerned at first that she might really be like her mother.

It had taken courage to do that duty, when they could easily have insisted she remain with Anne Penhall—now Anne Howard—in Virginia. And she had repaid them by stealing the money that was their surety against hard times.

"Thank you," she said softly. "I am truly grateful to be home again."

They ducked their heads bashfully over their plates, and she could not help but smile as the boys began to eat with an enthusiasm that owed more to the largesse of food than Aunt Mercy's return. She smiled at Nathaniel as he forked a slice of turkey breast onto her plate, and at Hephzibah when she suggested briskly she try a corncob, and at Sarah because she loved her.

She remembered something Soulange had said. In all things, however bad, there was some small blessing for which to be thankful.

****

When Mercy had returned to New Exmouth, the weather was too rough for Nathaniel to go out fishing. Instead he used his time to build a new little lean-to room at the back of the house, off the parlour and behind the stairs. It was now her bedchamber.

She had believed at first that he did it to lessen any influence she had over Sarah, with whom she had shared a room before she went away. But the real reason was much more pragmatic. Martha had outgrown her cradle and the crib, fetched in from the barn and dusted down, would not fit into her parents' room. Therefore the baby had to go into Sarah's room, and there was simply nowhere else to put Mercy.

They carried her trundle bed and wooden trunk down into the new room, furnished already with a little pinewood table and stool Nathaniel had also made. He informed her curtly that if she left the door into the parlour open at night she should not be too cold. Mercy had seen him build the walls of two thicknesses of planks and hammer up a plank ceiling below the new shingles. She smiled and said she was sure she would be warm enough.

Hephzibah gave her, without comment, a whole sheepskin, for which they had traded a small barrel of salted hake. Mercy knew her sister-in-law by now. Hephzibah would never admit it, but she was pleased to have the help of her hands again. Mercy made her own rag rug for the floor, and was almost comfortable.

However she was lonely. She missed the sound of Sarah's quiet breathing at night, and the comfort of her young body at the times when they had snuggled together for warmth. But for other reasons it was best she was alone. There were times when she wept, and her tears being no longer silent had to be hushed in the duck-feather pillow. And sometimes she had nightmares, and from these she now woke with cries that would have woken Sarah in a shared room.

Strangely enough the nightmares were not of Edmund's hanging, nor of her mother's. It was as if the recent death by the rope had cancelled out the other, older one. No, her first bad dream had been, oddly, of the time of her first captivity, of the pile of her own and Edmund's ruined clothing that Jedediah had fretted over outside the cabin of the *Thalia,* when Gorman had so nearly drowned them both. In that dream the red dye that had stained Edmund's shirt and her skirt formed a pool, which slowly thickened and darkened until it was blood...

The next bad dream, even more strangely, was of the beggar she had seen on the Charles Town wharf as she and Edmund had been rowed to the *Dart.* She thought she had forgotten the creature. Now she felt that she should know that malevolent face, yet she always woke a moment before recognising it. It puzzled and worried her at first, but in time both nightmares became less frequent and by the end of winter had vanished altogether. She decided that the bad dreams had been the last evidence of her grief.

The other, sweeter dreams were far more cruel. Some nights she was actually warm with the sheepskin beneath her and the quilt on top, with more warmth drifting in her door from the banked stove. Her sleeping mind then returned to the deck of the *Dart* and Edmund's arms around her, and the warmth along her back became his body...

They had been as aware of each other, there, as if there had been no layers of cloak and clothing between them. And yet they were comfortable with it, so close in spirit that the bond of touching bodies was only a part of the union of their souls...

There was an evening in New Exmouth when she fell into a snowdrift, and had to rush to change her wet things from the skin out. For a single moment before the cold overtook her she touched her own breast and wondered if he had felt that firm soft texture through her petticoat and woollen dress, on his arm...

On the *Dart*, near sunset, when it seemed certain she would have to stay aboard after all, he had given the helm to Ned Turner and taken her below.

Without any words they had closed themselves in the larger cabin again. He had laughed and said it was a good thing the sloop would be swamped with men that night - he would have no chance to be tempted to seduce her. And she had not so much as blushed... He had asked her then if she knew she had the most perfect, the most exquisite little round breasts, and had undone her wide collar to trace with gentle fingers their shape on her gown.

Finally aware of guilt, she had written on her board, I AM SINNING. And he had said sternly, *No, you are not, but I am. Forgive me, Mercy. The first woman I see after months at sea and weeks in prison is the one I love.* He had not hidden from her his face of passion, though he had fastened her collar again...

But those dreams also faded, during the weeks when winter closed over New Exmouth. Here was the bitter cold remembered from childhood, that she had dreaded in the autumn. They left the house only when they must, to tend the cow and the poultry in the byre and henhouse, to bring in wood for the fire, to sweep and shovel snow from the doorstep and the paths.

The boys crunched through wet whiteness to attend school, and all of them trudged across the square once a week to the unwarmed church and listened to John Hanson's brimstone sermons. Christmas-tide, not celebrated by Puritans, passed unmentioned. The world was edged with ice, or deep in snow, or blown with storms. There were few days when the sea was safe enough for Nathaniel to take the boat out.

Most of the season they spent in the parlour, where the central iron stove burned all day and all night. The two women and the girl prepared meals from the stores and preserves and salted fish, took care of Martha, knitted and sewed, turned wool into yarn on the spinning wheel and wove homespun on Hephzibah's little loom. Nathaniel whittled and carved, mended tools and furniture, made new nets and lines, heard the boys' lessons and read aloud from the big Bible.

The coldness of the world seemed to Mercy to freeze her very heart. At first she had keenly missed Soulange. Hephzibah talked only of commonplaces, and Sarah was shy of her these days. The memory of her friend's affection and intelligence warmed her for a while, then began to fade. Soulange was slipping into the past, part of a different world, just as Edmund had been. Even her grief seemed to belong back there. Her heart felt emptier with each passing day and she perceived herself only a shadow of the woman who had journeyed to Carolina.

There was a night when Nathaniel read to them from the latest copy of William's Chase's Boston *News-Letter*. After the London politics and a re-hash of last summer's battle for Queen Anne's war in Europe, he found a list of English prices and exclaimed crossly over the fact that there, lobsters fetched one shilling and a penny-halfpenny each. Mercy did not need to bite back a smile as she once would have done and thought bleakly that she was losing laughter also.

Nor did it help that the New Year of 1705 ushered itself in with a blizzard and no signs of hope for spring.

She could keep her hands busy and her mind a little, but she had wanted to live with courage. There was no courage needed in the plodding round of tasks repeated day after freezing day, only patience. And patience, though self-taught, was not part of her nature. Life was merely endurance, and 'life' was not a word she could apply to winter in New Exmouth, where the energies of the earth itself seemed extinguished.

More than once in her life she had decided to live and not to die. But now that she had tasted of life's best in the arms of a man she had loved, she knew too well that she was not, now, really alive. Winters and years would wear her down, her prettiness would fade and her body wrinkle, until even the men she did not want ceased to look at her. She would become just another sour spinster, and the life she had clung to so passionately would pass her by.

She knew this was all self-pity, which she had never allowed herself before, and knew that both Edmund and Soulange would have despised her for it. But she was as unable to prevent melancholy seeping into her soul as she was the powdered snow through the cracks between the wall boards of her little room, no matter how many rags she plugged into them.

****

Spring came at last, heralded by breaking ice on the New Exe stream, by brisk breezes that chilled but no longer died away to the stillness before snow, and by new buds stubbornly rising on every growing thing.

It saved Mercy from herself. Her youth and strong heart responded of their own accord to the season. At first she wondered, with the last of lingering sadness, if a time would come when the hope of spring would not move her. But for now the cow bore a new calf, fluffy yellow chickens and ducklings hatched and ran about, and the peach tree was pink with blossom. And it did not matter as much as it would have during winter that in April she turned four-and-twenty.

The women began to turn the house inside out to clear its mustiness. They aired clammy clothes and linen, beat mats, and even opened the rear door on days when the sun shone. On a morning early in May she and Sarah carried little Martha's wetted bedding out to dry on the roof of the hen house, slipped in a cold unseen puddle, fell into it, and ended up patched with water and mire.

Sarah had been timid around Mercy since she returned from Carolina Colony, but now looked at her and giggled.

"Oh, Aunt Mercy, you have mud on your chin, just like a naughty boy making mud pies!"

"And you, child, have it on the end of your nose, as if you were sniffing the pies!" Mercy pulled the girl to her feet, and then on sudden impulse scooped up a handful of the chilly muck and smeared her own cheeks and Sarah's with it. "And now we can both play at being Negroes!"

Sarah laughed, delighted. "It's so good to see you smile, Aunt Mercy! I thought you never would again, you were so sorrowful all winter. Didn't it make you glad, to get your voice back?"

Mercy felt her smile slip, and shook her head. "It has made no difference to anything." It was both easier and more difficult to talk to others without the necessity of writing. She had no buffer, now, between her thoughts and people, and no time to weigh her words. However she made herself pick up the smile again, for Sarah's sake. "It was strange for a time, not to have my belt and board and bag about my waist any more."

"It is different, Aunt Mercy. That is all, isn't it?"

"Yes," Mercy smiled. She retrieved Martha's pallet from the damp ground. "Quickly, Sarah, pick up the quilt. We must clean this mud off before it soaks in, and our faces too..."

"Mercy! Sarah!" called Hephzibah's appalled voice from the open door. "Wash yourselves at once in the bucket! Lay out the bedding, then come back inside!" Mercy thought her agitation exaggerated, but then Hephzibah added, "We have a visitor!"

Beside her a tall man leaned on the jamb, a richly dressed man in a new blond periwig. He grinned at the girls. "Faith, Mistress Burdick, don't berate them! It's many a year since I played at mud throwing, but I'd be tempted to join in, if it wouldn't be the ruin of my new clothes."

Large as life and bold as brass, it was, of course, Richard Collyer.

****

"I like your voice, Mistress Mercy. 'Tis a trifle husky, but that makes it sound seductive."

They walked, with Nathaniel's permission, on the foreshore road, a foot apart, in plain sight but out of earshot. Mercy thought with indignation that it was just like him to make such an immodest remark. It was also just like him to have cozened Nathaniel, who had been at home that day breaking with a plough the hard ground of his cornfield, into looking on him with favour.

Her stepbrother had at first totally disapproved of the dandified and un-Puritan stranger. Hephzibah, of course, he had won over again easily. When she had apologised stiffly that they had only poor fare, he had claimed with a laugh that he remembered very well how hard it was after winter to put together a decent meal with all that was left of the salt fish, stored flour and dried vegetables.

But he said he did not expect to be fed, having dined on shipboard, though he had brought some small gifts for the Burdicks to compensate for calling on them without warning. Like a conjurer he produced from his deep coat pockets a bottle of nutmegs, two jars of raisins, and a bag of dried oranges and limes.

Nathaniel had thawed like the spring ice then and there. He had read in the list of London prices in the *News-Letter* that raisins brought a whole shilling a jar. Collyer had then sewn up his host's approval by listening with apparent sympathy to a recital of Nathaniel's rigours when out fishing, and recalled his own times on boats as a young man in England.

Mercy strongly suspected that those times had been spent smuggling, not fishing. Yet Nathaniel had seen no reason, after that, not to allow Captain Alexander to walk with Mercy.

Richard was as splendid as a peacock. His coat, waistcoat and breeches were moss green, thick with gold embroidery and gilded buttons, gold lace at neck and cuffs, dark green stockings and gilt-buckled shoes. A gilt-handled small sword hung from a fringed baldric, and he wore a curly-edged hat trimmed with gold lace over his yellow periwig. Mercy wore the everyday dress of undyed homespun she had sewed during the winter and an old shawl.

"You did not come to New Exmouth to pay me doubtful compliments," she countered coolly. "Are you trading?"

A spanking clean-lined little two-master rode at anchor in the rushing brown waters of the estuary. William Chase, who had walked around her on eggshells since her homecoming, had bowed stiffly and frowned as they passed his counting house. She wondered idly whether Richard had hired the ship, bought it or stolen it, and decided she did not really care. "Booty from the Caribbean?"

He sighed noisily. "Why, ma'am, you do me an injustice. These goods are honest come by. Well, most of them," he added incorrigibly. "Yes, I am trading, but I do business in New Exmouth solely because Madame asked me to see if you were well. She has had no letter from you."

"There has been no boat to take one." Nor had she wanted to worry Soulange with the poor state of her spirits. Mercy ceased walking, wrapped her shawl more closely about her, and stared past the fishing boats' masts and furled sails toward the ever-moving cloud that was seabirds by the thousands wheeling over Rocknest. Soon the great flocks would be flying up from Carolina and the Caribbean again. "You have seen her, then."

"Aye, and been berated for not saving Edmund. Though what more I could have done, not being a wizard, I've no notion." Still at a respectable distance, he bent his head to look at her and said flatly, "You've grieved for him."

The word *wizard* had frozen her for one moment, but then she turned her head to meet the keen hazel eyes. Converse with Richard had the advantage that she had no need to dissemble, in most things. "Yes. But I find that even broken hearts mend, with time, and after a fashion." She saw that, for once, his expression was not even slightly humorous. "You grieved also, I think."

"Edmund was my friend. In many ways my only one, for all we're very different men. And for all he was sometimes too soft hearted." He scowled, though not, she thought, at her. "You'll want to know—we buried him on the beach. There's a cross over the grave, with his name and the year cut on it. Edmund Gramercy is dead, Mistress, but I know he'd not want you to be wasting yourself with grief for him." When she did not answer, he shrugged. "What do I tell Madame?"

It had been preferable when she did not know. The body she had held in her arms lay rotting in the sand. She shook her head, to rid her mind of the thought. His soul was in God's care and forgiven. "Why, that you found me well enough."

"You have shed a few pounds of flesh, Mistress. Your eyes have no spark and your step no bounce. That is not well."

She did not say that it had been a hard winter, that everyone had lost some weight. "I told you that I am mending. It takes time. She will understand that." She pressed her lips together. Talking of Soulange meant to miss her anew.

Richard did not answer immediately. He turned his back on the rocky shoreline and looked toward the town, then directly at Mercy again. "You may recover from sorrow, but you'll never fit here, Mistress. You never have."

"Who does, Captain?" She spoke with a flash of her old temper. "People live where they must, where their families are. I have no other home."

He smiled, as if pleased with himself for pricking a hole in her defences. "Madame also asked me to remind you that the offer to live with her still stands, and always will."

She felt the sting of a tear in her eyes, but shook her head. "I was settled here well enough, until you came and disturbed my peace."

"You'll be glad to see the back of me again." He glanced up to watch the far-off cloud of birds, and his face, for Richard, was grim. "I'll tell you something, Mistress Mercy. What happened to Edmund has disturbed my own peace—if that's the word for the life I led. I'm selling the *Prospero* to my crew—there's no bully-boy like our late friend Gorman keeping me there by threat. No, Turner and the others are taking her..."

"Master Turner is alive? Heaven forgive me! I've been so bound up in myself I did not think to ask after him, or Jedediah. What happened to Jedediah?"

"Jedediah's alive, for all he's lost the arm that was hurt."

She could somehow picture Jedediah going his phlegmatic way with only one arm. "Where is he?"

"Where he is has something to do with my own plans, which aren't settled yet, but he's safe and otherwise well." He rested one elegant leg on a stone, then rubbed his chin. "I considered going to Europe to fight as a soldier of fortune in the wars. But, damme, I must be getting old, for I found I'd lost my taste for such adventure. No, I'm for Virginia Colony. I'll use my ill-gotten gains to set up as a tobacco planter."

"You trust me with this information? Now that I can speak?"

"You've had chances to inform on me in the past, ma'am, and you haven't done it. Besides, I tell you this because I ask you to come with me."

She stared at him. "As your mistress? You know I would never do that. For Soulange's sake alone."

He grinned. "Oh, no, you and I'd not suit each other. Nay, come as anything you like. A passenger to Virginia, or my guest for a little until you decide what to do. But then, you don't trust me, do you?"

"I don't know if I can trust you or not, Richard. That is for myself. I know Edmund did." It hurt to say the name aloud, however pain was in the heart and her mind could think only—*Virginia*. It was a temptation. As once before, she did not know if Collyer was angel or devil. "It needs no thought. My place is here, with my family."

"Your stepbrother, not your brother by blood."

"That is beside the point. The point is that my life is now what it would have been, if I had had no truck with pirates."

It was impossible to offend him. He merely said softly, "But if Edmund had asked you, you might have gone." He saw her chin lift, and rubbed his own again. "No need to tell me your thought, Mistress. What's a scoundrel like me doing unhung, when Edmund, a better man, is gone?"

She bit her lip then faced him. It was necessary to lift her head up, because he was a good foot taller than she was. "I am sorry, Richard, to seem ungrateful. I know that, after your own lights, you are being kind. You are trying to do something for me for Edmund's sake. But it would be wrong of me to go with you, a sin. Surely you understand that?"

"I forget sometimes that you're a Puritan. Very well, lass, I'll say no more on it. But that's not all my business with you. Here." He took an oilskin bag from his waistcoat pocket, stood a half step closer and passed it to her behind the screen of her shawl. "Careful, don't drop it. 'Tis heavy."

Mystified, she received the thing into her hands, and looked about her. The town was west of them and at their backs, the estuary was before, and no one was close by. Of course, Richard the pirate would have made sure of that. She pulled the oilskin off a leather bag, and loosened the thong threaded through its top. No wonder it was heavy—it was full of coins, gold guineas on the top.

"What is this?" she whispered. But she already knew.

"I was able to bribe but five minutes speech with Edmund in the Guard-house at Charles Town. But he used one of them to tell me that if all else failed, one of us must get your money back to you. Forty Pounds."

Her eyes blurred. Edmund was dead, and still took care of her. She gave herself time to recover some calm by slowly pulling the thong and oilskin closed again. "I know he used all I gave him, therefore this is from you." She looked up at him. "It has troubled me that I owe so much to Soulange—not just help and friendship, but money. Please, give it to her."

"And cut her to the heart? If you're Madame's friend, you should understand her better. For years she was bought and sold. Even Monsieur bought her, after a fashion. She believes, without knowing she believes it, that love must be paid for. If you try to repay her with money, she'll think you love her no more."

"I would never hurt her," Mercy said slowly. Carefully she lowered the bag into the pocket of her gown. She would need to walk with caution, not to look weighted down. She managed to smile. "This is probably dishonestly come by. But I must accept, for the sake of Nathaniel and his family. Though now I am indebted to you also."

"No, Mistress, you're not. I gave my word on it and I'm keeping it, 'tis all. But what I want to know is, you went all the way to Charles Town with a testimony you knew would make no difference and forty Pounds. Did you expect he'd bribe his way out of gaol, past guards, and through a court of law, with so little?"

Strangely, she was not angered. "Richard, you loved

him and did what you could. I loved him, and did what I could."

"And we both failed. Let's not quarrel, Mistress." He glanced about him, at the estuary rushing with thaw, at the pale sunlight and the budding trees. "'Tis a fair enough day, for New England. Shall we stroll further? I like the company of pretty women, even if they don't like me."

"You are a strange man! Yes, we'll walk." A few yards further, along the verge for the middle of the road was muddy, she smiled again, this time without effort. "You raise unrealistic expectations in my kinfolk, I fear."

"I admire you, Mistress, but I wouldn't wed you, even in common law. I'm dam - blessed if I'll be shackled to the same woman for life."

She almost laughed. "You are reprehensible! As if they would let me leave with you, unwed." She inspected his face a second. "You understand Soulange. And she likes you."

"And dislikes me too, sometimes," he said flippantly. "The same as yourself. And you leave unsaid the fact that her husband is a sick man and unlikely to live long. Oh, I like her well enough, but I ain't the stuff husbands are made of."

"Will you go with them this summer, to the Penn Colony?"

"They should be safe to travel. The Quakers have taken pains to be at peace with the Indians, and the Frenchies are unlike to stir them up there. Virginia's quiet along the Tidewater, it's up in the mountains there's sometimes clashes. And I'll be busied for some time, with my parcel of land to turn into a plantation." He frowned back along the foreshore to his new boat. "I can send the ship, if they need it."

Mercy felt a stirring of mischief. "Is it yours, or did you steal it?"

He cocked an eyebrow at her. "Ain't none of your affair, Madam Nosy." But then he shrugged. "I bought it. Looks best that way, if I'm to turn honest. And I'm a wealthy man, from pirating."

She shook her head in bemusement. How strange the turns of life, that made her acquainted with such a man.

Yet she said only, "We are almost out of sight of the town. We'd best turn back." She stood and looked back along the road, where it passed the little wharves for the fishing boats, and wondered idly if the crab-apple trees on the way to the Mill would bear this season. From here she had a fine view of the orchards beyond the town, all alive with blossom.

New England can be beautiful too, she thought, and I had best learn to appreciate it.

Collyer stood beside her, still at a decent distance. "One more word before we return, Mistress. If ever you change your mind, and decide after all to go to Madame, or to come to Virginia, go to the Plummers' house in Boston, or send a message there." He did not wait for an answer, and offered her his arm.

She shook her head again. "Even my hand on your sleeve would be considered encouragement." They began to walk back the way they had come. She was oddly disappointed that he would soon leave. He was, at least, someone she could talk to honestly. She glanced at his pretty new ship. "When will you go?"

"With the tide this evening. Unless you'd like me to stay a few days to make the local swains jealous by pretending to court you."

"No." She did not smile. The less time he spent in New Exmouth, the less chance that someone would tell him about her mother. "As for swains, there are one or two." She knew she was foolish to say so, however he had annoyed her. And it was vain of her as well, because she did not want him to think she was totally unwanted here.

"I see."

They walked in silence. Mercy did not look at him. Those sharp hazel eyes might indeed see, too much for her comfort. They turned down the road to the town, passed the stockade and the warehouses and the budding maple grove. She arranged her shawl more loosely, to cover the awkward bulge in her pocket. Halfway to the square, she saw Master Barnard and John Hanson outside the smithy, watching them.

"There is one of my swains."

"Which? The smith, or the lean one like a vulture?"

"The blacksmith is a widower and needs someone to

take care of his house and children. The other you also met when you were here last, and you should speak of him with more respect. He is our minister, John Hanson." Though now that he had said *vulture*, her mind imagined John Hanson one of the turkey buzzards of Charles Town that hung over the meat market seeking carrion. "But last time you compared him to a crow."

"I recall. He watched you then, too. Why's he find you so fascinatin'?"

She admitted half the truth. "He still hopes I will make a mistake. In his opinion, I was let off too lightly for my escapade to Carolina."

"Faith, I'd like to give the old crow something to flap about! Hold your hand, or better, kiss you."

"Do not! I sometimes long to tease him myself, but it is not worth the trouble."

"And will you marry the smith? Mind, he's too big. He'd crush a little piece like you."

"No. And do not make indelicate remarks!" She tossed her head, and a vagrant fair curl escaped its braid and fell from beneath her cap. Absently she tucked it back. "Nor will I marry any of the young men who make calf's eyes at me."

"Spoken like a true woman, Puritan or no. But, why not? Wed is a better life for a woman than single. Or have you made of Edmund a saint, and are being true to him?"

"You have talked to Soulange!"

"Not about your person I haven't. I've eyes of my own to see things with. And I say you're a fool if you let memories from the past spoil your chances in the present."

"You have no right to tell me how to live!"

He shrugged. "So I haven't." They were in the square now, and as they passed the old stocks Collyer swept the minister and the smith a magnificent bow. He bent so low that his gold-laced hat almost brushed the muddy earth.

Master Barnard nodded curtly. John Hanson merely stuck his hands behind his back and frowned.

Richard sauntered toward the laneways, and observed dryly that he had shot happier birds than that particular buzzard.

Mercy had to bite back a smile. "He seems so, but it

229

is because he takes very seriously his responsibility toward his congregation."

"He's mean-minded, gills full of self-righteousness, and ain't got a breath of life's joy in him. Nor does he want any other soul to be any different. You used not to mince words, Mistress. At least not with me."

"I must live under his eye. And, now that I can talk, within his hearing as well." She noticed that Richard escorted her a different way home, behind the wooden walls of the close built houses behind the square. "You have taken the wrong lane."

"No. I've but scouted a place where we would be unseen for a moment." He stopped walking. They were in a corner formed by a window-less house wall and a pear tree. Its cloud of white blossom made a kind of roof.

Mercy looked up at him, momentarily puzzled, and was quite unprepared when he suddenly grasped her shoulders and pulled her against him. Quickly, before she could protest, he bent his head low and kissed her. At first she was simply too astonished to break away or to struggle. And then she discovered after a moment that she did not greatly want to. His hold was strong, but his lips were warm and undemanding, and it was not unpleasant to be so close to a man again.

However when he released her, his eyes twinkling, Mercy blushed scarlet. She whispered fiercely, "How dare you!"

"Oh, I don't pretend I feel more for you than any other good-looking woman. That kiss was to show you, Mistress, that, unless the lass loves elsewhere, one man's embrace is much the same as another's. Perhaps now you'll consider wedlock to someone not Edmund not quite so distasteful as you imagined."

****

Mercy walked to the shore road that evening, without asking permission, to watch Richard's ship leave New Exmouth. It was a fresh, brave sight in the spring breeze, and the tall figure on the quarterdeck doffed his gold-laced hat to her.

She lifted her arm and waved. No one could criticise her for that. He was an acquaintance, and as far as New Exmouth knew, with the single exception of William

Chase, not an improper one. She expected never to see him again, and held no real grudge for the kiss. In his own odd way, he had tried to help her.

It was not his fault it was impossible.

Chapter Fourteen

Spring advanced and New Exmouth worked. The townsfolk set out to sea to fish, broke the hard ground for planting, and beat the winter's dust out of the households.

The carpenter ventured up to the hills for wood again, and timber for the house to be built by the newly married son of the chandler was floated down from the saw mill. The town officer appointed to the task once more took the milch cows out to pasture each morning and returned them each evening. And the little squad of militia drilled and patrolled, not really expecting attack but aware that in Europe the great armies would have begun their spring campaigns.

The flour miller and his son went to check on the grist mill that would be used again come summer and autumn. They went on foot, by the muddy shore road, and on the way home stopped to talk with Nathaniel where he and Obed sowed barley and rye into the new furrows. Mercy thought nothing of this until the son, thin-shanked twenty-year-old Robert Hull, came bashfully one day with a crimson face and asked her to marry him.

She was mostly alive again by then, knowing it was due to Richard's prodding as well as the season, though no more ready to marry. The core of lonely sorrow for Edmund still lay in her heart, and the older reason would never go away. After her first astonishment—she had believed no man of New Exmouth would ever ask for her hand—she refused Robert, gently.

Nathaniel did nothing about it but roll his eyes heavenward. But John Hanson stopped her in the square the day after and asked bluntly why she had turned down a respectable suit.

Mercy's hands tightened on her basket of new-caught mackerel that Hephzibah had sent for the Hansons. The minister must have seen that she headed toward their house yet he had chosen to accost her publicly. Mistress Carey and a bevy of other housewives were within hearing, and although they might have lingered to listen to anyone else it seemed they did not care to eavesdrop on their minister. They hurried off, though Mercy barely noticed.

She knew the answer to the question in her own heart and mind, but it had been supremely difficult to speak it aloud to Uncle Jonathan and Nathaniel. To speak of it to John Hanson was near impossible. She had not forgotten his merciless exposure of her identity when she first arrived in New Exmouth, though then she had been able to distil her first dismay with the fact of her dumbness. Now she almost wished she was a mute again.

However she managed a calm countenance and a moderate tone, even while she wished for the freedom to show her anger. "I believe you know why, sir. I fear the taint that may be carried in me by my mother's blood." She felt she might choke on the words and be sick.

"So should you. But you must allow me to be the judge of things spiritual. You have shown no sign of witchery as yet. Your failings may be due to your own character and your loose upbringing." He let this sink in before he continued. "If your hand is asked for again, come to see me. I will pray, and tell you when it is shown me by divine grace whether it is safe for you to be wed."

Mercy met his cold eyes and hated him. She longed to throw the basket at him, to tell him that her marital status was none of his affair. She spoke stiffly. "If I am asked, I will remember what you have said." She set the basket down on the hard earth by his boots. "Here, sir. This is for yourself and Mistress Hanson, from my brother and my sister-in-law." She wished him good day through tight lips, turned on her heel and walked away.

"You may come to my house tomorrow, Mistress Penhall, and collect your brother's basket."

Unable to trust her temper, she did not answer. But she felt his eyes on her back as she crossed the square.

Of one thing, however, she was sure. He did not really want her to accept Robert Hull. He was a friend of Master Barnard's, and if the blacksmith asked for her would favour him. She entered the first lane and found herself striding by the pear tree where Richard had kissed her. She wondered for the first time whether she should have gone with him, or even stayed with Soulange.

But in the end, everything she did or did not do was for the same reason. Now, however, she felt that the inheritance of being her mother's daughter surrounded her whole life, like the walls of a trap.

****

Mercy woke at dawn the next morning from a lovely dream of Edmund lying warm beside her, and found herself embracing the feather pillow.

A tear wet each of her eyes. She wiped them away and pushed the pillow back under her head. She lay thinking then, and decided that while the old fear might have legitimate cause to shape her life, John Hanson and other people did not. No one could force her to do anything she did not want, and if she disregarded their wishes and opinions they could do nothing except treat her with disapproval. And she must not allow mere disapproval to trouble her. She must be strong.

How could others criticise if she chose to remain a spinster in her brother's house? Why should her character be more suspect than any other person's, because of her mother? No one else in New Exmouth was reproached for their weaknesses because of their parentage. If she was sometimes stubborn, or angry, or merry, why, that was herself. People must accept her as she was, and not blame everything she did on what she might be. She herself did not know what she might be...

Mercy shivered a little, then pushed back dread. She rose and dressed, and opened her shutter to see the sun rise before she began her chores.

By the middle of June she had heard the blacksmith's suit and rejected it, and had not asked the minister's opinion. He came to the house this time, white with anger, and berated her in Hephzibah's presence for both offences. Mercy listened to his tirade calmly, though not meekly, and from that day forward he was not merely watchful for her mistakes but was her implacable enemy.

He railed from the pulpit, the following Sabbath, about women who held, like heretic Quakers, that they were the equals of men and did not accept the guidance of the stronger sex. Mercy listened politely, ignored covert glances in her direction and did not look away when he glared at her directly. She left the church in the interval after the sermon, but so as a matter of course did many others.

No one ever did so before the bi-monthly taking of the Lord's Supper, and neither would Mercy have. She must be her own person, yet remain within the bounds of what was fair and just.

And she must not provoke the minister unnecessarily. John Hanson, in his own mind, still lived in the days when the rule of the clergy had been all-powerful. Even among the congregation some of the old attitudes remained strong. While those might change, it would be a gradual process that would probably take a lifetime. Therefore she could not afford to be openly defiant.

She could not help but wonder if it would ever cease to matter that her mother had been hanged for a witch. That too could take a lifetime. Uncle Jonathan had told her that public opinion had been outraged by the Salem trials and their savage aftermath, however he had also said it was unwise to speak of her own family's part in them. And that had been in Virginia. Here in New England, it was even more necessary that she be careful.

Mercy had made the mistake, in the spring, of mentioning to Hephzibah a piece of her mother's remembered lore. Young James had suffered during the winter from sore gums, a sign of scurvy. Mercy had suggested he be given the preserved lemons, since eating lemons and oranges and limes was a cure for the disease. Hephzibah had scoffed, and then looked at her sister-in-law with frightened eyes.

Mercy had needed to bite her tongue, and then watch James make a slower recovery than necessary. John Hanson did not hear of this. But he did of the treatment she gave Nathaniel for a different ailment, which laid her brother even lower than the original complaint.

She had brought home from Charles Town some dried root of horseradish, which was used at the de Vaugerets' table, finely sliced, as a food. Soulange had told her it was also useful to dry up the mucous of runny noses. Nathaniel had a miserable summer cold. He ignored it for a week to go out in the boat, but then it became so severe it kept him indoors.

Mercy did not consult Hephzibah this time. She brewed an infusion of the root and gave it to her brother as medicine. Within two days his symptoms began to be relieved. But then he complained of a burning discomfort in the stomach, and she gave him no more of it.

John Hanson made a duty call on his unwell parishioner, and heard the disgruntled patient complain of the remedy that had made him more ill than the cold itself. Nathaniel certainly meant no harm to Mercy, although he was cross about the business. But the minister immediately took issue with her over the matter and demanded to know what the medicine was. When she told him, with a calm face and a quickened heartbeat, he was grimly satisfied.

"From a Frenchwoman and a Huguenot! You had no right, Mistress, to try an unknown herb on your brother."

"It is possible it does not agree with Nathaniel's stomach. Its origin cannot have any bearing on that. The Huguenots were as persecuted in France as our own forbears in England."

"Nonetheless you have done him harm! I forbade you, when you first arrived here, ever to use your mother's cursed remedies. So now you defy me by drawing on those of others!"

Nathaniel interrupted uneasily. "My sister meant me no injury, sir."

"Your stepsister is wayward, Nathaniel! She not only uses these forbidden simples. She is disobedient and she is insolent. Nor has she ever truly repented that she ran off to Carolina. And she refuses the suits of church members, and entertains that of a popinjay of no known religious affiliation!"

"Why, hardly, sir. Captain Alexander has gone, and Mercy didn't seem to like him above half anyway."

This might have all washed over, leaving only one more grudge against her in the minister's mind, if Nathaniel had not become even more sick. The severity of his stomach pains, instead of decreasing, increased, and within another day he was forced to stay off the boat once more. He could do nothing except lie in his bed with a hand on his belly. He could eat no food without feeling the worse for it, and could drink neither cider nor ale, but only water and milk.

Mercy dared not suggest any more remedies and Hephzibah on her own gave him dandelion tea. This did not help either. Mercy could not let him suffer when she knew at least he should not take hot liquids into a sore stomach, and made sure he received the tea lukewarm. The pains subsided within a few days though he still could not eat. He began to lose flesh.

Nathaniel in his illness became extremely bad tempered. His children tiptoed around him and Hephzibah, since she bore the brunt of it, was frequently upset. Mercy, looking on, understood better. Half his trouble was that he worried about losing time from his fishing. They did not go hungry, since there were young vegetables coming on in the garden, and poultry to kill, and eggs. There was flour left, if a little weevily, and dried mackerel from the last catch.

But still, the larder was depleted and there were no fresh fish for barter. And there was always the concern that they might fall behind in provisioning for the next winter, a sharper worry in New England than Virginia and Carolina. Nathaniel, worried to distraction, pronounced himself fit when he was not and took the boat out. He returned without a catch, in worse condition and therefore even worse humour.

Hephzibah put him to bed, clucking as anxiously as one of her hens over a sick chicken, and went to warm some milk.

Mercy went down to her little lean-to room, barred the door and prised up the loose board by the wall where she had buried the money Richard gave her. She had hidden the oilskin-covered bag quickly, half in darkness, without looking inside it. Now she unfastened the thong and tipped the coins into the lap of her apron, thinking to use older pieces than the bright guineas on the top.

Her room had no glass window, and the summer light was diffused and pale. But it lit the gold pieces like a pile of little captive suns. There were no Spanish or Portagee coins, or even older English ones. They were all new English guineas with Queen Anne's plump head imprinted on one side, and when she counted there were fifty of them.

She very nearly said aloud, *a pest on Richard.* It was more money than she had given Edmund, which was generous, but how was she to explain a continuing supply of new gold? It was more specie than would have passed through Nathaniel's hands in years, probably more than anyone in New Exmouth but William Chase had to hand. Well, she must think of an explanation for the moment. For the future, perhaps Chase would help her to exchange it for other coinage.

She dropped two of the pieces into her apron pocket, wrapped three more in a kerchief in her wooden clothes box, and reburied the bag. She went out to the parlour and offered to Hephzibah to take the warm milk up. Her sister-in-law, near distraction with Martha who was cutting teeth, gratefully gave her the pewter mug. When Mercy knocked at the bedchamber door Nathaniel answered peevishly, and frowned at her as she came in. Obviously he had expected to see his wife.

He was in his long-tailed shirt, under a blanket, his face was gaunt and his eyes feverish. One of his heavy hands lay protectively across his belly and with the other he plucked restlessly at the coarse wool cover. The small room was stuffy and smelled of the chamber pot under the bed. Mercy always longed to push the little window open to the summer air, but both Nathaniel and Hephzibah refused to let the sash be lifted in case a pane of glass broke.

She handed him the cup and waited while he sipped at it. When he told her petulantly that she need not, she said softly that Hephzibah wished to know when he had drunk it all. However she pulled up the room's only chair so that she would not seem to stand over him. It was one of hickory he had made during the first winter of his marriage, in Salem. He drained the mug, pushed it at her, sighed and lay down again.

Mercy spoke then, gently. "I wish to say something, Nate. It will take but a minute, and will help you." He nodded curtly, not much interested, and she went on.

"Half of your sickness is worry about all the work not done, and how we are to manage if you are ill for a long time. I came to tell you there is no need for concern."

He said heavily, not looking at her, "Friends and neighbours have enough to do of their own."

"I know you would rather not be beholden to anyone." She set the mug on the floor, took the coins from her pocket and lay them on the blanket. "With this you can pay someone to work the boat, or a lad the field, or buy provisions. I have a little more if it's needed."

The guinea pieces caught sunlight that fell almost opaque through the small window panes. Nathaniel's mouth fell open, almost ludicrously. He said in a dazed tone, "I thought you had none left."

"I did use what I took from here." She wanted to set his mind at rest, without lies if possible, though also without allowing him to suspect 'Captain Alexander' might have given her money. "You see, Uncle Jonathan bequeathed me some for myself, besides that Anne sent for you. I should have repaid you sooner than this, but he particularly told me to keep my own laid by. He was always concerned that I might be left alone in the world."

That was the wrong thing to say. It upset Nathaniel. "He should have had more faith in me! I was always prepared to do my duty by you, sister." He glared fretfully at the money. "But if you had this, why did you rob the iron box under my bed, to go to Charles Town?"

She did not need to answer, then or ever.

Someone gasped behind her, and a board creaked sharply. Nathaniel's red-veined eyes widened to stare past her shoulder. Mercy turned slowly on the chair, feeling mind and heart begin to grow cold, knowing somehow—by witch's foreknowledge?—what she would see.

Hephzibah, pop eyed and with Martha snivelling on her hip, stood at the door. So did John Hanson, his hand on the knob. The minister's neck was flushed as red as a turkey buzzard's for all that his face was long, piously horrified, and triumphant.

****

As John Hanson pointed out to Nathaniel, he should rightly fetch the constable and turn Mercy over to the law.

That would mean the Boston Assizes, a whipping at the cart's tail, prison, or even the gallows. To Nathaniel's feverish insistence that his sister had acted within her rights to take her own money, Hanson pointed out, truthfully, that the law would not see it that way.

But, the minister said, he was mindful of the Burdicks' good name and the disgrace to it of a thief in the family. Therefore Mistress Penhall must be punished privately, in New Exmouth. She would be whipped, and taken out of this household where she might influence innocent children. She should be locked in the Watch-house, but it boasted only one cell and would be too public as well.

She could be confined for an indefinite time in the Hansons' house. The town would be told she had shown signs of madness. Given what her mother had been, no one would doubt it.

Hephzibah had run downstairs to give the baby to Sarah to mind and now came back, shut the door and stood silent, her look appalled.

Nathaniel sat up in bed, his cheeks flushed. "You cannot treat my sister so! She did wrong, yes, but after all it was to perform a Christian act. She has behaved well under my roof and worked willingly. Certainly she is sometimes forward, but I blame Jonathan Penhall for that." He coughed dryly.

Mercy had stood rigid and listened to all of this. Her knees shook and she longed to hold the chair back for support, but was too proud to do so. She felt as she had when she had heard Edmund sentenced to death, cold through and through, mind rebelling against what her ears told her and yet knowing it to be real. Now she began to be angry. She stepped back, laid a hand on Nathaniel's shoulder and addressed the minister.

"You are distressing my brother, sir! He is ill and you make him worse. Leave all this until he is better..."

Hanson rounded on her. "And who made him ill at the first, Mistress? You, with your witch's simples!"

Nathaniel wiped his dry lips with a shaky hand. "She has shown no sign of being such a one, Master Hanson! And God showed her favour by returning her voice."

"Nay, I'll not have that! She lost it when her mother

240

hanged and regained it when the pirate did. That is not Godly work, but devilish!"

"Oh, stop!" Mercy felt unutterably weary. "Nate, do not upset yourself any more. He is determined I be punished and will not rest 'til it's done." She felt her hand tremble on his shoulder, took it away and clasped it tightly with the other in front of her apron. "It is true enough that I deserve it."

Hanson actually licked his thin lips, though it was Hephzibah who spoke, in a frightened whisper. "But who will whip her? Surely not my husband..." Her voice faltered.

"Don't you see, Hephzibah, that he wants to be the one to beat me?" Mercy spoke with contempt, but had to grip her fingers harder together. "Let him, then, and in his own house. Certainly our children here must not be grieved. Might I inquire, sir, how you will explain my screams?"

"Madwomen scream, and are beaten. But you will be gagged. You escape lightly at that, Mistress. In all justice you should be arrested. I spare you from the law only for the sake of your brother and his family, who are decent church members. They took you in out of charity and were repaid with thievery. Be still, Nathaniel! It is either the whip at my hand, or the constable. You will do the wench no service by objecting."

Nathaniel fell back on his pillow, groaning. Hephzibah, pale and bewildered, hurried downstairs once more to fetch a hot rag to lay on his stomach. Mercy and the minister stood and stared at each other.

Hanson said softly, "You show your true colours, jade, by speaking to me so boldly."

"And you show yours." Mercy trembled inwardly, yet her voice was calm. Now that the worst had happened she no longer needed to pretend any respect for him. "You are a cruel and hard-hearted man."

"I am a man of God! And what comes your way is naught but justice. You were always bewitched and I say you bewitched the pirate also! Such a one does not set a woman free out of the goodness of his heart!"

"It *is* strange." Hanson had no way of knowing how close to the mark he had come. "The pirate treated me

241

well." She looked the minister up and down as if he was a piece of meat she suspected of being rotten. "But the man of God has no drop of the milk of human kindness in him."

Hanson's lips were white. "You will pay for that also, witch."

Mercy willed herself not to fall back before the word, and would say no more. Then Nathaniel groaned again, and she knelt by the bed and took his hand tightly between both of her own.

"Don't fret yourself for me, Nate. It is true you have been good to me, and true I have repaid you poorly. There are three more guineas in my box—take those as well. That much good at least will come out of this bad thing. I will come home, brother. Do not make yourself more ill over me."

Hephzibah returned with the hot rag, and had to stand passing it from one hand to the other while Nathaniel spoke hoarsely to their minister.

"I charge you, sir, not to be more hard on her than is needful."

****

Hanson whipped her in his own parlour. He first bid his wife to unlace Mercy's gown to expose her back. The leather thongs soon tore her shift to shreds.

She bit into a strap so that she did not cry aloud, and bit into it as hard when Mistress Hanson, distressed herself, at her husband's order reluctantly and quite gently rubbed salt into the open cuts. Mercy's body betrayed her resolution and shook at this treatment. Her eyes ran tears and she groaned, deep in her throat.

The minister grunted, satisfied. "You'll bear the scars of a sinner for the rest of your life, Mistress."

She drew on all her determination, spat the strap away and answered him, her voice thick. "It matters not. I'll never marry. No man will ever see them."

For that insolence she received one more slash, across her neck.

Nathaniel and Hephzibah came to visit her the next day. Nathaniel looked very sick, and she would not burden him with complaints, even though her back was so stiff and sore she could barely move.

"As you say, Nate, I've been spoiled. Mother never

smacked me unless I was caught in mischief, and Uncle Jonathan always preferred to lecture rather than hit. So I've now received in one beating all those I deserved in the past. And you know a penalty was due to me this time." She did not mention the punishments inflicted by her stepfather. Nathaniel knew; he had borne his share from his sire. Instead she asked about his stomach.

Nathaniel, hunched almost double and with a drawn face, did not answer.

Hephzibah told her he had taken at noon a little boiled fish. "So he must be on the mend." She was plainly ill at ease, though there was no mistaking the reason. The minister had not allowed them to see her alone. He stood within hearing.

Mercy made herself smile. "I am glad to hear that. But Nate, don't try to rush back to your chores. Give yourself time to get well."

Nathaniel's hollow eyes looked at her, then he turned to Hanson. "When will my sister be allowed home?"

"When I am satisfied that she has repented of all her sins and become a properly submissive female."

Nathaniel blinked. Possibly he could not imagine Mercy submissive, but he was too ill to argue. He and Hephzibah shortly left the house.

Mercy had received them sitting on a stool in the parlour, and Hanson now escorted her back to the quarters he had allocated. This was a windowless attic room, behind a locked door to which he alone held the key. There were fourteen narrow steps to the door and Mercy walked up every one of them without his help, since he merely marched behind.

It entered her mind that if she had been her normal healthy self, she could have pushed him down and run from the house. But there was no place to go where she would not be soon caught.

The room held only a smelly pallet of old straw with one coarse blanket, a chamber pot, and a hard little wooden chair. There was not so much as a bucket for water. The minister knew of her preference for clean skin, and denied her enough water to wash. Nor would he allow Hephzibah to bring her a change of clothes, or her horn-handled hairbrush and the new horn comb Soulange had given her, or her own quilt.

For the first week her sustenance was bread and water. Nathaniel baulked at this and thin soup was added to her diet. Within days, however, she began to lose the weight she had regained during the spring and early summer, and colour fled from her cheeks and left them pale again. After her back began to heal, hunger was the worst of her discomforts. Yet she was determined to win the battle of wills with Hanson and not allow her spirit to be broken.

She admitted from the first that she had done wrong to take the money, and would own to no other sin. But the minister had time, as well as every other weapon, on his side. Each morning he made her sit on the little chair while he alternately stood over her and paced the floor, berating her and preaching at her. She listened quietly, was not cowed, always looked at him directly and whenever possible in the eyes. He said this was impudence and struck her shoulder with the whip for it. Thereafter she kept her eyes on the wall, though she did not lower them.

For the remainder of each day she was left alone to contemplate various tracts and verses copied from the Bible. These were all on the subjects of punishment, judgment and the inferiority of women, and gave her no comfort.

In the tiny room she had nothing to occupy her hands or her mind. She tried to exercise by walking a certain number of steps each day, though that made her feel she was in a cell. She tried to think without dwelling on painful memories. She remembered, wryly, that a short time ago she had pitied herself for the dullness of life in New Exmouth. Now the everyday round of chores seemed a desirable dream.

After two weeks of Hanson's strictures Mercy began to wonder if after all God used this means to punish her for her part in Edmund's escape and her wanton conduct. She began to fear that the minister would have his way, remould her into a proper Puritan woman. She shook her head at these thoughts. But for how long could her pride and stubbornness keep at bay the erosion of her mind through constant nagging and close confinement? Would she weaken out of desperation? Or if she did not, would she go mad?

****

It was impossible for Mercy's detainment to remain unnoticed in New Exmouth. The town was small and self-contained, and everyone knew everyone else's business.

The townspeople had at first believed, at least outwardly, Hanson's tale of a mind unbalanced by blood heritage and sin. But the Burdicks did not confirm it. Nathaniel, his stomach pain easing, remained grim of face and close-mouthed on the subject of his sister. And Hephzibah was uneasy, the boys bewildered, and Sarah downright tearful.

A tiny tide of sympathy began to veer Mercy's way, and the elders asked more frequent and keener questions of their minister. Even his friend Master Barnard, when Hanson assured him of a malleable bride in the near future, backtrod by muttering that he had liked Mistress Penhall as she was, and a wan and spiritless shadow of her former self would not be acceptable.

William Chase, requested by 'Stephen Alexander' to keep a weather eye out for Mistress Mercy's well-being, sent two agitated letters care of the Plummer brothers in Boston.

One of these was forwarded to Madame de Vaugeret of Broad Street in Charles Town, Carolina Colony, and after a two-week voyage arrived at a house empty of all but cook, coachman, and maidservants. The Huguenots had departed at the beginning of June for their long-planned visit to Penn-Sylvania, and the letter was left on the escritoire in Madame's boudoir.

The other had not so far to travel, though to an area less civilised and its journey took as long. But eventually it arrived, much battered, at its destination, a plantation new begun north of the James River, forty-five miles west of Williamsburg, Virginia Colony.

****

In July, Mercy took ill with a fever.

She tried, at first, to remain on her feet and to keep her speech lucid, stubbornly resolved not to give the minister the satisfaction of seeing her give way to any weakness. That was pride again, she knew, but pride was

245

the only weapon she had left.

Within a day of forming this resolve she was no longer able to care for pride, or for anything. She fainted on the floor while trying to walk her self-prescribed number of steps. Hanson, apprised timidly by his wife after some hours of lack of sound from the attic room, found her there. He allowed Mistress Hanson to drag Mercy onto the pallet.

Mercy alternately burned and shivered and asked constantly and deliriously for water, yet was unable to hold it down after she drank. Mistress Hanson begged her husband to tell Master Burdick that his sister was ill, and the minister, afraid though refusing to admit it, sent the blacksmith's apprentice to the house with a curt message.

Nathaniel was out fishing, but Hephzibah went with some trepidation to look in on her sister-in-law. The severity of Mercy's symptoms frightened her, and she asked permission to stay. The messenger was sent back to tell Sarah to mind Martha and the boys, to prepare supper and to send her father to the minister's house when he arrived home.

When Nathaniel came, in the late dusk, John Hanson was pleased to tell him that his sister had lost her voice again. It was true. In the middle of delirious babble about a beggar, her throat had seemed to crack. She had been unable to do more than moan hoarsely since. In Hanson's opinion, if her restored voice had ever been a sign of God's favour, that favour had now been withdrawn.

"The curse of Jemimah Penhall has taken her once more! When she has recovered from this fever, I will have the stocks re-opened and lock her in them for a day!" His white face reddened with excitement and he waved his arms in the air. "Her hair will be cut short, to kill her vanity. Yes, cut hair is the punishment of an adulteress! But I have always believed she gave her body to the pirate, or cast a spell over him, so he would let her go..."

The terrible silence in the tiny room, his own browbeaten wife's horrified stare, told him he had gone too far. Nathaniel had knelt on the boards beside Mercy's restless body. Now he slowly rose to his feet. The light of the tallow candle had revealed to him her blue eyes burning with heat, her once-pretty face drawn and pale yet flushed along the cheekbones. Her fair hair, loose because her feverish hands had dragged off her cap, lay lank and lifeless and brown with dirt.

"She has suffered enough. We will take her home, and nurse her there."

"She has not repented one ounce! She still defies me! She will stay here!"

Nathaniel was neither clever nor particularly kind but he knew his duty. He was also tired from a long day, and his stomach still troubled him enough to make him irritable. However his awe for his minister held slightly.

"Then allow Hephzibah to remain with her, to wash her, change her garments and give her medicine. I will send Sarah back with those things, and clean bedding." He saw Hanson's blazing eyes and his voice did not falter, but firmed. "I do not wish to take her out into the night air, but tomorrow we will make up a carry-cot and move her down the stairs, and to home."

"She is a thief! I will tell the constable..."

"I will deny the charge. And has not this punishment been like prison? It is enough, John."

Chapter Fifteen

Hephzibah and Mistress Hanson nursed Mercy through the night, taking turns to rest.

After supper Sarah brought Mercy's own quilt and pillow and linen sheeting, and her flannel smock. The girl was overset to weeping when she saw her aunt so sick, and wanted to stay. Her mother sharply ordered her home to care for the household.

Mercy tossed and moaned for hours, while the two women alternately bathed her and covered her with the quilt when she chilled. It took the strength of both of them to force water and feverfew broth, drop by drop, down her throat. Then after midnight the fever broke, and she began to sweat.

The bedding was soaked and they had to change her back into her grubby petticoat then lay her again on the old blanket. Mistress Hanson hurried downstairs for linen of her own, and Hephzibah heard her voice raised tremulously against that of her husband. She returned, pale, but with a patched sheet to spare Mercy's skin from the rough pallet.

After an hour or two the sick woman ceased to sweat and fell into a sleep like a half death. Mistress Hanson went down to the parlour again, perhaps to pacify her husband. An hour after that Hephzibah, her head nodding on her hand, saw that her sister-in-law's eyes were open. Their blue was cool at last, yet seemed to look at something far away.

Then her gaze focused properly, she saw Hephzibah and actually smiled, if faintly. Hephzibah, very weary, snapped at her to go back to sleep. Mercy shook her head with a tiny movement sideways, and her thin hands felt at her waist. Hephzibah realised she searched for her old writing board.

She spoke less sharply. "You have lost your voice, Mercy, but 'tis only the fever. When you are well, you will be able to speak again."

Mercy pulled herself up a little and supported her frail weight on one elbow. She reached under the sweat-stained pillow and brought out the tract left by the minister the previous morning. She made a sign of writing.

"You will be home tomorrow. You can write then."

However Mercy insisted with the gesture, until Hephzibah feared she would use up her small strength and relapse into the fever. She went down the steep stairs to where Mistress Hanson dozed in her austere parlour. The minister was awake but had retired to his small study. Hephzibah could hear him pacing and muttering. She asked for a stick of charcoal and Mistress Hanson silently gave her one from the hearth.

When she returned to the attic she found Mercy still laying in the same position, with the stubborn look on her worn little face that Hephzibah had come to know. She took the stick eagerly in her wasted fingers, printed with painful effort four words across the tract and held it out.

Hephzibah took it and read, GOLD UNDER MY FLOOR.

She frowned at it. Mercy must yet be a little out of her mind, though to humour her she nodded and tucked the paper into her pocket. Mercy also nodded, apparently satisfied. Then she sighed, lay back again on the pallet and patched linen and fell straightaway into exhausted sleep.

She was still deeply asleep in the dark hour before dawn, when Hephzibah, yawning and near slumber herself on the small hard chair, heard a commotion downstairs.

****

Hours earlier, on the last of the evening tide, a little ship had anchored in the estuary opposite the wharves.

Ezekiel James the Watch-man had taken no special notice. For one thing he recognised it as one of the hired craft from Boston and New York which did business with William Chase. For another, it rode quietly on the water, lanterns lit at bow and stern. No one had yet come ashore

249

from it, but that raised no suspicion in his mind. Its master would wait until daylight to bring his goods in.

In these days of a distant war Ezekiel did not do the watch alone. His mate Peter Staple patrolled in the opposite direction. The Frenchies and their Indian allies skirmished inland and to the north, but not along the coast. No one expected New Exmouth to be attacked.

In the hours after midnight Ezekiel paced toward the square, holding his lantern in one hand and leaning on his staff like a walking stick. These small hours were the hardest, when the town was quiet as a graveyard and his eyelids grew heavy.

He did not see the boat that was lowered softly over the side of the anchored ship, or hear the dip of its muffled oars. He did not see it glide in to the shore, or see the wooden ladder that was used to scale New Exmouth's modest palisade.

The moon was not many nights past new and the square was ghostly beneath it. Ezekiel saw only two lights in the houses around, both in the minister's house. One candle glowed from the shuttered parlour and another flickered through a gap in the clapboards of the attic.

Ezekiel frowned. Like everyone else he knew Nathaniel Burdick's sister was sick, and like everyone else he had begun to think that perhaps John Hanson was not right when he said she was mad, witch's daughter or no. She had been a pretty, cheerful little thing, even when she had been dumb. Her history was a little strange, but that did not mean she was evil...

A brawny arm, strong as iron, suddenly encircled his neck from behind. From the other side another man's hand clamped over his mouth. The square he had thought empty was filled with dark figures. His staff and lantern were plucked from his grasp, his cudgel and dirk from his baldric, and his hands were pulled behind his back and bound with twine. He thought in panic, *the French!* He had a momentary hope of Peter Staple, then saw him bundled from a lane by three more men. They had already snuffed his lantern.

One figure separated itself from the others and stood before him. It spoke calmly, in a peculiar harsh tone, but, Ezekiel thanked God, in English.

"We'll do you no hurt, if you but point out the minister's house and nod if the Penhall woman is still there." The voice was that of a man used to command. "Jedediah, Ned, release him long enough to show us. Don't cry out, Watch, or you're a wounded man."

Ezekiel could feel the point of a dagger that dug into his coat below the ribs. He was shocked and frightened, yet attempted to do his duty. "What—what do you want with the lady?"

"You may believe it or not, but we mean her no harm. Quickly now, which house? The one beside the church? And she is there?" The voice allowed for nothing but obedience.

Ezekiel decided he had no choice. He nodded heavily.

The voice thanked him, then gave an order. The Watch-man was quickly and efficiently gagged, and the end of the rope that bound his wrists was fastened tightly to the hitching post before the smithy. Peter Staple was served the same.

They both stared, helpless, as the group of at least a score of men merged on the Hansons' unpainted dwelling. The weird light of the moon gleamed dully here and there on the naked steel of pistol barrels and cutlass blades. It showed the men in the rear acting as guard to those before them, turning constantly to scrutinise their surroundings.

A dog barked, and every one of them stopped where he was. But the sound came from a distance and was not repeated. They moved forward and surrounded the walls of the house. Three went straight to the narrow porch.

One of these was big as a bear, though one of his coat sleeves hung empty. The thin one called Ned, cutlass in hand, pressed himself against the wall beside the door. The man with the harsh voice and the stance of command, clad in colours dark as the night, thudded on the oaken door with his sword hilt.

"Master Hanson, open up! 'Tis a matter of life or death!" He stood back a pace then and waited, silent, yet alert.

In the stillness, sounds of movement could be heard inside the house. Then the door jerked open and the minister's face, white skinned and white haired, seemed

to float disembodied against the darkness. He held a
candle head high and it did not illuminate his black
clothes. He frowned and opened his mouth to speak.

They gave him no chance to utter a word. The big
man put his good shoulder to the door and shoved it fully
open. John Hanson's pale eyes widened in alarm. He
croaked the beginning of a cry.

The dark-clad stranger seized his arm and pushed
him into the house. The candle was plucked from his
hand, and the big man and the thin one followed their
leader in. They closed the door swiftly behind them. In the
square all was darkness again. The shadowy figures
around the house waited, and watched.

****

Hephzibah opened the low door of the attic room and
stared down the steep steps to the parlour. The noise she
had heard had been compounded of voices—unfamiliar
men's voices, John Hanson's voice raised in protest and
his wife's in a cry. Then a chair fell over. Hephzibah was
not afraid, simply wondered who had come at this
ungodly hour with bad news.

One voice rose above the others, harsh yet clear.
"Stay with them, Ned. You, sir minister, hush or you will
be tied and gagged." In a kindlier tone it added, "You also,
Mistress. Be quiet, that is all I ask of you."

Hephzibah saw in the dim candlelight a thin man
who pointed a pistol at both the Hansons. And then two
other men started for the stairs. The slim figure of the
first took them two at a time, and the big one of the
second lumbered behind him.

She backed into the attic room, frightened and
bewildered. They could not be French raiders, speaking
English so plainly—they must be robbers or pirates.
There was no internal bolt to the door, to close it. The key
to the lock was in John Hanson's pocket. Hephzibah
pushed the little chair against the door, and trembled.

The door burst inwards and pushed the chair over.
Suddenly the tiny room was filled with the figures of the
two men. Hephzibah opened her mouth to scream, but the
dark one said quickly, "Quiet, Mistress! We'll not harm
you." The other's left sleeve was pinned up and he bore a
pistol in his right hand. At the first man's order he

dropped it into his coat pocket. The dark man dropped to one knee beside Mercy's pallet, and stared at her.

Hephzibah had stood stock still, hands to mouth. But now she cried out, "Oh, sir, do not hurt her! She has been sick!"

"I see that. God in heaven!" Quite softly, the stranger's long fingers touched one of Mercy's white, wasted hands. He turned quickly to Hephzibah. "Who are you?"

She stammered like a child. "I—I am Hephzibah Burdick, h-her brother's wife."

The man's eyes reflected the candlelight but his look was cold. "Her family have done poorly by her." He wrapped Mercy in her quilt and lifted her into his lap. Hephzibah, frightened and not observant, yet saw that he cradled her gently. He was a sober seeming person, darkly clothed, with dark hair that appeared not to be a periwig.

"Sir," she whispered, "what will you do with her?"

"Listen to me, Mistress Burdick. I am a friend of Stephen Alexander's. He heard she was in trouble but was unable to come here himself. Tell your husband we intend her no harm, have come only to rescue her." His voice had a rough note, yet that must be by nature, since it was at odds with his words and manner. He frowned down at Mercy's small worn face. "Where is her cap? I don't wish to take her out in the night air bareheaded."

Hephzibah never knew why she did it, but instead of hunting for Mercy's grubby headgear she pulled off her own white linen cap and with trembling hands passed it to him. He smiled slightly and drew it over Mercy's dirty tresses, then whispered something, though so softly she did not hear the words. She was curiously unafraid now, reassured by his kindly conduct and the mention of Stephen Alexander. Even the big one-armed man seemed not threatening, more like a dog on guard.

"Shall—shall Captain Alexander wed her?"

"No. But someone will." He looked down at the unconscious woman with an unreadable face then turned to Hephzibah again. "We must tie you to the chair, Mistress, but only so that no one will think you let her be taken willingly." He passed a clean kerchief from his waistcoat pocket to the other man. "Gag her as well, but easily."

The large one grunted, lifted the chair from the floor and produced a cord from his copious pocket. Hephzibah was duly bound 'easily', sitting still, and then he turned to his master. "Gimme the lass. I can sling 'er over me right shoulder."

"No. There's nothing of her." The dark man was stronger than he looked. He rose to his feet with Mercy in his arms. Though she was tiny and thin, with her quilt she must have weighed near a hundred pounds. He smiled at Hephzibah. "You'll be found by morning. I regret your discomfort but it is for your own sake. Tell your husband he may keep the guineas."

Then he with his burden was gone from the room. The big man followed, pistol raised once more, and did not trouble to close the door.

Hephzibah heard their boots as they carefully descended the steep attic stairs. Then there were voices downstairs again, John Hanson's raised in fear and fury and his wife's weeping. The stranger's harsh tone ordered something then both voices ceased abruptly. She guessed that the minister and his wife were also being gagged and bound. She was sorry for Mistress Hanson, who was a timid soul, but she could find in herself no sympathy for the minister.

She heard the front door close quietly, and squirmed in the chair to get more comfortable. In the morning she must take Nathaniel aside and tell him his sister was safe. The dark man seemed benign for all his rough voice, and he was a friend of Stephen Alexander. Mercy would be fortunate, if she met up with the tall merchant again.

It would be hard in the household without Mercy's help, though she had Sarah. It was foolish to think it, but it would be good if they could afford a hired girl at the busy times... What had the man said, about guineas?

Hephzibah was not to remember his words until she reached home again and found the forgotten tract, with the words Mercy had charcoaled on it, in her pocket.

****

Dawn brought a hullaballoo. The Watch-men were discovered bound outside the smithy, the women found likewise in the Hansons' house, and Mercy Penhall was gone.

But John Hanson had been seen first of all. He was imprisoned in the old stocks, tightly gagged with a dirty kerchief and boggle-eyed with fury and humiliation. His breeches had been pulled down and his lean white rump was red with welts which, he told his rescuers in outrage, had been inflicted with the flat of a sword.

The smith's apprentice had found him and had not dared to laugh. But Master Barnard and the others who released him—it took some time since the chains of the stocks had to be cut through—were heard to snigger, later, behind their hands. Within days the sniggers had grown to open grins, and within a week the laughter caused him to resign his ministry. His wife was overheard one evening actually berating him, and shortly afterward they left to live with their daughter in Boston.

A young minister just out of Harvard College was sent to New Exmouth. He had a new young wife, and they whitewashed the house beside the church and planted roses by its porch. And, after consulting with the elders and the Town Meeting, he allowed cushions on the hard old pews of the church for the frailer folk and a fireplace built inside it. The first timber burned in it was the wood from the stocks.

One of the church elders was Nathaniel Burdick, newly elected. No one ever heard him speak of his sister again, and her fate remained unknown. Hanson had blamed the merchant Stephen Alexander for her abduction, yet no person of his description had been seen amongst her captors. Hephzibah Burdick maintained that the men who took Mercy had treated her kindly.

Whatever the truth was, investigation turned up no sign of the Penhall woman. Some of those who knew of her mother whispered that she had conjured up dark angels to rescue her, but the new minister called that talk superstition and suggested that it stop.

William Chase, in the autumn, delivered into Nathaniel's hands two letters that bore no return direction. One was for himself and Hephzibah, one was for young Sarah, and all three were seen to smile after reading them. The letters had come through the Plummer brothers in Boston, but Chase asked no questions. He merely wiped his brow, and prayed piously that he might never again, as long as he lived, set eyes on a pirate or a pirate's merchandise.

****

Mercy had lain dreamless down a deep well of sleep, yet now she did dream.

She dreamed she heard voices she once had known and a new harsh voice that tormented her because she should know it. Then she dreamed she was in Edmund's arms and struggled to wake because that dream grieved her. But the strange voice whispered, *Hush, be still, all's well.*

She had no more strength to struggle and lay still in the phantom arms. These bore her to a boat, and in a little while up the side of a small phantom ship. Perhaps she was not dreaming, but dead. Her mind recalled cloudily the Greek legend of spirits ferried over the River Styx, though she was a Christian... The arms settled her on another pallet and left her, so that she moaned at their absence. Then a hand she had once known stroked her cheek, and she sighed deeply and slipped again into unconsciousness.

She awoke to the arms of the angel—he must be an angel, if she was dead—settling her in a long sling. In this she was lifted slowly upward, up a higher ship's side. She dreamed fearfully then that Gorman would drop her into the sea again, and then the nightmare returned of the beggar's face in Charles Town. She moaned in her throat and tried to open her eyes. She caught a narrow glimpse of sails and stars, then the angel lifted her from the sling and she was safe once more.

She smelled the clean salt sea, and then ship's cabin smells of oaken walls and lantern oil. She was lain down, this time on soft bedding with clean linen and a feather pillow. She had not expected heaven to be so luxurious.

The odd rough voice said, *I pray you hear me, Mercy. You're safe now. Rest, we're going home.* The voice deepened, charged with feeling. *My poor little one, what have they done to you?*

The remembered hand touched her cheek again, then she felt the angel leave her. She opened her eyes to look for him, and saw the dark figure talk to another. This

256

other was a most incongruous angel, round and brown and soft, in a bright pink robe. The first angel vanished, though she heard a swift step she had heard before in her life...

The second angel leaned down close to her. Its voice also was full of emotion. *He gone to get the ship unner way, he want us far out on the sea when the dawn come. Now I goin' to clean you all over. Ah, my li'l baby, you shouldna ever lef' Virginia.*

Mercy was overjoyed to hear that voice, yet sad at the same time that Mam Felice had died too, like all those others she had loved. But she was selfishly glad to have her near again. The plump brown hands she had known as a girl touched a damp cloth to her face, unwrapped her from the quilt and stripped away the dirty petticoat... She slid down once more into the well of deep unknowing sleep, and the movement of the ship was like a rocking cradle's.

****

Mercy woke to sunlight that beamed softly through horn-paned portholes. She was not in heaven after all, but a large and well-appointed ship's cabin.

She had dreamed that she died. Yet she was not in the Hansons' attic. Where was she? Her tired mind could think no further than that, and she simply looked at her surroundings.

She lay in a single, wide bunk. By the door another, a narrow one, had been set. It was made up with a plump pillow and a linen counterpane of brightly coloured patchwork. A mahogany table stood against the bulkhead, half covered by a red cloth edged with gold tassels, and the solid chair beside it sported a red damask cushion with a gold fringe. On the deck boards beside them there was a big brass-bound chest, though more than that she could not see.

She was alive, but she was weak. She had been sick... She lifted her hand and saw it thin, yet it was heavy, and fell back. It touched her hair, and found her hair clean and smelling of chamomile. She had not washed her hair in chamomile water since she left Virginia Colony. Mam Felice used to help her with it—but she must have dreamed Mam. She had dreamed

Jedediah's voice, and Edmund's arms... Why were dreams so cruel? She turned her slow mind away from them.

Her clothing felt clean also, and the bedding. The linen was scented with lavender, her hands felt a blanket of fine wool, and the smock on her body was of soft white cotton.

Cotton. Cotton was unprocurable, because the English Parliament had passed laws—when?—three or four years before, prohibiting its use to protect the wool-weavers. Only a pirate or a wealthy man buying forbidden goods could purchase cotton. Therefore—her mind reasoned so slowly that it irritated her - there could be only one way she was aboard a ship. Richard Collyer had somehow heard of her plight, and kidnapped her.

She did not know whether to be glad or sorry. She supposed it was better than to remain in New Exmouth under John Hanson's thumb. But where would Richard take her? To Soulange? No, Soulange would be in the Penn Colony, this summer. To Virginia? He had told her he had land there. Would he expect her to be his mistress, after all?

She was too tired to think, almost too tired to care. And all she felt was a sharp pain at the memory of the dream of Edmund. She blinked weak tears.

She heard the door open and turned her head slowly to see who it was. A plump brown woman in a dress and turban of wide pink stripes closed the door. She carried fabric, more white cotton, and lay it down on the red cloth on the table, then came to look at Mercy. Mercy thought she was dreaming again.

The round face creased with a smile like a split in a dumpling. "You seein' true, Missy. It be your Mam Felice." She took Mercy's thin hand between two plump ones.

Mercy tried to speak, but merely coughed.

"I knowed you had your voice back, praise be the good Lord." She patted the hand she held, quickly and lightly, like a plump brown butterfly on a frail white flower. "You only lost it now 'cause of the fever. It will be come again."

Mercy's eyes ran helplessly wet, but she managed to shape words with her mouth. Mam had been able to read her lips, indeed had preferred it to the labour of reading her slate. *Mam, Mam, how are you here?*

"He buyed me, little girl, buyed me from your stepma an' her man Mus' Howard. Then he free me!"

She had told Soulange about Mam, and Soulange must have told Richard. She had not believed him capable of such kindness. She shaped with her lips, astonished, *Richard Collyer?*

"No, chil', not 'im." Mam's eyebrows rose, half circles over round button eyes. "Your man, Missy. Cap'n Mon..."—she had trouble with the pronunciation—"Montgom-ry." She frowned at the perplexity on Mercy's face. "You heared him las' night, an' seen him. I knows you did."

Mercy lay still. She knew no one named Montgomery.

What happened here? Had she been captured by pirates again? But how come Mam's presence? Her head swam, and she covered her eyes with her arm. Then Mam lifted her gently and supported her on the plump striped bosom, and it smelled as Mam had, of musky skin and dried herbs. Her arms were gently drawn into the sleeves of a blue dimity wrapper.

"He want to see you, Missy, but you has to be decent. He bring you here in your petticoat!" Mam's voice was as it had always been, thick and sweet like molasses, though at the moment stern. "I say, she has to eat an' drink firs', but he cain't wait. Menfolks!" Nonetheless she held Mercy on her shoulder and coaxed her to drink water, then eased her down again onto the pillow.

Mercy was glad of Mam, and certain now she was not dreaming. The water was shipboard water, fresh weeks before and now tasting of oaken barrels. She shaped her lips to form words. *Who is Captain Montgomery?*

"Bless you, chil', I tol' you. Your man, Edmun'."

Edmund is dead. It was painful even to mouth the words.

"No, no, chil', not him! He say, you tell her, Mam, seein' me straight off might fright her back inter fever. He said t' tell you, he didden hang proper, they didden make a noose of the cloth, jes' a knot. But he would of choked jus' the same, iffen Jed Bullen hadna hel' him up wid one arm, his other one all cut and bleedin', till Mus' Turner an' then Mus' Collyer could git t' him..."

259

Mercy made a sound in her throat.

Mam merely smiled. "It true. His neck weren't broke but he were half strangled an' coulden talk for days, an' even now him's voice still come hard." She chuckled unexpectedly. "Yes, chil', he be alive. An' you both cain't talk proper!" She patted Mercy's hand, then her cheek, and waddled from her line of sight.

Mercy's mind heard and believed, but her heart could not contain the tale and beat hard against her ribs. She heard Mam's short heavy footsteps, the swish of her round skirt and petticoats like dense shrubbery in a breeze, the molasses murmur of her voice as she spoke to someone at the door. The door closed, and she heard other footsteps, longer, swifter, quieter—and familiar.

She turned her head, and saw the dark slim man lean back against the table and cross his arms on his chest. He wore a white shirt with no lace on the cuffs, a high white stock around his neck, a long plain blue waistcoat, dark blue breeches, black stockings and steel-buckled shoes. His long, dark hair was neatly combed, his gold-brown eyes cool, his face expressionless. He wore the mask of Captain Gramercy again, but he was real.

"Mercy." It was the rough voice she had heard in the night, though under its damaged tone without inflection, as she had first heard it on the deck of the *Thalia*. "I told you once that Gramercy was not my born name. Montgomery is. I go by it now, and as far as the world knows the pirate is dead. You will think it cruel I let you believe so too. But believing me gone you could continue with your own life, find a man with a past inside the law."

She shook her head on the pillow, slowly.

"With your voice returned it seemed best that way." His look was no softer. "But then I intercepted a message to Richard. I feared for you, and have committed an act of unpardonable effrontery in abducting you from your home." He waited, stonily silent for a moment, and when she but watched him took a deep breath. "If you cannot forgive me for those things, then I will take you and Felice wherever you wish, and see you decently settled."

Mercy saw only one thing. He was afraid, afraid she would be angry that he had let her think him dead, and then taken her by force from New Exmouth. The manifestation of his physical self had stunned her, yet now she knew nothing but a rising tide of joy. He was alive! Nothing else mattered. She struggled to sit up, held out her arms to him and smiled.

He stared as if he could not believe his eyes, and then strode to the bunk in one long step and scooped her up into his arms. He held her body tight to his and her feet did not touch the deck. He kissed her forehead, her eyelids, her cheeks, her lips, gently but fervently, and his mouth was as warm as in her dreams, but real, oh, real!

Her arms somehow found strength and twined around his neck. The sweetness she had tried to forget flooded through her, body, heart and mind, and refilled the empty aching place left by his loss. She wept silently, with happiness utter and complete. But her weakened body could not contain her feelings. She gasped for breath and began to tremble.

He exclaimed, "I'm a fool! Poor little one!" He dropped into the mahogany chair with her in his lap, pressed her head gently onto his shoulder, stroked her hair and said, "Hush, rest," as to a babe. Behind the first harsh octave his tone was soft.

His body was a cradle for hers. She felt the steady beat of his living heart, breathed the warm air from his living lungs, felt his cheek warm on her forehead. All grief and trouble were behind her. She was safe, in the only safe place in the world, the arms that had borne her up in the sea, held her in other ship's cabins. She needed nothing else. But she wanted desperately to tell him so.

Her breath was regained, and her voice struggled up from her heart to her lips. "Don't," she whispered. No, croaked, hoarsely as a neck-wrung bird. "Don't let me go."

"I longed to hear you speak." The words shook, half with emotion, half with laughter. "Between the two of us we have a whole voice!" He held her more closely to him. "I will never let you go, Mercy. Never, never again."

****

Mercy and Edmund had never had enough time together for long conversation, even by way of her writing board. But on the voyage to Virginia on the *Prospero* they made up that time.

Mercy soon became used to the harsh upper tone of

his voice and learned to listen for the real one beneath it. Her own voice returned slowly, with rest and soft food. At first this was thin gruel and bread soaked in fresh milk. They had brought a nanny goat with them, for the milk. She found also that watered-down red wine soothed her throat.

For the first few days he sat by her bunk, or held her in his lap on the mahogany chair. Mam, at first, was shocked. Not because she believed Edmund would do her little girl any harm, but because Mercy had no clothing except the blue dimity wrapper over whatever shift or petticoat Mam's busy fingers had sewn for her.

"An' no cap! You been bareheaded!" Mam clucked in Edmund's hearing. "Where th' one you came on ship with? I have to sew you 'nother one now."

"In the trunk." Mercy almost giggled. "Mam, I intend never to wear a cap again."

Mam had never heard her speak before and was inclined to be lenient because of this, but muttered, "Not proper."

"Felice has a prim and proper soul," Edmund said solemnly, then continued with a smile, "And a brave one. She did not know me, but came with me for your sake. I freed her in Williamsburg, so that the choice would be hers."

"Like I woulden come, when my li'l girl need me!" Felice did not notice the subject had been changed.

"But," said Edmund later when he and Mercy were alone, "I should like to tell her we are betrothed, so she cannot fret that we aren't respectable." The laughter left his eyes. "Will you wed me, Mercy?"

He was afraid again. She lifted her face to look at him gravely. Somewhere inside herself she sensed a barrier to marriage, but with the sickness and then the great happiness that followed it, she had forgotten what it was.

"Yes." She smiled and slipped an arm around his neck.

"Ah." He exhaled his held breath and kissed her. In a few more minutes he told her, "There are Church of England parsons in Williamsburg. Though I understand that with Puritans marriage is a civil matter." He stroked her thin cheek, now beginning to bloom with a little colour. "We will talk more of it when you are well."

"Edmund," she whispered, flushed with kisses, "I will stay with you, wed or not."

He smiled so warmly it melted her soul further. "A maid's heart will always rule her head, though you have the strongest of both I ever encountered in a woman." He looked deeply into her eyes. "I hope, Mercy, that your head will not talk sense to your heart. If you had sense, you'd not stay with me."

"Why?" She smiled.

"You are strong enough now to know what you let yourself in for." He lifted her chin with a finger. "Edmund Gramercy is no more, and Edmund Montgomery another man. But I did not want to live in the fear that someone, someday, would point and say, *that man was a pirate.* Therefore I went to Governor Nicholson in Williamsburg, confessed to what I had been and asked for the amnesty." She did not move within his arms, just listened calmly. "If I do not return to my old ways within three years—two and a half, now—I will be pardoned."

A little frown creased the fair skin between her eyebrows. After a moment she asked, "Can your rescue of me be held against you?"

"It could. You see, love, a condition of my pardon is that I report each month to the Queen's officers at Williamsburg. I did so before I began this journey, and shall again once I am home. So far as they know I had business in Norfolk, which is true enough. I will return with a bride, and they will think I met her ship there. Therefore no one but you and I, Jedediah, Mam and Richard, must know I fetched you myself."

She frowned a little. "What of *Prospero?*"

"Ned Turner and this crew plan to take the ship across the Atlantic, to sail as privateers in Queen Anne's War. They part from us in Cheseapeake Bay, where we meet my own ketch. We'll not see them again."

She shook her head at him. "There are folk who know me in Williamsburg."

He smiled at her again, glad of her steady sense. "That is easy enough. You met Edmund Montgomery a year since in Boston, and sailed south to wed him. I know it is a lie, Mercy, but I must trust God will forgive me for it." He touched her lips with one slim brown finger. "He has much more to forgive me, as you know. I have bought my land, Mercy, with my share of pirate booty. It did not sink with *Thalia.* 'Stephen Alexander' salted it away in respectable banking houses."

"I will take blame for half the lie." She felt her eyes begin to swim with tears and her husky voice lowered. "Edmund, we cannot change the past." There was a faint echo in her mind when she said, *past,* but she hardly noticed it. "Could not Richard have come for me, to save you the risk?"

"Richard heard that Paul de Vaugeret was taken ill in Penn-Sylvania, and took his own little ship up the Delaware to escort Madame and their party home." He smiled at her. "I would have come anyway, little one."

There was a thing she must ask. "But if you had not heard of my trouble—would I never have known you lived?"

"It was for your safety. If I was pardoned after the third year, I planned to sail to Massachusetts Bay Province and find whether Mercy Penhall was yet unwed. If so, I could have asked for her hand as a free man. But I fear that if I found her with a husband, I would have seduced and abducted her just the same." He did not smile.

Nor did she. "I do not have it in my heart to tell you that is a wicked thought." She shook her head then leaned it on his shoulder. Against her will she was growing tired. "How shall we explain my voice, to those who knew me dumb, in Williamsburg?"

"Why, you had a fever, and in delirium it returned to you. That also is only half a lie." His tone was light, under its first harsh note. He stroked her cheek.

"Edmund." She was fast becoming sleepy, yet must say this. "In spite of everything, I am glad you came for me. It is worth all of it, to be with you. I am sure that God understands love."

He said nothing, though his arms tightened around her and he rocked her to sleep in his lap, like a child. He could feel against his hand, through the back of her shift, the raised welts from the whipping. If he had known, he would have given that black crow of a minister more than a child's beating with his sword.

He raised a hand to brush a fragrant fair curl from her face, to touch gently her thin soft cheek and pale rose lips. And heard in his mind her voice say huskily, *Past*.

She had forgiven him bloody-handed piracy. He then would forget her pain. They must start afresh.

Chapter Sixteen

No one looked at the face of a beggar. In his usual place between the brick paved street called The Bay and the wharf called a bridge, Elias Gorman huddled further into his rags and listened to the converse of the man and woman less than four yards from him.

The woman he had recognised as the Frenchie jade he had seen with the Puritan last winter. She had thrown coins to him, then. Now he had crept closer in the hope she would drop some again, and for no other reason. The tall silent tire-woman in attendance stirred no memory. The figure of the man twanged a vague chord in the dark ruin of his mind, though he paid it no attention. He needed money for rum and food.

"Do not fear for Mercy, Madame. Ned Turner left a message for me with the factor here, that Edmund was already on his way to New England." The man laid a comforting hand on the woman's russet sleeved shoulder and his voice lowered.

The beggar's clawed hand squeezed convulsively around his stick. His mouth fell open. *Mercy. Ned Turner. Edmund.* Edmund? He remembered now, the Navy sailors had hanged him. That confused him. *But he knew the names.* He stared at the man. He knew the cut of his jib, he was sure of it, but he could not remember...

"Ric'ard, I cannot help it." The woman's rich voice carried, even speaking low. "I fear for all of them, in such a venture."

"Naught will happen to Mercy when Edmund's there. And naught to Edmund when Jedediah's there." The man tossed his moss green cloak back over one shoulder and chuckled confidently. "He'll get her away safe from New Exmouth and they'll all be back in Virginia by the time I get there, never a doubt."

Jedediah. The beggar trembled. And now he knew the man, in spite of his brown whiskers and wig. *Collyer!*

"You know as well as I that any plan can go awry, in this world." The woman smiled, however. "But, dear friend, I choose to take you at your word." She turned to the dark maid-servant. "Sapra, the parcel, if you please."

The tire woman held under her arm an oilskin wrapped bundle. She passed it to her mistress, who hugged it a moment then pressed it upon Collyer. "These things are *Mercie's* own, that were left with me. I ask you to take them to her."

"I'll do that for you, Madame, gladly." Collyer eased the parcel into the crook of his elbow. "She'll receive it safe, I give you my word on that too. When, I ain't sure. I'll trade in Bath and Williamsburg on the way home, but I shan't take a great time about it." He indicated with his head a clean little two-master anchored off the wharf. "After all, I've a plantation to manage now, and I've left it in the care of an overseer."

"I have told you how glad I am that you no longer— trade—upon the high sea." The woman laid both her hands on his arm. "And I have thanked you for escorting us home. Monsieur said..." Her voice softened and the beggar could hear no more.

But he had heard all he needed. *All of them, in Virginia, run to ground.* He could kill them all! He slid forward past the pair and they did not notice. He rose within a few steps and shambled toward the little ship.

Ships always needed another hand. He might not be so strong as he once was, but he could do something, anything... And there were always wepons to be had, aboard a ship... He would keep his face out of Collyer's way, even though Collyer had not yet recognised it.

From the wharf's end the beggar looked back, to make certain they did not watch him. His brain did not work like it once had but his cunning was as instinctive as an animal's. They took no notice; Collyer was busy kissing Madame's hand. Half of Gorman's face leered in automatic reflex.

He remembered the Puritan. Gramercy had kept her for himself. Now the first mate would have her, when he found her.

****

In Cheseapeake Bay, Mercy was lowered by sling again to a rowboat, and felt no return of fear. In the boat Jedediah supported her awkwardly with his one arm and Mam fussed over her, while Edmund said thanks and goodbyes to Ned Turner and Richard's old crew. Then Edmund climbed swiftly down and took her in his own arms.

They all watched *Prospero* sail away, headed for the Atlantic and Europe, never to be seen in the Americas again.

Edmund's ketch, the *Dragonfly*, waited for them a mile distant, and the men who rowed the small boat were its crew. On the ketch Mercy was surprised again to meet its master, no other than young Ben Heslett, who had taken her ashore to Charles Town from the *Thalia*. Edmund had found him in the town of Norfolk, kicking his heels between voyages.

Mercy greeted Ben with a smile and he took off his cap and shook her hand, bashfully. She looked at Edmund over the boy's shoulder, and his eyes glimmered at her, and she understood. All those who had known him as a pirate were his friends, or in his employ, or gone.

They sailed gently up the great Tidewater of the James River, and then took to a wherry when it narrowed toward the Fall Line and the trading post of Byrd's Warehouse. The wherry at length landed them at a small timber wharf shared by Edmund and Richard, whose lands lay alongside one another. The journey was completed in a horse-drawn wooden sledge, which shook Mercy's frail body but lasted only a short time.

She was cross by now with her own fragility, yet could not deny her weariness. They arrived at the plantation at dusk, and she saw only a large house part-built on cleared land and a line of log cottages. Edmund carried her into the first of these, where she received a confused impression of small rooms. She would stay here with Felice, he told her. Still out of sorts, she answered that she wanted to be only with him.

"You are not yet well enough, nor is my house finished." He smiled and helped Felice settle her into a soft bed. "And I want you to lose no honour in the eyes of my work folk."

"Honour," she told him tartly, if tiredly, "is a man's notion. Women cannot afford it."

"Nevertheless, little termagant, you will do as I say in this matter." He bent and kissed her. "The journey to our own house is the last one you will make. Here is the end of all your travels. You are home. Sleep now."

Home. She forgot to be peevish, smiled at him, and slept.

****

For ten days Mercy drifted as if in a lovely dream, before the world intruded and shook her viciously awake.

She woke each morning to a sunny room where shutters in the opposite wall opened to a young honeysuckle vine and glimpses of green grass, treetops and blue sky. In the room, she saw the foot of her narrow bed of golden oak, a dressing table and stool, a rocking chair and a big armoire also of golden oak. The floor was polished pine. It smelled of beeswax, and her bed linen of dried roses.

From outside she heard bees humming, dogs barking and the lowing of livestock. She picked from the sounds alone cows, pigs, chickens and ducks and geese, the nanny goat behind the cottage and horses that whinnied further away. There were human sounds too, voices, some of them children's. Wood was sawed and hammered, at a far enough distance not to trouble her rest, only to be a pleasantly busy background. All these sounds were homely, ordinary, and contributed to her sense of wellbeing.

Mam was always there, in the rocking chair by the window opening where the sun could fall on the sewing in her hands. She frequently sang and hummed, and that was a sound of peace also from Mercy's girlhood.

Edmund came two or three times each day, often clad in rough workman's clothes of coarse indigo shirt and leather breeches, and always with a dark neckcloth tied high on his throat. If she was asleep, he simply sat and watched her. If she was awake, he talked quietly or held her hand. He smiled often, his eyes warm and golden. The cold-eyed pirate was indeed dead.

One day Jedediah knocked and tiptoed in, hat

crushed under the stump of his left arm, filling the room. He was startled when she spoke his name. She thanked him for Edmund's life and he was confused, as if he had been thanked for breathing. But he said he was content, and glad to have ceased roaming.

She ate more, solid food by the fifth day, chopped chicken breast or ham, mashed yams, strained soups, milk puddings. She drank sweet water from a new well, milk whey, and well-watered wine. She began to be restless, and snapped at Mam one day when the boars'-bristle hairbrush pricked her scalp. Then she burst into uncharacteristic tears, and begged Mam's pardon.

Mam merely chuckled, round chin wobbling like a turkey's crop. "You gettin' better, Missy, that be all. You ain't been sick since you was twelve and had the smallpox, and you's forgot. You's well enough t' feel like doin' somethin', but you ain't well enough t' do anythin'. It be pass, li'l girl."

On the tenth day when Mercy woke she decided, *I am well and will dress.* Mam was not in her rocking chair and Mercy padded barefoot to the window to look for her. She leaned out from the sill, saw a line of nine cottages to her left and on the rise of land before her the big house. It was partly of board and partly of brick. Edmund had told her they cut the timber from fallen logs in the forest, and baked their own bricks in a kiln beyond the cottages.

The house had a porch all along the southern side, as yet unfloored and with its shingle roof supported by squared trunks of young oaks. It would be a handsome house, and she could barely believe she would live there with Edmund, as his wife... The thought jarred against some blockage in her mind, but her heart shied away from it... She remembered that she had begun to look for Mam.

She turned her gaze to the beginnings of barns and a stable beyond the house, then across the clearing where more trees were being felled. White men and black worked together. Edmund had told her that he employed only bond servants and free men—he had seen slave ships.

She heard women's voices, and saw Mam at the next cottage chatting to a lissom young Creole woman with a child on her hip. Mercy smiled. *I must be well, if Man stays to talk. I will dress myself.*

It was simply a matter of finding clothes. She went to the armoire and pulled wide its doors. Two gowns hung inside, one of white Indian muslin over a white linen under-dress, trimmed with white lace and white bows. The other was of pale blue silk, with the swept-back overskirt, folded cuffs and lace half sleeves of high fashion. There were two pairs of shoes, one set high-heeled and fastened with blue satin ribbons, and the lower-heeled pair with slender gilded brass buckles.

Bolts of cloth lay folded on the floor of the armoire, she guessed to be sewn into more gowns. There was pink silk, primrose-yellow muslin, white linen, blue brocade, and woven wool for winter. There were lengths of ribbon and lace, and everything smelled of oranges and orris and cloves from the pomanders that kept them fresh.

Mercy almost wept with sheer delight, and searched further. She lifted a piece of silk, blue embroidered in pale gold, and found it to be a shawl, so delicate it could only be meant for warm summer evenings. There were also two hats. One was low crowned and wide brimmed, decorated with a white ostrich feather. The other was of soft grey beaver-felt pinned up on one side with a jaunty silken rose.

She tried this one on and inspected her image in the mirror hung over the dressing table. She had to smile. She looked odd in the calf-length white smock and the extravagant headgear. For a moment her smile slipped. Was it a sin, to abandon her caps and Puritan dress? No, she thought. She did not believe in God one jot less than she ever had, but she could not believe in the stern judgmental God preached at her by John Hanson and his kind. God was good. He had brought Edmund back to her.

She laid the hat aside and looked more closely at the dressing table. On it lay the silver-backed brush and comb Mam used for her hair, a silver tray for hairpins and a jar of rosewater. She opened the drawers one by one. In here, among dried rose petals, lay the underthings Mam must have sewn during the voyage to New England and back, fine cotton and linen shifts, cambric petticoats and lace-edged kerchiefs. There were stockings of cotton and silk, which would have been purchased in Williamsburg along

271

with the fine materials. Edmund must have been certain she would return with him!

She picked up the shawl again, draped it around her shoulders and inspected herself more keenly in the glass. She was pale and thin still, however the blue of the silk enhanced her eyes... In a little time she might look well enough to be a bride... She saw a dark figure behind her own in the mirror, and turned quickly, pulling the shawl more closely about her. But she was unafraid. She already knew who it was.

Edmund stood in the doorway, dressed for a day's labour in dark shirt and breeches, an old brown waistcoat, and as always a high neck-cloth. He smiled gravely. "I did knock, Mercy, but softly. I thought you might still be asleep."

She blushed a little, and was annoyed at herself. After all, he had seen her in her shift many times on the *Prospero.* "I am awake and, oh, Edmund, I feel well! I am even hungry! I should like to dress and walk." She smiled. "And I can assure you I am no longer invalidish cross."

"In that case, my lady, I shall be charmed to take you for a stroll. I will leave you to eat and change, and come back in a half-hour." He did not move, however, but stood with his hand on the wooden door-knob and watched her with frank pleasure, his eyes warm as honey. His voice lowered. "No, by heaven. 'Tis too much to ask of a mortal man." He stepped inside, closed the door, and walked slowly toward her.

Mercy stood where she was. Her cheeks were warm, though she was quite unalarmed. She saw him clearly, it seemed to her, for the first time since they had been on the *Dart.* Ever since he had taken her from New Exmouth she had been to some degree sick. He had held her, kissed her, talked to her, yet his presence had held some quality of the sweet dreams that had tormented her during the winter.

Now she saw his every feature distinctly—the dark brown hair sweeping back from forehead to shoulders, the long-lashed dark eyes full of gold light, the straight black brows, the slender strong structure of the bones of cheek and chin, the finely chiselled lines of nose and mouth. And his body, slim but strong; the way he moved, with the swordsman's sure grace and the unconscious authority of the ship commander.

She felt his physical presence with her whole body, and the soul behind his eyes reached out to her own with that remembered drawing of the invisible cord.

He stood close, not quite touching her. "You aren't afraid of me, Mercy. And you should be."

She shook her head and smiled. "I am always safe with you."

"I told you once that a maid is unsafe alone with any man. And I am a man like any other." He took her hand, brushed the fingers with his thumb and raised it to kiss. He smiled with slow mischief. "Do you have any notion how lovely you look, standing here like this?"

"I thought a moment since I seemed but a pale and skinny creature." She lifted her left hand to touch his cheek, and hardly noticed that the shawl slid off her shoulders.

He took her face gently between his palms and turned her chin upwards with his thumbs. He kissed her lightly, once each at the corners of her mouth, once on each lip, and then fully on the soft whole. Light kisses, but his breath came unevenly. "And I thought to live without my little Puritan two more years!"

She laughed and encircled his neck with her arms. Edmund's arms closed completely around her and drew her body softly onto his. He kissed her again more deeply, taking time, and then again with increasing passion. He loosened the drawstring of the shift and brushed his lips warmly down her neck, to the little hollow at the base of her throat...

Mercy forgot time, the world, everything but Edmund. She had never before been so aware of her physical self, her flesh seeming to melt like wax, blending with his. His body was warm and strong and solid, pressed tight to hers yet an extension of herself... His tongue gently parted her lips and caressed the inside of her mouth. Then he drew her loosed sleeve down to bare her white shoulder, and lowered his mouth to kiss the tender skin there.

His hand rose to the place where the soft fabric covered her breast and shaped to cup it for a moment, then brushed gently over the nipple... She clung to him, her breath ragged, felt his groin hard on her belly and was drowned in the sensual longing to be even closer, part of him.

He said, and his voice shook under the rough upper tone, "I press you too hard. Here, little one, rest." He drew the sleeve up again, wound the drawstrings together and tucked her head into his shoulder.

She leaned on him and it really was safe, because whatever happened she was where she wanted to be. Her quickened heartbeat slowed. She felt his heart thud under her ear, then he breathed deeply and it steadied.

She asked huskily, "Was that lust?"

"Puritan! Yes, it was. And it is allowed, between two people who are to wed." His mouth smiled on her forehead, then he held her away a little. "But if I'm not to claim you here and now, I'd best not hold you so close."

"You would make a Puritan yourself!" She lifted her eyes, and saw the dark kerchief above his collar. "But Edmund, allow me this." She reached up her hands, undid the neck-cloth and loosed the upper lacing of his shirt.

Below the Adam's apple the tanned skin of his throat was red and roughly scored, puckered all the way round by the sash that had almost choked him to death. Mercy stood on her toes and kissed it. She refused to remember the bloody sunset when she had seen him hanged. He was alive and they were together, that was all that mattered.

His hands tightened on her arms. "It is ugly, Mercy."

"So are the scars on my back." She smiled at him. "Neither can impede our marriage, Edmund." But there was something that could, her mind nagged from deep in itself, something in you that is uglier than scars...

"Mas'er Edmun'! You shoulden be in Missy's room afore she dressed! Shame on you!"

They both turned and smiled at Felice, who stood in the doorway with a breakfast tray that shook in her hands and threatened to drop.

Edmund laughed. "We are betrothed, Mam." He kissed Mercy without hurry, retrieved the silk shawl from the floor and draped it over her shoulders. "And Mercy feels well enough to walk. I'll go give orders for the day, and return for her." He kissed her hand and left the room.

Mercy's cheeks were pink with fresh blushes, then she smelled the breakfast of warm ham and coddled eggs and coffee and recalled her appetite. And after she had eaten she had Mam help her into a fresh linen shift, a cambric petticoat and the white dress. She drew on white silk stockings, fastened them with frivolous satin garters and slipped the buckled shoes onto her feet. These fitted quite well, and she asked Mam how Edmund had known what size to have them made.

"He say one shoe o' yours fell off on that beach, an' he keeped it. Now sit, Missy, an' I comb your hair."

Mercy closed her eyes a moment, to forget 'that beach', to cherish instead the thought of Edmund keeping her shoe and having others made from it in the hope she would one day accept his suit... Then she lost patience with the length of her *toilette* and refused to do more with her hair than run the brush through it once. Felice insisted she wear the hat with the feather in it and wanted to encumber her with the shawl as well.

But Mercy laughed, kissed Mam's brown cheek and almost ran from the little room, out through the front door and to Edmund, to explore her new world.

****

Within a half-hour Mercy was tired and though she would not complain, Edmund saw it. He spread his waistcoat on the bank of the stream and bade her sit and rest.

She protested the waistcoat. "I am not so poorly I cannot sit on summer grass!"

"I see you have never worn white before. The green would stain it, Mercy." He grinned.

"Oh!" She sat with care, smiled at him when he gave her his hand for balance and in the shade of native willows doffed her fine hat, which had been bothersome to balance when she was used only to caps. Edmund stretched beside her, propped on one elbow and at a decent distance of one yard. She teased, "Ah, yes, we are in full sight."

His eyes glinted. "Felice is pretending to hoe the cottage garden and will be here to defend you at any show of loose behaviour. And remember, madam, we are master and mistress of this plantation and must behave with dignity."

She laughed softly, and a comfortable silence fell between them. Around them the balmy air carried a medley of muted sound, from the chirping of birds and insects to the ring of axes on wood and the hum of human voices. More than thirty people lived in the widening clearing and she had been presented to many of them as Mr. Montgomery's wife-to-be.

All of them 'knew' he had gone down the Tidewater to meet her ship, that she had been seasick all the way from Boston and was just now recovering. Men's hats had been tipped to her, women had curtsied and children stared with round eyes until she had been downright embarrassed.

From the grassy bank Mercy gazed at the clearing to set in her mind a full picture of the establishment. Furthest away was the dark green line of wild woodland, which harboured deer and birds for meat. Next to it stood a field of growing corn, then the cottages with their vegetable gardens around them like wreaths. Before the big house two men, supervised and even helped by Jedediah with his one arm, unloaded from a sled cut planks from a saw mill upstream.

Her energy had flagged before she could enter her unfinished home, though from here she could see the avenue of oaks, seedlings too young to cast shade for another generation, that led to its imposing mahogany door under the incomplete porch. It was a larger house than her Uncle Jonathan's and a larger plantation, but she had no fears of being its mistress. She had helped run the Penhall farm when she was younger.

She looked at Edmund, who chewed a stalk of grass like a bumpkin, and asked why he had not yet planted tobacco. He said that they would grow some next year for a cash crop, however he planned to breed fine livestock, horses and bulls and milch cows, and perhaps build another ketch to carry the river traffic. Then he dropped the grass stalk and looked at her gravely.

"It is all risk, Mercy. But if I learned anything from the life I led, it is that nothing in the world is certain or safe. Also there is Queen Anne's War, which has come no closer to us than the mountains to the west, but which may last years longer. Yet I want you to live a settled and happy life."

"Edmund, I too have known change and danger." She reached for his long brown hand where it lay on his knee, and closed her fingers around his. "I am not such a fool that I think life will always be so kind to us as it is today, but let us be happy while we may! Today it is a marvel to me that you are near, that you will not go away to sea or to trial for your life."

He lifted her hand and kissed the small fingers. "A year and a month since when you were my captive, if I had been told I would one day sit with you in a Virginia clearing and hear you speak, I would not have believed it."

She smiled and slipped down to lean on her elbow, keeping hold of his hand. "Nor would I have. God has led us by strange roads, Edmund, to this place."

"And has blessed me to feel like a man again, allowed me to build and plant instead of leaving me to rob and destroy." He touched her cheek. "Mercy, it may be soon to ask, but do you wish to remain a Puritan?"

She shook her head. "That would be awkward, would it not? I saw many faiths side by side in Charles Town, and I have learned that Puritans are not more perfect than others. God does not change because he is preached differently. I will convert to Church of England, and God will hear my prayers as He has always done. We are both Christians, Edmund. That is enough." Something in the back of her mind cackled cruelly, then in the next moment Edmund laughed, and she forgot it.

"Perhaps we had both best turn Quaker and remove to Penn-Sylvania!" He added thoughtfully, in that real voice under the damaged surface tone, "I agree with them at least on two things. Women are of as much import in the world as men, and I cannot abide slavery any more than they. Richard has slaves, but has too tight a business head on his shoulders to treat them any way but well."

His voice went on, speaking of homely things, land and tilling, hunting and houses. Behind them the hundred sounds of people and farm, field and forest, combined to a harmonious whole that lulled her to drowsiness. Edmund's hand was alive and strong and connected her to him, so that there was no longer any need of the invisible cord...

She felt his fingers stroke her forehead and smiled at him sleepily. "I am so lazy."

"Tired, litte one. Time to return to your bed." He stood, and pulled her gently with him.

She leaned against him, though when he slipped an arm under her shoulders ready to lift her she protested. "No, Edmund! I shall never be well if I do not make myself exercise."

"Stubborn, prideful and short-tempered," he pronounced solemnly. And then, "Be damned to Felice!" He kissed her, quickly and hard.

Mercy giggled and kissed him back.

"A touching scene," said an amused, remembered voice, behind them.

****

Mercy's eyes flew open and Edmund laughed, not even surprised.

It was Richard, of course, tall in blue broadcloth and blue-feathered hat, the white lace at his neck and cuffs limp in the heat. He wore the short brown beard he had affected in Charles Town and a brown periwig instead of a blond. But there was no mistaking the hazel eyes or the look in them, undoubtedly entertained.

Edmund's arm still circled Mercy's waist. He extended the other to shake Richard's hand, and smiled. "I had not looked to see you for another se'ennight at least."

"Oh, 'twas a speedy journey. I flew like a knight-errant to the lady's rescue and she had taken charge already. I met their craft halfway down the Delaware and she thanked me for the escort, but I felt assuredly *de trop*. Monsieur's a sick man, though, and I believe I was of some service assisting them to home." He inspected Mercy without pretence and with a lopsided smile. "Edmund left a letter at my house, telling me he'd gone to fetch you. You're skinny, Mistress, but becoming, in that gown."

She smiled and offered him her hand. "I never know whether to laugh at you, or set you down! But since we are to be neighbours, it seems I must bear with you."

He bowed with a flourish and kissed it. "I am pleased to see you also, ma'am. And my name is now Dick Camwell."

Mercy drew herself straight on Edmund's arm. "I am pleased to make your acquaintance, Master Camwell." Her eyes twinkled. "Does your beard really grow that colour, or do you dye it?"

Richard flung up a hand in defence. "God save me, you were easier company when you had no voice!"

Edmund laughed outright. "He is no more really fair, Mercy, than a brown bird in white feathers." He looked his friend over, saw a bulge beneath his left sleeve, and his voice sharpened. "You're injured. What happened?"

"I should like to say that Monsieur was jealous and shot me. But he's no thought for anything except finishing his work, and his fever was only calmed when Madame promised to assist him herself. The dough-faced Dupuis was most put out, but he didn't do this either. Nay, it's a knife cut from an Indian who judged I paid him too little for a bearskin. And indeed I might have, considering what trouble it is to kill a bear..."

"Spare my lady, Richard! I will take her to her nurse, and you may tell me your tale at the house."

Mercy was indignant to be so dismissed, even though her wretched body was tired. "I wish to hear how Soulange is!"

Richard smiled lopsidedly again. "She is in fine health and looks, Mistress, and was mightily anxious when she arrived home to find a letter telling of your troubles. But I'd a message of my own from Ned Turner and was able to convince her you were safe. She sends her love and a letter, and a parcel which she says is yours." He waved toward a big bay gelding tethered to a sapling, which bore two canvas-wrapped packages behind its saddle. "One is yours, the other's the bearskin. Which I suppose I must give to Edmund as a wedding gift."

At the word *wedding* Mercy's knees suddenly trembled, and a small dark cloud seemed to blow across her mind...

Richard's keen eyes narrowed. "You seem a little shaky on your pins, Mistress Mercy."

"It's true I am tired for now." She shook her head to

clear it. She was leg-weary, that was all. "But I will walk again tomorrow."

"Indeed you will. But now you will rest." Edmund's arm tightened around her waist and he turned to his friend. "Richard, go up to the house and send Jedediah to care for your horse. There is a bottle of wine there cooling in a water-cask. Pour a cup for me." He began to guide Mercy toward the cottage.

She looked at Richard over her shoulder. "Richard! I have not thanked you, for saving his life."

His eyes glinted with humour. "Nor berated me for not telling you he survived, when I saw you last." He bowed, cocked an eyebrow, and wandered off.

Mercy watched him go with slight annoyance. "He always manifests himself when least expected!"

"His most endearing trait." Edmund grinned and his eyes crinkled at the corners.

Mercy's irritation vanished and she smiled back. Never again would she harbour hard thoughts of Richard. His conscience was elastic and his other faults many, but his loyalty to his friends was absolute. However, in the cottage, as Edmund bent to take off her shoes, she remembered something else.

"In New Exmouth—he kissed me!"

They were alone, he having sent Mam to collect the parcel Soulange had sent. He stood and looked down at her, eyes darkening. "I know, he told me. You may lay that at my door also, Mercy. I told Richard not to tell you I was alive and to convince you to marry elsewhere, if he could. It seemed at that time the wisest course." But his mouth twitched. "Naturally, he chose the most outrageous means!"

"It does not matter now." She pulled his shirt sleeves with both hands, until he bent over and kissed her himself.

"That cancels it out, does it?" He kissed her cheeks as well, and when he straightened his eyes were warm again. "Sleep, little one. We'll sup together, later." He left the room with swift quiet steps.

Mercy loosened the laces of the gown's bodice and lay back, just as Mam bustled in with the package. Under the twine-tied canvas was another covering of oilskin, and beneath that a length of linen. Inside it all, fragrant with spice bags, was the pink brocade gown Soulange and Sapra had made for her in Charles Town. With it was her writing board. Mercy hugged that to herself a moment, then lay it beside her. It carried a wealth of memories, and gratitude that she no longer needed it.

A small velvet bag, when opened, revealed the dainty necklace of pearls and sapphires she had tried on with the dress—how long ago it seemed! With it was a note in Soulange's flowing hand that read: *A bride gift.*

Bride... She did not know she frowned a moment at the word. Then in another oilskin packet she found the letter, and forgot that prick of uneasiness. She was, however, too tired to read. It would keep for later. She closed her eyes and slipped into peaceful repose.

****

Why did the nightmare return, now when she was so happy? Had she been too joyful? Were John Hanson and the other old grim ministers right after all, and happiness a foolish foible in the stern business of life?

She dreamed that the face of the beggar of Charles Town hung over her, then it became Elias Gorman's bearded visage that leered as it had on the deck of *Thalia*, then the two melted together into one image... Mercy tried to open her eyes, and found she was already awake.

But she must be dreaming, because the face was still there, framed in lank hair and breathing foul breath onto her. Its greenish bloodshot eyes were mad as a rabid dog's.

Mercy screamed and heard only the old bubbling groan escape her throat. An arm clad in stinking rags dragged her from the clean bed.

She staggered as her stockinged feet struck the floor. Then she saw Mam, lying face down and very still on the polished boards. Half a tree branch lay across her back and a trickle of crimson blood seeped from under her turban.

Mercy reached toward her but was caught by the filthy arms of the interloper. The overpowering smell and solidity of the bag of rags, its voice that rasped and cackled, convinced her at last that what she saw and felt was real.

"I got you, mute, I got you! I can nay git near 'im for 'is watchdog, but I got you! Left me t' die in th' sea, they thinked. They beat the hangman, they thinked. Maybe I can nay git them, but I got 'is Puritan, 'is dumb whore!"

He did not know she could speak. The discovery was like ice on her brain. It chilled panic before it could rise up. She must scream for help - but not here. Here she might not be heard by any save women and children. She must get outside, get past him to the front door of the cottage, be seen and heard from the big house. She tried to push the face away. And when she lifted her hands she found her wrists had been lashed together with twine.

She kicked out at the creature's shins. One of its hands struck her on the arm, though the other still held her fast. She kicked again, but Edmund had removed her shoes when he lay her down and her foot had no more effect than a babe's. It was useless to resist, for the moment. She must find some other way to escape him...

She felt her gown, loosened for sleep, slip down her arms. She tried to shrug the sleeves up again. Her shoulders were seized cruelly hard. Fingers like blunt talons dug into her bare white flesh. The face thrust closer, yellow teeth bared.

"Kept it for 'imself, would nay let me 'ave it. But I'll 'ave it, I will. Now, on this nice sof' bed? Nay, nay, got to git away first, 'e might come. I'll 'ave it in the woods, then sell it like we shoulda done... Or slit its throat, leave it for 'im to find..."

The horrible words quickened her instinct to defend herself, to fight. But no, no, she must think, she must be careful. Gorman was mad but he knew he could do nothing here, so close to other people. She must be passive, until he took her outside—then she must free herself. She stood still and tried not to flinch. She turned her face away to breathe cleaner air than his breath, and so that he could not see her eyes.

The hand held her shoulder, like a beast's claw would a kill. The voice muttered, more to its owner than herself, "Like t' wait an' kill 'im... He'll be comin' to visit it, nights." The cracked lip wrinkled lecherously. Gorman had no notion that Edmund had never taken her body. "Tie 'em up, gag the nigra, have 'em both, hide, kill 'im when 'e comes?" He actually scratched his head with his free hand.

This animal planned to rob her of the gift that was for Edmund, and to hurt Mam as well. Mercy sickened inside, yet she tried to twist away from the one hand that held her. Then she saw a pistol and a cutlass hung across his rags, and held still. He could kill her. And she very badly wanted to live. But she had seen Felice's striped bodice rise and fall with the breath of life. She prayed he would not notice it.

With one ear she listened to the creature's meanderings. With the other she strained to hear sounds from beyond the cottage. There was a lazy buzz of humanity and insects... It must be near noon, and the people here ate in the middle of the day. There was no sound of hammer and saw from the big house, but Edmund and Richard were probably there...

Gorman chuckled suddenly, a sound like the rattle of a rusty anchor chain. His voice, like her own and like Edmund's, was damaged, as if some like curse bound the three of them together...

"Collyer, he nay knew me," he bragged, half to Mercy, half to himself. "I knew 'im, though, knew the cut o' his sails, 'spite o' 'is new colours. Like t' kill 'im too. An' Bullen. Collyer, 'e 'ad a liddle new ship there in Charles Town. I heared 'im, talkin' t' that Frenchie jade on th' wharf—no 'un takes notice o' a beggar..." He coughed thickly then spat on the clean floorboards.

Mercy remained motionless. She breathed slowly. She hoped and waited for the madman to become bemused by his own wanderings, to give her a chance. He shook her shoulder and cackled rustily again. She steeled herself not to shudder.

"Needed 'nother hand, they did, an' I came up to V'ginia on 'is own craft. Kep' my face outter his way, but he nay saw me. Stopped at Will'msburg they did, then came to 'is wharf 'ere. Slipped overside I did, an' follered 'im." He sniggered at his own cleverness.

Mercy hoped this long-winded boast would continue. He might lose his train of thought, forget his threats. Then Felice stirred and groaned on the sunlit floor. Gorman's mutterings ceased. He scowled down at her and

Mercy braced herself. If he threatened Mam, she must leap between them. But instead he pushed Mercy ahead of him, out of the bedchamber. Mercy noticed that he limped, badly.

He talked to himself some more. "Only a nigra, nay worth trouble. We'll git out by back, same way I come in. Move, Puritan! An' nay try t' run off, or I run you through." He drew the cutlass with his free hand...

Chapter Seventeen

Mercy's room opened into a modest kitchen-parlour with nothing in it except a pine table, a bench and a few iron pots in an open fireplace. As Gorman pushed her along she saw Mam's room to the right of it. The parlour opened into a small store room, and in its back wall a narrow plank door stood open. Gorman had simply walked in, then. Mam would not have thought to lock it, in this quiet place...

He jerked her outside, onto a path of beaten earth between sweet-potato mounds and rows of growing squash and beans. The back garden had a wall, green saplings cut off at a height of six feet. Edmund had told her, one day as she listened dreamily to his voice, that he had ordered it built to give her privacy. Instead, it had aided Gorman to slip in unseen.

Mercy bit her lips. She could not allow Gorman to cause Edmund any more grief.

A gate of saplings stood open in the fence. Beyond it she saw the nanny goat on a long rope, grazing a strip of cleared land. Beyond again was uncleared woodland. He pushed her against the saplings while he peered out. Even the way he swivelled his neck to look made him seem like an animal.

Mercy panted a little, to seem weak. But the quick breathing dragged terror up into her throat. She had to breathe deeply again to calm herself. *Think.* He would drag her into the woods. Therefore she must break away from him outside the gate and run for the sledge track. Her cottage, she thanked God, was first in the row, and right beside the track. And she wore the white dress. She would stand out against the green summer grass like a moth in a cabbage patch.

He stared out to his right. Someone must be in sight.

She did not dare run now, he would stop her with ease. His smell filled her nostrils, churned her stomach. There were small sharp pains in her shoulder where his fingers dug into it. Then suddenly he dropped them and seized her bound hands.

"She gone inside. We walk like friends, proper folk, to th' trees. No hurryin'. You unnerstan', Puritan?" Her chin jerked down in a nod and he pulled her forward. His big dirty paw hid the twine on her wrists.

Two small Negro children in coloured shirts played with straw dolls on the back stoop of the cottage two doors away. They looked up, but were plainly too young to understand that anything was wrong.

Ten yards to Mercy's left ran the shallow ruts of the sledge tracks that led to the big house. It was imperative that when she cried out the call be loud. It must alert all within hearing. She did not know if her voice was strong enough. And Gorman's hold on her small wrists was like a bear's. She would need to surprise him somehow, to make him release her. Then she must if possible avoid both the cutlass, and the pistol—if it was primed.

Halfway across to the wood, she prayed. She decided what to do, swallowed her fear, and acted.

"Elias Gorman, take your filthy hand from me!" She tried to copy Edmund's voice, clear, cold, and commanding.

He turned toward her in slow surprise. Then he realised the dumb woman had spoken. His glittering greenish eyes popped to show the whites, all yellow. He moaned as if he saw a ghost. But the grip of his fist tightened.

Mercy was desperate. She spoke again, the first words that came to her head. "Drop your weapons! Edmund Gramercy and Captain Collyer are behind you, and armed!"

He shrieked this time, when he heard her. Then the meaning of the words sank into his deranged mind. He swivelled about to face his enemies. He raised the cutlass and grabbed for the pistol. He was probably not even aware he released her hands to brandish both weapons.

Mercy ran for the track. Her body was unevenly balanced with hands tied before her and she stumbled, but she ran with all her heart and strength. This was her only chance.

She heard a high-pitched oath as Gorman saw no enemies behind him. Then over her sharp breathing she heard his feet pound as he started after her. His step broke and he wildly cursed the nanny goat for getting its tether in his way. She heard the animal bleat, then heard the pistol crack.

He had killed the goat! But others would have heard the pistol shot... She ran straight a few more steps. She reached the place on the track that was abreast of the front door of her cottage. She screamed with all her strength.

"Edmund! Help! Help me!"

The unfinished house—home!—lay two hundred yards before her, warm and solid and peaceful in the mid-day sun. Mercy saw the two men rise from beside a deal table near one of the oak columns of the incomplete porch. She saw tankards fall to the table, chairs flung aside. Richard turned back a stride to seize a wooden stave that leaned against the wall.

Edmund flung his body from standing to running in a single instant. He ran toward her, weaponless.

Mercy tried to scream again, who it was behind her, that he was armed. But her over-taxed voice failed her. The words emerged only as breathless cries. Then she heard the thudding feet at her back, one step long and one step short in a limping run. She heard the voice shriek like a beast's again.

She had thought Gorman would head for the woods, to escape. She had not taken into account that he was mad and did not think sense. She tried to run faster. Her stockinged feet caught in the white gown's hem. She stumbled, but did not fall. Behind her she heard the cracked voice shout again. Its pitch was insanely high.

"I'll do for you, you witch! An' then for 'im!"

Witch!

The word caught her between the shoulder blades like a pistol ball, like a thrown knife. She tripped in mid-stride and this time fell. Her tied hands struck the dirt, her head fell onto them. Her legs tangled in the petticoat. And her courage drained from her. A sob of pure fear tore from her throat.

She struggled to her feet again, but slowly. Her legs felt like lead and had to be dragged forward. Everything else seemed to move slowly too, as if her mind and eyes were caught by the same weight as her limbs. The running figures of Edmund and Richard took an age for each step, and Jedediah, rounding a corner of the house and lumbering after them, was a huge tortoise. Negro folk and white emerged from the cottages, lifted their arms to point, and cried out, all as slowly as in a dream...

Her vision narrowed to one figure only, Edmund, as he leaped ever nearer, face set hard beneath its tan, dark hair streaming... The world sped again. And her ears heard how fast the unmatched steps pursued her and how fast came its breath, in screeches like a swooping bat's, and how fast came her own breath, in sobs...

The thing behind her was beggar and pirate and all sorrow from the past and she must run faster, reach Edmund before it caught her, reach Edmund and be safe...

The beast had the lesser distance to run. It caught her skirt, dragged at it. She twisted her body away, heard and felt the thin muslin rip. She staggered two more steps, weeping, then a beast's claw tangled in her hair and jerked her head backward. She tottered, off balance, and her hair was freed but the arm-shaped rags seized her waist. She was hauled back against the foully clothed body.

The creature's other arm flung around her as well and her breath choked with the stink. But this arm bore the cutlass. The dirty blade, murky even in sunlight, struck upwards over the white lace on her ribs and between her linen covered breasts, sliced more fabric until its point rested like a snake's tooth at the base of her throat. Cold steel kissed the very place that Edmund's warm lips had caressed short hours before.

The speeding picture before her eyes froze into a tableau. Edmund stopped, five short yards before her. Every line of his body was taut, except for his hands, which hung unnaturally loose at his sides. His lips were thin, his eyes dark. Richard, one step behind, stuck the end of his stave into the dirt of the track, frowned and shoved his hands into his pockets. Jedediah came to a halt like a great horse reined in.

Edmund shouted to the people from the cottages, "Stop!" without taking his eyes off Mercy and Gorman. The running farm folk stayed where they were, stared and murmured. Edmund's eyes for one second were haunted, he saw a ghost from the past. Then the cold mask of Captain Gramercy froze his face.

"Gorman," he said flatly. Then, his rough voice icy and calm, "Let her go. You can't escape all of us."

"But I can kill your doxy first—Cap'n." The creature panted hotly above Mercy's head, then it cackled with hysteria. "I heared—folks talk in front o' beggars like they's nay there—I heared Collyer say they did nay hang you. Jus' strangled your voice box a mite, it seem. Like mine wit' th' fire an' sea water." The shaggy head turned back and forth, took in the number of its adversaries. "Nay. I'm takin' her wit' me. Don't nobody move or I cut 'er throat." He began to back off, lurching on his bad leg, dragging Mercy with him.

Edmund stood unmoving as a rock. "If you do, I kill you myself, if I have to follow you to hell." His voice was harsh through every tone. "Loose her."

"You'll nay do anythin' that'll git 'er kilt. Unreasonin' soft on 'er, you always was." Gorman backed another step in the sledge rut, then halted. His breath rasped like a saw through a log. It had done him no good, to run.

With every rising breath, Mercy felt the point of steel prick the skin of her throat. But anger rose in her, stronger than fear. This vile creature had no right to her life. She had missed her first chance to escape him. Now she must try again. Edmund and the others could do nothing while the cutlass threatened her. If she wore shoes she could kick backward, if his hand was closer she could bite it. But then he would kill her before Edmund's very eyes.

What could she do? Her flesh crawled at the touch of the dirty body. Yet she felt the labour of his chest on her back and knew he was near winded. If only her hands were unbound... Very slowly she moved her tied wrists to the right. If she could get one elbow clear of her body perhaps she could drive it backward into his belly, make him drop the blade for one instant, long enough for her to run...

Edmund's eyes met hers. For a moment he looked into them deeply, and she saw a glimmer of light in his. He spoke softly and intimately, as if they were alone. "Keep your temper, little one."

He meant for her to be still, to do nothing, to leave everything to him. Her anger switched even to Edmund. Surely he had sufficient faith in her to know she was ready to do what she must, when she could! However she winked one blue eye, with a trembling lid, to let him know she had understood. She was unable to nod—to do so would draw the cutlass point into her neck.

Richard casually joined the strange conversation. "How come you're alive, Gorman? We all swore you'd drowned."

As an attempt at distraction, it failed. Gorman did not even glance at him. Mercy could feel by the angle of his hairy chin that he never took his gaze from Edmund. He cackled, as if Collyer's words were a joke, but uncertainly. Perhaps he had begun to see that he had no chance of escape. The claw that held the cutlass shook.

Edmund's eyes, now fixed above Mercy's head on those of his former lieutenant, narrowed. He spoke this time with cold control. "Leave her be, and I give you my word I'll let you go alive. With a handful of guineas to boot."

The creature screeched in a passion of hatred. "Your word! Aye, you'd gimme money, then take the woman an' kill me, an' take it back!" The cutlass wavered dangerously.

"No. That is what you would do, not I." Edmund extended his left arm and pointed south, toward the James River. "I'd want you away, yes. But I'd have you taken down the Tidewater to Norfolk. I'd give you passage money to England, and more. The choice is yours. Money in your pocket and away from here with a whole skin, or harm the lady and be killed."

"I nay trus' you!"

Richard said mildly, "But Edmund's a man who keeps his word, you know that. It sounds like a fair trade to me, Master Gorman."

Jedediah, who had loomed large behind Edmund all this while, spat contemptuously to one side. "He woulden know. He never did have no brains."

"You, Bullen, you great donkey! I'll cut your other arm off!" Gorman was so enraged he actually shook the cutlass in Jedediah's direction.

Mercy saw the blade swish through the air in an arc. It was quite six inches from her neck. She felt the arm that held it quiver violently. *Time to act.*

She bent her head sideways then threw her small body to the left. The arm dragged on her waist. She swung her tied fists around and hit Gorman in the midriff. He no more than staggered. She knew she could not hurt him, only distract him.

And distracted from the others he was, with a vengeance. He screamed foul words then struck at her. She felt the cutlass slide across the back of her neck. But the blow was wild and did not have the madman's full strength behind it. The blade tangled in her thick fair curls. She felt only a burning sting, like John Hanson's whip... Then she lost balance and fell sidelong into the dirt.

She was there for the barest instant. Edmund had leapt forward the second he saw her move. He seized her shoulders, jerked her to her feet then backward with him, and thrust her behind the shelter of his own body. Gorman plunged toward them, slashed the cutlass madly from side to side.

Edmund ordered coldly, "Stand where you are, Gorman!" He counted on the effect of his voice, the voice Gorman had obeyed during ship actions.

The madman did waver a moment. But Edmund was unarmed. The pirate grinned horribly and stumbled one step closer. The arc of the cutlass narrowed, swung now to the width of Edmund's body.

Jedediah drew from the ground the stave Richard had set there. He stepped up beside his master and pushed the point toward Gorman. Richard took his right hand from his pocket, and in it was the smallest pistol Mercy had ever seen. He pulled the hammer back. The tiny sound was as distinct as a shot in the tense silence of the clearing.

Gorman halted before the weapons. His eyes blazed with a sick green fire and his breath hissed through the gaps in his teeth.

Richard spoke, in his normal equable tones. "You may have escaped the sea, my lad. But you're a dead man now."

The pirate's eyes dilated, greenish and yellow like rotten eggs. His face contorted with thwarted rage. He shrieked and rushed at them, swinging the blade.

Edmund pushed Mercy at Richard, who caught her on his free arm. He held the pistol steady in the other hand but did not fire. Mercy wondered wildly if it was even loaded.

Edmund sprang forward. He stepped to one side of the thrusting cutlass and seized the arm that held it. He swung the ragged body completely around, away from Mercy and the other two men.

Richard released her and turned the pistol around to grasp the barrel, to use the butt as a small club. *It was not loaded, then.* Jedediah pointed the stave to Gorman's chest.

Edmund shouted to both of them, "Leave him! He's mine to kill!"

He squeezed the thick wrist. Gorman grunted but did not release the cutlass hilt. Instead with a maniac's strength he barrelled his whole body into Edmund's. Edmund fell. He still held the sword arm and deflected the cutlass past him harmlessly into the dirt. Gorman was brought down with it and fell on top of Edmund.

His breath expelled in a whoosh. He had enough strength to pummel his former captain with his left fist, and all the while tried to wrench the other free of Edmund's grip. He wasted breath screeching and swearing, but Edmund ignored both his words and the wild blows that fell on his face and chest.

Without loosing Gorman's wrist he lifted his whole body sideways. They saw his face tighten with the effort but he took the heavier man with him. Gorman, unbalanced, suddenly found himself on his back like a tortoise flipped off its feet. Edmund dropped to sit astride his body.

The three onlookers saw the creature's mouth open

and heard it groan for air. Gorman had exhausted even the unnatural strength of the insane. He lay spent and gasped for breath. Edmund tore the cutlass from his grasp.

They saw his eyes roll as Edmund raised the blade in the air. They heard his last groaning scream as Edmund brought it down strongly and swiftly and plunged it into his chest. They heard the terrible crunch and suck of steel as it scraped on bone and then entered flesh.

The body shuddered along its whole length then flopped like a scarecrow and lay absolutely still, without life. Like an obscene afterthought red blood spurted from the wound like a fountain, then sank back into a crimson pool that stained the filthy rags. The cutlass leaned from the thing at an angle, like a crooked grave marker.

Edmund stood slowly. His chest heaved and his eyes were fixed on the body. Blood stained his hands red and darkened the front of his shirt and breeches.

Richard was the first to move. He strode forward, bent over the corpse and after a moment said, quite matter-of-factly, "Dead." He planted one boot on its chest, drew out the cutlass carefully so that the blood did not stain his clothes, and dropped it back flat onto the bundle of rags. Jedediah stood and stared, licked his lips a little. His breath rasped and he leaned on the stave with his good arm.

The silence in the clearing was now one of shock. Then the watchers broke into movement and sound, men's voices pitched high, a woman's hysterical cry cut short, a child's squall hushed.

Richard called to them, "Go back to your meals and your work. The madman's dead, whoever he was. 'Tis finished." He returned the pistol nonchalantly to his pocket.

The people drifted away to their cottages. Some looked back over their shoulders. Two or three men stood looking for longer, then shrugged and departed after the others.

Richard told Edmund coolly, "None of them were close enough to hear what was said."

Jedediah grunted. "Anyways, they knows which side their bread's buttered on."

"It doesn't matter." Edmund did not look at either of them. He took two long strides toward Mercy.

She had stood frozen during the brief fight, had felt nothing except fear for Edmund. Now that it was all over she felt her legs shake. She was drained of strength, but she stumbled toward him.

He tore the cord off her hands and seized her by the shoulders. One was still bare, and beginning to bruise where Gorman's fingers had grasped it.

He demanded hoarsely, "Are you hurt?"

She shook her head jerkily. She trembled all over now, and completely forgot the sword scratch on her scalp. She saw Jedediah go down heavily on one knee to close Gorman's staring eyes, and choked.

"Mercy, don't lose your voice again! Say yea or nay."

"N-no, I am not hurt." Then she understood suddenly the fear in his eyes. "Not—not in any way."

He closed her tightly within his arms, kissed her face and whispered fiercely in her ear. "God be thanked! I thought I had lost you forever, this time." He felt her tremors, held her even closer and pressed her head onto his shoulder.

She noticed vaguely that his shirt was wet, however had remembered something far more important. "Edmund, he was on the wharf at Charles Town, when Soulange took us through the gate and we boarded the *Dart*. I did not recognise him! And it must have been he who sent the Navy after us!"

"Yes," he said slowly. "But be easy now. It's over, already past." He spoke over her head to Richard. "Take the body away. I won't have it buried on my land."

"Aye, lad. 'Tis the least I can do. But how did he get here?"

"On your own ship," Mercy whispered. "He boasted of it."

"And I didn't see him. Well, no matter now." Richard rubbed his beard, then asked Jedediah to hitch a sled behind his horse and bring both here. His hazel eyes were intent on Mercy and Edmund. "I shall visit in a few days, to see how your lady does." He smiled oddly. "You would make a good soldier, Mistress."

She shook her head numbly, clung to Edmund and

felt anything but brave.

Edmund said in a voice still harsh, "Yes, Mercy. You kept your head, and then you used it." He felt her shoulders heave and whispered hoarsely, "Cry if you wish. Tears will wash it all away."

Strangely enough, she did not want to cry. She shook her head again. Richard's hand gripped her arm an instant then she heard his steps, long and brisk, follow after Jedediah's plodding ones. She looked past Edmund's arm, to reassure herself that the clearing had indeed returned to peace. She saw a man, grizzled and square-faced, who had been one of those who watched longest and said least, drop a ragged blanket over the dead thing...

Then suddenly she recalled Felice, and jerked her chin up to look at Edmund. "It is Mam who is hurt! He hit her with a club!"

The square-faced man said stolidly, "My woman an' Marta gone in to see to 'er, already."

"Thank you, Jotham. Go now, help Jedediah and the Captain with the sledge."

"Aye." He stumped away.

Edmund swung Mercy up into his arms and bore her to the cottage, only yards away. She saw her torn skirt fall aside, saw how dirty it was and said witlessly, "The gown is ruined."

"Be damned to it! There are more gowns in the world. Your senses are scattered, Mercy. It happens to soldiers, after a fight." He carried her in through the open door. On the floor of the little parlour two women tended Felice— obviously they had pulled her out from the bedchamber. They had unfastened her turban and her tightly curled head rested on a cushion. He asked curtly, "How does she?"

One of the women was the young Creole Mercy had seen talking to Mam only that morning. The other was older, one of the white bond-servants, and it was she who answered.

"She got a liddle crack behind the ear and still be stunned. But her woolly head and her turban saved her from worser." The woman was pale, though not agitated. "What of Mistress?"

"Mistress is only spent, Bab. I'll take care of her 'til

you have seen to Felice. Can you and Marta lift her onto her own bed? Or do you need my help?"

"No, sir, we can do it."

Without another word Edmund carried Mercy into her room, shut the door with his foot and dropped with her down into Mam's chair. He rocked her like a child.

Mercy felt him tremble and forgot her shock and exhaustion. She wrapped her arms around him, pressed his head onto her breasts and dropped kisses on his hair. Equally as much as she needed him to hold her, she wanted to hold him, to give comfort. She whispered husky endearments and repeated his own words.

"Hush. It is over, it is done."

"Mercy, love, he should not have been able to reach you at all!" He lifted his head and took her face between his shaking hands. "When I came here the garrison officers in Williamsburg advised me to build a palisade around the home clearing, in case of trouble with the French or Indians, at least to keep out wolves and bears. But I would not." His eyes fired with anger, directed at himself. "I wanted to live like a free man, not a prisoner. And that foolhardiness almost cost you your life!"

This was not a thing to be chased away with a finger on the lips and the word, *past*. She smiled and said, "I prefer danger with you than safety elsewhere. Remember that. As for a barricade, build one if it is sense. But do not grieve over it." Her throat was hoarse, and she coughed.

He reached behind him for the water jug, made her drink from it, set it down and held her to him again. "It is not only that." He spoke slowly, unused to talking of his feelings. "Little one, it is as if a curse follows me. That the past will never release me." He felt her suddenly still, and swearing at himself for his inconsideration he stood with her in his arms and lay her on the bed.

"God!" He stared at her, and then at his own clothes and his hands. "The blood—it's all over your gown. And on your cheek and shoulder. It came from me." He set his mouth grimly, lifted her to a sitting position and quickly drew the unlaced gown over her head. He rolled it into a ball, but not before Mercy saw the crimson patches of Gorman's death blood on its sleeves, its bodice, its skirt.

Edmund saw her face white under the streak of red,

and thought he understood. He took a handful of lace-edged kerchiefs from the dressing table, dipped them in the jug and knelt beside the bed to wash her face and the satin skin of her shoulder. He dabbed carefully at the long scratch under her hair, and became calmer himself, believing he could reassure her.

"You are the practical one of the two of us, yet I hope I learn. I will burn the gown and the things I wear. Then it only takes washing and clean clothes, and we start over again. We were both right, it is already past." He smiled at her. "What happened has done us a favour, by showing our lack of defences. Captain Gramercy would have taken military precautions, but Edmund Montgomery has been a fool. I will order trees lopped for the palisade, and the work to start."

Mercy could find no words. It cost her effort, but she nodded.

"Mercy, Gorman was the last ghost that could trouble us, and he is gone." His eyes began to glint with the gold lights she loved. "Nothing can now rob us of the future."

She could not look at him, and stared past his shoulder. However he had turned away a moment to rinse his hands and did not notice. When he turned back he saw only some pain in her eyes. He took her small limp hands in his, thinking again that he understood.

"You're exhausted. Rest. When you wake the world will be as it was again. Better." His voice was calm under the rough first tones. He bent and kissed her eyelids and lips, lightly.

Before he could wonder at her lack of response, a knock sounded at the door. At his word Bab bustled in with a basin of water and clean linen, and he kissed Mercy's hand and went out. He scooped up the red and white bundle of the spoiled gown and took it with him and told Bab he would send brandy down from the house, Mistress might need it.

Mistress. At last the pain closed Mercy's eyes, and she did not see Edmund go. She only heard his footsteps fade from hearing.

She opened her eyes then, yet comprehended nothing that they saw. She moved stiffly as a doll at Bab's directions, was washed more, had the thin line of her own blood rinsed from her hair and salve smoothed onto the cut across her neck. The woman brushed her hair in merciful silence, avoiding the mark of the cutlass, and stripped off her linen petticoat. It also was lightly stained, and when Bab drew off her stockings Mercy saw they were torn and dirty.

The woman washed her feet, helped her into the shift she had taken off that morning, so long ago, gave her more water to drink and eased her back onto the pillow.

"You be well soon, ma'am," she said kindly. "Dose o' brandy'll help, I leave it beside you when Master sends it down. But you sleep it all off, now."

Mercy pretended complete weariness and closed her eyes. She heard the woman tiptoe out. But then she could not bear the darkness behind her eyelids, and lifted them. The sunny room, the fair summer's day outside, the workaday sounds and smells that drifted in through the window—all mocked her. Clean clothes and clean skin would not help, sleep and the kindness of others and Edmund's love would change nothing.

Witch. Gorman had said it as a curse, not knowing its truth. She was still what she was. It was she who was the curse, she who had brought her tainted blood into Edmund's new life. This lovely little world of theirs, that had barely begun to be built, might as well be lying about her in ruins. She had been sick, then happy, and had actually forgotten.

She could marry no one, least of all the man she loved.

****

Mercy told Edmund the next day that she would not wed him, and that she wanted to leave his farm.

She had intended to do it the evening before. He had come then to tell her he had arranged a roster of the men to stand guard at her cottage day and night until the big house was fit for her to live in. There had always been a watch at night, and to extend it into the day took men away from their work. But that would be the price of safety, until the palisade was erected.

"It's likely a case of closing the stable door after the horse has bolted." He had smiled. "But I'll not put you at one ounce of risk, Mercy, before we are wed or after."

It had been the ideal opening, yet her courage had failed. She had merely nodded. She knew from her mirror she was pale and sad, but he clearly believed it was from the shock of her experience. He did not stay long and left her to rest, kissing, gently, no more than her cheek.

Mam, getting about with an even thicker turban from the bandage beneath it, heard her weeping that night. She patted her hand and stroked her head and sang to her, and plainly thought the same thing Edmund had.

Mercy had read Soulange's letter before candlelight. Only one day earlier she would have rejoiced at the loving good wishes which her friend had written in the first sentence. But the rest of the letter touched on the thing that beset her mind, and seemed to confirm that her decision was the right one.

Cherie, there is no need now to offer you a home with me. But do not forget that if ever life takes one of its strange turns, a refuge awaits you under Monsieur's roof.

For now, dearly as I wish to be a witness at your wedding, I cannot undertake another journey while Monsieur needs me. I see his frustration at his own weakness and must help him all I can with his work. And I am fond of him, as well as in his debt.

Mercie, since my own marriage has changed in form, I presume on our friendship to advise you on yours. From the very first day of our acquaintance I sensed a reserve in you, something about yourself you held back, even from me. When you regained your voice it remained, a thing you would not speak of.

Ma petite, your marriage will be different from mine because it begins with love on both sides. But Edmund Montgomery is like Riccard, like myself. He has lived too hard to be easily deceived. There must be nothing less than truth between you.

If there is something you fear to tell him, I pray you will draw upon that great courage of yours, and speak it out. Because, living closely together, he will soon perceive that reserve and question it. And any secret you bear is best told him from your own lips.

You know that I write this hard thing out of love for you and concern. I look at the words and they seem but errant imaginings, set down so nakedly. But in my own heart I know there is something in yours that must be brought into the light of day, and vanquished. Courage, courage! Think of my own case. Nothing can be worse than that.

I beg that you and Edmund visit us in Charles Town when you are able. Before that, send me a letter. My friend Riccard will travel this way at some time, and will carry it for you.

I remain always your dear and loving friend, Soulange.

No, Soulange, thought Mercy miserably, there is one thing worse than having been a whore. I cannot tell him the truth. Better he hate me for leaving him, than recoil from me because of the evil I carry.

She slept little that night, and called herself a coward because she had not told Edmund what she must. In the morning she could not eat, or drink anything but a few mouthfuls of coffee. *Ninny-broth.* She remained silent when Felice scolded her for her poor appetite, then pushed her cup away and asked Mam to help her dress in the gown of pink brocade Soulange had sent.

The blue silk gown in the armoire, all the pretty things Edmund had bought and Mam had made for her, must be left here. She had no right to them. Even so, she needed to borrow a shift, stockings, petticoat and shoes. Her own torn and dirty underthings had been thrown overboard from *Prospero.* All these bride clothes, all he had done to bring her from New Exmouth, were for nothing.

In time, she told herself, he would forget the ungrateful Puritan, and now that he was a landed gentleman would have no trouble finding another wife... On the pain of this thought she sent Mam to fetch him.

Chapter Eighteen

Mercy sat on the oaken stool before the dressing table, clasped her hands tightly in her lap and blanked her mind of everything but what she must say. She closed her heart behind a shield of her will. His presence must not melt her resolve. It was for his own sake.

He knocked softly at the open door. She stood, and asked Mam formally to wait outside while she spoke to the Captain. Mam went off, puzzled and grumbling.

"How pretty you look!" Edmund walked to her with confidence and gently grasped her shoulders. His eyes were golden with admiration and his smile equally warm. "Why did you want to see me, Mercy?"

He wore his workaday indigo-dyed shirt and leather breeches. His features were relaxed, his hands strong. The feel of them, now, was sweetly familiar. His closeness still stirred her blood just as it had on *Thalia.*

"Sir, I must ask you not to touch me."

His hands tightened and he frowned. He stared into her eyes, and she hoped he found them cool. Yet he did not seem overly perturbed. He probably thought she had some female peevishness on her mind, or some residue of fright to tell him of. Obviously he was prepared to humour her, because he dropped his hands.

"Tell me, little one, what troubles you." His voice was gentle. She hardly noticed now its rough upper tone. "Then walk up to the house with me. You've not yet seen inside it, and there are things I wish your opinion of."

"That is not necessary. I will never live there." He would not believe her unless she said it baldly. Her hands, gripped together over the pink skirt, tightened. "Sir, I regret that I led you to believe otherwise, but I find now that I have made a mistake. I cannot, I will not, wed you. If I disappoint you, I beg your pardon. But I will not

301

change my mind."

The warmth slowly drained from his eyes, and the smile faded from his mouth. A look of wariness took their place, as if the pirate had discovered an enemy in his camp.

"Why, Mercy?"

"It does not matter why." She could not say she did not love him. That was a lie she knew she could not carry off. "I ask only that you arrange passages for myself and Mam—if she chooses to come with me—to Charles Town. I will stay with Madame de Vaugeret. If that does not suit, I may return to New England." She did not really know where she would go, however that was not this moment's consideration.

"It does matter." He crossed his arms over his chest. Now his look was grim and his voice harsh through all its tones. "Yesterday you loved me. Today you say you will not be my wife, that you wish to leave me. *Why, Mercy?*"

"It is finished, that is all." She lifted her chin, to seem haughty. That was difficult, when one was small and needed to look up at the other person. But she must make him accept her words and not probe further, because there was no explanation she could give him. She added desperately, "I find I have been mistaken in my regard for you, after all."

"You spare my feelings and will not speak it aloud. Therefore I will be the one who says it." The cold mask of Captain Gramercy was almost back in place. But his voice, though hard, was charged with passion. "Yesterday you saw me kill a man as I would a mad dog. You saw blood on my hands and I stained you with that blood. You have remembered that I was a pirate, and find you cannot forgive me for it after all."

It had not entered her head that he would think such a thing. He had protected her from Gorman, saved her life. And she had always understood that he had been as much a prisoner on the *Thalia* as she had been. But—if he chose to believe that, then she would make it easier for both of them by allowing him the belief.

She said coolly, "If you wish," and forced a shrug.

They stared at each other. She stood rock still and apparently was calm. He seemed to search her face for a ray of hope, and when he did not find one he turned cold, cold. He bowed suddenly, stiffly.

"Very well, Mistress. I should have known. Once a Puritan, always a Puritan. I will send a message to Ben Heslett to ready the *Dragonfly* to leave for Charles Town. Are you certain you are fit to travel?" The voice was expressionless at last, icily polite.

"Yes, I thank you." She also was coldly polite.

He spun on his heel and marched to the door, then halted there, his back straight as a ramrod. He turned abruptly. A hint of feeling warmed his voice once more, and lit tiny sparks in his eyes.

"Mercy, I have never begged before in my life. But I beg you now, with all my heart, to forgive me for the crimes of my past. You are my reason for trying life anew. You are my hope to live like a man, and not a beast. Do not leave me." He held his hand toward her, plainly not knowing he did it.

She had known her heart would break, but not that it would crack so wide she would feel as if her body split in half as well and fell upon the floor in pieces. She shut all that away, and willed strength into her voice at least.

"Sir, one single person, even a wife, cannot be responsible for another. I believe you have sufficient character to build your plantation here on your own. If you need a woman to provide you with heirs"—*ah, how that hurt!*—"as a land owner of substance you will find a wife without trouble." She made her shoulders lift in another shrug. "I wish you well."

"Very well then." His hand dropped and the mask settled at last into place. It was worse than cold, it was bitter. His eyes flashed briefly with another flame, the one that had been reserved for Gorman his enemy, and cruel circumstance. "It is finished."

He walked away, and left her there alone.

****

It was Bab's husband, Jotham Paddock, who took Edmund's message to the James River mooring and returned the next day with Ben's answer. This was that it would take at least two days to complete some small repairs on the ketch and to provision her for the sea journey south to Carolina.

Therefore, for that day and for the two after it, Mercy did not stir from the cottage except to exercise in the enclosed back garden. She felt a prisoner again, and longed to be away, to cut clean that invisible cord that bound her to Edmund. At the same time she despaired, for where in the world could she go, after she left Soulange?

The marvel was that though her heart was sick, her stubborn body regained its health. Her mind believed she could not eat but her flesh hungered for food. She helped Mam to prepare their meals at the little hearth and ate well of them. She thought, *if he hears that I dine with such appetite, he'll know for sure I am heartless.*

If only she had remembered on the *Prospero* or while she lay here sick, that to marry Edmund was impossible! But she had not and had lived in a fool's paradise, until that one word had destroyed it. Before she met Edmund she had not believed that a woman needed to love a man to be happy. Now she must prove that again to herself. Old maids often lived long and she might survive many more years.

And what could she do to support herself? Become a children's nurse or governess or housemaid? A woman could not live alone...

However at present she had no heart to plan any future. Nor did it help that she knew Edmund must feel the same. She prayed he really would find a woman to marry, yet jealousy spoiled the prayer. She could not imagine Edmund trusting any female but herself to see the tender soul under the armour of the pirate.

Because she knew his heart was soft she also knew how much she had hurt him, and the knowledge increased her own pain. Their short hours of happiness had now cost them dearly. As Soulange had said, the prices one paid in life were always too high.

During those days he did not approach her. Work on the big house and the beginnings of the palisade did not cease, but rather increased in intensity. Mercy understood that. Like herself he did not have the temperament to sit in corners and grieve, therefore he sought solace in work.

She wished that she herself had some task to occupy her hands. She had seldom in her life been idle, and not to be busy meant that the mind wandered...

She borrowed an apron from Mam and pulled up every weed in the garden. She milked the goat, that Edmund had sent to replace the one Gorman had killed, each day. She set the cottage in order. She could have spent all her time sewing garments from some of the materials in the armoire, if her pride had not baulked at making clothes for Edmund's future wife.

On the second morning Mam told her that Cap'n Montgomery had ridden into the woods alone, with a flintlock and a knife, to hunt. There were wildcats there, she reproached, as if the presence of beasts was also Mercy's fault. However he returned safely many hours later with the carcass of a white-tailed deer across his saddle, and courteously sent cuts of venison for their dinner. No message came with the meat, but Mam thanked pointedly the Negro youth, called Elisha, who brought it, and instructed him to thank the master.

Both Mam and Jedediah treated Mercy as if she were a monster. Felice went about with a long face and complained Mercy left her no work to do. Mercy informed her coldly that she could remain at the plantation if she wished, instead of coming on to Charles Town. Mam, in a tone of long-suffering, announced that *her* place was with Missy. Somehow she managed to insinuate that Missy's place was with the captain.

Mam could be excused because she had known Mercy only in Virginia, and had the barest knowledge of her childhood in Massachusetts Bay Province. Only Uncle Jonathan had known what had happened to her mother in Salem.

Jedediah did not hint or sulk. His reproofs were blunt. "He tol' me not to talk to ye, but I've disobeyed him before for his own good. Why you doin' this to him, Mistress? You know you breakin' his heart, and you don't care. I thought better of ye than that. He'll go to the divil, wit'out somepin' to live for."

"He has his land," she said stiffly.

Jedediah shook his shaggy head. "He don't hardly care 'bout it now. Aye, he works harder than a slave, daytime. But of nights, he jus' sits, and drinks. Wine an' brandywine an' Jamaica rum. He don't get loud when he's drunk, like other men. He'll jus' up one day an' do somepin' wild. I'm afeared he'll go t' sea ag'in, and how's he goin' t' report to th' Queen's officers then? You got to stay, or he's a lost man."

"You are wrong, Jedediah." She had learned from Edmund how to seem cold outside when one's inner self twisted with turmoil. "I know you hint he will return to piracy. But he'll not go back to that life. He is not such a fool. Nor is he the first man to be disappointed in love. So far as I have seen, folk recover from it. Nor will he leave what he builds here. I have never yet seen a man to whom his property was not more important than any woman. He will come about, and likely in a short time."

Jedediah remained obstinate. "You've taked away his hope."

Mercy saw it was of no use to argue with him, and simply went inside. The exchange had taken place at the back gate of the cottage garden, out of sight of the big house. She did not go into the garden after that and remained in the cottage. But in there the hours dragged.

The future seemed bleak. She began to wonder, in those days, why she had chosen to live when all her life was blighted by what her mother had been. During the nights she lay awake and dared not even weep, unless it was a very little and stifled deep in the feather-down pillow. She did not want Mam to hear her cry and perhaps suspect her mistress was not quite so out of love as she said. A great dam of unshed tears built up in Mercy's soul, and she could only hope it would not burst until she had left this place.

Nor could she sit again at the window when sleepless. On the first night, through the cracks of the closed shutters, the big house up on the rise had stood plain to see, and in the moonlight it looked finished. It had seemed to her to be waiting, waiting for its mistress... She had even wondered what name Edmund would give it.

The house had been dark and silent, except for the lonely light of one candle that had flickered through an opening. Too easily she could imagine Edmund, also sleepless. Her whole being had wanted to run to him... And then the man on watch had sauntered past the cottages, musket over one shoulder and a lantern in his hand. She had drawn back, and looked no more into the night.

On the fourth morning, her nerves strung tight from the waiting, she took some linen and lace from the armoire and cut them into sizes for kerchiefs and trimming. She no longer cared if another woman used them. She must do something or go mad. She sat by the parlour window that looked out on the sledge track, and sewed. Mam's eyes rounded in surprise then narrowed in suspicion, however she merely rolled them once and said nothing.

Mercy jabbed the needle through the fine cloth with increasing violence. The work gave movement to her hands though it did not still her mind. If only she had money! She could go to England, or Jamaica, where no one knew her. But she did not delude herself that a change of geography, though it might hold novelty for a while, would provide escape from what she must take with her—herself.

She was grateful that her thoughts were diverted, quite soon, by sight of one of the sailor-boys from the *Dragonfly*. He ran up the sledge track, doubtless to tell the Captain that preparations on the ketch were complete and it was ready for its passengers. She sewed thread through lace and wondered what Ben would think of it all. Yet it did not matter. She needed tell him no more than she had Mam or Jedediah, and he was shy enough of her to leave her be if she so asked.

She tied a knot in the linen thread, and upon the act Jedediah came to the front door. He brought sour word that she was to pack up her things, that the wheeled cart would take her down to the wherry, and the wherry to the ketch's landing on the James. She thanked him calmly.

It would not take her long to pack. Nothing in the cottage was her own, except the letter from Soulange. The necklace she would return to her though, since it was no longer a bride gift. She stared at the writing board, then decided it must stay here; it carried with it too many memories. She wore the pink gown and Hephzibah's cap, and had no choice but to don another shift and petticoat from the well-stocked dressing table, and the pair of shoes

307

with the steel buckles. If Soulange would loan her other things, she would send all these back from Charles Town with the ketch.

Mam made up her own bundle and had no compunction about taking with her all the clothing given her by Edmund. Mercy, when she looked in the mirror, saw Felice with her belongings in both hands, and herself the mistress with none, and began to laugh. However she realised the laughter could become hysterical, and might lead to tears. So she near choked herself to swallow it all. She must not cry– not yet.

She walked stiffly out the door of the sunny bedchamber, and did not look back. She opened the front door of the cottage and stood on the stoop. The cart, with Jotham Paddock holding the reins of a plough horse standing between its shafts and Jedediah beside him on the plank seat nursing a musket on his good arm, waited.

She had not intended to look at the big house, either. But against her will, compelled by that cord that always stretched between them, her eyes were drawn to gaze up the rise.

He stood by one of the oaken pillars of the unfinished porch, stood quite still, watching. He did not wear his everyday leather and indigo but fine black breeches and a coat and waistcoat of blue, with white muslin tied high on the throat and lace falling beneath the cuffs. The mid-day sun shone on silver buttons, on silver buckles on the shoes. He was bareheaded. He did not wave.

Mercy turned her head away. Her throat was unbearably tight. Perhaps if God was angry, or even had compassion, He would take her voice away again, or strike her dead. She climbed onto the cushions set behind the driving bench, and stared at the stream and the woods.

Jedediah turned and dropped two heavy purses beside her. "There be fifty guineas in each one. They're for you." His voice was thick with anger and contempt.

She wanted to scream at him to take it back. But her will prevailed. It would prove to Edmund she was mercenary, if she took it. The gold would burn her fingers, because it was evidence Edmund loved her and worried about sending her into the world without provision. She sat and said nothing and did not touch it. She wondered if Jedediah would shoot her, he was so angry.

Felice embraced Marta and they both cried. Bab Paddock stood behind them, puzzled, and beyond Bab was a haze of other faces, all staring.

Mercy cleared her throat harshly and ordered Mam sharply to come. Mam climbed in, crying, and waved to Marta and Bab. Jedediah curtly told Jotham to move, and the cart lurched forward behind the horse.

Mercy did not look behind her yet she felt Edmund's eyes on her back, until the cart lumbered into the wood. She knew he would stand like a statue, his eyes dark, until he saw and heard them no more. She knew he would still see them in his mind's eye long after they seemed to vanish. She knew it because she would still see him, with the eye of her heart, all her living days.

****

The track to the wherry landing was but two miles long. The cart was more comfortable than a sledge, and was the only wheeled vehicle on either Edmund's land or Richard's.

Perhaps Edmund had had it purpose built for her convenience. All other supplies were drawn by sledge, and on the plantations tobacco was rolled along in great hogsheads. People walked, or rode.

Richard was riding, when after one silent and jolting mile they met him coming their way. He did not ride sedately. He galloped as if pursued by Indians. Nor was he well dressed, he wore a shirt half open without a neck-cloth, and deerskin breeches. And he was not only hatless but without a wig or even a kerchief on his head, his scalp prickling with short bristly brown hair. But he bore weapons, a sheathed sword in a baldric slung over his shoulder and a brace of pistols in a waist belt.

He saw the cart and pulled his horse up so violently that the animal slewed around on its haunches and plunged its head under the bridle. He took a moment to bring his mount under control, and Jotham reined in the cart-horse.

Mercy stared and saw Richard's face as she had never seen it, set and grim. The hazel eyes snapped and there was no trace of humour or indolence in them. She

309

thought for one heart stopping second that the grimness was for her, that he had heard she was deserting his friend.

But he said only, urgently, "'Tis no time for a jaunt in the woods now, Mercy! There's soldiers coming for Edmund from Williamsburg and they're but half an hour behind me. God be thanked they went by way of my holding, and I gave them friendly refreshment. They don't know I'm acquainted with Edmund as anything but a neighbour, and the officers made no bones about their business." He cursed at the horse to keep still.

Mercy was too deeply shocked to do anything but cry out, "Soldiers! But why?"

"Can't you guess?" Richard's voice hissed with urgency and impatience. "There's been an information laid against him, that he raided a town in Massachusetts Bay Province and abducted and ravished a helpless woman. A message received a week since, they said. Only one person could have told it—Gorman. And his flesh rotting in my cornfield, damn his soul! Turn back, Mistress!"

Mercy was on her feet and did not recall having stood. Stunned, she could still think. *If they prove he has broken the amnesty, it is all up with him!* And she had the presence of mind not to say it. Jedediah mouthed profanities, but that was mere background noise. She caught Richard's eye, and indicated with her head Jotham Paddock on the driving bench.

"Be careful what you say, sir!"

"Don't fret about Jotham! He's an old crewman of mine, and knows how to keep mum! Mercy, go home, an' behave peaceful. Lie in your teeth, if you must! Tell them you're here willing, that Edmund met you by arrangement down the Tidewater. Don't let it drop that he's been to New England, for the love of God! If they take him, it's another trial and a hanging for sure. Except Edmund'll not let himself be taken alive, not again, or I've never known him!" He pulled the bay's head around and the horse leapt up the track.

Jotham had already begun to turn the cart-horse. There was enough space. The woods were thin here and the sides of the track grown with nothing but high grass, sprinkled wildflowers, and dogwoods. Then as the cart moved, Mercy, her mind now in commotion, put out a hand to stop him.

It had cost her so much pain, to leave! She could not return, face Edmund again... And nor could she let him be arrested. Her hand dropped.

If they could save him, then she must tear her heart out once more to leave him after. If not—she could think no further. The cart jerked as it turned into the sledge track again, and she almost fell. Her heart thudded, she wanted to scream, Jedediah still cursed, and Mam's voice quavered questions in her ear.

"Mam, hush! You too, Jedediah! Swearing helps nothing! Let me think! Oh, God, help me!"

While the cart rolled she tried to calm her mind. An information, and only Gorman could have laid it, when Richard's ship had stopped at Williamsburg. But Gorman had been dead four days. If the garrison had believed him, they would have arrived here with him. That they came so late could only mean that the commanding officer had not taken the information seriously, yet felt duty bound to investigate.

Therefore, if all of them acted naturally, the soldiers would be even less inclined to believe the tale, or to arrest Edmund. She prayed that Richard would not do anything rash.

What else? Would the farm people be questioned? How much did they know? To her knowledge, only Mam, Jedediah—and Jotham - knew Edmund had travelled further than Williamsburg. There had been no wedding as yet because she had been sick. But what of her departure today? How had that been explained? They would all know Edmund had not visited the cottage for three days, and all of them had seen that he and she had not exchanged farewells.

"Jedediah! Did your master tell anyone why I was leaving? That I was going down to the ketch?"

"He got too much pride for that." Jedediah's voice was surly, half with anger and half fear. "He told 'em nothin'. I didn't neither. *I* weren't lettin' nobody know a fool woman had changed her mind, for no good reason."

His accusations did not even hurt, she so

311

concentrated on the task at hand. "Jotham? What did people say about my going away?"

He grunted stolidly that he minded his own affairs, though Bab had been puzzled. He tickled the horse's rump with his lash and it pulled a little harder.

Mercy turned to Felice. Her brown button eyes were very round and she held tight to the cart's side with both plump hands, against the bumping. "Mam, what did you tell them?"

"I don't blab your bizness, Missy. I tol' Marta we was goin' down to Byrd's Trading Pos', to find some laces an' satins for your bride clothes, if they had anythin' good 'nough. *Ow!*" The cartwheel had turned over a stone. "Miz Paddock, she lif' her eyebrows at that, 'cause she seen some o' the fine things in your li'l room, but she not say nothin'."

"But you cried when we left! Marta must have thought that strange, if we weren't going far. And you've brought a bundle of your clothes." Mercy was sharply thankful she had no luggage herself.

"I tol' her I cried 'cause I had a achy head still, an' didden feel like goin' nowhere." Mam sniffed, and her voice thinned from its normal molasses pitch. "An' this mornin', I sort of hint we might needs go to Williamsburg, for proper silks an' such. That were for when you not come back. What Master tell them then, that be up to him."

"Good! Thank heaven no one has said any more! I have only to show myself, unharmed, let the soldiers see I am there wil-willingly." She was afraid herself, that was why she stuttered. "Jotham, tell the other folk I tore my gown, and returned to change it. Or felt sick with the movement of the cart—anything! The rest we must leave to Captain Collyer, and Ed—Captain Montgomery."

"If he do anythin', Mistress." Jedediah turned on the seat, balanced himself with the stump of his arm over the plank, and glared at her. "He don't care much, no more, what happens to him."

"You exaggerate, Jedediah! He is not a total fool, to throw his life away. Now, put that musket under your seat, and leave it there! You will offer no violence to the soldiers, unless Master Edmund orders it."

He obeyed, if with bad grace. He threw the weapon

down on the cart boards so hard that Mercy thought it would fire. But it did not.

"Missy!" Mam's voice shrilled with hope. "If you does that much for Master, iffen they not take him away—you be stayin' here, after?"

"No! Nothing has changed! I owe him my life, twice over, and I will but discharge the debt. And I want to hear no more about it from either of you!"

They both sulked then, but in their silence she smelled fear. It was hard not to catch fear from them, like plague... Jotham whipped the horse again, into a clumsy trot. She gripped the side of the cart with both her own hands to keep from falling and prayed in her mind, like she used to do, *Help me, God. Help us all.*

****

Mercy told Jotham to let her off at the edge of the wood, so that she and Mam could slip into the cottage through the gate in the sapling fence. She caught a glimpse of the big house, but could see neither Edmund nor Richard.

She ordered Jedediah to take the cart the long way around the clearing to the unfinished stables, and he answered sullenly that he and Jotham could think of that themselves.

Mercy ignored him and ran inside.

The first thing she did was to cast Hephzibah's Puritan cap into the hearth and instruct Mam fiercely to burn it. "Hang a pot of water on the rod to explain any curl of smoke from the chimney. And then come help me change!"

She had decided already on her appearance. She must present herself as respectable and attractive, as unlike a Puritan as possible. The pink gown was crumpled and grubby from three days' wear and from the dust of the track. She tore open the door of her recently deserted bedchamber and ran in, mind racing as fast as her feet.

For one haunted moment the room was quiet and neat... She set her teeth and quickly turned it inside out. She flung open the bottom drawer of the dressing table and threw the two purses of gold into it like so much rubbish. From the other drawers she drew out yet again a

313

fresh shift, silk stockings, a cambric petticoat. She must change from the skin out. She was over-warm from the sun but must now appear cool, like a lady who did nothing more than sew and read.

There was water still in the pitcher. She tipped it into the basin, remembered to add rosewater from its jar, stripped off and splashed it over her whole body. The linen towel she had used that morning lay on the stool, and she patted herself dry. She must not be hasty, must not perspire again. She had the shift and petticoat on when Mam came in, and she sat on the stool and stared at the mirror.

Neither braids nor her disorderly curls would suit her purpose. "Mam, can you dress my hair high, like the women of fashion wear it?"

"'Course I kin!" However Mercy needed to instruct her how to pile it up and pin it as Soulange and Sapra had done, and not allow her to cover it with more than a tortoise-shell comb and a scrap of lace. She sat still while Mam worked and willed her pulse not to race. *How much time did she have?*

The question was answered by sounds outside, the clop of horses' hooves and the jingle of their harnesses. Mercy drew on the dimity wrapper, and walked, did not run, to the window of the parlour. She peeked out beside the shutter, careful to keep her face behind the jamb.

Two smartly-coated officers in tricorne hats and high cuffed boots rode at the head of a squad of some dozen mounted dragoons. The older officer wore the insignia of a major and the younger was a cornet. The dragoons' coats were dyed every shade of red from rose to crimson, the baldrics across them were hung with little leather pockets for musket balls and bayonets tapped at their sides. All carried sabres and muskets in leather scabbards over their saddles. Their formation was not tidy, but the rutted sledge track was responsible for that.

A hundred yards behind the mounted men a line of eight pike-men marched behind a sergeant. They all looked uncomfortably hot in steel helmets and with steel cuirasses over homespun tunics.

None of the faces revealed anything except boredom with the march. But even if they believed their errand

314

unproductive they were soldiers, and more than a match for an equal number of servants and former pirates. And the officers were backed by the authority of Queen Anne's government. It might be possible to mislead them, but not to resist them or to defy them.

Her heart rose into her throat, but she coughed and made it be quiet again. She must not be afraid! She must do everything she could to prevent any suspicion falling on Edmund. She watched no more, and returned to the bedchamber.

She pulled the blue silk gown from the armoire, drew it over her head and bid Mam help her lace it up. She stared at herself in the glass, seeking not beauty but the appearance of social consequence. The colour blue looked well on her, but something was missing—jewellery. She searched furiously through the discarded pink dress, found the velvet bag and lifted the sapphire and pearl necklace from Soulange to her throat. She was unused to wearing such things and Mam had to close the little gold clasp behind her neck.

Still Mercy was not satisfied. There was no need for great hurry, she knew. Men being men, the officers would expect, and receive, a courteous reception before they stated their business. In normal circumstances she would have had faith in both Edmund's and Richard's cool heads. But Edmund was in an unknown mood, and Richard would stand by his friend.

How to improve her looks? She was still thinner than normal, and there was no knowing what tale Gorman had told. Had he known that the abducted woman had been very sick? The necklace suited her, a perfect foil to the white skin above the straight lace-trimmed neckline of the gown. But it also drew attention to her collarbones, delicate but prominent.

She recalled the fine silk shawl and riffled through the armoire for it, disturbing the bolts of linen and satin and silk. Then when she drew it out, something tumbled from its folds to the floor, clattering. It was her writing board.

She whispered, "Put it back, they must not see it." Gorman may have also told that the captive woman was a mute.

Mam tucked it away under the lengths of fabric, but the sight of it had unnerved Mercy completely. She stared at the armoire, caught by memory.

The board had been made on that beach where the *Thalia* had been repaired, after she had been captured. Too easily she remembered Edmund sitting by her on that beach, too easily she recalled the look on his face, that stern and moody detachment which she now knew had been controlled despair. And she remembered herself there, writing in the sand...

No! She must keep her mind centred on the necessities of the present. She forced her thoughts elsewhere. Much depended on whether they questioned the servants. These might say Master and Mistress had appeared to quarrel. But they had also seen the killing of Gorman... She trembled all over, leaned her head on the armoire door, and repeated, "Oh, God, help me!"

"He will, Missy. He a good God." Mam seemed to have lost her fear, found again her placidity. "A li'l angel been whisperin' in my ear, all be well."

Mercy laughed shakily. Mam undoubtedly believed what she wanted to believe, yet it would do no good to tell her that all was not well, rather totally uncertain. She drew herself straight, however, and draped the shawl lightly about her shoulders. It drew the eye away from her collarbones neatly enough, but she now saw that the whole gown hung slightly loose.

"Mam, I look too thin. What can we do?" She was strangely calmed by these pragmatic considerations. A queer fatalism had descended on her mind. She could only do what she could do— beyond that all was in the hands of God.

"Tuck some kerchiefs down your li'l bosom, make it plumper. An' I pull in the waist wit' some pins, seein' it already laced tight as kin be." These improvements were rapidly worked, then Mercy drew on the hat with the perky rose on its brim, picked out a fan of ivory and painted silk from the dressing table and slipped her feet into the shoes with the blue bows.

She stared at the fashionable little lady in the glass, who stared back and uttered, echoing Soulange, "'Tis too much."

"No, Missy. You jus' used to your plain Puritan clo'hes. Pretty ladies like you, they dress up more'n that. But I take the fan. You not used t' it, and likely make the shawl slip iffen you waves it." Mam put her head on one side in critical examination. "Your cheeks still pale, an' your mouth. An' your eyes smudged underneath from losin' sleep. Oh, yes, I heared you in th' night, tossin' an' turnin'! There some rice flour in the kitchen we kin put over them smudges. An' there no face paint here, but your white cheeks be pink by time you walk up to big house. Your lips you kin make red by bitin' 'em."

Mercy's legs trembled and so did her insides. She wanted to sink onto the rocking chair or the bed, and not go through with this. And it was not the soldiers she feared. She would fight with her bare hands for Edmund, if they tried to take him. No, it was he... What would *he* do?

Coward! It was as if Soulange was with her, and spoke.

Her throat was dry, yet she spoke firmly. "Mam, when you fetch the rice flour, bring me a drink of water from the kitchen pail. I must stay as cool as I can, and keep my voice."

She sat still for the flour to whiten the skin under her eyes, and bit her lips to make them red. Then she took a deep breath. She told Mam to come with her, but to say nothing, merely to act like any respectable lady's tire-woman. Felice opened the front door and Mercy stepped through it.

She minced rather than walked. The shoes' heels were too high and she was not used to them.

Chapter Nineteen

Mercy stepped daintily up the grass-grown verge of the track, Mam respectful behind her. She hoped that her face and bearing exhibited the casual curiosity of a lady who has been informed of the arrival of unexpected guests. She hoped it was not evident that she was afraid her high heels would trip her, or that her hat would fall off...

The dragoons had dismounted fifty yards from the house, and allowed their horses to crop. But each man stayed by his mount, alert. The pikemen sat on their haunches in a ragged line behind them, their vicious long axes angled over their shoulders with the hafts resting on the grass.

Jedediah moved slowly among them all. He carried a wooden bucket and a ladle in his one hand, from which they helped themselves to water. He wore the stubborn look that was usual with him when he obeyed orders he did not like. Jotham and the Negro youth who had brought the venison, Elisha, performed the same service for the horses.

The Major and the Cornet sat with Edmund at the deal table under the roof of the unfinished porch, a wine bottle and three pewter mugs before them. There was no sign of Richard, nor had she expected to see him. She could easily imagine him inside the house, pistols cocked, sword at the ready...

As she walked she concentrated on her steps, yet at the same time watched Edmund. He must not seem surprised when he saw her. Richard would have told him he had met the cart, but how much would Edmund have had time to tell Richard?

He sprawled carelessly in his chair. The blue coat was slung over the back of it and his waistcoat buttons were undone. The embroidered muslin at his throat was loose, though not low enough to expose the rope burn. As she drew closer she saw that his eyelids were half closed and his face was expressionless. His Captain Gramercy mask was in place, yet casually, as if it might slip at any moment, and he would not care if it did...

Her heart beat a little faster, and she halted for a second and pretended to adjust the lace beneath her sleeve. She must remain calm, all depended on her. It was she who had dealt him the blow that made him unheeding of his life, only days before. He had not yet had time to pick up the threads of existence. And she recognised another aspect of his physical tension. From that position, if he chose, he could leap up as swiftly as a cat. But whether, if he moved, it would be to save himself, or to make certain he was shot, she did not know.

She lifted her chin, and strolled on.

She had seen Marta and Bab and the other farm folk around the cottages and in the fields, and had wished they would not stare. Now the soldiers saw her, then Jedediah, and Jotham and Elisha. The officers, whose backs were toward her, were the last to notice, and turn.

The mouth of the Cornet—he was very young, and wore a periwig of black curls under his hat—fell open. The Major, floridly good-looking and with his own grey hair, frowned, but also watched the approaching apparition.

Edmund glanced to see what they stared at, without much interest at first. Then he saw her and his eyelids lifted. His fingers, that had drummed slowly on the table top, stilled. So too did his body, like a statue's. His eyes were wholly dark. If Richard had told him that Mercy would return, he had not believed it.

She did not need to worry, now, that her cheeks might be too pale. She felt them slowly colour, with so many eyes on her. The dragoons stared at her as if they had not seen a woman in a year. But she must not be distracted. She fixed her mind on what was necessary and her eyes on Edmund, and willed her mouth to smile. This alone might do the thing. If they had heard he had taken a captive by force, her very act of walking openly to them would cancel the tale. She reached the shade of the porch.

"Faith, 'tis a warm afternoon. I should count it a

favour to be offered a chair, sirs." She smiled sweetly and indiscriminately upon all three men. "My betrothed seems uncommon slow in his attentions, today."

The officers rose, the older more slowly than the younger and still frowning. But Edmund, though he seemed scarcely to stir a muscle, was up before them. He drew out his own rough pine seat and held it for her. As she sank into it and spread her skirts with exaggerated care, he bent over her with apparent solicitude. He said nothing and his face gave nothing away, yet there was a strange light at the back of his eyes.

She had never seen it before and could not read it. She risked a single pleading look, then changed her face as he moved away. He took her hand, very lightly, and turned to the two standing men.

"Gentlemen, may I introduce my affianced wife, Mistress Mercy Burdick. Mercy, this is Major Roger Blaxton, and Second Lieutenant Daye, from the garrison at Williamsburg. Felice, be so good as to fetch your mistress some water." Mercy could not read his tone, either. Under the first harshness it was cool all the way.

Both officers bowed to her, the younger man more deeply than the older. His eyes expressed appreciation. Mercy inclined her head lazily in acknowledgment, took off her hat and lay it on the table before her. It might give him her blonde locks to admire, but she was unused to hats and found the elaborate headpiece difficult to manage. It would be one less thing to be careful of, and now that she sat she need not mind her heels either. She clasped her hands demurely before her.

"I am prodigiously pleased to meet you, gentlemen. 'Tis exciting to have visitors, and you are my first here. And military men, no less. Though I take it 'tis not a social call? Is there trouble with the French, or Indians?" She waved a languid hand at the dragoons, and tried to look a little anxious.

The men reseated themselves. Edmund, to her intense relief, released her hand to draw up a stool. His touch troubled her now more than it ever had. It was Blaxton who answered her, heavily polite, his eyes steady on hers.

"No, Mistress. We had word of a pirate, hereabouts."

"A pirate ship? In the woods, perhaps?" She managed a small laugh, met his look, and wondered where she had found the ability to play act.

Daye squirmed slightly, yet Blaxton was not easily put off. "One pirate, ma'am. They do run to ground, if they escape justice, and they seem to prefer to hide far from the sea." Clearly he fished for a response, though his frown deepened. Perhaps he asked himself not only whether she was genuine, but if she was, how much she knew of the past history of her husband-to-be.

"Oh, la, yes. Edmund tells me he would be quite happy if he never set eyes on salt water again." She raised her eyebrows. "Surely it is not he that you seek? You must know he has renounced the life, is under amnesty and reporting each month to Williamsburg, I understand."

Blaxton asked sharply, "You have known him long, ma'am?"

Unsure what to answer, she fluttered her eyelids coquettishly and smiled warmly at Edmund. It was heart-rendingly easy. "Long enough, sir."

Edmund's face remained expressionless, but the gold sparks grew brighter in his eyes. He answered for her. "Eleven months, Major. I met the lady in Boston, during my first honest foray into the merchant community there. I am pleased to say her family favoured my suit."

He lied for her because he knew she did not lie well. She felt her smile waver. Then Felice saved her by appearing at her elbow with a bone cup filled from the well. Mam set it on the table and withdrew to stand a step behind her chair, like a plump watchdog. Mercy saw the pretty fan that dangled from her brown wrist and decided suddenly that her prominent collar bones mattered less than the need to hide her face.

She dropped the shawl onto the chair back and said pettishly, "Give me the fan, Felice. I am warm. I vow, you would stifle me in lambs-wool if you could."

Mam opened the fan and placed in her hand without a word. Mercy waved it slowly before her face. The Major's scrutiny remained critical, behind a courteous countenance. She met his eyes calmly over the shield of painted silk and allowed her gaze to pass idly and meet that of Daye, which was frankly admiring. She sipped at the cool water.

The young man asked eagerly, "Would you prefer wine, Mistress?"

Edmund lifted the bottle and trickled a little into Mercy's cup. "Mistress Burdick is not fond of undiluted wine."

Blaxton took a careless swig from his own tankard, and his voice was bland. "Do Puritans object to wine, then?"

Mercy did not need the sudden pressure of Edmund's knee on hers, to recognise the trap. No Puritan woman would be dressed as she was. "What have Puritans to do with anything, sir? Though they are not monks—they like wine, and beer and spirits."

"I wondered if you were of Puritan stock, ma'am. Boston is a Puritan town, and Mercy a Puritan name."

"You know little about Massachusetts Bay Province then, Major. Or your information is out of date. There are more folk than Puritans there now, and indeed Puritans themselves are softening their ways. But I am Church of England, like Edmund. And my sisters' names are Patience, Charity and Virtue." No need to mention these last were Nathaniel's sisters, her stepsisters.

"And you were born in Boston, ma'am?"

"Why, yes." That was also true. She had been taken to Salem by her mother and stepfather when barely two years old. But not to save her life would she mention Salem. She dropped the fan to meet his look squarely. "Why this curiosity, sir? I begin to feel like a victim of the Papist Inquisition."

Edmund said calmly, "And I begin to object, Major, that you question my lady like a criminal."

"I must do my duty, Montgomery." Blaxton's lips thinned to a straight line. "I have told you our business, and I will now tell it to Mistress Burdick. We had an information, ma'am, that this gentleman, whom we know to have been a pirate, attacked a New England town, New Exmouth, and forcefully abducted from there a Puritan woman." Daye coughed behind his hand, and his superior glared at him.

"If I had wanted a woman," Edmund continued in that same calm voice, "I would not need to go so far as that."

Mercy curled her lip. "New Exmouth? I know of the place. Believe me, sir, no pirate would trouble with it, who could plunder the Indies, or Brazil, if he chose. Really, someone has teased you. My ship anchored off Norfolk, and Edmund met me there." She yawned. "A foolish tale." She waved the fan lazily, aware that her pulse quickened. She hoped the Major was a man to believe what sounded sensible even to her own ears.

Blaxton's voice smoothed. "How come, ma'am, he did not go to Boston, to wed you among your family and friends, before you left?"

Mercy felt her face turn pale. She managed to maintain her expression, but could find no immediate answer.

It was Edmund, again, who replied. He had leaned back against the porch post, balanced on two legs of his stool, thumbs hooked in the waistband of his breeches and apparently quite relaxed. Yet there was now an edge to his voice.

"Mistress Burdick has journeyed here in good faith, Major, so that I did not need to take time away from building my farm here. She has her father's permission. She does not need yours. Do you suggest there is anything improper in the fact of her presence here, in one of the cottages, and chaperoned by her maid?"

Blaxton's face reddened, however he continued stubbornly. "I do not question the lady's reputation, sir. I merely make inquiries so that the charge against you be proved either true or false. You were both by Williamsburg, then, but did not wait to be wed before you came on here?"

Mercy snapped the fan closed, a thing she had once seen Soulange do when irritated. "We did not, Major, because I was vilely seasick during the whole of the voyage to Virginia and had not yet recovered. I am only now able to take normal food and drink, and have barely begun to regain the flesh I lost. I devoutly trust that you are now satisfied, and will cease to persecute us." It was not difficult to feel anger. And anger was the easiest emotion with which to cover fear.

She tapped her foot against the table leg, pouted then

glanced away, swinging the fan on her wrist. She saw
between Edmund and Daye some of the nearer dragoons.
Their expressions were too neutral, as if to prove they did
not listen.

Blaxton's face had reddened even more, yet he
persisted. "I beg your patience a moment longer, ma'am. I
must be certain, you understand, that you are here
willingly. Would you swear, Mistress, that you came of
your own accord, and to what you have said, on a Bible?"

Edmund did not move, but his voice hardened by two
tones. "By heaven, Major, you go too far!"

"Do not lose your temper, my dear." Mercy found that
she could affect anger and boredom both at once. "Sir, I
would swear that I came here happily on every Bible in
Christendom and in every court." She took a mouthful of
the water and wine to steady herself, and saw over the
rim of the cup Edmund's eyes. They were full on her, and
coloured amber.

He said without inflection, "Happily."

She dared not look at him longer. She returned the
cup steadily to the table and waved her fan in a gesture
that encompassed the whole clearing. "Do I seem like a
captive, forced to pretend otherwise?" She was oddly
reckless now. Fear, then the little amount of wine and the
play-acting, had gone to her head. "Since I am not,
perhaps you had best search the servants' quarters and
the fields and woods. It may be Edmund has hid a Puritan
maid somewhere for his amusement, and told me not of
it." Her voice dripped sarcasm.

The Cornet blurted suddenly, "It cannot be this lady
anyway, sir. The report said that the woman was dumb."

Mercy leaned back in her chair until the pins in the
gown's waist pricked her skin. She looked from one officer
to the other and used her haughtiest voice. "Dumb? Not
able to speak? An admirable advantage in a captive, I
imagine. I, then, am a mute. And you, sirs, are Red
Indians, and Captain Montgomery a bear."

Edmund spoke quietly and still calmly. "Do you
accept now, gentlemen, that the report was false? But I
would like to know who made it." His stool was yet tipped
back, and to Mercy's eyes it was the cat-stance from which
he could move quickly, any way he chose. She glanced

324

aside at the dragoons. Jotham still moved purposefully among them, watering the horses. Elisha had disappeared. Jedediah stood apparently idle, the heavy bucket swinging slightly in his one hand.

Daye forgot himself again. "The veriest ruffian! I did not see him, but Sergeant Wallis did. He said he was a shaggy ragged creature with a matted beard and stinking breath, half a cripple! And mad to boot—he swore he dared not turn his back on the brute!" He caught Blaxton's eye and subsided, abashed, lifting his tankard to hide his face.

Edmund shrugged against the post. "Then the mystery is solved. It would have saved time, Major, if you'd told me of him earlier. The madman came this way four days since, shot at Mistress Burdick, and tried to do for me with an old cutlass. I killed him."

Mercy did not need to act out feeling sick and upset. She turned her face away and pressed a hand to her cold lips. She could see down to the cottages, and noticed that the women there had all found chores to do at their front stoops. And she saw Elisha heading for the corn-field, an ostentatious hoe on one shoulder. Had Jotham sent him with some message for the men?

She glanced back at Edmund and this time could read his expression. Her mind cleared. *Of course.* His words had not been recklessness, but a calculated risk. She had feared that if the farm folk were questioned the tale would come out. Now Edmund had said the thing aloud... What would happen? The whole clearing held its breath. In the quiet she could imagine she heard Richard, ten feet away through wood and brick, lift his pistol hand. She found she held her breath, and expelled it. Yet she said nothing. Edmund must know what he was about.

Blaxton thundered, "You should have reported it, sir!"

"So I would have, when next I reported to Williamsburg." His hands rested loosely on his knees. "It was self-defence. You may ask any of the people here. They all saw it. If it was murder, Major, I'd have fled by now."

Blaxton gulped wine then wiped his mouth. "You are telling me, Montgomery, that a stray lunatic found his way up the James and then to your land. That he knew enough of you to leave at least a garbled story with the garrison—and that you did not know him?"

"I did not recognise him. He may have been a former crewman, or someone who held a grudge against me. Enemies are made easily in the Brotherhood. And I made no secret of the fact that I would leave it. But I doubt I'll meet any more of his kind." He looked directly into the officer's eyes. "My only desires now are to build my farm, marry my lady, and raise horses and children."

Mercy wondered if it would help his case if she had a fit of hysterics. It would not be difficult... But she saw what it was that Edmund conveyed to the Major by way of his words. Every new holding in the Colonies was a gain for England, another buffer against the French who infiltrated the mountains to the west. And that not all of the great plantations had been settled by respectable men. Even the College Of William And Mary, in Williamsburg, had had its building fund fattened with three hundred pounds in fines from the pirate Edward Davis. Any doubts Blaxton might entertain were worth little, when weighed against the advantages of letting Edmund be.

She opened the fan again and spoke stiffly. "My betrothed has told me that he did not—enjoy—his former occupation, sir. Like many others, he was forced into it to save his life."

Blaxton, however, held out a little longer. "And yet I understand you prospered at the game, Captain. Why give it up?"

"It is a short-lived career, Major. I preferred to survive. And I met a lady whose goodwill I ardently desired." He turned his head to look fully at Mercy.

She blushed, and Blaxton, watching her, seemed to thaw a little. "And when will the marriage take place, ma'am? You'll need to travel down river to Williamsburg then wait for the banns to be called. If I know the date, I shall be honoured to dance at your wedding."

"So shall I, ma'am!" Daye confirmed eagerly. His face was flushed. Perhaps he did not have a strong head for wine.

Mercy felt her blush die like a rose under snow. In

the urgency of the need to save Edmund, she had not thought of this. But of course it would seem strange, now, when this apparently devoted wife-to-be suddenly deserted Edmund and his farm and fled away...

She said carefully, "Why, sirs, I am flattered. But we have waited for my health to improve before we name the day, and have not yet done so." Perhaps, she thought wildly, they would hear much later that Edmund Montgomery's betrothed had run off from the capital, had left Virginia altogether. They could put what construction they liked on it, then. Men had been jilted before...

She straightened her spine. All that was for later, not now. But her throat was dry and she was afraid that her voice would weaken. She drank a little more, and like Daye was grateful for the cup that hid her confusion.

Edmund lost no particle of his coolness. He tipped the stool forward and imbibed deeply from his own tankard. "Our wedding plans are our own affair, Major. I take it we are now to be left in peace?"

Blaxton drummed his fingers on the table. "The tale does not fit, does it? Very well, we shall see you when you report next month. But we trust you will have your lady on your arm, if she will deign to visit us."

Mercy needed to call on all her courage, to meet his eyes. Her ability to play-act seemed to have deserted her as suddenly as it had arrived. It was the fan, now, that she used to hide half her face. "Perhaps, sir. Though I find the thought of travel wearisome, in this weather. I am accustomed to the cooler north, you understand."

"You will grow accustomed to Virginia also, ma'am." He glanced at Edmund. "It is afternoon and there seems no point in continueing our march today. May we pitch camp on your land for the night? My men would be grateful for the rest, and fresh food."

Mercy's heart thudded. To play a part for a short time had been hard enough, but what would she do if they stayed? At a loss, she glanced over the fan at Edmund. And by his darker eyes and slightly lifted brow she read his thought. Blaxton did not impress one as being more solicitous of his subordinates than any other army officer.

"I regret, Major, that I do not have enough provisions in store, to feed so many. Much as I should like to be hospitable."

"Hmm." Blaxton was annoyed and his face showed it. "The pikemen have slowed us down, but the Colonel said they needed a march." He rose suddenly to his feet. "And they shall have one! This is not England, with short routes and passable roads. Our work is to patrol for signs of French and Indians, and that we shall do! Sergeant! Get the men to fall in. We are leaving."

The soldiers came to their feet with obvious reluctance and poor Daye, who had begun to look comfortable with his chair and his wine, seemed in much the same state. Mercy was a little sorry for them all, especially the pikemen on foot, but utterly relieved that they were leaving. Edmund stood, came to her side and took her hand. She rose to stand by him like a good hostess. Only she knew that her legs trembled, and not only because she balanced on the high-heeled shoes.

Edmund said smoothly, "I regret that we are unable to entertain you, Major."

Blaxton bowed stiffly, but managed a polite tone. "Perhaps next time we come this way you and your wife might have a larder better stocked, and we provisions as well. For tonight, we can shoot a deer and bivouac by a stream." He turned to Mercy and extended his hand. "Mistress, a pleasure to meet you."

She had sufficient wit left in her to hold out her own. "A pleasure always to make new acquaintances, sir."

The officer surprised her by kissing her wrist, though of course he was no Puritan, to merely shake her hand. With the exertion of some self control she forebore to withdraw it. Then when the Cornet followed suit, she found she could favour him with a little smile.

"At least you do not bear the Colours today in this heat, Master Daye."

"Not necessary, ma'am, unless the whole regiment's turned out." The young man turned impulsively to Edmund. "Faith, sir, you'll have a fine and pretty wife!"

Edmund drew her hand firmly into the crook of his arm and smiled. "I know that. But thank you."

Mercy felt a stirring of alarm, then comprehension. Now that the crisis seemed to be past, she saw that Edmund believed his danger had caused her to change her mind, that she had returned to him for good. She needed to disenchant him as soon as possible! But for now she must stand at his side, watch the dragoons remount and the red-faced pikemen fall into rough formation again. A corporal led up the officers' horses, and Daye swung up into his saddle.

Blaxton delayed a moment. First he brushed dust from his hat, and then glanced over at the growing pile of sharp-ended logs intended for the palisade. "I am pleased to see that you look to your defences, Captain."

"It seemed wise, after the madman came among us so easily." Nothing, it seemed, could ruffle Edmund's calm.

Daye pranced his horse away a few yards and called out cheerful and quite unnecessary orders to the dragoons. The Major set his hat on his head then looked straight at Edmund.

"You know, Montgomery, he even had your name wrong. He described you, but called you Gramercy."

Mercy's fingers tightened involuntarily on Edmund's arm. Without haste, he covered them with his right hand. "Then the poor fool must have confused me with someone else. I had heard of another pirate of that name. I have also heard that he is dead."

"You would know, sir." Blaxton turned away without another word and drew himself easily onto his mount. He took his place at the head of the small column, gave the command to march, and saluted as he passed them. Daye saluted also and behind his superior's back risked a grin. Edmund acknowledged both gestures with courteous nods.

Mercy stood as if dumb once more. The horses, the straight backs of the dragoons and the slow steel ones of the pikemen, retreated down the sledge track. She stiffened her knees. A worse ordeal was yet to come. As the last man reached the edge of the woods she spoke, forcing her voice to be cold.

"Sir, you may release me now. They are almost gone."

He held her hand to his cambric clad arm more firmly still, though he did not look at her. His eyes were intent on the flashes of colour and metal still visible through the trees.

He said only, "No."

329

****

Jedediah upturned his bucket and sat on it. He drew pipe, flint, and tinder from his waistcoat pocket and lit the tobacco in the bowl. Jotham, who had previously vanished, reappeared with the musket from the cart under his arm.

He asked Edmund laconically, "Follow 'em?" When Edmund nodded, he clamped his hat to his grizzled head and strode down the track.

Mercy whispered, "Why?" The last hints of the soldiers' presence had merged with the landscape.

"He'll pretend to be hunting or seeing to traps. If we hear a shot, it'll warn us that they are returning."

"But why would they?"

Richard sauntered out from the house and joined them. He lay a pistol on the deal table beside Mercy's hat and helped himself to a deep draft of wine. His eyes, also, watched the place where the column had disappeared. He grinned at Mercy.

"They won't. But pirates, and soldiers, get to be old by suspecting all possibilities. Edmund and I are old pirates, and our friend Blaxton's an old soldier." He drained his tankard, the same one Daye had used. "Mistress, you gave as fine a show as I've ever seen in a play-house, and mostly they believed you."

"An uncommon combination, a very junior officer and a very senior one. It smacks of surmise, not certainty." Edmund turned to his friend. "Daye doesn't count. Blaxton made it plain that he suspects there was truth somewhere in the report yet has chosen to let the matter lie. We are safe so long as I set no foot wrong. Though I plan to be the most law-abiding citizen in the Colony from today onward."

Richard wiped his mouth then rubbed his beard as if it itched. "Aye. He'll confirm her tale. But if ye both act staid and steady there's nought to worry about."

Mercy was alarmed. "Confirm my tale? How?"

Edmund clasped her hand where it lay imprisoned on his arm. "They'll not send to Boston to ask of you. But I'll wager a doubloon that tonight they'll pitch camp not far from here, and send a scout back in the small hours to see where you sleep."

Richard grinned, and stretched his arms to loosen tense muscles. "It was a lie, by the by, that they carried no rations. I saw inside their saddlebags, at my place."

Mercy barely heard him, and turned big eyes on Edmund. "You mean they will spy on us? To make sure that I am truly here of—of my own free will?"

"Yes." Edmund looked down at her and his voice, under the first tone, was soft. "Tonight a strange face will peer in at the window of your cottage. And they will make sure I am in the house, for good measure." He smiled wryly. "I ought to let our own sentries surprise them at it, but I want them to report back to Williamsburg that all is as we said." He added to reassure her, "You need not fear you'll be molested. Their watchers will be watched."

That was the last thing that concerned her. She was appalled at the prospect of staying another night. In the morning she would need to find the strength to leave again, and she was afraid her resolve might melt. *No— wait!* If she left the next day, and Blaxton heard of it, he might not keep his suspicions to himself. She must wait here until she and Edmund went to Williamsburg for the fictional wedding, and then escape... No, that was too long a time, she could not! She must contrive some incident, to get away, join the ketch tomorrow...

Her head whirled, she could not think. She felt her legs give way and leaned her hand, the one not held prisoner by Edmund's, on the porch post.

"She gonna faint, Master!" It was Felice's voice, behind her yet seeming far away.

"I am not," she whispered. However Edmund lowered her to his stool and supported her with his arm. He knelt, which brought his eyes level with hers. They were warm as melted honey, but still unreadable. She begged, "Please. I must speak with you alone."

"Soon, little one. Here." He took up his tankard of neat wine, held it to her lips and made her drink a mouthful. Her mind remembered the cabin on the *Thalia*, when he had done the same thing and said he would not harm her. No, he would not, but he did not understand... Felice had taken the fan from her, and plied it vigorously above her head.

Richard said quite kindly, "It's not a weakness,

Mercy. 'Tis the same as the other day, after Gorman was here, the shock that follows a fight."

Jedediah rose and plodded toward them.

They surrounded her. She could not breathe. She leaned her head back to seek air, and it came to rest on Edmund's arm. She did not have the strength to remove it.

Edmund said roughly, "Stand back all of you, or she may indeed faint."

Mercy wished she could. It would be a brief escape. But her giddy mind sheered toward, of all things, Edmund's voice. "Your voice, Edmund! Do they know how...?"

"They think it my natural one, hereabouts." He touched her cheek gently, and then suddenly and softly laughed. "I'm more concerned that young Daye has fallen headlong into calf-love with you!"

Richard chuckled also. "That were most entertainin', from where I stood! The young pup! You'll have to watch him, lass, that he don't make advances when next you meet."

She stared blankly at both men, unbelieving.

Edmund said with tender amusement, "You don't have a vain bone in your body, do you?"

She shook her head wearily. It did not matter. She would never see the young officer again.

But Edmund continued lightly, "They'll watch us for some time, to be sure we wed and settle down, finish the house and work the farm."

The loving words were hot irons to her soul. She stared at him. But she saw only the fan fluttering like a trapped bird, Jedediah frowning heavily above Edmund's head, and Richard's narrowed eyes. She pressed her hands to her temples. "Stop! Let me be!"

Edmund's tone remained even. "Felice, go begin your mistress's supper. Jedediah, bring Richard's horse around."

Mercy heard Felice sniff and Jedediah snort, however Mam flounced away and Jedediah stomped, seizing the bucket as he went.

Richard, however, was not so easily dismissed. The hazel eyes flicked sharply from Mercy's face to Edmund's.

"Now what's to do, here?"

"It's between Mercy and I, Richard. You'd best not stay the night. Blaxton's scouts will wonder when you came."

"You want me to go home, you mean." He laughed, and ran a hand over his close-cropped scalp. "Well, my head's discomforted and craves its wig. I'll go! But may I kiss your lady first?"

"Don't forget, the lips are mine only, now." Edmund stood, drew an inert Mercy with him to her feet, and reached out to grip his friend's shoulder. "Thank you for the warning."

"We ceased keeping count of favours a long time since." Richard bent and kissed Mercy's cheek, which startled her. She had expected him to salute her hand as the officers had done. The keen eyes gleamed down at her. "You're a good woman, Mistress Mercy. Almost you convince me I should take a wife myself."

Mercy momentarily forgot her own plight. Nor did she misunderstand him. "Oh, Richard, would you really marry Soulange? I should be so pleased!"

"Softly, softly." He frowned slightly. "Madame's the only woman who'd never bore me, but Monsieur's not dead yet."

He slapped Edmund's arm, wished them good evening, and strode to meet Jedediah who had come from behind the house with the bay gelding. Within a minute he too was riding down the track.

Mercy fixed her eyes on him, and wondered if this was the last time she would see Richard as well... No, of course not. Wherever Soulange was, Richard would sometimes be. If she went to Soulange... The future was uncertain, but it was the next few minutes she must survive.

Edmund remarked easily, "Madame is too desperate for respectability. Richard will chafe, pressed too hard or held too tight. Best advise her, when you write, to settle for being his mistress or common-law wife. He's a man who will only be secured by a loose line and a light anchor."

"I will see her, to tell her, soon enough." Mercy found courage that had only one source, the knowledge that what she must do was for Edmund's own sake. She swallowed, and tasted neat wine on her tongue. When Richard and the bay were invisible among the trees, she spoke with great care. "What happened here changes nothing, sir. I have merely repaid you for my life again." She tried to tug her hand free, and could not. Her voice rose in a cry, "Edmund, let me go!"

"I have already told you, little one. No."

Chapter Twenty

Edmund seized Mercy's other arm and swung her round to face him. His eyes glittered and his voice under the first rough tone was as unyielding as a wall of oak.

"You cannot now convince me that you want to leave. I was ready to release you because I believed your love had turned to hate. But what you did for me today can only have been for love."

She made fists of her hands and tried to beat them on his chest. The trap was closing and she must escape.

He caught her wrists and held them, continued inexorably, "Therefore, Mercy, there is some other reason that you left me. Tell me what it is."

"No!" Her voice was hoarse. She tried to collect her scattered wits, tried to lie. "I do not love you anymore! I will not be a pirate's wife! I will not live here in the wilderness, in fear of Indians and the French! I..." Her voice failed and she choked.

A loud '*Halloo*' was called from down the track. Edmund turned and saw Jotham, who waved his musket over his head. He held Mercy hard with one hand and waved back. "The soldiers have gone."

Mercy did not care. The most dangerous person in the world now was Edmund.

She watched Jotham stroll to his cottage, give the musket to Bab, who stood at the door, then cross the clearing to the field. Marta ostentatiously swept her front path. Felice stood with arms folded across her plump bosom before the door of the first cottage. Elisha and the other men glanced their way now and then from the fields.

Edmund commanded quietly, "Come inside, Mercy, away from all these eyes." He led her in through the mahogany door, which Richard had left open.

She could not resist because her hand was held fast, she was as imprisoned as when Gorman had tied her. And there was nowhere to run, where she could not be easily caught. The steps were temporary ones of planks on bricks, and she stumbled a little in the high-heeled shoes. But he supported her with an arm around her shoulders and guided her in. Then he firmly swung the door shut.

In the single moment that he was off balance she wrenched herself away from him. They stood in a large, bare entrance hall. One day it would boast a set of stairs to the upper floor, but was for now occupied only by a ladder.

There was a door to her left that stood ajar. She ran through it. However it only led to another room, a large room. Edmund strode steadily behind her and into it, shut that door as well. There was no other entrance.

The trap had closed. Yet the room gave Mercy pause, like a hunted animal's breathing space.

The afternoon sun poured in through tall south-facing windows with square glass panes beaded together with wood. It caught dancing dust-motes and glowed on a floor of polished oak and oak wall panelling. A brick fireplace with a carved mahogany mantelpiece was set in the midst of the north wall, with a mirror in a gilt frame hung above it.

Part of her mind recognised for the first time that Edmund must be wealthy, to have bought so much glass and have it transported here. She turned her head slowly, and saw canvas-covered shapes scattered about untidily and pushed against walls, table and chair and cabinet shapes. A long settle with a tapestry seat stood half uncovered.

Under the window nearest the porch stood an elegant little rosewood side table, its holland cover dropped beside it on the floor. A sword lay incongruously on top of it alongside a pistol, the twin of the one Richard had left outside on the deal table.

Edmund crossed the room and calmly unloaded the pistol. "We must take these back to Richard. It will be an excuse to visit. You've not yet seen his house."

"What is all this?" she asked witlessly.

"Our parlour, little one. In the wilds here, it will be

more convenient to situate it on the ground floor than above stairs." He took the cover from a chair. "And these are our furnishings." Like the small table, the chair was neither the plain solid shape of New England furniture nor the heavy carved Jacobean style in the de Vaugerets' house, but a slim outline with simply curved legs and with the seat cushion fixed instead of loose. "The style is called after Queen Anne. And I bought it all, Mercy, because I found it like you, lovely in itself, without adornment. And because I believed you would like it."

"Then you must trust another woman will like it." But she recognised his manner, that beneath his gentleness he was implacable. He would not let her go without hearing an explanation he could believe without a scrap of doubt. She must think of something he would accept, and she must speak it quickly. Yet he would know a lie, from her. And she could think of nothing.

She saw the sunlight gleam on the steel of the sword blade. There was nothing left but that...

She sauntered slowly forward, pretended to look at a rolled carpet, at a bolt of brocaded cloth, at a box of silver-gilt candlesticks. Then she pretended to look out the window at the sunny clearing... When she was abreast of the weapon, she turned quickly and snatched it up.

He had moved away from the table when he showed her the chair. But it was not far enough. He caught her in three long swift strides, seized her hand as it closed round the hilt and forced her fingers from it. The sword clattered to the floor. Mercy cried out, then shut her mouth. Nor, though her pride was flailed, would she weep.

"As bad as that? For the love of God, Mercy, trust me!" He pinned her arms to her sides with his arm over her elbows. She struggled to escape, but she had forgotten once more how strong he was. With his free hand he pushed her chin up, as the pirate had done.

"Still a virgin's eyes." His own were amber. "Mercy, the only thing a woman fears to tell her husband is that some other man has taken her. With you, it is not that. But I tell you it would not matter to me, any more than Madame's past matters to Richard." He released her chin, encircled her with both arms. "Tell me."

Tears slid down her cheeks of their own accord, but

she barely noticed them. She was spent, had no place left to turn when all she wanted in the world was to remain in the refuge of his arms, to rest her head on his shoulder... The gilt buttons of his waistcoat pressed into the silk and lace bodice of the gown. She wished the buttons were knives, so she could die there. She shook her head wearily on his chest.

"Mercy, it's of no use to run away from me, or to hide anything from me." His voice above her head was soft under its rough edge. "Think, little one, look back. We have parted how many times? Three, and then four, today. And yet our paths have crossed again in spite of all." His tone turned relentless. "It ends here. We make a stand and we live in this house as man and wife. Nothing you can say to me will prevent that. Nothing."

"Nothing?" Her voice was bitter. She jerked her head up and stared into his gold-brown eyes, his loving, determined face. "If I tell you the truth, you will let me go. Like a snake, like filth. I will tell you what I am, and then you will never willingly touch me again. Let me loose. I will not be pushed away." She shivered all over.

His eyes were fixed on hers. They were merely troubled and unyielding, not yet shocked. He slid his hands down her blue silk sleeves and their frothing lace, over her wrists and hands, held her fingers a moment and then released them. She backed away, bumped against the uncovered chair.

"No, Mercy, no further. I'll not touch you, because you ask it. But you will stay within arm's reach."

Her legs shook within the silk and fine cambric. She clasped her hands together so tightly that her knuckles whitened, though she did not see that they did or feel any pain in them.

"I am a curse," she whispered hoarsely. She tried to say why but her voice died in her throat. She uttered the bubbling groan of nightmare, and pushed her clenched fingers against her mouth.

The sunlight made a gold halo around his brown hair, and found gold lights in his eyes. "It has to do with your voice, doesn't it? You said you lost it because you were sick. And yet you regained it when you saw me hanged." He held up one hand in unconscious gesture, a man groping for truth. "Mercy, I charge you, for both our sakes, speak it out!"

"*I am a witch!*" Mercy thought she screamed but the words, torn from her inmost soul, came out in a strangled shriek. She turned blindly and ran, tripped against the long settle. She had forgotten her shoes, with heels too high for running...

She collapsed onto the tapestry seat, curled her arms around her body and trembled violently. Her neck lost strength, her head fell forward and then the long fight with tears was lost. She wept as if her soul had split and the sobs burned her throat. She scrabbled at her hair with her hands, tore it loose from comb and pins until the fair curls fell around her face and hid it.

Other hands took hers–long, strong, familiar hands— and held them tightly. Shocked that he touched her she cringed away, backed against the canvas over the settle, afraid the hands might strike her...

"Don't! Don't fear me! I would never hurt you, for any reason!" The harsh-surfaced voice, stern and passionate, cut like a sword through the fog of her fear. "Do you think I will accept such a statement without question? Why do you believe it, Mercy? It is not true."

"You do not know!" She almost choked on tears, swallowed them. She had no strength left to pull free of him but twisted her head away, so that the curtain of her hair fell between them. "You don't want to believe it, but it is the truth!" The last word came out in a cough, but she must speak, must make him understand. "My m-mother was hanged at Salem, thirteen years ago, tried and condemned! She was a witch! I am also a—a..." She could not say the word again. Her body sagged.

Then the hands jerked her straight. "Your own mother, hanged? Did you see it?"

"*Yes!*" This word she screamed.

"God in heaven! That is why you lost your voice. And why it came back to you, when I was strung up... Poor little soul, my poor little one."

"My voice does not matter!" she cried desperately. "You must listen! She was a witch! I must leave you because I am—I am..." Once more she could not say the word.

"No, Mercy! You are not a witch! I have felt no shadow of evil in you. My heart would have known." He had breathed hard before but now took air deeply into his lungs, then continued more calmly. "If you will not look at me, you will listen to me. Let us reason the thing out. A real witch is as rare as a hen's tooth. Did your mother practise the black arts? Do you?"

"No!" In her frenzy she knew only she must somehow convince him. "But she knew the magic of plants and herbs, and taught it to me from when I could walk. I have not forgotten it. I know all the herbs of healing. But I have barely dared to use them, since she died." She tried again to free her hands but he would not let them go. She tried to shock him into releasing her, to save himself. "Perhaps I put a love spell upon you, or gave you a potion, on the ship, to save myself!"

"Foolish little one! You are half out of your wits! I needed no spells or potions to love you!" He shook her hands, hard. "Nor is there any magic in plants! If God made the good green things and put virtues into them, how can it be evil to use them? Mercy, look at me!"

She had not thought of it in this way before... Perhaps a hope began to stir in her heart. She dared to lift her eyes a little way to peep through her draggled curls. She saw that he knelt before her, reached his arms across her crumpled silken lap to hold her hands. His face was keenly thoughtful, passionate, angry, and yet—the anger was not for her.

"You—you cannot tie yourself to me," she whispered brokenly. "I no longer know what is true and what is not, but I know you cannot take the risk. My blood may be tainted with witchery. I cannot risk that it may taint you—or a child." Her throat caught. It was the first time she had allowed herself the thought, that she would dearly love to bear Edmund's children...

"You see the beginnings of reason in your mind? You were certain before, but now you are not. Little one, listen. I will be your advocate, since you are your own accuser." He rose and sat beside her on the tapestry seat. His face was grim, as the pirate's had been when he duelled words with his enemy. "I remember the witch trials at Salem discussed in a tavern in Bideford when I was a young man. The tale had been brought by a ship just come from New England."

Her heart thumped unevenly. "What—what did they say?"

"They said it had begun when young women were accused of concourse with the devil. That alone was superstition, not Christianity! But they did know that the proceedings were unjust. Hallucination and hearsay were accepted as evidence, and not proven. The trials were halted by the Royal Governor because of public outcry. It became evident that those hanged were innocent of anything but their neighbours' foolish fears." He lifted one hand to brush her hair from her face, to look directly into her eyes. "Mercy, your mother was hanged because people feared her knowledge of medicines, and did not understand it."

Mercy heard the words yet could not take them in. She stared at him as if she was dumb again.

"The question is not whether you are a witch..." She flinched and he pressed her fingers. "But why you believe it." His eyes were sombre with deep thought. "The women and men who were hanged at Salem, some of them must have had children. Do any of those children believe themselves accursed as you do?"

"I—do not know." This aspect of the matter had simply never occurred to her. "Uncle Jonathan took me away to Virginia, almost straight afterward."

"You do not know. There have been no more witch trials in New England. Therefore none of those children are witches. Why do you think you are? Did your uncle say so?"

"No, never!" She did not think to flinch now, because Edmund said the word over and over without fear. "He was angry with the clergy, the court, for so using his brother's widow. It was not he who said it."

"Ah, then someone did say it." His dark amber eyes searched her own while his long brown hands held her still. "Who, Mercy?"

"My stepfather." Mercy drew in a painful breath. Edmund's insistent words had opened a door in her mind long years closed. "Nathaniel's father, Isaiah Burdick. He hated her for disgracing him. He made her be tried under

341

my father's name, Penhall. He hated me because I was her child, and lived. My mother had borne him a son but the babe was stillborn. My stepfather—made me watch her die."

It was the nightmare, but she had remembered that much. She had forgotten what came after... She did not want to remember it. A great sob tore from her throat.

"Courage, Mercy! Do not falter now. I am here."

"He beat me!" she cried. "He took me home and he beat me, he said to drive the devil out of me. And with every stroke of the stick, he shouted, *"Witch! Witch!"* I wished him dead, and five years afterward Nathaniel wrote that he had died. I ill-wished him!"

"No, you did not! Not after five years." Edmund's eyes were bright with anger but the anger, again, was not for her. "He laid your so-called curse upon you. He spoke the word 'witch' into your soul, and it festered there ever after." He breathed deeply. "Look at it now, Mercy, in the open and the light of day. It cannot stand, can it? It was untrue and unjust, the word of a man who was angry and afraid."

She did look at it, and what he said was sense. But she dared not believe it. She had carried it too long within her. She clutched tightly the fingers that held so hard to her own.

"I want to believe you, Edmund! But—I do not dare!"

"You must let go of it." He took her wet face between his palms. "Listen to me. Take my words into your heart in place of those others. *You are not a witch.* Your mother was not a witch. Your mother was tried unjustly and unjustly put to death. *You are not a witch.* Say it aloud."

"I..." Her voice stuck in her throat.

"Say it!"

"I am not a witch," she whispered.

"Louder!"

"*I am not a witch,*" she shrieked.

A remarkable thing happened. Once the words were uttered into the air they seemed to depart, to be gone. Stillness descended upon the sunny room. The evil spoken upon her so long ago had been cast out, and peace entered in its place.

She stared at Edmund, at his lean tanned resolute

face, his bright brown eyes, his dark hair flowing over the white shirt and neckcloth. It was as if she had never seen him properly before. She needed to touch him to be certain he was real, and lifted her hands to his shoulders. She felt his flesh warm and strong beneath his shirt. She smiled.

His features relaxed and his hands gentled. "From now on you need not carry that burden. It is behind you." He pressed two fingers onto her mouth. "Past." He smiled into her wide blue eyes. "You are more speechless now than when you were mute! Agree with me."

"Yes, Edmund. It is past." She linked her hands behind his neck, and felt the beat of his pulse, slowing down.

"Past, thank God." His arms closed around her. "I never fought a harder battle."

****

Mercy and Edmund rested quietly together. Neither knew for how long, though it could only have been a few minutes. At last he sighed and loosed her, and she sat back a little and smiled at him. She wiped at her damp cheeks with her hand. "I despise women who cry easily!"

"Those were hard tears," he told her quietly. "We will clean them away." He raised his lace-cuffed sleeve.

"I have kerchiefs," she said demurely. She drew two from inside her bodice, where they had padded out her breasts.

He laughed and blotted her cheeks with them, then stroked her damp fair hair off her face once more. His fingers tangled in her curls and he held her face up to his. His eyes were grave for a moment, but warm, warm...

"When I saw you walking up the track, looking so beautiful, I forgot to breathe. Mercy had shown me mercy after all." He kissed her softly on the lips.

Mercy shamelessly pressed him closer and kissed him back. It was as sweet as something new and something familiar, both at once. Then she opened her eyes on his shoulder, and saw the sunny room with fresh eyes also.

"It is home! It is really home!"

His lips smiled on her ear. "Yes. And you will be a busy wife. You must set the house to rights, and be mistress of this plantation, mother to our children and a gardener of healing herbs. Ah yes, and my lover." He kissed her ear.

She sat back. "Edmund, I don't wish to wait until the house is finished, to come into it. Where do you sleep?" She stood up, shook out her silk skirts, and when she wobbled on the high-heeled shoes kicked them off. Then she reseated herself with soft rustlings, but in his lap, and wound her arms again around his neck.

"I have always suspected that you had it in you, to be a baggage." He smiled slowly, his eyes all amber. "But this former pirate intends to be the most straight-laced of men. You will sleep in the cottage tonight, for that knave Blaxton's sake. And in the morning, since the ketch is ready, we will go downriver to Williamsburg, to be wed."

"Hmm." She balanced on his knees, wondered if she could pout then decided not to try. "I must wait, it seems. But we will tell the parson we are busy here, and cannot wait for the banns to be called." She smiled slowly. "There are folk I once knew in Williamsburg, and my step-aunt outside it. Perhaps from one of them we can beg a room for a night."

"Be damned if we will." He grinned mischievously back at her. "Better we send Ben ashore, and that the cabin of the *Dragonfly* serve for our bridal."

"A ship's cabin will be most fitting, sir, since I have known you best in them!" She laughed and kissed his forehead. "But when we get home, what here? The cottage?"

"No, we will start as we mean to go on, in this house." His hands stroked her silken middle. "There is a great four-poster bed in pieces, but it shall stay so until the bedchamber is ready. Will a pallet in here suffice, covered with Richard's bearskin?"

"Admirably!" she laughed, and nuzzled his neck...

"Missy Mercy!" Neither of them had heard the door knocked on, then opened. Mam Felice stood there, hands on hips. "You been by yoursel' wit' the Cap'n too long by half! Folks will wunner what you be doin'. Ain't you got no sense of what be proper?"

Neither Mercy nor Edmund troubled to move, and Mercy giggled. "No. But we will be married soon, so I do

344

not care."

"Well, I should t'ink so!" Mam's round face could not stay stern for long. "What bother you got in your li'l brain, wantin' t' go away, I not know. But it be time to get supper soon—an', goodness, you ain't got your shoes on!"

Jedediah's face loomed like a great craggy moon over Mam's head. He demanded suspiciously, "She made up her mind t' stay?"

"Yes, she has," Edmund told him in a voice losing patience. "And you will bring both our suppers in here, and then I will escort Mercy back to the cottage before dark." He glared at them. "Lord, what a pair of watchdogs you are!"

They went off grumbling, and Edmund kissed Mercy again... But *lo!*, in one minute the watchdogs were back, Felice with Mercy's hat and shawl, and Jedediah's one arm carrying the wine-bottle and cups, Edmund's coat and Richard's pistol. Jedediah started to tell his master that he had unloaded the pistol.

Edmund roared, "Out!"

They dropped everything on the rosewood table, and fled.

Mercy laughed helplessly. "It is the first time I have known either of them not to have the last word!"

"It will not be the last time!" Edmund said grimly. Then he smiled and lifted her chin with one brown finger. "Mercy, we may not always have a good life or an easy one. The world owes us nothing for past grief, and we must carve our own corner of it, here. But we will do it together."

"Yes," she said softly. "No longer pirate and Puritan, but man and woman, husband and wife, farmers, of Virginia Colony." She pulled his head down, and finished the kiss they had begun. She had learned how to do it, and parted her lips to caress his mouth with tongue and nibbling teeth.

"Baggage," he breathed. He did not know it, but his arms, for the first time since they had met, held her easily, not too tight. At last he believed she was his for a lifetime, that the world would not separate them again.

Mercy laid her head on his shoulder, in the place that had always seemed made for it, and gazed out the window. The late afternoon sun had mellowed to rich gold, and once would have reminded her of pirate booty. Now it seemed like a hearth fire. They would light a fire in the hearth here under the mahogany mantel, and with careful tending it would burn for all their lives.

"A baggage for you alone. To the world, merely Mistress Mercy Montgomery."

A word about the author...

Mary Clayton has lived all her life in south-east Queensland, Australia. She decided to be a writer at age 6, began writing at 11, sent short stories to magazines at 13, and won a local story contest at 15. Finished formal education before age 15, accidentally educated herself by voracious reading. She has always been an incurable reader and deeply interested in history. She took 30 years off writing to raise her family and only a few years ago began to scribble again then learned to use a computer. Married to Arthur when she was eighteen, they have four married children, thirteen grandchildren and two great-grandchildren, all of all of whom she finds fascinating for their differing characters.

Printed in the United States
206660BV00004B/1/A

9 781601 541192